Hope Lyda

HARVEST HOUSE PUBLISHERS

EUGENE, OREGON

Cover by Left Coast Design, Portland, Oregon

Cover illustration by Krieg Barrie Illustrations, Hoquiam, Washington

ALTAR CALL
Copyright © 2006 by Hope Lyda
Published by Harvest House Publishers
Eugene, Oregon 97402
www.harvesthousepublishers.com

Library of Congress Cataloging-in-Publication Data
Lyda, Hope.
  Altar call / Hope Lyda.
     p. cm.
  ISBN-13: 978-0-7369-1590-8 (pbk.)
  ISBN-10: 0-7369-1590-7
  1. Weddings—Fiction. 2. Bridesmaids—Fiction. I. Title.
  PS3612.Y35A79 2006
  813.'6—dc22

Printed in the United States of America

06 07 08 09 10 11 12 13 14 /BP-CF/ 12 11 10 9 8

*This book is dedicated to the friends
who helped me down the aisle
when I took the plunge:
Dawn, Kim, Jeri, and Jackie.*

*And to Marc, the good man who was waiting
at the end of that aisle
(and had no idea what he was getting into).*

Acknowledgments

Thanks to...

The readers of *Hip to Be Square* and the retailers who carry it, for encouraging a new author.

Hap and Julia Lyda, for generously allowing me to use the coast cabin as my personal writing retreat. It truly saved me!

Glen and Elaine Lyda, for their hospitality, encouragement, laughter, and kindness. And for the many meals at their special table with the best view along the Oregon coast.

Kim Moore, my generous and supportive editor, who has a good eye for scenes and a great heart for her work and her authors.

To all the women in my life who have taken big steps this past year and inspire me to take leaps of faith. To Andrea—thanks for the road trip adventure and for modeling courage and faith even when you didn't feel it.

And to my cousin, Randy, for the tours of DC, your hospitality, and for great conversations at a rooftop restaurant, a cabin table, and on a fabulous porch.

Introduction

"Lots of faith."

This was my answer several months ago when a reporter asked me how a previously antisocial, hopelessly outdated girl ended up the creator of Tucson's biggest social gala in years.

Well, he didn't phrase my status exactly like that, but I *was* on the verge of social extinction as I approached my life goal date of thirty. But on the cusp of thirty, I discovered I had faith, purpose, and best of all…potential. I turned an inheritance of vintage clothing into a fund-raiser for Golden Horizons Retirement Center that is still being talked about today. I ended up with the job I used to take for granted and now love. And I met Beau, a great, datable guy (stuff of urban myth), and through a strange turn of events he proved to be a humane, stellar boss as well.

For the first few months of my new and improved existence I was certain that the center would drop like a faulty Times Square New Year's ball and crash into a million glittery pieces.

My friend Angelica Ross, a former college pal who has known me through thick and rarely thin, pointed out to me that while our friend Caitlin Ramirez is a "glass half full" gal, I am a half-full-with-a-twist person. When I say the proverbial life situation glass is "half full," I say it like an accusation—merely to point out that by being half full it is indeed half empty.

She was right.

At least I used to be this way. My dear friend Tess Childers, who passed away last year, taught me how important it is to don an attitude appropriate for the life season. And this is a good season. Brilliant with sun, and I don't just mean the Tucson blaze above, but rather the brightness of hope for good things. From Tess I inherited the fabulous collection of designer wear and a deeper capacity for joy. As a reminder of all she taught me in our time together at Golden Horizons, I wear the key to the clothes trunks on a bracelet. It isn't a fashion statement by any means, but it is a faith statement.

I owe my chance at this new life to Angelica, Caitlin, and Sadie Verity. Last year was all about me. I was on a quest for the good life. At one point I even had a job at Majestic Vista Luxury Resort and a car with real payments, not just bills from the mechanics. Of course, this new life I was so desperate for did not take into account the fact that I really did love my old life, including the work at Golden Horizons. I don't know why I never comprehended how much a person goes through when they work against their purpose.

Faith, combined with a desire to shake up my old life and find a new one, led me to this place of contentment. I am grateful. But this year, in the fairness of a carefully orchestrated universe, it is someone else's turn to step into the limelight.

Sadie is five months into an eleven-month engagement, so she is the obvious choice. Her fiancé, Carson Curtis, is kind, handsome, successful, and generous. Sadie glows with happiness. But I have noticed a slight imperfection in the normally flawless veneer that is Sadie. In the throes of wedding plans she is a bit…scattered, moody. Dare I say unstable?

I sense she is about to crack, but I don't mention this to her face in case she does pull a Humpty Dumpty. I would feel responsible.

Every book I have skimmed on aisle 4 at the bookstore says that her

change of personality is typical behavior for a bride to be. It is completely normal for the woman to get a bit nervous and unglued with each step closer to the altar of commitment. That book, however, says nothing (and I checked the index) about whether it is normal for the friends surrounding the bride to act equally deranged. Sadly, I could only deduce that the absence of the topic indicated that our individual quirky responses were either very weird or so taboo of a subject that the author and publisher behind *The Blissful Bride* could not bear to shed light on it.

Chapter 10 of the aforementioned book says that Sadie will indeed survive this time of emotional upheaval, identity change, and a million-and-one little decisions to achieve her time of bliss. But I'm beginning to wonder if the rest of us can survive the next six months.

Dang. That glass always gets in the way of my progress.

Dating the Boss

"Mari, would you tell your boyfriend that this rotation schedule is killing my love life?" One of my coworkers, Lysa, rubs her red eyes and adjusts her tousled Golden Horizons Retirement Center uniform, which is on backward.

"Maybe your lack of dates has a little more to do with your faulty closet-eye coordination," I suggest, laughing.

"Or the fact that you started taking night classes again," Sonya, the yoga instructor, chimes in as she enters our small office area.

"Yeah, you are probably right." Lysa takes a gander at her misfit outfit. "But I prefer to blame someone else, if you don't mind."

Sonya and I raise our hands in submission. "Go right ahead," I say. "You can blame Beau anytime."

"Hey, I heard that." Beau strides down the hall toward us. As he gets close to me I stare into his eyes but then force mine to drop to his name tag, which says "Director."

Overall I'm starting to feel more comfortable with the idea of sharing my life with someone. Even this too-close-for-comfort scenario has begun to reveal benefits. When we are not able to go out after work, we see one another throughout the day. We steal glances and sweet conversations about life, my friends and their latest antics, and our favorite residents at Golden Horizons. When I go to bed at night I try to recall our best exchange of the day. Lately, I have been going to bed mentally balancing my checkbook. But every relationship has a natural dip after the initial, mutual wooing.

In the past I've engaged in relationships that had little chance of surviving. Sometimes they had a natural expiration date, like college graduation. Other times they were such absurd pairings that they just had to end...a Julia Roberts, Lyle Lovett kind of thing. But this...*this* thing with Beau pulls the real me to the surface. Fighting and screaming at times, but deep inside I know this is the adult relationship I have always been afraid to hope for. And as sappy as it sounds, my belief in love came alive the day I let my guard down.

Beau heads toward his office, which has no door. His first decision six months ago, when he became director and subsequently my boss, was to declare an open door policy forevermore. In a mock-ceremony our small staff gathered around while Beau dismantled the hinges. Party favors from the dollar store were involved.

As I get back to my file purging, Beau spins on one heel and backtracks two paces. He gives me a smile, steals a kiss, and grabs the remaining maple bar from the Sugar Fix box before disappearing into his doorless den. "As you were," he says.

I doubt that is possible.

Crowning Glory

M iss Verity, more champagne or sparkling cider?" The ever-pleasant bridal shop hostess makes another round through my friends with her silver tray and tempting hors d'oeuvres.

I stop staring at her visible happy lines and respond. "You mean Mrs. Curtis to be." I reach for a cider, completely ignoring my desire to grab the bottle of champagne and run for the door. I have had these five months to get used to the idea of my friend's pending nuptials—and I still desire a numbing agent to keep my mixed emotions at bay.

"You aren't falling for the whole change your name bit, are you?" Angelica inquires while eating pimento loaf on a cracker topped with a bit of judgment, it seems. I know she is playing devil's advocate. Her horns are showing through the silk-and-lace veil she has chosen to model for us.

We all hold our breath. Well, I hold my breath and give Angelica a look that could melt the spot of misplaced cheese resting on her nose. Has she *not* noticed that Sadie is on the verge of an emotional breakdown these days? One does not ask a maniacal maiden to second-guess any of her decisions.

Caitlin, always the first to crack during a moment of uncomfortable

silence, seeks a distraction. "This would be heaven." She reaches for a tiara and places it on Sadie's perfectly shaped cone of hair.

Like anyone living on adrenaline and anxiety, Sadie is quick to respond to new stimuli. Especially when it sparkles. With a blink of her pink frosted lids, Sadie's expression goes from annoyed to overjoyed. She radiates from within as she offers the mirror her silhouette.

I half expect animated blue birds to appear and encircle her head.

"Oh my, that is beautiful," I say.

"Breathtaking," Angelica adds.

Sadie gives a slight shoulder shimmy to see if the sculpture will remain in position.

It stays. I am certain we have nicely maneuvered the minefield of Sadie's panic buttons…until Sadie's face falls. Crumples, really. And she starts crying as she runs for the dressing rooms.

Our hostess hands the tray of goodies to Angelica—just as Angelica is about to grab the last shrimp puff—and rushes after the bawling bride. I do believe it is the three-thousand-dollar tiara that has made the hostess break the record for the one hundred in heels and not empathy.

Angelica keeps eating, Caitlin explains the situation to a security guard responding to the alarm set off by Sadie's expensive getaway carats, and I go after my friend. Recently, it seems many of our heart-to-hearts or spill-our-guts conversations take place in public restrooms, dressing rooms, or the lobbies of our preferred restaurants.

Val, our attentive attendant, feigns concern for Sadie's hair. She gently brushes loose strands back into the fold of Sadie's shiny, black updo before casually removing the tiara. I think I see beads of sweat on Val's nose. But she needn't worry about losing the tiara or offending a customer. Sadie is caught in her reoccurring cyclone of self-doubt, fear, and whatever else brews in that pretty head of hers.

A false eyelash sails for the shore of her chin. I catch it before it wanders to the brilliantly expensive gown she has on. Val smiles to show her appreciation and hands me a narrow towel used to protect dresses from the mascara and foundation of blushing brides.

I take the towel and drape it over Sadie's now reddish neck. She is trying to hold back the sobs, but I know they soon will escape their prison of privacy.

"Val, can we have a minute?"

"Certainly. Can I bring you anything? Aspirin? Valium?"

We both look at our incredibly helpful hostess with troubled concern. *What kind of joint are you running here?* I want to ask. Our obvious preference for none of the above is made and Val takes her leave.

"Why is it that when one of us breaks down it leads to drug use?" I say in jest. Though last year my breakdown at a slightly less desirable locale did indeed lead to an emergency room visit and a mild narcotic.

Sadie's quick smile fades as she likely recalls that last time *she* was the one in control of her emotions. That was normal for us. Me whimpering, sniveling, and caving in to my constant angst while Sadie was assuring, comforting, and advising. But this scene was the opposite of normal. And I know I am witnessing a glimpse of things to come.

"Would it be too inconsiderate if *I* asked for the valium?"

Sadie does not offer a laugh but holds the towel closer to her throat as if chilled by her outburst.

"Maybe it's hormones," I offer.

"Um, I'm pretty sure that is said to comfort or disregard *pregnant* women, not engaged women. Unless you are suggesting I am so old that my hormones are out of whack," Sadie sneers. This is definitely new behavior territory for Sadie.

"No. No. I would never suggest that because I am a nice friend," I pause, "and because we are the same age."

This gets a laugh. I close the fabric curtain a bit tighter so my friend can open up. "I'm really doing well, Mari. At least I have been managing, don't you think?"

Kinda. "Yes!" I assure her.

"I have been juggling the wedding details, handling my inner fear that this is too good to be true, and dealing with the pressure at the Tucson Botanical Society to generate more donations."

I nod.

"Then over spaghetti at Vauldi's last night, Carson tells me that Harry will be flying in quite early to have quality father-son time before the wedding."

I understand the shock value of this news, especially when you are enjoying lamb meatballs and looking forward to your next bread basket refill. However, my first thought is that a father *should* spend time with his son...especially before such a big life transition. Instead of giving volume to this viewpoint, I make appropriate listening sounds. "Oh. Hmm. Uh-huh."

Sadie needs me to hear her worries, not determine their merit.

"There is more...but I just cannot discuss it now. Not yet. I'm still trying to pray before I jump into my first response to...this other news."

Her first response has clearly already come and gone. But I say, "Um. Hmmm. Uh-huh," and keep my thought life to myself.

It is the right thing to do.

Piece of Mind

The plush and lush lobby of Majestic Vista Luxury Resort welcomes the wealthy, the pampered, and today even the underpaid. I can hardly believe I worked here for a short while last year during my life makeover efforts.

That was then. This is now.

As I walk through the rock garden entryway, I am merely a guest of this place of high-priced juice cocktails and hot-rock treatments. Today I want to revive my connection with Beau. I figured a spa day complete with mud masks and pedicures would give us lots of time to talk. I enjoy the independence of our dating relationship, but I need a little peace of mind about us.

Halo, one of my first friends at Majestic Vista, quickly finishes a conversation with a spa client and rushes over to present me with a tray of beverages—spring water with lime, orange juice, and wine spritzers. She greets me with a kiss on each cheek and an up-and-down look over. "Darling, you look fantastic. I swear your thighs were much larger."

Did I say friend? "People remember me fat. But thanks."

"Care for a beverage before you begin your romantic spa day?"

"I'll wait for Beau. Is Lionel around? I'd love to thank him for this comp

treatment. I quit on the guy, and he gives me a gift certificate. One of us is crazy."

"Lionel's at the spa in Mexico checking out the new chef. He'll be sad he's missed you. The man still talks about reviving your bingo night." Halo cups her ear piece, looks up to concentrate on the invisible communicant, and then turns back to me. "There is a call for you, Mari. Here, just use this." She transfers her headset to my head which, it turns out, is about three sizes bigger than hers.

"Hello?"

"Mari, it's me." Beau's voice is distant.

"Hey. Are you stuck in traffic? I noticed it was backed up over by the courthouse."

Beau says something, but I am sure I haven't heard him right. I step out from beneath the alcove hoping for better reception.

"I'm stuck here. My reports to the state commission are due tomorrow. I'll be burning the midnight oil as it is. You should go ahead with it."

I move three steps to the right hoping for better answers. "But it's the romance package. And Lionel was so sweet to give me this free pass, I'd hate to ask for a rain check." I sigh with exasperation and quietly add, "Besides, it hardly ever rains."

"You deserve to be pampered, Mari. Please go for it. I would feel terrible if you missed out. Invite Sadie."

"Yep," I say, instead of giving him a piece of my mind, which goes a bit like *You want me to give half of my romance package to the one friend who is actually in a happy romance? The one person who would only serve to remind me that I am dating the guy who is never around?* "I will invite Cailtin. Not Sadie."

He doesn't want to notice my attitude, which I am a bit ashamed to be exhibiting so openly. "Well, Caitlin can thank me, then. I guess I will have to plaster my own face with mud pies."

I imagine a cream pie soaring toward his handsome features right about now. I cannot figure out how to respond. I'm not good at the letdown part of a relationship. Beau is so great—so perfect—that I hadn't expected these kinds of surprises.

Sadie told me not long ago that grace seems to be the biggest requirement in a real relationship. I decide to try it. "Okay. Go burn your oil. Do you want me to bring you something to eat later?"

"No. You will be ready for a nice leisurely afternoon. I'm jealous."

I click off the phone and head over to the receptionist's cubicle. "Halo, can I bring in a sub for Beau?"

"Sure. The whole day is covered for two. Are you okay?"

"Yeah." As I dial Caitlin's number and switch my expectations from a romantic date to a girl's day out, I have a déjà vu moment.

Caitlin listens to the offer and is ecstatic. "Yes! I'd love it. It will be just like the old days—you know, when you were single."

I knew this felt familiar.

Between Phone Lines

I twirl my fuchsia phone cord and wait for my mom to pick up on the other end. Caitlin bought the Barbie princess phone for me as a humorous and congratulatory gesture when Beau and I started to go out. From Angelica it would have been an insult.

"Hello, my dear! Right on time." Mom answers our weekly call with her usual energy.

"I had to set my alarm," I say, looking at the clock. It is just after 8:30 for me but 11:30 for Mom and Dad in Washington, DC.

"I don't believe you. You were always such an early riser."

"I was?" Probably so I could get a hot shower. Sharing three showers with a dozen kids from the shelter did not allow for much warm water, not to mention privacy.

"You and Marcus were the only ones to help out with breakfast on weekends. He still is such a big help."

Mom makes a point of mentioning Marcus Dean at least three times a conversation. Not just because he is a nice guy who is helping at the shelter while working on his PhD, but because he was my high school sweetheart and a former resident of the shelter. Mom sees him as her success story and would love our story lines to intersect.

"Have you made your decision about running for city council?" I change to the only subject that will distract her.

"I just sent my official candidate application yesterday. Are you proud of your mother?"

"Yes, of course! It is great news—especially for the neighborhood." Mom has long been a pursuer of change and a vocal advocate for youth resources in Washington.

"Once my application is approved my campaign must start right away. These days, they don't give council candidates much time to be visible. I'm kicking it all off with a meet and greet at your old grade school. Marcus is going to help. Isn't that nice?"

Two down, one to go.

"Hey, did I tell you that Beau was selected for a special mentor program? Only five directors of assisted care facilities are chosen in the nation."

"Beau is such a good man. So he gets someone to help him do his work?" Mom inquires. She likes him; she just has a blind spot the size and shape of Marcus.

"Actually, the mentor is really someone who collaborates with him. The assigned professional communicates with Beau and reviews his ideas, projects, whatever. At the end of the program, the mentor and the director create a series of papers and pursue grant funding for further development."

"Outstanding. Outstanding." Mom's voice is muffled.

"Mom?"

"Yes, dear. Development. Excellent."

"I need to get going. I'm meeting the others for breakfast in just a few minutes." Mom's attention span is worse the older she gets. Too much going on, and she is so easily distracted by the action of the youth shelter. Frustration carried over from childhood bubbles up in me.

More muffled sounds and a man's voice in the background. My dad usually wants to say hello.

"Put him on," I say, checking my clock again. If I forget makeup and just put my hair in a ponytail, I can still get to breakfast on time.

"Certainly!" Mom says to me and then I hear her gleefully turn the phone over with, "She wants to talk to you."

"Mari?"

It is Marcus. Thanks, Mom.

"Hey, Marcus. I thought you were Dad."

"Just me, I'm afraid," he says, a bit put out.

"I didn't mean that…I was just surprised. So how is school going?"

"Good. Good enough. Isn't it wonderful about your mom running for council? She is going to do great things."

Marcus is as much of a cheerleader for Mom as she is for him. It is a club I didn't always feel a part of.

"I really have to get going, Marcus. My friend Caitlin will be here any minute to take me to breakfast."

"How is Bo-Bo? No, wait—Bono?"

Yeah, I'm really buying this act of indifference. "His new CD is great. And he's helping pay off the debt of third world countries. So good of you to inquire."

He laughs.

I don't.

"Tell Dad I'll catch him next week. Good luck with your classes, Martin."

I slam down the phone, but the fluffy fuchsia princess receiver only makes a very dissatisfying thud.

It isn't until I slam the passenger door of Caitlin's car with a very satisfying thunderous "WHAM!" that I wonder if my overreaction is something other than anger.

Green Light

"Where did all the good parking places go? I know this is my punishment for trading in my bus pass for a car again. This is ridiculous. Let's just go somewhere else for breakfast." Caitlin's nostrils flare with frustration.

"We can't go somewhere else. What if Sadie and Angelica are already inside Freddies?"

"Weren't you wanting to change to the Sante Fe restaurant?"

"That was when I was trying to change everything in my life. I'm over that. Like the curb you just jumped," I note as a pedestrian throws coffee at Caitlin's windshield in retaliation.

"Look. I drive one time in months and people hate me. The universe hates my decision."

"Please. Not the universe talk again. You do realize that such grandiose generalizations only remove you from a personal connection to God."

Urrchhh.

The car stops, but my head and backpack do not. I nearly nail the dashboard with my face. We are nowhere near a parking place or a stop sign. "What on earth!" I shout, but I know perfectly well why she is ticked. I did

hear what came out of my mouth. Good grief. I don't know what is wrong with me lately.

"Don't preach at me, Mari. I have faith, you know. You don't have to judge everything I say and decide whether it is godly or not. Okay?"

I want to stand up for myself and tell her I held my tongue with Sadie just the other day, but I don't want to prolong this discussion of my judgmental ways. If it turned into a debate, I would lose. I liked it better last year when Caitlin and I discussed how Sadie can sometimes be judgmental.

"Okay. Sorry." I turn to look out the window and notice a Jeep backing up just down the block. "Over there is a parking place."

"Good eye." We run over the edge of a median but Caitlin's speedy reaction secures the spot.

"Any other Saturday and I would have gladly gone to a different place. But Sadie is giving us our wedding assignments today."

Caitlin removes her seat belt and slumps in her seat.

"What is it?" I reach out to pat her shoulder, which is adorned with leather fringe the color of watermelon.

She rolls her head in my direction. "I forgot that was today. I don't know if I feel so good."

"Caitlin?"

"I'm not like you. You are so supportive of Sadie's life situation, but it is not easy for me. I mean, you have Beau and he's amazing. And he's your hope for a future. I haven't had that with anyone in a long time."

"So, this isn't about having a vehicle?"

"Aren't I just the worst friend in the world? I cannot be happy for her because my life is like…like *this*," Caitlin makes a big circle with her hand.

"A hoop earring from the seventies?"

A laugh slips from her stern lips. "Well, a loop-di-loop. I meant like driving around looking for a parking place. I've been wandering around in circles for years trying to land a guy. I thought maybe Jim the Cop was a possibility, but he hasn't called in weeks, and the guy practically lives in Nogales."

"Or impractically," I try for humor and get no response. "Maybe if you had stopped using terms like 'land a guy' or introducing *the* guy as 'Jim the Cop' to everybody..."

Caitlin's look reminds me I am back on my way down judgment lane, so I adjust my tone. "The idea of marriage affects all of us, Caitlin. Have you seen the way Angelica has been eating lately?" I laugh, but the visions I have of Angelica stuffing her face since the engagement border on scary.

"And you?" Caitlin asks pleadingly.

I don't particularly want to reveal the underbelly of my nature, but I see it is needed. "All right. But you cannot say anything to anyone."

Caitlin sits up expectantly. I cannot disappoint.

"Lately I have felt that something is off between me and Beau."

She looks sympathetic but not appeased. "Like?"

"Well, that's the problem. I'm not sure what it is. It might be because we don't spend as much time together as we did the first few months." I stop before the next words can form fully in my mind. I began this assessment to pacify Caitlin, but a truth emerges. "I feel disconnected from him."

My mind starts to sift through a mental cupboard of filed away moments when Beau and I seemed to talk over and at each other but not *to* one another. Caitlin interrupts my troublesome tangent unaffected by my revelation.

"That is just part of a relationship's growing pains. It isn't the same as having ill feelings toward a friend's happiness."

We step out of the car and head toward Freddies. The line to the restaurant is wrapped around the building. Somehow, when we weren't looking, our once humble hole-in-the-wall diner turned into a popular hangout.

"I didn't finish my confession." I hike up my jeans. I am not getting thinner as Halo suspected; I just recently bought a new pair of fat pants.

The awning of Freddies is up ahead, so we step to the back of the line of weekend breakfast eaters. Caitlin leans in, ready to hear my secret.

I clear my throat and continue. "Well, when I was thinking about me and Beau and wondering if we have what it takes, I started to think of Sadie and Carson the same way."

Blank stare.

"I started projecting problems onto them—totally out of jealousy. I began

to scrutinize their relationship. See? I'm not so perfect. I should be thinking happy thoughts about the happy couple, but I analyze, twist, and deconstruct what they have instead of focusing on my own problems."

Caitlin's eyes light up. This pleases her. "I know what you mean, Mari. I have done that too. What is it about a friend's engagement that does this to us? I don't want to be a jealous person."

"Let's keep each other in line." Have I just agreed to accountability?

My last words fade in the sound of the crowd as Angelica comes rushing toward us. "What are you guys doing at the back of the line? We are about to be seated. I am starving. I barely had any breakfast this morning."

"It's 9:15. This *is* breakfast."

"Oh, yeah. You're right. Gosh, I've been eating a lot lately. I don't know what my problem is."

Caitlin looks at me out of the corner of her eye and we try not to laugh.

Pew

While subtle doubts about my dating relationship might exist, I don't question my commitment to making it work. Beau, or Beau-and-I, is the best thing I have ever had. My church relationship, however, is a different story. I go. Religiously, even. But I am keeping my distance these days. I have avoided the singles group. My only claim to involvement was a stint on the Grandparents' Day greeting committee. I love the hymns, praise songs, the communion, the sermon—and the very quick departure out the nearest exit.

Nobody ever explains how introducing love into your life means introducing your loved one into your life. Each time Beau's presence makes me stop and contemplate my typical behaviors I realize I have given myself lots of grace in lots of areas. For example, while my pew seat is cooling before the benediction, Beau is the type to actually stay for the fellowship time between services. I am unlocking my car door, and he is reaching for a sugar cookie and the fresh pot of mint tea. I am turning my cell phone back on and playing any messages, and he is politely asking for a refill of the tea and directions to the new children's wing because he agreed to be on a vacation

Bible school advisory team. I am grabbing the folds of my stomach and wondering which restaurant we will go to for lunch, and Beau is recruiting more members to the advisory committee and is sitting down to play a game with several kids waiting for parents to retrieve them.

I am bad. He is good. This is what runs through my mind while mild hunger turns to seemingly fatal pangs of starvation. I get out of the car and start walking—not toward the church but toward Vinnie, a hot dog street vendor—and I realize how little I have changed my previous single life patterns. As I bite into a beef dog with extra relish and mustard and a spot of mayo on a whole wheat bun, I wonder if I should change or whether a real relationship makes room for two individuals to have their separate behaviors.

There is little that I want from this life. I want happiness, contentment, joy, meaning, and…

"Hey, love, you got enough mustard there?" The vendor shakes his head and lets out a hearty laugh.

"And love." I say aloud with my mouth full of hot dog.

"What?" Vinnie's cheeks and lips scrunch toward his nose in confusion.

"I want love."

"Sorry, darling. This beefy wonder is married."

Mid-deluxe dog I realize that I need to get back to Beau.

I wipe my greasy fingers on the edge of my sweater. I must rush to the church, find Beau, and say something committal like "Can I be president of the children's wing fund?" or "Sign me up to take the middle school class on a mission to Mexico." Somehow I need to show Beau that I am a loyal, committed, and equal partner in this relationship.

I am winded by the time I reach the long flight of stairs to the fellowship hall. I pretend to tighten the straps on my sandals so that I can catch a few extra gulps of air. When I look up, a silhouette blocks the stained-glass image of Mary Magdalene talking to Jesus. It is Beau—his face shrouded by the shadows. I wonder if he is mad that I left the service so quickly or that I didn't stand by his side as he signed away his next fifty Saturday afternoons to serve on committees and boards. I consider that he might be upset because of everyone he met today, only two people knew of me, and they were the ladies who serve doughnuts right before service starts. But as color-filtered light is replaced by full sunlight I see the face that puts my worries to rest—that makes my anxieties ashamed of themselves. Beau is smiling a broad, lovely grin acknowledging that it is moi who stands just a few steps away from him on a narrow staircase.

"Sorry. I kept trying to find a way to leave so I could get to you," he says without an ounce of judgment.

"Me too," I say. But as I wipe away the definitely real mustard and the possibly imagined problems with a swipe of my hand, I am judging myself.

In Print

"Are you interested?" my friend and former neighbor Yvette Patterson whispers her proposal for the second time through the phone. "The Tucson Talent Night will benefit the local animal shelter. Come on. Do it for Elmo."

I pet my cat. "No fair. Elmo has a home." I pause, but I know this is no argument. "Beau might not be able to. He's super busy these days."

"I know it's hard to plan months ahead, but the advance ticket sales help us plan the budget for the shelter." Yvette's laryngitis seems to clear. "It also helps support the Veterinarians for Octogenarians program, which provides discounted vet care to the pets of the elderly."

I roll my eyes and roll over in submission. "Okay. That got me."

We hang up. I regret any more commitments, but I realized halfway through the conversation that Yvette could have guilted me into helping her. After all, last year she and then-boyfriend, now-hubby Zane came to the rescue for my big fashion show fund-raiser. They handled all the Internet promotions and sales and made the show an international success. How can I not support their cause of the year?

A knock at the door reminds me what I am doing today. Caitlin has asked me to go to the library once again to research the how-to's for a business start-up. I'm starting to wonder if she will become one of those people who forever researches an idea but never has the courage to act on it.

I open the door to find my friend, who looks as though her clothes have been dipped in red Jell-O. My tortured expression asks the questions going through my head.

"It's a new, nearly breathable plastic. Isn't this incredible? Feel this." She holds out a gelatinized arm.

"I'm scared." I tease my friend and avoid touching her new creation.

"It will be all the rage in my new shop. You know, I still need a name. What do you think of Caitlin's Closet?" She sweeps her hands across the air above like a Midwest girl just off the bus in Los Angeles.

I duplicate her movement. "Kinda cutesy."

Her smile fades. "Really? It seemed clever, but probably only because I was watching the late night shows and eating a bag of nacho cheese tortilla chips. I never think straight after bad jokes and junk food."

I gather my notebook and shove it inside a soft leather briefcase alongside my recently purchased, lightweight laptop. "A name will come to you. First we need to establish a business plan and a marketing plan. If you are going to get noticed by either a bank or outside investors, you must look like you mean business."

"This isn't my strong suit. I just want to make clothes and get people to think outside the boxed shoulders. You know?"

"Bus or heap?"

"Heap."

"Your heap or mine?"

"Yours. I had to bus here."

We walk out the door simultaneously like a staged Abbot-and-Costello moment.

"Well, this is a fine mess," I say.

We enter the library and I breathe in the scent of books, paper, and coffee. The coffee cart is just past the entrance, followed by a small cafe and vending

machines. Libraries sure have changed since my childhood. I recall being forced to stand in a corner between a large fern and a wastebasket because I would not spit out my gumball. Now they practically have full-service restaurants. Coffee cups and ceramic plates holding pastries are carried everywhere, from fiction to biography to periodicals.

Normally, I am a traditionalist. But joining the comfort of food and the comfort of books is a wonderful exception to make. I place an order for lemon pie for Caitlin, and I wait at the end of the granite counter.

I have sent her ahead to the business section because it takes the girl twenty minutes to get settled. She brings colored pencils, rulers, fountain pens, and several styles of paper products. The aesthetic value of her collection is considerable. The productivity value of her ritual is zilch. She procrastinates with flair, I'll give her that.

I am licking whipped cream off of my finger at the condiment bar when a woman approaches who looks familiar. I cannot place her until she pours skim milk into a big ceramic cup.

It is Cruella the Gruel Slogger, my little pet name for our usual waitress at Freddies—back when the place was clear of many paying customers. I stare at my pie until I can think of her name. Name. It's a real name. Aha. "Samantha!" I say, delighted with my memory recall.

She spills some milk onto the blue saucer and looks up with a start. "Yes?"

"Mari." I say, and then realize this probably means little to her. "Senior Sunrise Surprise breakfast."

Samantha puts her cup down and surprises me by walking over and offering a handshake. "Of course. This is out of context."

"Exactly. It wasn't until I saw you pour the milk that I figured out who you were. How are you? Are you still at Freddies? We usually go on weekdays now, if we go."

She pulls her hair back, and with a few flicks of her wrist ends up with a nice updo. "I put in a few hours a week just to help them fill the schedule. But I am interviewing for jobs—which feels like a full-time job."

"That's right. You were finishing your master's degree in psychology."

"Very good. Well, behavioral sciences, but basically the same."

"What kind of job does someone do with that?"

"Most of my peers are using it for marketing and advertising jobs."

"Makes sense."

"It does. I just want something a bit more serious. My wish list includes mostly research institutes that focus on trends and behaviors of people in relation to social issues. I find that fascinating."

"Is that what your thesis was on?"

She walks back to get her coffee and sighs. "No. My advisor was a celebrity in our department—full of himself and his ideas. Sadly, I went with his suggestion."

"What was that?" I am most curious because last year Cruella…Samantha had told me she used some of the regulars at Freddies for her case study, and I was one of them.

"Consumer Choices: Limited by Life Perspective. You were one of my primary case studies for my subset group. Did you know that?"

I take a bite of pie and focus on the word "limited." "You mentioned I might be a part of your research, but I was scared to ask for details." I laugh, but she nods. "Should I be worried about what you figured out about me while I sat there enjoying my eggs and toast?"

Now she laughs to reassure me. "No. Not at all. Actually, the library houses published papers and thesis projects from the University of Arizona. Do you want to go take a look?"

"It's here?" How many times have I walked by an examination of my life? She starts to head to the far corner of the main floor. I follow, mesmerized by this news. "For the whole city to check out and read?" I ask, worry setting in.

"Not to burst your image of the master thesis as a source of entertainment, but the only people reading these are the students who wrote them and students doing research."

We walk among the ceiling-high metal shelves until Samantha stops abruptly in front of her shelf. "Grab that stool, would you?"

I follow her instruction, and she steps up to retrieve the bound thesis. She hands it to me casually.

"You should be so proud. You are in the library. Incredible," I say while skimming the table of contents and looking for my name. "How amazing to have accomplished something like the degree, the thesis, and..."

"You're number twelve."

She does know me. I quickly thumb through to the subset research study evaluation. Right away words catch my eye because they catch my heart as well:

> *Subject 12 is unlike the other subjects in that she seems to be aware of repetition in her consumption choices and life habits and seems to express regret, anger, and hostility about this understanding. Noted in the early section on change and routine, this subject remains unique because she seems to desire change, whereas subjects 1–5, 9, and 14–18 did not indicate tension with their routine. On several occasions 12 expressed mention of a life's "rut" and seemed bothered by this self-exposed truth. Twelve's efforts to make changes seemed based on societal pressure that was internalized rather than a true desire to be different. My conclusion about the above subject is that she desires to know herself—her instincts as well as know what the best option is in all situations. She desires truth, but she bases her definition of it on the cultural standard and not on self and self-understanding. I attribute this to a lack of belief in her place and purpose outside of societal norms and expectations. This comes from research conversations listed in Appendix C. Please reference.*

I take another bite of pie and swallow with some difficulty.

"I haven't read it in a while. I hope it isn't too offensive. And you have to know, this kind of study and assessment is more my advisor's style, not my own. I was winging it, basically."

I let out a big sigh that sends dust particles from other thesis projects flying. "Well, you did a good job for winging it. The whole desire for truth and looking for it in society's expectations—that's...that's pretty darn accurate."

"You've changed a lot, though. I can see it." She hesitates and examines my face. "A slice of life study does not allow for examination of changes over time. This is one small picture, a moment." She is using her education to calm her subject down. Samantha uses a gentle, yet firm tone.

I let my life examiner believe this, but I know better. I flip through to appendix C and note the date of the conversation she references. "I had better get the last piece of this dessert up to my friend or she will never forgive me. Thanks for showing me this, Samantha. You really are good."

She blushes. "Thanks."

I sense she knows I am bothered by the profile.

As I make my way to the business section upstairs, my eyes glaze over and the muted library sounds become even less distinguishable. However, my mind is noisy. It is shouting phrases like "You're frozen. You have the same problem that you did two years ago. You thought you had grown."

I look down at my What Would Old Mari Do bracelet, a gift from Caitlin last year to remind me of old behaviors.

Old Mari would believe those things my mind is screaming at me. Old Mari would wonder if she would ever change. But new Mari...new Mari wants more out of her life than disappointment and a "lack of faith." She wants to embrace her purpose, even if it isn't what people expect of her or what she expects of herself. She wants to listen for God's leading...

"You took so dang long," Caitlin scolds, staring at the measly portion I have handed her. "This is one pathetic slice," she says, stuffing the sliver into her mouth eagerly.

"It will get better," I promise myself.

Choices

"Do not make eye contact," I mumble out of the side of my mouth in the direction of Angelica.

Her blond head immediately turns in the forbidden direction of the man in a tuxedo just a few tables over from us at Chez DiDi's. "Why? You don't want a coffee refill?"

"He ain't waiting; he's our magician," I sing-talk.

She looks again, this time with her brows half raised. "A what?"

"Magician. It's sort of their thing here. They have had a magician harassing patrons every Friday night for the past fifteen years."

Angelica yawns. "I wondered what magicians outside of Vegas did for gigs. What are you ordering?"

"Salmon, I think. With lemon garlic sauce. You?"

"I just want dessert."

"Since when did you stop eating for twenty?"

Mean look.

"Sorry. That came out wrong."

"There was a right way for that statement to leave your lips?"

33

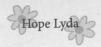

"Point."

"You are correct, though. I'm troubled." Her eyes catch mine to keep me from commenting.

"Go on," I say politely.

"I've been in a Bible study at church for the past six months. And it has been really good for me during my…" she pauses. I assume it is to find the right word to describe her break from dating.

"Sabbatical?" I motion for the waiter while the magician has his back turned.

"Yes, that's it. The study, it has been really good. Very disciplined but good. They asked me to lead a spin-off group."

The waiter arrives and stands at attention. "Cheese plate and garden salad, please. Paulie?" I question his name tag. "With crackers," I add, unable to help myself.

"What happened to the salmon with lemon garlic sauce?" Angelica eyes me.

I shrug. "The waiter is waiting."

"He's good at it," Angelica looks at her patient, silent DiDi's representative. "I will have the steak and red potatoes and mixed greens."

"What happened to just dessert?"

"Medium well. The steak, that is." Angelica adds.

"Yes, I got that." Paulie marches off.

"He ain't no dumb waiter." I fake-chuckle for my friend who is troubled.

"Enough about Paulie. This possible authority role just doesn't feel right. If I lead the group, I become the nurturer instead of the nurturee. I might not be ready for that."

"Have you said yes?"

"Not yet. I have to tell the coordinator tomorrow."

"Have you considered saying no?"

"I hate to disappoint this woman. She's been a big help to me while I've been trying to get my act together."

Dilemmas like this did not exist for Angelica a mere year ago. She never worried about what others thought or expected. "I like this side of you."

"You have been really supportive of my decision to abandon an incredibly successful social life. Now we have switched places," Angelica points out.

"It is my pleasure to reverse roles with you. However, I went from *no* dating to dating *one* guy full-time. So, I never had what you had...the speed dating thing. The different guy every week for a rotation of lunches, dinners, and dancing. Your roster of men waiting to escort you to a business function. Your..."

Angelica holds up her manicured red nails and places one to her lips because my lips are too far away.

"How is Peyton?" I drive right over her intended speed bump on memory lane.

"So, what should I do?" Angelica tries to ignore my comment, but her red face is far from ignorable.

"Maybe this opportunity would take you to the next level, but I don't know the answer. I do think six months of avoiding Peyton is enough time. Couldn't you end your fast of men, or at least of one man?"

Angelica sighs and twirls the ends of her perfect hair. She is avoiding eye contact with me and by doing so makes eye contact with the magician.

"Now you've done it. He's coming this way. Act like we are deep in conversation." I speak in hushed spy tones.

"We are."

"I mean deep in *deep* conversation. Cry."

Angelica is not at all fazed by this command. She obliges with short, mousy sobs that slowly evolve into howls.

"Ladies. One of my favorite tricks is to turn tears into a smile." Elusive Lyle wants to earn his tips tonight.

Angelica stops midcry and rolls her eyes.

"Pick a card, any card." Lyle fans his deck.

"Don't let your ability to choose be restricted by your life perspective. Believe me, I know this," I whisper.

Angelica looks at me with a "you're weird" glance, takes a deep breath, and with impressive confidence, makes her decision.

Falling

"How do I turn this thing?" I screech down the bulletin board-lined south hallway of Golden Horizons while standing on a motorized creation with smooth wheels. Smooth except when they hit the seam lines in linoleum or discarded pencils.

"You don't want to turn. Keep hauling forward," Beau hollers, safely hidden behind file cabinets.

In a moment of insanity, involving a chocolate bribe, I offered to be a guinea pig for this latest project, "Moving Toward New Mobility," but only because I thought it would turn Beau's attention back to me.

"Watch out!" I shout, but it is too late. I have collided with the library cart. Beau rushes to save a copy of *Anna Karenina* from landing in the fountain. I, on the other hand, am allowed to fall flat on my face.

"Ouch. Ouch." I moan extra long for effect.

"You leaned too far forward while accelerating," Beau explains as he places Tolstoy back on the cart.

I wanted a rush of sympathy, not an explanation for my predicament. His lack of caring sends a power surge through my veins. "Thanks so much," I say sarcastically and add this to the ever-expanding file of Beau's faux pas and wipe away imagined dust from my sore behind.

It is then that he sees injury beyond my pride.

"Your elbow…it's bleeding. Oh, Mari. Are you okay?"

Finally. Proper attention. "I'll be all right. It's nothing." I morph into a good sport now that Beau has shown he cares.

"Let's get that taken care of. Come on." He grabs my hand and takes me to the staff room, where a first aid kit hangs on the wall. I never even knew the kit existed until Beau got this grant. My knees, toes, fingers, and head have all been tended to from this white box with the red cross on it. I have tested circular wheel chairs, aerodynamic walkers, and even luxury scooters.

Lysa walks by and does a double take.

"You know," she says, enjoying my humility, "if you would just follow your passion, you would have a career you love and better income."

"What would that career be?"

"Crash test dummy." She stares at me with complete seriousness. Only Beau laughs at my new job prospect. He ends up in tears, which finally causes Lysa's facade to crack and my reluctant smile to appear.

"Sure, mock me. Both of you. But at least I am contributing to mobility science research. You two just sit back and observe. I am giving heart, soul, and blood to the cause." I raise my now-bandaged elbow up in salute to my courage.

"I'll bet you had to wear a special helmet as a child, didn't you?" Lysa offers one last punch line and exits shaking her head.

"No!" I call after her indignantly and deeply hope that she never sees our home movies of me as a three-year-old with protective head gear and thick glasses to correct my wandering eye.

"I like your clumsiness. How else could I take care of you?" Beau leans in and gazes at me with his deep eyes and a look of tenderness.

That's twice today I've fallen.

Remembering Me

Elmo has just told me in so many meows that he does not like it when I throw crushed ice at his head.

"But I'm bored," I say, defending my actions. Poor cat.

The expanse of an entire weekend is laid out before me. I used to like being alone. In fact, I lived for it. All day at work I would fantasize about being in this personal space, away from the demands of the residents, the commands of my former boss, Rae, and even distant from the expectations of friends. This used to be my sacred ground.

But my apartment has lost its appeal for me. For the past several months my time has been spent working, running errands with Sadie, meeting up with Beau for quick meals between his meetings, and hanging out at the library to help Caitlin research how to start her own business. Everywhere but here. The place has been neglected and exudes sadness.

So what changed? Does a woman's investment in a relationship completely void her ability to enjoy solitude?

"I think not!" I shout at Elmo just when he has forgiven me.

Suddenly, I want this time more than anything. *Ever.*

I pull a napkin out from underneath a Sara Lee carrot cake box and start to jot down the things I miss doing with myself.

1) Going through my books and choosing my top ten.

2) Watching old movies till dawn.

3) Practicing handstands against the wall in my living room.

4) Eating slightly melted ice cream with saltine crackers.

5) Purging my kitchen with plans to start a new diet tomorrow.

6) Going to matinees alone and ordering a large popcorn.

7) Playing CDs and dancing (with curtains closed).

And perhaps the most important of all:

8) Wearing pajamas and eating Chinese takeout.

Within five minutes I have ordered chow mein and hot and sour soup from Chin Ye's, put my hair in a ponytail, and changed into my worn flannels. Nobody in Tucson wears flannel to bed, I'm sure. But I am a still-single girl enjoying a night to herself, and I will wear flannel.

Elmo is figuring out that I am actually settling in for the evening and begins to purr. He too has been neglected. It is as if I have been blind to my former likes, my past pleasures, and even my thought life.

Like Sadie.

Goodness. Is that what has happened to me? To her? All along I thought her new state of pandemonium was caused by the engagement, by wedding pressures. Maybe a scattered life is not caused by the adding of things to one's already heavy workload, but is really caused by the undercurrent of loss. Losing oneself to the cause of love.

This is why Beau is probably the best thing in my life. When left alone, I get too reflective. I could live here forever. Not in this apartment, but in my head. And I sense it is a dangerous place.

By the time the Chinese food arrives, I have called Angelica and Caitlin to come over so that I will not be left alone with my thoughts. But as fate would have it, they are busy. Of course they are. They have learned this lesson themselves many times over.

Caitlin has committed to spending Friday evenings at her parents' house for dinner (very *Gilmore Girls* of her, considering she has rebelled against her wealthy parental units for years and is just now willing to reconcile). Angelica is studying so she can lead her first group tomorrow morning. Apparently she said yes to the woman she didn't want to disappoint and said no to Peyton, who has been waiting six disappointing months to go on a date with her.

It seems we all have been making sacrifices lately.

Misstep One Two

How is anything other than a two-step possible? I mean, we have two feet. One. Two." I showcase my pair of Dansko clogs.

"Nice." Lysa presses down the ruffled layers of her square dance skirt.

"Still fluffy," I say. "I cannot believe you own this getup."

"It was my mom's. I would only wear this in public for you, Mari."

I fold my hands over my heart. "Wait. In public? Does this mean you loll about your apartment in this?"

Martin, a resident who insists on wearing his chenille bathrobe all day, approaches Lysa from behind and taps her on the shoulder. "Wanna dance?"

"Sure, Martin. This dress isn't getting any more attractive, so I might as well put it to use."

"But your knees are quite nice." I wink at my friend before she is whisked away. "And keep your robe closed, Martin!" I holler after them.

"Ready for a twirl, my dear?" Beau loosens his tie and his mood after a hectic day of conferences with his supervisors.

"How'd the meetings go? Were you able to make any headway on the recent restructure proposal?"

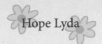

He hesitates, rubbing the back of his neck. For a moment I recognize him as a man. I have thought of him as a guy, then as the guy I am dating, then as my boyfriend…but I don't often acknowledge him as a man. I am about to tell him this, but something in his by now quite lengthy pause gives me cause for pause. Does he think I don't want to hear about his work? Or worse, does he think I don't *get* his work.

"Sick of talking?" I give him an out.

"Yes, I guess so." He grabs it.

The music takes an upward polka turn but my mood takes a dive. I cannot help but review the past few months of conversation with Beau. We ride the surface of everything and never dig deeper. Stuck in Pleasantry Ville is fine for acquaintances, toll booth operators, and occasionally parents—but not for us. In our early months we talked about everything, even the hard material, like our doubts about life and love.

For the next forty-five minutes Beau and I dance with each other and a few of the other residents. When together, we manage to maneuver our way across the makeshift dance floor with forced ease.

I even make it through the do-si-do.

It is the so-so nature of our relationship I keep tripping over.

All About Spin

Overall, the wedding plans are going well. I'm just trying to keep my head above water at work. No wonder brides run away. Planning the big day is like willingly signing up for a second job—without pay."

"There's a payoff. You get to saunter down the aisle in a beautiful white dress and link arms with a wonderful man."

"You are right. It is the preshow that is questionable." Sadie is walking in new heels she bought for the reception. She wants to be a stiletto pro before trying out any dance moves in them. A crack in the sidewalk causes her to grab me for stability.

"You'd think you would get training heels first," I joke.

We are walking along downtown Tucson and nearing our destination. A large sign shaped like a book with a neon bookmark appears just as we pass an ice cream shop. "There it is, Prologue. It is my new regular bookstore."

"Got any Band-Aids?" A quick flip of her ankle positions Sadie's foot in my line of sight. I am not sure what she expects me to do.

"Should I blow on it?"

"No, but can you tell if a blister is forming beneath the ankle strap?"

I pretend to look but am really eyeing the small group of people trying to get by us on the sidewalk. "Tell you what—I guarantee that once we get into Prologue we will not have to walk for at least an hour. Coffee is on me, and there is a fabulous reading room with leather chairs. I'll deliver books and magazines, and you will feel like a queen."

The foot goes back to its natural position and Sadie straightens her shoulders and gives a quick shake of her black hair. This is her "buck up" posture. I open the door for her, and she limps ever so slightly past me into the air-conditioned store.

Before Sadie is seated in the biggest leather chair with an ottoman, I have an iced passion tea ordered for her and an Americano ordered for me.

"Mari?"

I look around me, unsure which direction the voice is coming from. It is a male voice and a bit tentative. My eyes scan the small clusters of people seated at wooden tables with laptops and scones and stacks of books for research and pleasure.

"Over here!" The volume of the voice raises and so does the hand of Kevin Milano, fashion photographer and the man who captured my personal fashion metamorphosis last year. He is seated with a rather tall, striking woman with deep-set eyes and nearly bronze hair. Small, stylish glasses perch on her nose seemingly for visual affect and not visual assistance.

I grab my drinks and walk over to the smiling man. I am feeling good that he recognizes me.

"So good to see you, Mari. Where is your friend?" He asks, motioning for me to take the open seat next to him.

"You mean Caitlin...the one who designed my outfits last year?" I am so excited he asked about her. Caitlin could use some encouragement right now.

"Oh, right. No. I meant Sadie. I saw her walk in with you."

"She is putting her feet up. De-stressing for a bit."

"Weddings can take a lot out of anyone. And really it is right around the corner."

Kevin's comment takes me by surprise. "You know the wedding date?"

"Are you kidding? November 19 is engraved on my calendar. Carson Curtis' wedding will be one of my biggest shoots this year. Besides, I captured his proposal to Sadie last year, and I was thinking I could create a wonderful black-and-white photo essay of their relationship."

"Goodness—you are so powerful you can crash exclusive weddings." I mean it as a compliment, but it sounds a bit judgmental. I am about to revise my phrasing when Kevin speaks up.

"I'm invited. Carson talked to me months ago about attending."

"As the wedding photographer?" I'm wondering why Sadie has never mentioned that she will have *the* Kevin Milano as her own.

"Strictly for PR purposes. The Curtis family was more than a little willing to bring me on board for this event. Carson was a popular bachelor, but people cannot stop talking about his engagement to Sadie. It comes at a time when his family could use some good publicity. He chose well."

He chose well. I picture Sadie all dressed up and placed on a large store shelf with other possible brides as Carson carefully considers his best option—finally pointing to the tall, slim one with a great smile. "Why do they need the publicity?"

Kevin's face reddens and he stirs the remaining cappuccino foam in his green ceramic cup. He checks his watch and looks at me. "I just meant that they position their many companies as family owned and family oriented. It looks good for the oldest son to be married, and I'll bet old man Curtis feels the same. But that is just my opinion."

"Enjoy your coffee," I say to Kevin's table partner. Kevin looks relieved that I am not asking him to elaborate. "I will tell Sadie hi for you," I say in an overly friendly voice.

But as I head back to my *pied*-challenged friend, I know that I won't be mentioning the conversation that just took place. I highly doubt Sadie knows her special day is considered an excellent PR move for the Curtis family—but that is just my opinion.

My cell phone rings. It is the theme from *Star Wars*, the original. "Sorry," I say to Sadie who is devouring the ten new bridal books I have brought her from aisle 4's offerings. "I just got this dang thing and I don't know how to change the ringer. I want to put the theme from *Ice Castles* on there just to bug Angelica..."

"Just answer it." She says and flashes me a glossy photo of a bride running along the edge of a canyon. Sadie's hazelnut-glazed nails are pointing to the veil which has large colored flowers sewn into the edging.

I scrunch up my nose, shake my head, and squelch the ring song. "Hello?"

My mom's voice comes through with only a bit of static, but I sense lots of friction in her tone. "Mari, glad I got you. I wanted you to know that your father is going in for some blood tests today."

"Why? What's been going on?"

"Well, even you mentioned how tired he seemed at Thanksgiving last year. He's just not himself lately and cannot seem to catch up on his sleep or energy. We want to be sure he's fine so we can rule out anything worrisome."

"If that is all it is, why are you calling me?" I come off cold, but I'm trying to force the truth.

"Honestly? Because Marcus told me to."

"So, Marcus knows about all this and I find out…when? While you are in the waiting room?"

I hear my dad in the background. He knows me well enough to guess how I took that bit of truth. "Honey," his voice is weak but light with his usual charm.

"Dad. I want you to tell me what is going on." Sadie now squeezes my hand and offers a look of concern.

"There is nothing to report other than your father has taken up napping. I will call you as soon as we find out which vitamin or diet I need to alter my life with. And that is bad news. You know how I like my ice cream with potato chips." Dad puts a positive spin on his possible news.

"You might not confess that to the doc. Please keep me informed. I can handle it. It shouldn't take Marcus to motivate you and Mom to tell me what is going on."

"Got it. We messed up. No more. The stewardess is waving me in."

"Be good to the *nurse,* Dad, or she won't find your vein on the first try."

He laughs and hangs up, but I can't seem to put the phone down.

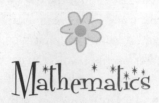

Mathematics

No rice, no bread, no starch carbs, no dairy. Let's see, what else?" Sadie counts on her fingers the foods she is eliminating from her diet for the next six months.

"No fun," Angelica mumbles, devouring another french fry. "So po-taw-toes are out?"

"They are about as starchy a carb as you can order. It all comes down to numbers. That's Renee's theory, and it obviously works for her. Calories in and calories out. I've decided not to look at losing weight as an emotional thing. I'm too sensible for that. If I examine my nutrition as a matter of math—pure mathematics—I can handle it."

"You and Zellweger are on a first name basis now?"

Sadie gives me a sideways "not the point" look.

"Here's some math for you, Sadie. You need to lose zero pounds. You look fabulous." Angelica extends a no-cal offering of sweet praise, but Sadie refuses even that.

Caitlin reaches over to grab one of Angelica's starch bombs. "It's nice having Freddies to ourselves again."

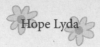

"Yeah. Tuesday night is the only time this place is empty anymore. I miss Samantha," I lament.

"Who?" Sadie nibbles at her Cobb salad.

"Our former waitress, Cruella the Gruel Slogger. She only does the morning shift."

They all nod and we reminisce about the days when we gathered weekly. Pre-engagement. Before Beau and I were serious. Back when Angelica dated with a vengeance, and Caitlin wore the craziest concoctions trying to find the style that would put her on the fashion map. Well—wears. Today she has on a rubber vest the texture of corkboard. And earrings that resemble bottle caps. I think "Dumpster Diva" but leave it in my humor-for-self-only mental files; they need to be purged soon.

"How are the business plans?" I ask the friend I feel the least connected to lately.

"And how is Jim the Cop?" Angelica inquires.

"Those weeks of no calls—turns out he was visiting his grandmother, who is on her deathbed in a small town in Central Mexico. No phones! We have a date next week."

"Great." I cheer.

Sadie, who has been lost in thought for a moment, points her fork in Caitlin's direction. "Carson thought he saw you on an airport shuttle. But when I quizzed him he said the woman had matching pieces of luggage. I told him, 'You don't know Caitlin. She tries never to match.' Then he laughed…"

"It was me," she says sheepishly as she raises a piece of falafel to her lips.

"What?" we ask in unison. Apparently none of us know Caitlin these days.

She puts down her utensils and leans in. "You know Isabel Rossi, that woman in New York who helped us price for the fashion show?"

"Yes."

"Well, she invited me to see her setup in New York." Caitlin's eyes get big. "It was fabulous, you guys. Her collection of vintage and contemporary clothing truly is to die for. And she does tremendous business as a high-priced specialty buyer. I think I could do it. With Isabel's established roster of wealthy women, she barely has to leave her incredible, luxurious apartment in Manhattan to promote the business. It is…"

I interrupt, "But inquiring minds want to know why you didn't tell any of us. You know we all love to live vicariously through one another when it involves travel."

"I'm considering going into business with her. She would like to extend her line and her clientele to the daughters of these women and to the up-and-comers on the New York fashion scene."

Sadie waves her napkin to give us all air. "Oh, Caitlin. They won't pay attention to what you are doing in Tucson. They only want something from Europe or…"

"I would move to New York."

There is a serious silence as we all catch up to this news.

I turn the situation back to me. "I thought all your hours…let me rephrase that, *our* hours at the library were so you could start a clothing store *here.*"

"Amen!" shouts Angelica. The fry-grease that she only eats when it can tempt Sadie seems to be giving her unearthly energy. She claps her hands in succession like one of those organ grinder monkeys with cymbals. I want to set her free, but I am too busy trying to imagine how Caitlin, who dresses to her own beat but depends on everyone else's opinion for everything from toothpaste to apartment decor, has pursued a business venture on her own.

"Now I know how your mom felt the first time you used a rope ladder to escape your bedroom to go dance in dilapidated discotheques." I exaggerate a dab to my eyes with a napkin—but I mean it. Just a little bit.

"Do Mr. and Mrs. Ramirez know about this?" Sadie refers to Caitlin's parents this way because they happen to be two of her biggest donors for the Tucson Botanical Society. They each give from their respective bank accounts every quarter.

Caitlin looks up with her big brown eyes and long lashes. Her mouth

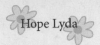

shifts to one side. She looks twelve. "Not yet. But they are the reason I am considering this. *Somehow* they got wind of my desire to open a store." She scans our faces looking for guilt. "Now they want to finance it to secure my future so I don't make a disaster of my credit record in the business community."

"If you take away the put-down part, that is really quite nice."

"But with my parents you cannot omit the parts you don't like. You have to say 'Hey, this is worth it just like it is. Just like they are,' and go from there. That is how I survive my relationship with them."

"Parents like to help their kids. It's natural." I feel myself stepping over to the wrong side of this argument. My friend needs support, but I don't want her to leave.

"Speak for yourself," mumbles Angelica, who has moved on to an order of onion rings.

"Instead of calling it bad, consider that they might want this opportunity as an investment. They believe in what you are doing enough to back it financially." Sadie raises her eyebrows like a parent trying to convince a grade-schooler that maybe liver is the superfood of Olympic gold medalists.

"I still want to claim my purpose. Isn't doing the right thing in this case about doing it on my own and not relying on my parents? I want to show them I can depend on God in my life and that happiness isn't about the numbers in my bank account or my credit rating, but about how faithful I am to my calling."

"Now, that thinking could be a bit dangerous. God doesn't want you in debt." Sadie is missing the point. I make eye contact with her and shake my head.

I jump back over to Caitlin's side of life and extend a hand to shake. "We will support you and your leap of faith, Caitlin."

Silence returns. We eat our desserts with effort and unease. Nobody wants to imagine what life would be like if our perfect table of four turned into an awkward party of three.

Aftermath

How long has it been?" Beau peers at me over the tub of buttered popcorn on the armrest between us.

"Ages. Our last official date was twenty-three days ago. But who's counting?" I take a breath and a slurp of my large soda and regret how I declined the gigantic refillable option. "Though it occurred to me that maybe you had broken up with me and hadn't had time to officially tell me." My hand reaches for yet another mound of artificial yellow kernels.

His face turns toward me and his lips move but a blast of surroundsound obscures his statement. The vertical crease between his eyebrows suggests it was not a reciprocated laughable comment.

I pull the tub toward me and clear our speaking space. While the pop cans and licorice ropes are dancing on the screen, Beau leans in. "I meant since we started going out. This is our nine-month anniversary." He shakes his head.

"Oh. I knew that. I've been looking forward to it all week. I marked it on my calendar at work. You can check. Circled in red. Right there on the seventeenth of June."

It is no use. I have killed his effort at romance with my surly comment about our nonexistent dating pattern.

The movie begins. The movie I have been so excited to see that I circled its preview date in red months ago is now running on the screen before me. I cannot hear the intense dialogue about how a very unnatural disaster is about to hit the coast of Florida. I cannot enjoy the handsomely square jaw and brilliant blue eyes of the lead male. Even the fake butter flavoring turns to battery acid in my mouth. I have squelched Beau's attempt to get our love life back on track.

It isn't until much later—until the leading man and leading lady are flying in a helicopter over debris and see a limping golden retriever and they brilliantly land on the precarious roof of a former post office to rescue the dog that Beau grabs my hand in his long enough to calm my racing thoughts but briefly enough to keep them revved.

I cross my legs rather than go to the restroom because I don't want to leave his side. Not until we have resolved this. I regret my tendency toward one-liners, but surely by now the guy's nervous system is immune to my under-the-breath musings, my offhand remarks.

Twice I catch Beau looking over at me. There is a touch of regret in his eyes. Is it a reflection of my own or all his?

Credits are running by the time I get the nerve to nudge his elbow. He mouths, "Sorry" and closes his eyes. Placing the tub down between my feet so there is nothing between us, I lean in and kiss him.

The kiss is so great I wish we had started cliché movie date kissing earlier.

"Did you really remember it was our ninth anniversary?" he asks.

How to answer. How to answer. "Yes." Pause. "After you mentioned it. But I loved the movie. Who knew *Aftermath* would be that ever-so-special combination of thriller, disaster movie, and big-screen romance?"

He laughs and I know it is safe to offer him the unopened Milk Duds—the gesture I was afraid he would reject earlier.

"I want us to spend more time together, Mari. I know that I have been selfishly caught up in the program. Let's find a way to get back to our old way."

"Should people have an old way to do anything at nine months?"

"We can," he says optimistically.

I try to focus on his positive attitude rather than the depressing thought that we are at a place in our relationship when we need to strive for, work toward, hope beyond hope for connection to reemerge.

Maybe I need to readjust my version of relationship. Maybe real love never measures up to romance in the movies—even disaster movies.

Emphasis on Maid

For the fourth time this week, I am running errands for Sadie's wedding. My maid of honor assignments just keep coming. But at this rate, one would assume we were racing against an altar deadline of tomorrow.

I'm happy to help my great friend, but it can be awkward handling some decisions and discussions with bridal industry representatives. Half the time they assume I am the bride. The woman at the bakery said the "Sadie + Carson" sugar cookies needed to be paid for up front. She actually grabbed a sample chocolate marshmallow cookie from my hand which was on its way to my mouth and held the treat for ransom. I immediately wrote a check for $150 on Sadie's behalf—because she is good for it—but mostly to get my cookie back.

My car complains with each turn of the wheel, so much that pedestrians look at it with an accusatory expression. I shrug once in a while to make it clear that I don't know what it is saying exactly, either. But if it is taking cues from me today, it is whining.

"Purse Strings," I read from a sign decorated with silk strings and vintage floral appliques. Maybe this will be one of the best tasks yet. After all, I am here to pick up our bridesmaid gifts. Sadie, on a business trip, was appalled to ask me to pick up my own gift, but the shopkeeper told her that there was always the possibility our gifts would be mistaken as new inventory and sold to the general public. I think it was the phrase "general public" that really scared Sadie into action.

Everything I see in the storefront window changes my formerly martyr mood into a very hopeful one. Daintily embroidered clutches, monogrammed silk wrist purses, even a cashmere drawstring evening bag doesn't seem over the top among this collection. As I step into the vanilla-scented store I can feel myself breathe more deeply. I'm happy to do this. I'm happy to be here, even though it meant leaving Angelica to completely manage the monthly birthday party at Golden Horizons. She insists that she did not mutter "cake fight" under her breath after I asked her to help me.

"Mari?"

I turn around expecting to see a salesperson, but instead I see the man sold on dating Angelica. "Peyton!" We embrace with genuine affection. I've been rooting for him to win over Angelica's confused heart for nearly a year now.

Once we are standing face-to-face, the juxtaposition of him against the backdrop of silky, shiny women's accessories raises a few questions. "So, Peyton. Whatcha doin' in a place like this?" I spread out my arms to reveal his true surroundings in case he meant to walk into the magazine store next door.

"I love it here."

I motion for him to keep talking.

"They have the most exquisite pieces in town."

"I know that. Apparently Sadie knows that. And probably so do the best-dressed *women* in town. But how do *you* know that?"

He laughs and shakes his head. "I give my top clients a special purse every year for their birthday."

"Female clients, I hope."

"It should go without saying that my top pharmaceutical reps are all women."

"Touché. Well, I give my best clients at Golden Horizons a huge, sugary

cake from the Shop Club. In fact, I'm not even doing that today, Angelica is…" I stop midthought.

"It's okay. Angelica and I *do* work in the same corporate office. I have to hear her name plenty."

"Do you see her? Talk with her?"

"She avoids me whenever possible. If we make eye contact it is only accidental. It is as though I did something to hurt her instead…"

"Of the other way around. I know. And she knows. She doesn't have ill feelings for you at all, Peyton."

"My self-esteem just soared."

"I mean—it is the opposite. I am still convinced she is very attracted to you and wants this eventually. I cannot believe you are holding out for her."

"But you can a little, right? We both know what she is like when she lets her guard down. Wonderful." He looks so sincere and smitten.

"Sir, your purses are ready." The sales manager looks at me. "Are you with him?"

"No. I'm Mari Hamilton, picking up for Sadie Verity."

She smiles a curious grin and puts her palms together in a very Japanese way, though she looks more like a California beach transplant. "Yours are available too. Won't you both join me over here?"

"We'd love to. Shall we?" Peyton grabs my elbow and ushers me toward the side of the store where a counter has two large pieces of velvet folded over like envelopes.

"Ladies first." Peyton offers graciously.

"Let's look at what *your* ladies will receive."

"No, we should honor Sadie," Peyton returns.

The saleswoman seems to fear that we will go back and forth like this all day, so she opens the envelope nearest Peyton. We both suck in our breath in pure appreciation.

"Clearly, by the monograms, these are not for me and the girls."

"You are right. These beautiful pieces are for Mr. Foster."

"I cannot wait to see mine." I look expectantly at her and notice that funny, nearly mischievous grin again.

"Here are your very *original* choices."

When she unveils them, I quickly say, "Not my choice. Sadie's choice."

"They are very unique," Peyton says as we all stare at the delicate yet strangely bulbous creations made of silk, lots of tassels, and—now I see the cause for the facing palms gesture—Japanese writings along the seam line. But it isn't the cultural flair that surprises me. It is the odd striping combination of a creme de menthe green and a sunless tan lotion orange which makes happy words difficult to come by.

"Um. Hmm. Wow. They are…wow."

"You can say that again," Peyton and the saleswoman say in unison.

"I take it these are for use after the wedding. I love the shape. They are surprisingly roomy." Peyton opens one up and reveals a hollowed out bowl fitted with more silk, this piece the color of a cranberry.

"I thought they were to go with our dresses. But I must have misunderstood."

Saleswoman of the year shakes her head. "You understood. These came from our sister store in San Francisco, where the dresses were ordered."

This makes me most curious about the dresses, but I trust my friend Sadie, the classiest gal I know. "Cover them up, please," I say shortly. "To protect them from the sun."

Peyton's hand brushes over the purse with Angelica's initials. "Would you mind if I put a note inside this one before you protect it from the elements?"

"She won't see this until the day of the wedding. This purse is a surprise."

"Sure is." The saleswoman takes her parting shot.

"That's perfect," Peyton says.

I open and close the bubble purse so that it is talking. "It's your heart, go for it."

He smiles and reaches across the counter for a pen. On a blank receipt slip he scribbles out a note to the girl who won't let herself love and places it into the silk wishing well.

Digging

"Keep looking. I know it is here somewhere." Sadie's voice and upper body are buried in an old refrigerator box filled with photo albums, lace doilies, and collector spoons representing tourist stops to exotic places like Michigan and the Oregon sea lion caves.

I talk to her rear portion, which is three feet away from me and my box of Sadie's heirlooms. "It is a picture of your parents and grandparents...at your parents' wedding?"

"Yes. I know I have it somewhere. I want it to be on my guest book table. I've got to have it. Why didn't I pay better attention to this photo? It is priceless, and now look at me...I've gone and lost it." She stands with her hands massaging her lower back. I see that she is starting to cry. She adjusts her bangs to cover.

"Do you want me to call Val for Valium?"

"You worry me sometimes."

"Keep looking." I turn to a new box and begin sifting through belongings representing Sadie the single gal—books about men, dating, not dating, praying for a future mate, and a surprising one entitled *Building a Log Cabin for One.* I hold this one up. "Isn't Caitlin coming over? She should take this one."

"Hey, that is a great read," she self-mocks, "and Caitlin is buying material for my veil today. Didn't you look at the master wedding task list?"

"Couldn't lift it," I mumble.

We dig, plowing through many images. You can learn amazing things about a person through the photos they keep. Most of Sadie's are of her receiving awards, certificates, trophies, and other praiseworthy items. In every shot she is poised, standing a model stance with one foot angled in front of the other and showcasing her amazing posture.

The duration of this engagement might be the only time in my friend's life when she has not been completely perfect. I think of my helmet and Clark Kent-glasses photo and wonder, for the millionth time in the past few years, how Sadie and I became friends. Sure, we met at a Bible study...but why did she ever agree to go out for potato skins at Freddies with me and Angelica afterward?

"I'm such a loser—literally. How will I break it to my mom that I lost that image after I begged her for it after my college graduation?"

"Why'd you want it so badly?"

She returns to an upright position and smiles with a look of disbelief. "I actually thought I would get married soon after graduation. That is how naive I was. Dad had passed away a couple years earlier, and I guess I was hoping the man of my dreams would come into my life soon after to fill the void. Remember how we all thought our timelines would include marriage and kids by now? And here I am just getting started."

"Speak for yourself. My plan did not involve children at this point. We are all right on schedule for what needs to happen, don't you think?"

She shrugs and does the fake wipe of the bangs again. "I suppose you are right. I'd like to believe that."

"Time for everything, right? Like...finding a missing photo!" I raise my hand and the sought-after image with a victorious shout.

Sadie drops to her knees and crawls three paces to come and sit next to me. For a moment, we are both holding the photograph. "This is amazing. Look how your parents are looking at each other's face. It is with utter..."

"Wonderment," Sadie finishes my sentence and we sigh in unison.

Somehow a black-and-white photo better captures our idea of romance than any of the bridal magazines, chick-lit books, or even personal diaries that grace our nightstands.

"Do you think love is really so different for us these days? I mean...do we have a chance at this?" As I finish my sentence I realize it could be a bit insensitive, seeing as how Sadie is nearing the altar. Surely she believes we have a chance.

But my friend who spent her growing up years in the limelight of accomplishment expresses her own shadow of doubt when it comes to *amore*. "I think it is different. Look at what I am entering into. Not what I imagined for myself."

"But still good. And just think...you really will be caught up to your timeline because you will have a stepson. Last I checked that counts as a kid. And you will still be thirty when you tie the knot."

She nods as if I have really shed light on the situation for her.

"Maybe the early arrival of Harry and his mom will turn out to be a good thing. A chance for us all to..."

"His mom is coming?"

She peers over at a year-at-a-glance wall calendar hanging from her bookshelf. "Yes, early."

"Where will they stay?"

She gives me a look.

"Not *with* Carson?"

Sadie reaches toward her bangs, but I grab her hand and hold it. She cries for a while. I've been around her for the waterworks so many times during the engagement that I have figured out her pattern. Shake. Shake. Breathe in. Exhale cry.

"You have nothing to worry about. I'm sure Carson just wants his son close. You should see that as a sign of responsibility."

"Can't he responsibly get them a hotel—a nice hotel?" She waves her hands in the air with exasperation and then folds them back in her lap as though worn out. "I don't really feel that way, Mari. His son should be with him. I'm just not sure where the boundaries should be with Harry's mom."

"Have you discussed it with Carson?"

"Not at all. I found out through his mother. She called to go over the rehearsal dinner arrangements and mentioned that Harry and Leila should probably be invited since they will be staying with Carson."

"Well, our history is always with us. As I recall, you had a former boyfriend on the invitation list. Ghosts of romances past."

"He was my first and only long-term romance before Carson. But Carson was married. Married." Sadie repeats the word in case I didn't get the significance. "I thought girls like you and me would be safe from such things. And that women like Angelica, who find love around every corner, would be the haunted ones."

I sigh and yet cannot help but laugh with her. I have such warped thoughts too. "Sadie, do you realize that the two of us have bought into the existence of a picture-perfect life hook, line, and sinker?"

"Is that wrong?"

"It's like women running around using a magazine's latest rules to change their dating life. Now, that might totally work for them. But the sad part is that all of us want to believe so badly in one cookie-cutter story line that we are willing to follow rules or trends instead of God's leading."

"I already blew the perfect timeline concept, so I might as well allow a new story line to unfold."

"Exactly. The story *intended* to unfold." Just then my phone rings to the *Sesame Street* theme. "It is probably Caitlin, drowning in tulle."

"Answer it. That ring is no better than *Star Wars*."

"Let me talk to my *real* friend!" I pretend to be insulted. "What happened?" I say instead of hello.

"Mari? It's me. Nothing happened." Beau's voice crackles through a bad connection.

"What?"

"My mentor flew in a day early..."

"And boy are his arms tired," I punch line.

Beau doesn't seem to notice my incredibly accommodating sense of humor. "So I'm afraid I will be out of commission today and on through the weekend. Sorry about dinner. I'll have to cancel because my mentor..."

"Yeah. I got that part. That's okay."

"Are you sure?"

Like I have a choice. "I'm bummed because we hardly see each other anymore, and I had reserved a table at that new Thai place…" as I hear my voice I realize I sound needy, but I don't really feel that way. "I do understand, though, how much work is involved in this program, Beau. You know I'm supportive of it, right?"

"Thanks. I'll call ya later. Sorry about canceling. She didn't give me any warning."

"She?" That neediness tone just spiked.

"Yes. Paige."

Paige. I sense a hint of preplanned nonchalance.

"It's just business, Mari." He sounds very male about now.

"I realize this. So why didn't you mention it was a *she* before? Like when I made the mistake of thinking it was a *he* a moment ago? Or the forty million times we have discussed this mentor program and your mentor. Your mentor-ess. Which sounds like…"

"Don't be silly, Mari. I'm sure I mentioned Paige by name. I really have to go. We're okay, right?"

"We're okay. I'll call you later." I decide not to dig any deeper into this topic while in front of Sadie. She has just unveiled her secret, but I cannot expose mine. Though I want to assure us both that while the love we receive might not be exactly as we pictured, it can still…

"I had better call you. We'll be in a meeting."

End of conversation. Beginning of suppressed questions.

"Bye, Beau," I whisper with a tinge of melodrama and hang up the phone.

Sadie clears her throat. "Mari, you have nothing to worry about with Beau. He's like the ideal guy."

"As in *like* but *not* the ideal guy?"

"Uh-oh. You're in quite the mood."

"Yep. I had better be going home. I have lots of weekend plan revisions to make and comfort food to pick up." My voice falls away, as do my thoughts and a little hope.

Sadie seems to notice. "It will pass."

We hug and she gives me an extra squeeze.

I grab my sweater from the hook by the door. My silver ring gets caught on the sleeve, but I'm too impatient to detach myself so I wave the cardigan like a flag as I gather my purse, a few bridal magazines, and the box of books about dating and cabin building. "It was worth looking for," I say on the verge of tears. The fact that I *know* I am overreacting does little to calm me.

"What was?" Sadie comments absently, a bit too baffled by my sweater dance to recall how we just spent our Friday evening. "Oh, love."

"Right." I meant the photo.

The soothing evening air kisses my face, and I pull the door closed.

Tutu Good

Sometimes it is when a friend says nothing that you can discern the loudest cry for help. When Angelica decided to swear off men and get her life back on the straight and narrow, I think she narrowed life down too far. This is my realization today as I watch her sluggishly move from the escalator to the china department, where I have just printed thirty pages of registered gift listings for Sadie and Carson from a kiosk.

Angelica has always had an edge about her but never, ever lines. Until now. Beneath the fluorescent lights and above the glow from crystal displays fine creases appear in surprising numbers around her mouth and about her eyes.

"Tell me this is the novel you always wanted to write," she pleads.

"Afraid not, fellow shopper. But the good news? I had them printed out in ascending price order. We can get rid of these." I scan the pages and toss twenty-eight of them in the recycle bin.

"What does that leave? A 'first year of marriage' Christmas ornament?"

I return my gaze to the list. "Pretty much."

Among the salad bowls and the beach-themed weekend plate sets we

wander, pick up random items and scrunch our noses. Nothing suits our friend. "You think the only good choices were in those last chapters?" Angelica asks, sighing.

"These gifts are for people who don't know her," I groan.

"You're right. Let's go. We won't find *it* here."

We make our way through the crowd of registering almost-brides and commission-frenzied saleswomen to the heat of the afternoon.

"Let's go in here." Angelica points to a restaurant on the corner. I'm too hot to say I just ate lunch.

When we step into the cool, I realize this is Nonconformity. Angelica and I have a history here but she does not say a word. She nods to our hostess, who is wearing a tall Abe Lincoln hat and again to our waiter, who is dressed in a tutu.

Angelica's eyes glance over the decorative walls and large booths we had first seen on a Friday night last year. She had left the place early with some other friends and Peyton had remained behind with me to profess his feelings of admiration for her. It was when Angelica was dating anyone and everyone except for guys who had potential to make her stop and consider what life would look like through the lens of love. I had consoled Peyton and wondered why I was always the girl having love for her friends professed to her. Even in high school, this had been my role in the dating wheel.

"Nachos and diet soda." Angelica hands her menu over to tiny dancer and motions for me to order.

"Lettuce wraps with the orange salsa and an iced tea."

Our waiter curtseys and walks off toward the kitchen. Only now do I notice he has on turquoise Converse sneakers.

"Are you going to tell me what is going on?" I say with blunt force.

Shock. Surprise. Innocence. They all make a brief appearance on Angelica's face, but the looks of acknowledgment, guilt, and self-loathing remain. "Yes. I know this is where Peyton told you he liked me. Can't a girl eat wherever she wants during a busy shopping day with a good friend? The kind of friend who doesn't bring up sore subjects?"

"I think you are pining."

"Pining. Pining?" She first says the word quickly and then the second slowly, trying to make sense of it. The friend formerly known as "Angel" to her in-crowd groupies never had to nor desired to pine for anyone. "That is ridiculous. Nobody pines these days. When have you known me to pine?"

I look down at her fingernails. Just as I had suspected. Brittle, unpolished, and completely her own jagged stubs. "Let's see—perhaps it was the last time you went out in public without a manicure."

Those hands pull back toward their owner and disappear under the table.

"Angelica, when are you going to let yourself take a chance? At least call the guy and let him know if he is waiting in vain. You know he hasn't dated anyone."

Her eyes soften and her mouth draws together with worry. "Is he mad?"

"No. Just hopeful and a bit enamored with a girl he has never gone out with. What a nut, right?" I lighten the mood by insulting the object of my friend's secret admiration.

She laughs and raises her eyebrows, which also have returned to an au naturel state. "I promised that I would take a break from dating and see what God gave me to fill that void." She pauses as our waiter returns with our food. "It turned out to be a lot."

"Too much," I add. "Need I list all the volunteer activities you are involved in? Your time helping me at Golden Horizons alone would qualify as a part-time job. I appreciate it, but combined with the church stuff, fund-raisers, food bank, and sponsorships of children in Africa, you have no time to..."

"What? Say it." Angelica dips a chip deep in the sea of orange and awaits my response with accusatory eyes.

"To know yourself, I guess. Wasn't that your objective?"

She drops the chip back into the bowl and sips her drink. "What if I return to myself and become self-absorbed again? You know what I was like before."

"Uh, yeah. But this extreme swing of the pendulum is throwing you off balance too. Getting your faith and personal life back on track does not

require you to pay penance this way. Have you left forgiveness out of your theology?"

She nods and retrieves the abandoned, soggy chip. This time she devours it. She looks up a bit hopeful. "You're probably right." While she chomps away with revived hope, a slight wince crosses her ruby mouth.

"What is it?"

"A couple months ago I was at a store buying a baby shower gift for a woman at church. The girl at the counter said, 'Happy Mother's Day,' and I said, 'No, thank you.'" Angelica traces her finger along the edge of the table and seems frustrated. "I said it like she asked if I wanted pickled herring."

"Pickled herring?"

"I hate pickled herring."

"I've never had…"

Angelica interrupts my digression. "The point is that my response was so immediate. 'No, thank you.' I mean, who says that? Do you really think this is the kind of woman Peyton wants? Deserves?" Angelica points a hangnail in her direction.

"He deserves a lot. You're right." I look directly at my friend. "But, Angelica, you are amazing. You have so much to offer someone."

"You are just saying that so I will buck up and stop being the downer in Sadie's fairy tale."

"Not true. I'm saying it because I don't want to show up at your apartment someday and see you in fetal position, on the couch, with Tori Amos or Kate Bush music playing in the background."

"That happened *once* in college," she states for the record and cracks a smile.

"Would it help to know he is still waiting for you to emerge from your dating coma? This is recent and accurate news."

"He's too good." She shakes her head back and forth as though this is actually a bad trait.

"Is this what you are trying to do?" I add up her recent behavior and compare it to what she has just said. "Are you trying to become good enough for Peyton?"

"Maybe," she shrugs. "That sounds crazy out in the open. In my mind it made sense." She laughs at herself. "I wish I understood why Sadie's engaged bliss has sent me spinning."

The friend I thought was immune to jealousy and peer pressure has just confessed to conforming to the confusion all of us have experienced since Sadie's engagement.

"Well, join the club, sister. I have yet to feel good enough for Beau."

"But you have what Sadie has."

"Don't be so sure," I say quietly, not wanting to go deeper into my own doubts.

"You haven't answered my question. How do I find my way back to myself without going overboard?" The last chip is devoured and Angelica licks the salt from her fingers.

I look up and see the tutu coming toward us. He has added one of those propeller beanie hats to his outfit.

"Ask him. He seems to have found the key to moderation and mental health."

"Funny." Angelica tosses a toothpick with yellow cellophane toward me. It sticks in the weave of my top.

For a moment I have hope that my friend is on her way back to herself.

What Goes with Chartreuse?

I look at my latest wedding responsibilities written out in purple ink on vellum—Sadie's elegant way of dictating our lives. It would be a welcomed touch if revised lists—in calligraphy—did not arrive in my mailbox regularly. I've taken up origami because the paper is too pretty to toss in my produce plastic bag-lined wastebasket.

We are all seated on a silver bench awaiting Valerie, the overzealous bridal consultant who is going to show us Sadie's choice in bridesmaid dresses. Sadie had to go out of town for a national botanical society conference, but she made us promise that we would call her with our reaction as soon as we saw the dresses. She said we might be surprised by the style she went with, but she knew we would grow to love them.

This last comment and our collective closets full of pink lace sweetheart necklines and wide-load, rear-end bows make us all nervous. Angelica is biting her newly manicured nails, Caitlin is tracing the pinstripes on her pants with a dime, and I am willing Valerie to make her sedative offer to me just one more time.

"So perfect of her to be gone." Angelica rolls her eyes and returns to her Bible study notes.

I try to defend the defenseless. "Sadie wanted to be here. Can she help it if she is so well known in her field that she was asked to speak on designer gardens of the twenty-first century to her peers?" I wish I had nails to bite. All I can think of are those dang awful monogrammed purses made to match the creation we are about to see.

"Sadie has great taste. I mean, a bit sedate for my preferences," says Caitlin, "but we have nothing to worry about. Besides, she has been in more weddings than all of us combined. She knows better than to offer us garments of fluff and no substance."

"Excuse me, Valerie?" I call out to our MIA hostess.

The second in command happy girl rushes into our viewing room on heels that are toothpick-thin. "Yes. Can I help you?"

"Did Valerie go to lunch?"

Happy girl the clone realizes I am kidding but impatient. "Of course not. You're funny. Ms. Verity's dresses were special ordered, so we are transporting them from the shipment cases to the preview trolley."

"This is bridal shop speak for Valerie is unpacking boxes and loading a roller rack, am I correct?"

Nod.

The nice version of me returns for one last try at nourishment. "I'm sorry. We are all on our lunch break and very hungry. Could we have that tray of appetizers come through here again? And could you at least ease our angst by assuring us that the dresses are not made out of taffeta stiff enough to walk the aisle by themselves?"

She takes in my requests and rings for more food. "I don't want to give away too much, but I promise you that there is not a thread of taffeta on these unique dresses."

Angelica looks up from Philippians, which is now painted highlighter

yellow in her travel Bible. "Wait. Classic is rarely described as unique. Get Valerie in here pronto."

The squeak of the preview trolley arrives just ahead of the creak of the snack cart. The dresses are draped in opaque garment bags and the veggies are wrapped in wontons. I have a hard time remembering which I am actually here for.

Valerie pulls one from the pole and positions it to face us. She begins to unsnap the seams.

Snap.

Snap.

"I feel like we should have a drumroll," Caitlin whispers.

I am about to joke "we have egg rolls," but now the dress is revealed and I cannot think of anything except "bold stripes."

"You've got to be kidding me!" Angelica snaps.

Caitlin rubs her eyes and repeats the motion. I know this doesn't help because I just did the same and the dresses are still…

"Vibrant Vixen." Either Valerie speaks with self-absorbed alliteration or she names our gowns.

"Excuse me?" Angelica says, incredulous.

"Aren't they fabulous? These are hard to find designs from Europe."

You mean hard to look at.

"Nobody has ever splurged on these for a wedding."

You mean nobody in their right mind.

Only Caitlin still has her wits about her. "Could you leave us alone with—those. There—the dresses."

"Or better yet, take them when you go," Angelica adds.

Valerie thinks we are joking. She tolerates our lack of appreciation and waits next to the most colorful, horizontally-striped, silk kimono of a thing ever witnessed this side of the psychedelic seventies.

"Do we have to try these on?"

"This isn't a fitting," I clarify. "It's a—sighting."

"Like a UFO."

"Is that a band of pistachio green?"

"You mean the stripe next to the chartreuse one?"

"Shouldn't we have 3-D glasses?"

"At least a black light."

"Maybe she didn't want to actually *choose* a color for her wedding?"

"She said they would grow on us…" I try my supportive voice.

"Like fungus," Angelica interrupts.

By now Valerie understands we are not kidding but very, very serious. She pushes our fashion fate out of sight and closes the curtain behind her. We are left alone with our first impressions, and they aren't pretty.

"Who was responsible for selecting dresses with her?" I demand an explanation other than the one about our friend being captured by alien fashionistas who want to ruin good taste one fabric at a time.

We all refer to our calligraphy lists.

"I think her sister went with her. Is she color-blind?"

"Uh—try blind-blind."

Angelica groans. "How can we call her with our response now? I'm not a good liar anymore. Mari, you do it."

For a moment this makes sense until my mind does a double take over the insult.

Just then my phone rings. I shove it toward Caitlin. "You are the one who kept the secret about your New York trip. And you know all those fashion terms. You have to stall for us."

"Is that the stupid theme from *Ice Castles?* Make it stop." Angelica grabs the phone, presses the talk button, and thrusts the phone to Caitlin's ear.

"Hello? Sadie! How is the conference going? Congrats on being selected to speak to the directors about…what? Yes. We are at the bridal shop right now. We *just* saw them, Sadie." Caitlin raises her eyebrows at me and shrugs. I motion for her to keep on talking, but the deer-in-headlights look I'm getting is my cue to grab the phone.

"They are dream dresses, Sadie." Or to be more accurate…costumes for performances of *Joseph and the Amazing, Technicolor Dreamcoat.*

"I'm so glad you like them, Mari. I was worried. My sister chose them when I visited her in San Francisco last month. We've never shared style preferences, but by the time we got together I had assigned all the big jobs, and *you* are my maid of honor, so when she said she didn't fit into my life anymore..."

My friend's stammering explanation is explanation enough. It is clear that we all feel the same way about these dresses. "Then this is the right dress for us," I offer.

Angelica kicks me; Caitlin stifles a cry.

Lie-brary

What do we need this time? Haven't we read the entire business section?" I chase after Caitlin, who is wearing a bright yellow raincoat, matching hat, and very interesting tiger-striped sandals, which move at a rapid pace despite their spiked heels.

"I want that business plan book again. The one with the questionnaire to help us create a 'unique and successful' mission statement."

"And why are we running?"

Caitlin stops midstaircase and turns to face me. "My parents and I had another inspiring talk."

"Meaning—a fight?"

"Correct." She does a half bow, which gives me a chance to straighten the plastic daisy on her hat.

"Got it. We have a mission." I reach into my purse and pull out my favorite pen to show her how serious I am.

We both step into the same slice of revolving door and push together with a bit too much force. I get out in the right spot, but Caitlin ends up stuck in for another spin. I don't even bother fixing the daisy when she emerges.

"Get busy," I say, pointing toward the resource center.

"I need you." Caitlin's hands are on her hips. She's all business in her Paddington Bear getup.

"And I need coffee. I'll bring you a coconut bagel." I wave my serious pen again.

"With the pineapple cream cheese?"

"Nothing less."

We part ways at the escalator, yet another moving apparatus for Caitlin to get caught up in. I watch until she is safely upstairs.

A server with book-shaped earrings and braces excuses herself to the back room to look for the pineapple cream cheese. I count straws in one of those self-painted vases and then pennies in the spare change dish—a very savant thing that I do. Funny how I could barely pass geometry but my mind spins with numbers like a roulette wheel that never stops—or pays off.

"Bingo!" Nice girl emerges with a small plastic tub of cream cheese.

"Goodness. That is a rare thing to hear outside of my day job."

She cocks her head to the side. "What do you do?"

I laugh self-consciously. I hadn't intended to solicit further conversation about myself. "I'm the recreation director at Golden Horizons."

"Oh my gosh!"

"Now *that* is a rare response."

As she spreads the yellow-and-white mixture on the bagel she can barely contain her power of knowledge. "I know that place."

"You do?"

"They had a big fashion show last year. Do you remember? It was quite fancy. I had to work, but my mom and dad went."

"That was my fund-raiser!"

"This just gets better, doesn't it? I bought my wedding dress there. It was something I would have never dreamed of getting. My dad called me from the auction and took a picture with his camera phone. And I said 'don't let it get away.'" She reaches her hand toward me. "I'm Tanya, by the way."

"Mari. Small world, isn't it? I actually thought my friend Sadie would buy it. She is the one who modeled it."

"I copied her look for my wedding. I like things a bit funky. I have a picture...can you wait?" She pushes my order toward me and rushes back to the storage room.

Sadie's style has never been called funky; that is, until last week when we met the go-go dress.

When Tanya returns she is digging through her purse.

I don't have the heart to tell her that I know the dress well. I stared at it for quite a few hours during the days before the fashion show. Everyone thought I should keep it. After all, it was part of my inheritance from Tess, but somehow it seemed too self-assured to buy a wedding dress before there was a groom. Beau and I were long-distance dating at the time, but I was afraid to hope we would become serious.

I don't want to see the dress that should have been mine. The dress I should have had faith enough to keep. But instead of saying anything, I smile. Big and confident and full of what I hope appears to be great faith.

A wallet-sized photo is handed to me and what I see surprises me. "This one?" I blurt with relief. "I mean, I love this dress. It was one of the highlights."

In my hand is a beautiful shot of Tanya and groom leaning against a bridge rail. They are looking at one another and the sun is setting behind them. It is a romantic image, but what my eyes cannot veer away from is the floor-length velvet dress with horizontal satin piping. The colors are yellow and green. It is funky, and it is the formal dress Caitlin modeled.

"It is cool and unconventional. My dad said he put a bid in on an actual bridal gown as well so I could choose, but someone else bought that one. Things work out, don't they?"

"Yes, they do. Thanks for showing me the photo. And for the coffee." I raise my cup to her. All of a sudden I feel overwhelmed by memories of last year—the times when I wasn't sure if I was ready for a serious relationship. Then the happiness. And now...more of the confusion. Is this what love is?

My feet move toward the escalator while my mind skips around to scenes from my relationship with Beau. I cannot help but smile. The guy is sweet, even if we never see one another these days. Even if I spend my Saturday at the library with Caitlin and he spends his Saturday at the office slaving over his reports, compiling research and writing page after…

"Paige! Over here. You'll love these architecture books." Beau's voice bellow-whispers from the other side of the glass cubed wall.

I duck instinctively as though I have been caught doing something wrong. I am already moving on the escalator and soon I will be high enough for Beau and friend to see me. A little boy and his mom stand behind me on the narrow stairs. There is no escape.

I crouch down lower, keeping my eyes on the steel ridges of the step. Head in sand. Head in sand.

"What's wrong with her?" The little boy says quietly to his mom. I imagine the stern look and raised eyebrows she offers him as her only explanation. I mean, who wants to think they are in the presence of demented individuals at the happy library…the wonderland where books and bagels coexist.

I glance down to my right, unable to resist one more moment of suspense. I see a bit of red hair leaning in toward Beau's dark hair. They are peering over what must be a fascinating book of architecture. Architecture? Since when is Beau interested in architecture?

The stairs run out before my stare does, and I am thrust onto the red-and-purple checked carpet. Pineapple cream cheese becomes a face mask and my coffee does a double half twist beyond my reach. The curious little boy steps over me cautiously in case I plan more erratic movements.

"What took you so long?" Caitlin looks up at me from her notebook.

"I had to stop at the bathroom."

She looks me over and then to my hands, which are empty of offerings. "Where's my bagel with pineapple cream cheese?"

"They were out."

"Where's your coffee?"

"Drank it." Wore it.

She gives me a curious look, seemingly unsure of whether to buy into my lies. "Did you see Beau? He's here," she looks around at the stacks of books, "somewhere."

"No. But he said he might be here today."

Liar, liar coffee-stained pants on fire.

"I thought he was at his office?" She says with a curious lilt.

Clearly, Caitlin the Spy saw *the girl* and wants to know who she is.

"He was for a while. Then he and his project mentor, Paige, were coming here." I say this to protect him, to save my pride—and once out of my mouth, I believe it.

"Oh," she says still questioningly. "Don't you want to go look for him? Them?"

"No. I'm sure they are busy. And so are we. Let's get going on that mission statement. We have a goal, girlfriend!"

Caitlin must want to move past my inner cheerleader as much as I do. She pulls out a chair for me and motions for me to sit. "As long as you are fine with it."

"Totally!" I say this with a large half-yodel *O* in the middle—and once out of my mouth, I don't believe it.

Favorites

"The diabetic club had their activity," Lysa states as she places a large cookie in front of me.

I stare at the huge mound. "A bake sale?"

"They see it as their outreach."

I take a bite and chew slowly. "Applesauce…carob…and something tangy."

"Lemon zest."

"Ah, I've always wondered what my chocolate chip cookies were missing."

Lysa sits at her desk, which is just outside of Beau's office. "How was your weekend?"

"Oh, same-o. I helped Caitlin with her business start-up research. She has to turn in her proposal to the Small Business Association loan review board next week. And Beau had to work. Turns out his mentor was in town again. Who knew I would become the jealous type? I have my life, my interests, my friends—but lately he is either working or working with her. Which means, it really isn't working for me. I'm morphing into one of those women who is needy. Needy is my current second-least-favorite word."

"What's the first?"

"Paige. Which brings me back to needy."

I realize I am more upset than I expected. I try to reexplain my circumstances to make us both feel better. "You know, it is good timing, though. I have Sadie's wedding to deal with. I gladly help Caitlin. And I have had more time to enjoy the solitude I used to love before I got so caught up in Beau. It's good. What did you do?"

Lysa pauses and half shrugs. "I worked too. Just a little." She seems uncomfortable. "Before I forget, Rose Waverly was asking to see you. She has a new idea for the afternoon craft group's project."

"But she's in the morning craft group."

Lysa points her index finger at me like a cheesy game show host. "Exactly."

"Now be nice," I get up from my seat and gladly step away from the shredder and my exciting activity for the day. "Rose is actually so much sweeter now than back when I knew her at church. She was my least-favorite pew neighbor. She scared me."

"And now?"

I laugh. "Okay, her control still scares me. But the first day she walked through these doors, she was fragile and broken. I'd rather see her happy and in charge any day. And I can confidently say she is one of my favorite residents."

"Well, good—because she wants to turn your desk into a float for the end of summer parade."

I walk over to Lysa's larger desk. "Why use my little pooper-scooper float when she could have the star of the show?" As I pretend to take the measurements of the old roll-top-turned-convertible workspace, I notice a miniature yellow rose plant.

Lysa notices me noticing and casually pushes some books in front of it.

"Good try. Who's the guy?"

"That rhymed."

"You know everything about my relationship with Beau. I just spilled my guts, for Pete's sake. You finally have one admirer who sends flowers, and you say nothing." I goad her a bit, but I'm really quite happy that she has a new friend.

"I will let the word 'finally' slip because..." she looks down and feigns a hangnail. One of my personal moves of avoidance.

"I'm waiting. Who is he?"

"I worked here all weekend because I ran reports for Beau and for…"

"Least-favorite word?"

"Yeah. I already knew you felt a bit left out of this project, so I didn't want to rub it in that I got to work all weekend." She stops and laughs.

I laugh to ease her discomfort. "Oh, don't worry—I'm nuts. I'm surprised I have a boyfriend."

"And since I think working all weekend is cause for jealousy between us—I'm not surprised I *don't* have a boyfriend."

My eyes scan the hallway, and I quickly glance into Beau's office to be sure we are alone. "So, why were Beau and Paige at the library on Saturday if they were supposed to be here working?"

Lysa looks relieved. "I sent them there. I had to run five reports, and they were standing over me. So I insisted they leave for half an hour to give me peace. How did you know?"

"I saw them. Sort of. I saw Beau and half of her head. And then I hid."

"Why? You are his wonderful girlfriend. The girlfriend he talks about all the time. You should have gone right over to them and laughed and shaken hands and acted like it is no big deal."

"Yeah."

"Because it is *no big deal.*"

"I should have, you're right. But I also think he should have made a point of introducing her to me before now. Don't you think? He's quite a polite person by nature. So the fact that I have not met her makes me nervous. She's pretty, isn't she?"

"I might have a third-least-favorite word for you."

"Uh-oh. Bring it on."

"Stunning."

I act as though a dagger has gone through my heart. "Where is the protective nature you exhibited moments ago? Now you are throwing images at me that my little head does not need right now."

"I'm not finished. She's stunning and a bit severe. I think Beau spends half of his time with her trying to regain control of his own project. Despite the yellow flowers of friendship on my future float, she is not a warm person."

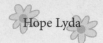

"At least I feel better about why they were at the library. But if he doesn't introduce us next time..."

Lysa looks past my shoulder and pinches my leg. "Beau!"

"Hello, Lysa. Mari." Beau nods at us both. It is the first time I have seen him since I tripped off the escalator.

Lysa stands up and starts down the hallway rather quickly. "I will go tell Rose that the desks are off limits."

"Nobody can call that woman subtle," Beau says and motions for me to go into his office. As I walk in front of him, he places his hands on my shoulders and gives me an affectionate rub.

I turn and face him and wait for whatever he wants to say. Usually I make it easy for him to be a man of few words, but I want to hear something that will turn my thoughts around.

He starts off haltingly. "I'm sorry I missed church."

Okay.

"I should have called you," he continues.

I remain silent. Anything I say will come out wrong, harsh, or just plain crazy.

"Good news, though. The project is coming along nicely."

"So you will finish sooner?" I break my vow with hope.

"Sort of. We'll meet our goal early enough that we can complete our second pitch for funding. It's beyond what our expectation was for this project."

I remember when "our" was a happy word in the dating vocabulary. It has just bumped "needy" for second place on my least-favorite list.

Since I broke my silence, I decide to plunge forward into the abyss of relationship mystery. "Beau, I don't know if I am supposed to say this. It might be stupid or unnecessary at best—but I think I should meet Paige. In fact, I'm surprised it didn't happen that first weekend."

His face softens into worry. His hands go back to my shoulders. "That isn't stupid. You shouldn't have had to ask. I'm so caught up in my new work that I'm missing out on the reason I moved back to Tucson in the first place."

"The fancy office and sizable bonus?"

He hugs me and kisses my hair. "You, silly. I adore you. Next time, I will introduce you to her."

Is it terrible that I wanted him to introduce her to *me*?

"And we will go out on a date soon," he promises.

"The three of us?"

"Mari, you are my top priority." He leans in and kisses me on the lips. "And you are my favorite person in the world."

I don't even worry whether coworkers will see us kissing. That's all I needed to hear. I set aside my reservations and kiss him back.

Sudden Moves

It taunts me, hanging there flashing all those stripes and colors." Caitlin motions with grand gestures at her dress in her closet. We are sitting on leopard-print beanbag chairs on opposite sides of the living room playing badminton over her metal coffee table. As each serve sends a rush of wind over a PEZ dispenser, the Superwoman's head rolls around with a "ping, ping" on the copper-and-aluminum surface.

"I decided that we should think of ourselves as backup singers to Sadie's finest performance." It is a stretch, but I like my new perspective.

"We won't have to worry about being overlooked, that's for sure."

"We'll look like a Broadway version of the Partridge family bus."

"Or waitresses in an Austin Powers movie!" We laugh and bat the birdie back and forth.

Ping.

Ping.

"How real is New York, Caitlin?"

"That's what Jim asked me last night."

"Oh, yes. Your reunion date. How was it?"

"Like all early dating reunion dates—a bit like starting from scratch." She retrieves the birdie from a potted plant. "That isn't true. I was nervous because I had thought we were over before we started, but he seemed comfortable and really glad to see me."

"I think that is why people have dogs. They are always happy to see you." I put my racket down to concede the match.

"That was left field. Racket up. No quitting until we have a winner."

Caitlin lobs the birdie toward the ceiling. "Jim does have big brown puppy-dog eyes. And he is so kind. He brought me something from Mexico. Hold on." She interrupts the game and walks over to a small vintage jewelry case. I watch her smile broaden as she removes a piece and brings it over to me. She walks as though carrying precious cargo.

I stare down at a jewel-coated bug broach. The shape is disturbing, but on second glance, I see how delicate it is. "Exquisite," I say.

"His aunt in Mexico makes them. I guess she is a well-known artisan." She flips the bug on its back and there is an inscription: "The amber is for my brown-eyed girl. The red is for my affection."

"Flip again." I direct her actions so I can see the red stone in the center of the bug. It is a heart. "Caitlin, you have found a guy as romantic as you are."

"I know. And we do have a connection. Well, other than those endless couple of weeks when I thought he had deserted."

"It also seems fast. I mean, fast to receive a bejeweled beetle."

"Like you and Beau—romantic matches *and* it happened just like that." She snaps her fingers.

"We are not romantically balanced. Beau is far more about flowers and stealing kisses than I am."

Or he used to be.

I ignore my mental digression. "But yes, it did happen fast. Faster than I would have…"

Caitlin narrows her long-lash adorned eyes. "You aren't going to become dissatisfied with life again, are you?"

I shake my head. "Wouldn't dream of it."

This is as far as I can go in conversation with any of my friends or family these days. After my desire for a bigger life last year brought me full circle to appreciate what I have, people act as though I used my one free pass to life exploration. I like my life. I'm thankful for Beau. I appreciate my friends. But I don't feel my phase of sacrifice or growth is over. I learned priceless lessons during my makeover, and I don't think God is finished with those lessons yet.

When does the sometimes helpful discomfort with life become the destructive seed of discontentment? I have nobody to ask these things. Everyone is tired of analyzing my life with me, but there is so much going on in my mind and heart these days.

My life is obviously a retired topic, so I return to Caitlin's life. "What if the New York scenario becomes only working with or under Isabel? Will that be enough for you?" I start up our game again with a fine serve.

"I think it is better than the alternative—allowing my parents to run my life. I have been making it on my own without depending on my parents' wealth or connections. Why would I want to go back to that feudal system?"

"I believe in you, Caitlin. Whether you start your own place or partner with Isabel, you will find your groove."

"My groove? Are you under the spell of the dress or something?"

My phone rings "Stayin' Alive," thanks to Angelica, who thought it would match our wedding attire. "Good timing," I say and answer before Caitlin starts her Travolta moves.

"Mari, it's Mom."

I swing and nail Caitlin on the nose with the birdie before putting my racket down. "How is Dad? What did the doctor find out?"

"Mari, it isn't great news. Not the worst, so don't get frantic, but your father is restricted to bed rest right now. He has a blood infection of some kind. Nobody seems to know how or when he contracted it, but chances are he has had it for a while. His fatigue is so much worse. He can't work. He can barely walk across the kitchen without becoming breathless."

"Oh, Mom. How are you doing? What about the shelter?" I take in a breath. "And your campaign?"

"Marcus is here. I will be fine. And the campaign can wait," she states with conviction, but I don't believe her.

I hear Dad yelling, "I won't let her quit!"

"I thought Marcus was finishing his program at the university this term."

"He is. But Dad will be good in no time, Mari."

I hate to do this, but apparently I must. "Put Marcus on the phone."

My mom is flustered but she follows my instruction. If Marcus is the one who told Mom and Dad to initially call me about this, I know I can trust him to give me the actual home scenario. If Marcus is anything, he is straightforward.

His first words make my head tingle. "I'm sorry about the news, Mari. We certainly were hoping it would be different."

What? Marcus is speaking on behalf of the family as though I am a concerned neighbor or a distant acquaintance. My tone comes off less perturbed and more scared. "Marcus, can they really do this without help? More help?" I clarify.

"I will stay on longer if need be. My situation in Chicago is somewhat flexible."

"Marcus, take the phone to the roof deck. Then we'll talk." While I wait for him to climb the stairs to the top of the youth shelter, I walk into Caitlin's dressing room, which is an actual bedroom. A year ago she decided that extra space for all her fashion creations and purchases was more important than splitting rent with a roommate.

For a few moments I only hear Marcus breathing in the foreground and the sounds of daily shelter activity in the background—kids discussing the chore chart, asking questions of Mom and Dad, slamming the front door on their way to school, sports, and the nearby Metro stop.

"I'm here." Marcus' voice is warmer now. I picture him seated on the bench with flower boxes sprouting lavender and rosemary on each end. A trellis of yellow roses is his backdrop—the nation's Capitol, his view.

"What do I need to know, Marcus. I trust your judgment."

"Straight out, Mari—he's not good. And if your mom plans to go ahead with the campaign, and I think she does, this place could be in trouble. I'd

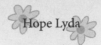

like to think I alone could manage everything, but I'll be working on my dissertation…" He pauses long enough for me to formulate my revised life plan. He hears me sigh heavily.

"Mari?"

"It's sinking in, that's all."

Marcus assumes I am talking about my dad's health. "He'll be okay. He just needs absolute rest, which you know is a nightmare for him."

"No, what I need to do next, *that* is sinking in. I'm coming to DC for as long as it takes."

In the living room, a shout from Caitlin is followed by a loud crash.

"Mari, hold on. I could check in with you every week, and then we could assess this kind of change later. It's not like you can just quit your job."

"Thanks, Marcus, but these are *my* parents. And I won't have to quit. I'll take a leave. You forget that the guy I was dating, *am* dating, is now my boss."

I hear a siren on the Washington, DC end and then Marcus' voice. I can tell he is cupping his hand over the phone. When his words come to my ear they are close, intimate. "Mari, not a day goes by that I forget."

My heart catches a beat.

Telling

The walk to the Tucson Convention Center seems to last forever—as though I am trudging along on the bottom of the sea. My feet drag, my legs resist the pressure to keep moving, and my lungs are heavy. I could blame it on the heat, but it is the news I've received about Dad and the news I will need to give Beau that weighs on my limbs.

I didn't call Beau last night and tell him over the phone. I have asked for more connection in our relationship, and here I am planning to leave. But I know he will understand.

After a restless night's sleep and a shower, I decide to surprise Beau after his meeting with the city commissioners today. He's joined one of their task forces as an advocate for special populations' services.

I wave to a little boy who is selling lemonade on the corner. As I approach his card table-turned-storefront, I can see swirls of sugar on top of the full pitcher. The ice has melted and the boy is ready to. After digging into the accessible part of my purse for a one-dollar bill I crammed there, I pull out a ten. Now I remember asking for cash back at the market last night. Last night when I left Caitlin's I just wanted to be alone. I didn't call Beau, nor Sadie or Angelica. I just lay down on the couch, opened a quart of ice cream, and stared at my ceiling fan wondering why or how I made this big decision so easily.

I give the boy the ten. We talk for fifteen minutes about the rigors of owning one's own business. I tell him my friend might open a clothing store. He is unimpressed because stores come with bathrooms and air conditioning and new merchandise. I nod and down my warm lemonade, but I remind him that he can close up shop at any time without worrying about firing employees or paying the lease.

He nods and refills my glass.

As someone who is not particularly fond of kids, my time with Bronson is enjoyable. Sometimes people are uncomfortable at the thought of what I do all day—hang out with the elderly—because they see it as sad. But it doesn't feel that way to me. Once you find a kindred spirit or two or three, you don't notice the age spots or the slow pace; you only see something of yourself in the other person. Or, sometimes, what you aspire to be. Surprisingly, I'm finding the same comfort level with Bronson.

I talk about my dad. Not about the current situation, but about my growing up years and how he was always making life fun for all the kids. Bronson tells me about his dad, who is in the military and brave. He has story after story about his dad's courage and warmth.

"Is he your hero?" I ask my little friend, expecting a "yes."

"Are you kidding? My hero is Batman."

Bronson pulls a bunch of comic books and graphic novels out of his backpack. His eyes are huge with excitement; he is pleased to show me why Batman is the obvious choice.

As he reads the small frames of adventure, I realize that the people we are afraid of and the people we make heroes have something in common—they are often the people we don't know very well.

So engrossed in the comic book story line am I that I don't notice Beau walking by us. Only when I look up to resituate my lawn chair do I see Beau standing at the corner, waiting for the light to change.

"Gotta go, friend. Thanks for sharing your piece of the sidewalk and your comic books." I down the last of my sugar water and rush to get to Beau. I pray for some supernatural help through my fear of things to come.

Guarded

I need someone strong." Caitlin is standing between the main doors of Golden Horizons and my car door. I can almost hear the eerie whistle of a Western showdown.

"Not so strong," I say, pointing weakly to my heart. "Won't your parents think it odd, me tagging along to dinner?"

"No. Besides, you are leaving town soon. If they are offended, it won't matter."

"It will to me. I like your folks. Both times I met them, I liked them."

"Please. This is my big conversation where I stand up about my choice to go to New York."

"Where's your car?" I scan the lot for Caitlin's car, which is as recognizable as my own beater.

"I had Mary Margaret from work drop me off. See, you are my transportation to my parents' house. You'll love the house, by the way. It is beautiful. I try not to go gaga over it in front of them, but it is breathtaking."

"I am going—not because of the whole house of luxury pitch, but because I want to support you. But aren't you still evaluating this?"

"Don't be on their side."

I mime locking my lips and then unlock the passenger door.

Our drive to the outskirts of town and toward the ritz of the hills is filled with conversation.

I'm not a part of it, however. Caitlin is hashing out argument points with her parents who, I point out, are *not* in the backseat of my car.

The driveway up to the gated community is miles long. As Caitlin enters her code in the security box and waves to the security guard staff, my palms start to sweat.

"I'm not dressed properly, am I?"

She laughs and points to her own outfit, which is something like an inside-out denim jumper with a tool belt cinching her tiny waistline. "Believe me, they will respect you because of your work. Your profession. There is nothing they like more than someone who earns poverty-level pay for the greater good."

"Don't sell yourself short. You are within reach of government cheese."

"Ah, but my goals are about making a name for myself—at least that is their take. Clothing is a nonessential. They don't want to hear my philanthropic ideas of combining social conscience and style."

"Which one of these huts is your family's?" The landscaped, rolling lawns and giant houses make me feel as though I have stepped into a pop-up book. An expensive pop-up book.

"See that gazebo by the large saguaro patch? Take that driveway."

Three gates later we pull into a garage as large as my apartment wing.

"What? No valet parking?"

"Only during parties and holidays."

I look disgusted. "We are slumming now."

We are three courses into a very long meal when Caitlin gets the nerve to bring up New York. She doesn't use the words "I want to move to New York," but says something more along the lines of "I love New York. Public transportation is so economical and really serves the masses."

My kick under the table is useless because Caitlin is seated across from

me at least two yards past the length of my leg. I cause the centerpiece and her father's head to shake.

"You know what I love about New York?" I add. "The opportunity around every corner. And there are so many humanitarian organizations based there."

"It is noisy and dirty. And the streets aren't safe." Mrs. Ramirez subconsciously puts her hand up to her diamond studs. Her line seems rote, as if she too has had advance imaginary conversations.

Caitlin assumes her folks are in the dark, but I sense they know something. They share worried glances as they politely pass a fancy version of mac and cheese with olives and tomatoes. Twice I witness Mrs. Ramirez signal to her husband as if provoking conversation.

The chocolate soufflés are announced, and we are asked to retire to the air-conditioned patio facing the backyard.

We walk in a procession to our seats. Looking back at Caitlin, who takes up the rear, I mouth, "Say something."

Caitlin yanks on my shirt and pulls me behind a curtain that covers a large section of wall. "We'll be right there!" she yells to them and turns to face me. "I think it is going well."

"Think again. Caitlin, I am not sitting through dessert unless you promise to state your plan."

"I was warming up to the topic. Then Mom had to mention crime."

"She knows."

"What?"

"She knows. Her comment about New York was intentionally mentioned to squelch the rest of your conversation. But she was trying to get your dad to say more. I could tell."

Caitlin's mouth drops. "Not possible."

"Possible. Are you sure you haven't implied this move? Maybe a long time ago when this seemed like a pipe dream?"

"I'm sure. I've been wanting to say something for so long, but I..." she stops short of a full thought.

"Figure it out?"

She squints and pounds her forehead with the palm of her hand. "I used their computer last week to book my next flight to New York." She snaps her fingers as the evidence builds. "And then I used the phone to call Isabel. But they were out of town."

"She wouldn't have to be suspicious to run across the list of recent Internet searches and to read her own phone bill. You always said your mom was meticulous. The woman is going to notice an extra long-distance charge. She might be rich, but I'll bet she knows where all the money goes."

"How do I get out of this?"

"You don't, young lady. You take advantage of her knowing something is up and you dive right into this. Or I'm walking. No, wait. I drove. If you don't do this I will drive back to a place without gates and security guards."

"And to think I brought you here for moral support."

"Correction—you brought me here for my strength. And sharing my strength is precisely what I am doing. Now let's go, missy."

I stand behind my friend and force her to shuffle toward the soufflé and her future.

Something Old

I cannot believe I am losing two of my bridesmaids. I'm tempted to eat carbohydrates."

"Don't do it!" Caitlin protects her pretzel with extra mustard. "And I don't know about New York yet. I'm visiting one more time before I make a decision."

Sadie is chewing beef jerky, which is absurd since she is a filet mignon filly and even more comical as she is sitting on a child-sized chair at the city park—the only place we could all get to for an emergency meeting.

"Did Beau take it better than Sadie?" Angelica straddles a rocking mini-dolphin while sipping her lunch of iced tea. Since seeing the scary horizontal stripes of the bridesmaid dresses, Angelica has been living on wheat grass, wheat germ, and green tea.

I dig through my brown bag filled with grapes, yogurt, and tortilla chips. Nothing is appealing. "He was great. First we had to get through about fifteen minutes of apologizing for recent behavior." I balance a plastic spork on my nose.

"I'm so sorry about your dad. I think it is great how you are willing to give up work and love to help your family," Caitlin said, romanticizing my actions.

I hold up my hand in protest. "Wait. I'm not giving up any of those things. Am I? I can go home, be of help for a few months, and return to everything. Who knows, maybe I will be back before the wedding. It is strange, but I didn't even have to think about it."

"Well, I could not leave that to chance. Here." Sadie hands me a piece of paper with a lot of digits.

"Lottery numbers?"

"No." She looks around shyly as if having second thoughts. "These are the numbers for Carson's mileage account. He insists that you fly home, Tucson home, once a month. Or more, if you want to."

I stare at the paper. In my mind I visualize a United States map and a cartoon plane leaving dashes in its wake as it moves from DC to Tucson and back again. "This is too generous, Sadie. Carson barely knows me."

"He is doing it for me too. His life will be unbearable if my maid of honor is not available at my beck and call."

"I'm a beck-and-call girl now? Uh-oh, maybe these aren't my lucky numbers." I tuck the piece of corporate envelope into my pocket. "Thanks, Sadie. Tell Carson how much I appreciate this. It will help ease the hurt of being away from you guys and the residents. I will miss them."

"And Beau," Angelica prods.

"Of course Beau. That is a given." I hedge back to an appropriate answer. I will miss Beau. But I've been missing him for several months, and we are in the same town.

"How will they do without you at Golden Horizons? You put in tons of hours there these days."

"Well, that isn't all diligence. Beau is working a lot, so I stay late. But I've been training Sonya to take over some of my responsibilities and," I nod toward Angelica, "our friend and her little sister, Rachel, are volunteering to cover the reading hour, music sessions, and the Scrabble tournament."

A round of praises for Angelica. "You stuck it out with the Big Brother, Big Sister program?" Sadie asks, impressed.

"I quit quitting, don't you know?"

"How long do we have you?" Caitlin asks me a bit reluctantly.

"Until the end of the week. Everything is set. Beau is even taking some time off from his busy schedule to hang out with me..."

"About time," Angelica mumbles somewhat loudly.

I ignore her and continue. "And remember my former neighbor, Yvette? She and Zane are going to use my apartment while they wait to move into their new house."

"No pouting during your last week. Everything will turn out fine, Mari. Your dad will be back to good health soon, and before we know it..."

"Get off! You're too big!" A little and yet loud voice interrupts Sadie.

"And old!" Another annoying set of vocal cords adds.

Our impromptu gathering is invaded by the three-foot-and-under set. A young girl in a neon purple swimsuit with turquoise piping pulls on Angelica's leg while a little boy pokes his index finger in Sadie's ear. They are both armed with suckers.

"Well, you heard them, ladies. We're fat and old. Guess we'll go eat worms."

"Gross." The Mini Me bathing beauty confuses her universal signs and pinches her nose between her thumb and forefinger.

"Where's your mother?" Angelica insists.

"Where's *your* mother?" The girl bellows back in the same tone Angelica used.

"Let's go. If the police get involved, we'll lose. I guarantee it." I motion for my friends to follow me before this turns to Blow Pops.

"Can you believe kids today?" Sadie brushes grass off her slacks and rubs sucker residue out of her ear with the hem of her blouse sleeve.

Angelica starts laughing uncontrollably. Between fits and starts she manages her joke. "Sadie, at least your 'something old' is taken care of for your wedding."

Blind Faith

I have chosen Ray Charles followed by Al Green as the soundtrack for this last night in my apartment. My mood is melancholic and spiritual. I'm surprised how right this feels and how calm I am about this choice. A few years ago, even if my decision was a meaningful one or a no-brainer, I would torment myself about other possible paths.

Just to show myself how much I have changed, I limit myself to a medium-sized roller bag and my computer pack. No packing for every possible scenario once I get to DC. No second-guessing my packing list and tossing in six more clothing items at the last minute.

By the time Al Green is exposing his soul in the confines of my apartment, I am finished and, amazingly, have some room left in the case. I look around at my bookshelves, mementos, and jewelry case. Nothing seems important enough to take with me on this pilgrimage. Each piece has special meaning in my home but does not warrant a place on this particular journey.

My last bit of business is to write out instructions for the care and feeding of Elmo. Yvette and Zane are happy to take care of Elmo as part of their stay at my place. It's funny. When I met Yvette, I would never have guessed

that within a couple years she would be married, happily adjusted to married life, and looking to move into her very own house. My apartment has been home ever since I decided to make a life in Tucson, far away from my family. I view it as an extension of me. But for Zane and Yvette, it is a transitory location. A waiting room with its own bathroom and refrigerator. I examine the minimalist rooms warmed by lots of bookshelves and colorful pillows, rugs, and vases. But for the first time I see that it is livable, yes—but also leavable.

Do we only notice such things when the time is right?

I check the clock. Nearly nine o'clock, the time I asked Beau to come over so we could have a short time of prayer together. He will be taking me to the airport in the morning, but departure days are too crazy, intense, and public. This will be our true goodbye. The one I will need to set aside in memory while I am on the other side of the country.

It strikes me that this goodbye will be one of our few shared memories lately. Even with our best intentions, life's busyness has kept us apart. Neglect doesn't start out as a choice, a preference, a decision, but when it enters a relationship, it certainly dictates all of those.

I drape a scarf over my blouse for a bit more elegance and let my hair out of its captive state on top of my head. The slight natural curl and the kink from my barrette give me a wild look. I am wearing my long black jersey skirt, trying it out for comfort and wrinkle resistance to see if it should be my travel attire. The overall look is very "granola," as Angelica would say.

A sharp knock at the door startles me.

I twirl a couple times to fluff out my skirt and tame a few curls by my face. The mirror by my door shows pink cheeks and warm skin from my evening of packing and tending to details.

"Entree," I say while opening the door and bowing down low to the ground.

"Kiss our feet!" A female voice surprises me, and a I fall back onto my sandals. Through the veil of hair over my face I see Angelica, Sonya, Lysa, and Caitlin standing in my doorway.

"What are you guys doing?"

"You are coming with us, little harem girl." Angelica brings me to my feet with one harsh yank on my wrist.

I start to protest. "But I'm seeing Beau, and I am packing." I add the packing part hoping that I could get a tad bit of sympathy about the daunting task before me. I kind of want to be alone with my thoughts on this last night.

"Oh, you'll see Beau—ouch!" Caitlin rubs her arm where Angelica punches her for giving away part of their unfolding secret.

Caitlin self-corrects. "I mean, you will see Beau tomorrow. Tonight, however, you won't see anything for awhile. Get her, girls."

Sonya and Angelica show their hands and the several bandanas they have been hiding from me. The strap of Angelica's lavender bra and her silver-and-turquoise cross are the last things my eyes get to take in before I am nearly hog-tied and led to a car that is running.

"Keep the blindfold on!" Lysa hollers at me from the front seat of her old Buick while Angelica and Caitlin hold me down in the backseat. She is playing up the drama.

"I can tell where we are by your turns."

"Nuh-uh," copilot Sonya insists.

"You are on Tanque Verde...just about to pass the tofu yogurt stand."

"You're cheating!" Angelica elbows me in the side and I decide to play dumb the rest of the road trip. It is clear they are headed for Golden Horizons, and I am glad. All week I have been avoiding any acknowledgment among the residents or staff about my departure, yet, in some small way, I need to have a goodbye. While held captive, I have time to think about my life and my captors.

Last year may have been about learning to walk in faith, but this year is all about blind faith—for all of us. Angelica is just figuring out that blind faith is the ingredient she needs in order to trust her feelings for Peyton. Sadie is in love and is afraid of all the unknowns. For someone very much in control of her life, her marriage will be the most wonderful and difficult thing ever. And Caitlin is maybe the most courageous of us all. Her blind faith

will likely lead to her dream of the New York fashion scene, and she wants to do it completely trusting in God and not in her parents' connections.

"What are you laughing at? This is a serious abduction," Angelica says sternly but with a hint of humor.

"I was just thinking how being blindfolded is the perfect symbolic gesture for what is going on in my life right now."

"This is not the time for you to get philosophical. Don't you ever turn off that part of your brain?" Lysa swerves around in a circle a few times to get me good and dizzy and confused. I know we are in Golden Horizons' parking lot.

"So what is this time for?"

The car comes to an abrupt stop. "This is your time to dance, my friend."

I am escorted in through the security doors, which open and close with electronic wheezes. For good measure, Caitlin and Angelica spin me around and catch me when I am about to topple over.

"Good thing for you I didn't eat a big dinner."

Once the forced-motion stops and my thoughts calm down, I prepare for a chance to enjoy this night with everyone who means the world to me. With three people guiding me, my first steps into what seems to be the courtyard are sure and quick. Maybe blind faith is not as scary as it seems—not when you have the support of good friends.

Water Under the Bridge

Let the music begin!" Beau calls from somewhere off to the right, and a band to the left kicks in with Van Morrison's "Moondance."

The blindfold is removed and I am able to take in the graceful courtyard adorned with Christmas lights and cardboard cut outs of Washington, DC, monuments, including a quite tall mini-Washington Monument at the end of the man-made pond.

Before I can look for Beau, the residents usher me over to the buffet table and each person stands before their creation. Rose asks me to try her capital cream cheese bars. Wanda presents her presidential panini with pepperoni. Chet beams with pride before his Georgetown peach pie. Bite by bite I consume enough calories to jog to the East Coast. Even my stretchy skirt is beginning to rise up in resistance.

My eyes are covered from behind by slender fingers. I am holding a slice of Linda's Lincoln lemon cake, so I use my free hand to gain clues to my new captor. The huge ring on the left hand is a dead giveaway. "Yes, Sadie? I've already been kidnapped, but if you choose to steal away my seventh serving of dessert, you are most welcome to."

The hands fall away and Sadie about-faces me and stares at my offering. "Are you kidding? And risk not getting into my designer gown? I've been sucking on carrot sticks all evening. You've been here less than an hour, but I've been here for several."

"I knew you were behind these decorations. Fabulous. They are so romantic. If only I could locate Beau."

"You will. But right now the girls want a few minutes of your time over by the south fountain." She points to Lysa, Sonya, Caitlin, and Angelica, who are waving their DC-licious drinks and shouting "Cheers!"

"We had best get over there before they start a ruckus."

Terra-cotta squares with intermittent topaz-colored tiles adorn benches that are built into a sloping hill that separates Golden Horizons from a golf club. The girls are lined up and kicking their left leg, right leg, left leg in unison.

"Too late. The Rockettes are well-past ruckus and have moved on to stage show," I say as I sit between Caitlin and Angelica.

Sonya clears her throat. "Mari, honorable guest of honor, we wanted to give you a token of our esteem, a measure of our adoration, and a memento of memories before you leave."

"Here, here," says Lysa.

"And here it is." Caitlin reaches beneath the bench and emerges with an extravagantly wrapped gift. A rainbow of ribbons cascade over a deep burgundy box.

"You shouldn't have. This makes me feel like I am leaving for a long time."

"Yes, we should have. Even if you are back in a week after discovering your dad is one hundred percent recovered, we would want you to have this gift," Sadie comforts me with kind words.

"You didn't let me finish. I was going to say 'You shouldn't have—but I'm glad you did.'" I smile and accept the beautiful box. Someone takes a flash picture from a distance; the music playing is an old Ray Charles tune. And I thought I would spend the night alone with Ray C. and Elmo in my apartment. This is so much better.

I tear into the ribbons, the pretty wrapping, the delicate tissue paper, and beneath all of this adornment there are two velvet bags. One large, one small.

My hand goes to the small one.

"Other one first," Angelica directs.

Sadie shakes her head and shrugs. "She's probably right."

I undo the drawstring of the large satchel and hope and pray this isn't one of those bridesmaid purses. I reach in while trying to read everyone's faces. There are no clues, only excitement.

A leather journal full of creamy pages with delicate borders feels the perfect weight in my hands. There are four sections to it, and each divider page has a double-sided photo window. The first has a photo of all of us at the fashion show last year just after Sadie got engaged. The second is a shot of Beau and me leaning against his Golden Horizons office door the day before he took it down. We are pointing to his name on the door and looking at one another with overzealous surprise like we are in a forties romantic comedy.

"It's amazing. I love it."

"We figure the other photos will be of the memories you make while back with your family," Sonya says, pointing to the empty cellophane squares.

I look down at the remaining gift. "I shouldn't get anything else. This is too much."

"True. But this one was my idea, so you must. Now open it before we are all old enough to get residency here." Once again Angelica directs the scene.

"Okay. Okay." I pour the contents of the small bag into my hand and the gentle sound of chimes seems to follow this action. I look down and discover a beautiful charm bracelet with colorful jeweled pieces: a cactus, a sun, a cross, and tiny but elegant initials for each of the women around me.

I'm speechless.

"Well, I would do anything to get you to quit wearing that darn single key on your wrist. I know it was from Tess and has sentimental value, but sentimental women can still have taste."

And I was worried that Angelica would completely lose herself to her new leaf.

Caitlin rolls her eyes at our boisterous friend and returns us to a happy place. "If you will notice, there is a large vacant area on the links. This is so you can add Tess' key," she smiles broadly and sits up tall. "That was my idea."

The band beckons residents and other guests to step up and step out onto the dance floor. I recognize the group as the one Beau used to be a part of. They formed during their college years to pay for tuition, and I suspect, to meet women. Due to the demand now they play oldies, but all of them are under the age of thirty-five. Romantic songs inspire the women to locate their dance partners and direct them to the special area marked off by potted yucca plants. Caitlin is with Jim the Cop, Sadie is with Carson, and Angelica is swinging with Chet.

My eyes scan the scene until they find Beau. It isn't hard. He is the hand-some guy, in a suit, standing on the far side of the bridge with a bouquet of flowers resembling the one he brought me on our first real date. I put my hand over my heart and walk toward him—and he toward me.

We meet midbridge. It is the very bridge where I first figured out he was *the* Beau who worked as recreation director at Golden Horizons before I took that job. The other day outside of the convention center we exchanged "I'm sorry's" with sincerity, but these are our first and simultaneously exchanged words tonight.

I laugh, but he is very serious as he says, "I am sorry about our anniver-sary date tension, I'm sorry about canceling out on several of our weekend plans..."

"Numerous." I prod, half joking.

"Yes, numerous. And I am very sorry about..."

I know where he is going with this. "It's okay. I overreacted to the whole thing. I'm not a deeply jealous person, yet I sounded so much like a person

I don't want to be. That girl is hypersensitive and untrusting." As I say this, another thought runs across the back of my mind, *I didn't expect so many apologies to be a part of a good relationship.*

Beau's eyes go from serious to sentimental. "This girl reacts just as she should." He points to my chin.

"With the geographic distance we will have, it is going to take effort from both of us. You are so busy, and once I am living at the Urban Center, helping Mom, Dad—things will be hectic." Even during my rambling, my mind censored adding Marcus to the list.

"You are right. It will take more effort," he says gently and places my hand on his heart. "I vow to be better at this dating thing so that when you return, we will be back on track."

This statement jolts me a bit. What does that mean to a guy like Beau? We are just beginning to figure out how to apologize. Surely he doesn't mean to imply…

"It's our song. By request, of course." Beau interrupts my derailed thoughts.

"Fly Me to the Moon" is our cue to stop talking, to stop assessing our relationship. And for me, a clear signal to stop obsessing about hypotheticals once again.

We start to dance, holding each other cheek to cheek. It feels good to be so close. Recent arguments and misunderstandings have swelled beneath us and sent us off balance. Now, under the stars and the spell of the music, we are steady and close. And those trivial things are hard to recall.

Security Measures

So I got to thinking about what you said last night. About the distance and how hard it will be to feel like we are together, and…"

"Do you have my ticket? Wasn't it in the front pouch of my laptop case?" I am sweating and tired and a bit anxious about the day of travel. I check my watch for the zillionth time and realize we are considerably early. Which Beau annoyingly points out.

"It isn't even six o'clock. And your ticket is still in that pouch."

"Maybe I should have come on my own this morning." I get agitated with myself on travel days. Trying to be pleasant with Beau, who is just trying to be nice, is making me more frustrated. Something about the maze of people, lines, gates, and flashing boards sends my heart rate flying. "There's the line I need to be in." I dash down the airline lobby and get behind a woman with two little boys, each with his own roller backpack.

"Anyway, I created a travel kit for you. But first you have to open this." Beau removes a small nylon mailer envelope from his backpack. There is a small bulge in one corner.

"What's this?" I say, verbally shooing it away. I had just prided myself on

packing the ideal bag. The journal from the girls was the missing piece to fill my case perfectly. "There's no more room." I crane my neck to see who is holding the line up.

"I know. It fits in your laptop bag. I already measured it."

The guy measured his gift for me, and I am worried about being late for a flight that is likely still midjourney from Florida. "That is sweet. Will you open it for me? My hands are full."

Beau grabs my suitcase handle and reshapes my tight grip around the package.

I detach the Velcro opening and peer inside. A small flip phone with a bow on it is the bulge, and there are several other items tied up with string.

"I have a phone." I explain a bit like Mr. Rogers might. "You've called me on it."

Beau's eyes get wide and just when he should want to slap me, he gets more excited. "I know, but this one is under my plan so we can talk free anytime. There is no limit on minutes between our phones. Now you can always reach me."

I resist asking him if the phone also has a tracking device because it wasn't my phone plan that made him difficult to reach lately.

"Keep looking, honey."

I crack a smile. How can I resist such enthusiasm? I dig further and first pull out a calling card. One of the two boys in front of us falls over and the other knees him in the back. We help the one up and direct the antagonist toward his mother.

"That is in case you cannot use the cell phone. You could use the shelter's line and not charge them. And I was thinking that when you are out and about there might be places the signal doesn't cover, and you could use the card at a pay phone to check in with me."

Check in?

"Good morning. I'm Clarissa, your Fly Right representative. Thank you for choosing Fly Right flights for your flight."

"That must be difficult to say all day." I smile to make up for my bad mood.

"A pleasure," Clarissa says without an ounce of it in her voice.

"Like flying," I return.

"Has anyone asked you to carry anything for them or assisted with your packing?" Clarissa says her next line as she accuses me over her dark-rimmed glasses.

"No."

"Please step over there." Clarissa points in the opposite direction of the gates.

"What's over there?"

She sighs and points with a firmer thrust of her finger. "Extra security measures. You were seen receiving that package while in line. Please go."

I give Beau a stern look. A "this is your fault" grimace so he too will worry that maybe my one and a half hours of extra time won't be enough for me to make this flight.

While my nylon bag is searched, the third gift is removed by the security guard and held up for all to see—a very large necklace with an oval of mother of pearl. As it spins in the breeze of air-conditioning, I see that one side is scary. Beau has affixed a close-up photo of our faces on that side.

"It's so you can wear us all the time."

Wear us? What are we now, Dolce & Gabbana?

The guard gives me a sympathetic smile and motions for Beau to stay behind a blue line three feet away.

"Did I mention the cell phone is a camera phone? You could send me pictures anytime. And I got one too," he says, holding up a matching phone, "so I can show you what I'm doing…" Beau's voice trails off and in its wake his unspoken thoughts rise and take shape. Now I understand. This pocket full of communication tools is more about the state of *us*. He is making up for the fact that I heard the name Paige through the phone line. He is making a peace offering, a guilt gifting.

When I finally get through security, I understand he is just helping me through my insecurities. And maybe a few of his own.

I place the necklace over my head after going through the metal detectors. While an elderly man is getting his hat searched I call out over my fellow travelers and tell Beau the gifts are wonderful and sweet.

And I blow him a kiss.

Welcome Matt

My name is Mari Hamilton. Everyone is expecting me." I have bellowed this same sentence four different ways into the intercom speaker outside the gate of the Urban Center.

The young voice on the other end is that of a boy trying to sound a bit older. He coughs every few words to add gruffness to his vocal impression. "We don't let anyone in when they aren't approved."

I try again. "My flight was delayed. I traveled all the way from Arizona. Because I got stuck in Chicago for a while, the Hamiltons had to go on to their doctor's appointment. So I took a cab from the airport."

There is static on the other end. My counterpart has forgotten to push the "talk" button again. I cannot hear his rebuttal.

I press my talk button and try my last attempt before walking down to a café a few blocks away to wait out the return of people who want me here. "Who am I talking to?"

Static. Then "Matty. I mean Matt."

"Matt, I really need a bathroom. I've been traveling all day, and I never use airplane bathrooms. I'm too claustrophobic. It started when I got stuck

in a sleeping bag at camp and I've never gotten over it. Does your breathing ever get shallow and your chest hurt with panic? It isn't fun." Good grief, give me a captive audience and I turn it into a counseling session.

Static. "Nope."

"Matty, look over the soda fountain counter and you will see a big photo of the Hamiltons and me taken last year at the Thanksgiving dinner—maybe you were there? Then look at the security monitor, and I will make the same hand signal as I am in the photo. A stranger wouldn't know what that is. But I do because I am not a stranger. In fact, I will be living at the house for a while. We'll be buds." I may have pushed a bit too far on that one, but my idea must be logical to his young mind.

"Okay. Do the signal."

Placing my suitcase on the ground, I spread both hands wide and make moose horns with them. To add to the authenticity of this test of identity, I also cross my eyes. Some folks worry about the day when everywhere we go we simply hold up our thumb for print identification, but I believe I would welcome this technology about now.

There is a faltering buzz and the gate unlocks. I quickly shove my things on through and shut the gate behind me. If the gate is left open too long, an alarm sounds.

By now it is late afternoon and I am hungry, tired, and in need of a post-travel shower. I pity Matty if he tries to stop me.

I can already see the signs of Dad's illness. The rose garden to the right of the walkway is scorched from summer sun. The grass is brown and the fountain is sputtering instead of flowing. A bit of frustration rises up in me. How long has he not been able to do this work? Why isn't Marcus on top of caring for the yard? I come all this way, leaving a great job, romance, and circle of friends to find the place in disarray. Someone should have called me to come much sooner. I find my emotions bouncing back and forth between my martyr and my savior complexes.

Considering how the gate conversation went, I decide to knock before entering the house. Before my second tap a large boy answers the door. He has rosy cheeks, blue eyes, and a shock of red hair. His appearance makes me smile.

"Matty, I presume?" I hold out my hand, which he shakes firmly. "I'm Mari. Can I come in and get settled?"

"Sure," he says, as though he has not been the stern gatekeeper for the past ten minutes.

I look around at what used to be three individual rooms but is now one large multipurpose area: the kitchen, dining room, and meeting area. My eyes and heart take it all in. Funny how a place that seemed to offer uncertainty as a child now provides the strongest sense of home and peace.

"If you are looking for the bathroom, it's that way." Matty points to the back by the walk-in freezer.

"I used to live here." I reinforce that fact in case he didn't make the connection.

An expression of curiosity crosses the boy's features. It is a "why are you still talking to me" look, not a "that is interesting, keep going" invitation. I make my way to the bathroom.

Once the door is closed behind me in the one-stall room I revert to old behavior. I start holler-talking to those in the main room. "So where is everyone? Since when do they leave you kids all alone?" I want to gather information before I lay into Marcus about letting things fall apart before I could get here.

About the time I figure Matty has left the room I hear his voice filled with confusion about the boundaries of this conversation through a bathroom door. "I'm not a kid. My fifteenth birthday was last week."

"But still. We have strict policies about leaving any child alone in the house." I return to the main room wiping my hands with a paper towel. "I want to know what has happened to house rules, to proper conduct, and to professional treatment of the residents. This is unacceptable."

Matty holds his hands up in the air. "Okay. If it makes you feel better, our house folks are at the doctor's—which you seemed to know—and Uncle Marcus took everyone to the roller rink. I, however, got a D in my summer school math class, so I was supposed to stay behind with some giant, angry woman who was going to be here earlier, but she never showed."

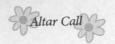

I realize he is talking about me. "And who described this so-called large person?"

"Giant," he corrects. "Marcus."

"Yes. Sweet Uncle Marcus." I roll my eyes and sit down at the large farm table. I can see Marcus avoiding the use of my name, but my parents? Wasn't anyone excited about this huge decision I made to come here and help? I thought I would come in and be welcomed with open arms, balloons even. Instead, I am alone with a kid who has only heard me referred to as big and mean. Correction: giant and angry.

Matty reaches into the fridge for bottled water. "And I'll probably get kitchen duty for a week for letting you in."

"I will stand up for you."

He looks me up and down for a moment and seems to assess that I won't have the clout to ease his fate.

"Just to give me a fighting chance, would you please stay here in the main room until they arrive? No outsiders are allowed in the study room," he points his fruit of choice toward the side porch that has three rows of antique school desks.

"Math?" I ask the obvious.

"What?"

"No, not Matt. I asked if you are doing math because I am really good." I lie a bit to make connection with the boy who will be my housemate for who knows how long.

He raises his eyebrows to indicate I'm weird and moseys on to his studies while I sit at what was once my place at this huge table. I reach underneath and feel around until I find the area where years ago I had drilled tiny holes into the wood with the tip of a ball point pen.

Anything to avoid my math assignments.

Pass the Role

Mari!" A chorus of one word—my name—rings loudly in my ear. I have fallen asleep at the dining table and can barely rouse to consciousness even with the earsplitting vocal alarm.

"What time is it?" I wipe a bit of spittle from the corner of my mouth and "Uncle" Marcus takes a picture of the awakening grouchy woman.

I punch his arm hard. Angelica would be proud.

"See, what'd I tell you?" Marcus shouts to the gathering of kids who stand behind him trying to get a look at me. "Well, maybe she is petite, but I was right about the angry part!"

My heart is still racing. I am unable to defend myself in the moment. This seems to be the reaction Marcus was hoping for. He winks at me and leads the kids in a dinnertime hand-washing-and-food-preparation drill while I struggle to my feet too slowly to regain my composure.

Just what I needed—to start off feeling like the loser girl.

I am weary and feeling tousled in general, but instead of doing what I want, which is run and hide, I decide to step in line and find my place in the dinner routine. Marcus calls out orders for the color-named teams. Red team prepares vegetables, blue team breads the chicken for frying, the white team scoops up portions of potato salad from an industrial-sized container, and the green team sets the table.

Since the long, narrow kitchen space is filled with teens, I opt to be green. Thankfully the silverware is in the same oak buffet in the corner. Turns out Matty is green; I follow him as he sets mats at each place setting. Every couple paces he looks back to see if I am still following. I think I am growing on him.

The sounds of this chaos are stimulating and relaxing, like surprisingly rhythmic white noise. Matty and I finish our task facing the soda fountain bar, which divides our area from the kitchen. "Hey, Matt. Could you tell me everybody's name?"

He considers this. I can almost see the rule about not talking to strangers flashing behind his blue eyes.

"I was the one who was supposed to be here when you got home from school. I'm sorry I was late. And I'm not just a friend of your housefolks, I am their daughter. I grew up here. We have something in common." I motion between us, drawing an invisible thread from his heart to mine and back again.

His hand goes to his chin in a very adult gesture of contemplation as he thinks it over. "Left to right—Tara, Jon, Liz, Camden, Elsa, Grant, Josiah, Lou..."

"Lou?"

"Short for Louise. Katie, Alf—short for Alfred, Ben, and the little guy on the end is Wallace."

"When I was here the girls outnumbered the boys. Good thing I came." I give myself a reason to feel good about being here, even if nobody else will.

"Music. Music. Music." Red team refuses to cut one more carrot until Marcus approves stereo usage.

His walk over to the sound system involves passing by me. I have not made eye contact with him yet, and I hope to keep up the avoidance. During my last visit here, Marcus mentioned having feelings for me, or at least the hope of developing feelings. I want to make it clear why I am here. For the sake of my parents and the kids, nothing else.

"Our special guest will make the music selection for this evening." Marcus comes behind me and pulls me by my shirt until I am standing next to the rather large collection of CDs.

A large groan comes from the kitchen.

"Order in the galley," Marcus hollers back.

I play up the importance and pressure of the decision by pacing along the bookshelf containing the music options. The kids stand watching me, grimacing as they anticipate some oldie from way back in the eighties or something equally disgusting. I break my initial rule and look to Marcus for a clue, but he looks past me and shakes his head no. I notice a few CDs are sticking out a bit from the shelf as though someone quickly put them back after use. I reach for one of these.

When U2 comes blaring out of the stereo the restless cooks send up a cheer. I even get a high five from Matty. The ice is broken, and I am no longer staring in from the outside. I know there is a long way to go before I am accepted as part of the group. Many times I watched a new child enter this home, uncertain and worried. The boys often acted tough and insensitive, the girls often shy or nervous. Always it took time before they became themselves among the brood.

The ring of the bell attached to the front door announces the arrival of my parents. I watch my mother's eyes light up with joy as she sees the kids in motion, working together and creating a meal. Before she can notice me, standing in the corner, I notice Dad following behind her. His face is hollow and narrow. Even the smile which reflects his pleasure in the scene before him does not reflect the sparkle it once did. My news of his illness has been so recent I had not expected to see such a frail person.

Marcus notices my expression. He gives my elbow a squeeze of support. And as he does, my parents scan the room and rest their eyes on me. They rush over to give me a hug. My arms can practically reach around the both of them.

"Yeehaw! We are thrilled you are here. Hey, kids," Dad shouts, his voice a bit strained, "this is our daughter, Mari. She's the one who insisted I build that clubhouse out back."

"And the library slash phone closet upstairs," Marcus adds, laughing.

I notice Lou, Elsa, and Ben clap. Looks of recognition and appreciation cross the faces of the others. Wallace walks over to me shyly. "Are you the Mari who invented the poetry pizza night?"

I lean over to look him in the eye. "That's me. Do you enjoy the pizza?"

He nods earnestly, shaking his black curls. "Yeah, but mostly the poetry."

Mom kisses Wallace's forehead and looks pleasantly surprised by his social interaction with me.

Dinner is just like old times. The chaos doesn't bother me. I actually enjoy the experience when there isn't attention on what I am eating. If Beau could see me here, with these kids devouring platters full of food, he would laugh at how similarly we all eat—quickly and as much as possible.

I find myself looking at Dad often, trying to readjust my sense of him and his health. They reported that today's doctor's visit was a positive one. If Dad follows his diet and medication plan, his recovery will be surprisingly fast. Periodically, Mom will check his plate to be sure only baked chicken is resting next to his salad.

Before the strawberry shortcake is brought out by the blue team, Marcus stands on the fourth stair leading up to the bedrooms. "Since the green team got to make the music selection, they also have kitchen cleanup."

There is a groan, and this time I am joining in. It isn't easy being green. But for a moment, I have high hopes of spending this visit home being me.

Ground Rules

"What's wrong with you?" A little hand taps my forehead several times before I open my eyes.

"Where'd you come from?" I struggle to prop myself up on my elbows.

"I'm Daisy, from New York."

That isn't exactly what I meant, but it will do for now. Perhaps she is the child of one of the volunteers. "Your mom is probably worried."

Her eyes get big. "Really?" she whispers.

"Daisy!" Lou rushes into the small guest room where my cot is set up and seems flustered to see me. "Daisy, you woke her up. I'm sorry."

"Whose is she?" I ask.

Lou seems a bit put off. "She's mine, that's whose she is."

I realize my mistake and feel bad about mentioning Daisy's mom. Chances are, there is no mom worrying about her. I try to cover.

"Let's go see Mom Hamilton so she doesn't wonder where you are." I reach for Daisy's hand and scout around for my slippers.

"She was asking about you, actually," Lou says and takes Daisy's hand from mine.

As if on cue, Mom's voice floats up the stairwell. "Breakfast, dear."

I check my watch. It's five o'clock in Tucson, and I feel it. The household is in high gear. Kids are stuffing books in backpacks, grabbing brown lunch bags from the counter, and waiting for their school buddy to walk out the door with them. My presence among them goes unnoticed. I point to the calendar. "It is not even August."

Mom and Dad look at me and nod.

"Since when does school start in July?"

"Marcus started a practice school day drill. They all get ready, walk to the school, and then go to the park to play games. It really helps the first day jitters and eases any kinks out of the morning routine. They do it once a week."

"Interesting."

Soon it is just Mom, me, and Daisy seated at the table. I lift the line up of cereal boxes one by one—only Cheerios remain. I do the same to the milk cartons…soy it is. Instead of missing children featured on the side panel, there is information about endangered species.

"It is so good to have you here. Your dad was beaming all evening. His physical therapist even noticed he seemed peppier this morning."

"Therapy this early?"

"They are trying two short sessions a days until he builds up strength and stamina," she says with a cheery tone.

"How about you? Do you get two sessions—therapy, perhaps?"

She laughs. "It isn't so bad. We are thankful to have good news. He promised to do the work it takes to get back to health."

"Dad said you were second-guessing the city council race. Is this true?"

Mom begins to braid Daisy's long hair and then looks directly at me. "I want to do it, but I worry about Ted."

"You need to do it, Mom. I'm here to help for as long as it takes."

She shakes her head slightly and starts the braiding over. "But you have Beau, your friend's wedding, and those dear people at Golden Horizons."

"This is where I want to be. And I will go back and visit as often as I need to. I have all that covered."

With practiced flair Mom ties Daisy's braid off with a band and forms a clover-shaped bow with yellow ribbon. "Yellow for Daisy. Now you go do your art project, my dear. It seems Mari is here to stay for a bit, so no need to treat her like a novelty." Mom winks at me and turns Daisy's shoulders toward the study room.

Once the girl is out of earshot, I whisper, "Since when did you start taking in kids that young?"

"I did break my own rule for Daisy. When I met her and Lou, they were with their aunt, who is not physically able to care for them. There is no father in the picture and their mother died. I want all children to have opportunities, but these two," Mom pauses and gets teary, "with all they had working against them, these girls should get their chance."

"Then they will."

She smiles. "Yes, they will."

I watch her smile fade and her down-to-business look take its place. "Mari, I meant it about your life. You have important, lovely things going on right now. This time is also your chance for happiness." She takes my hand in hers. "Promise me you will come to me if and when the distance causes a problem of any kind for you. We have Marcus and we have other options for help after he leaves."

I do a Scout's honor salute.

"Were you proud of us for not sending Marcus to the airport to pick you up this time? I had to talk your father out of it."

"I'm with Beau, Mother."

"Believe me, we are thrilled about your relationship with Beau. Certainly there was a time when we wanted you with Marcus because he is such a good boy. And you two made a great couple until you..."

"Broke his heart."

She feigns shock. "I was going to say moved to Tucson."

I sigh, "This is *my* rule for this visit—there is to be no forcing together of Mari and Marcus. There is to be only great respect for the relationship Mari has with Beau. No jokes, no subtle comments, no insinuations in front of the kids."

She mimics my earlier salute and starts to speak.

I place my finger to her lips to silence her. "This concludes the Marcus-Mari conversation."

"What about Marcus and Mari?" Daisy calls out from her perch at the littlest study desk.

Teaching Old Dogs

I could be gone a while. You're sure about this?"

"Mom, you are leaving me to hang with Dad, not with a tyrannical toddler. Go to your first candidate meeting, would you? I've been here a couple weeks. If you aren't going to trust me now, you never will."

"It isn't trust, sweetie. I am just a doting mother and wife. What can I say?" She is flush with excitement. I wonder how many years she has dreamed of becoming more involved, more influential for the sake of what she believes in—education, equality, fair housing, and funding for kids.

"Don't forget your special lunch. Josiah and I packed it this morning." I hand her a bright red lunch box covered with stickers. The night before, Marcus asked the kids to decorate white labels with campaign slogans or reasons why Mom should win a seat on the city council.

As she reads these for the first time, she puts her hand to her mouth. I can tell she is about to cry.

"Nobody wants a tardy and bawling councilwoman."

With a blue scarf draped around her shoulders and her lunch box in

hand, Mom kicks open the screen door and walks out into the mild heat of the late morning sun.

"I'd vote for her," Dad says as he approaches me with careful, slow steps. His favorite trick of sneaking up on people is thwarted by his illness.

"Did you do your exercises with Fabio?" Dad's therapist, Bernie, doesn't really resemble Fabio other than in the long hair. But the lean and slightly bookish Bernie seemed flattered by the moniker I gave him when we met.

"All done. Watch." Dad does a partial jumping jack for effect.

"I'm not sure how to interpret that move, Dad, but I will give you the benefit of the doubt. Do you have the educational tape of your choice with you?"

"All set up in the study room. Shall we?"

I loop my arm through his and we hold our heads up high. We invented this formal walk so it looks less like I am holding him up and more like he is escorting me around the neighborhood.

"I do believe you are gaining some bicep muscle, Father."

We enter the empty room and each take a seat at a desk. I have fresh notepads and sharpened pencils ready for use. As part of our deal, Dad has not told me what we will be studying during his time of recovery. As he shuffles at a turtle's pace over to the old boom box setting on a bookshelf, I can only hope we will not be learning to tango.

"Here's lesson one."

"Hit it, DJ Daddy."

Through speakers torn and splattered with paint from past uses, the first words of our learning adventure fill the space between me and my father.

"*Bonjour,*" says a rich female voice.

"Bun-jer," repeats my father with an intentionally horrific accent.

I take the crisp first sheet of paper on my pad, wad it up, and toss it at him. "French? This is what you have selected to make use of our study time?" I talk over the seductive voice as it works through various ways of greeting fellow countrymen.

"You said I could choose. This is what I choose."

"Do you speak any language other than English?"

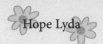

"Non." My father says with pronounced nasal effect.

"Wouldn't Spanish be more useful?" I throw my hands up in the air. I was all prepared to learn carpentry, Latin cooking, or astronomy.

As I am about to say "What on earth are you going to do with French?" my father quietly says, "Your mother has always wanted to go to Paris."

From that point on, I learn to shut my mouth—*fermé la bouche*—and pay attention to the life lessons my father is trying to teach me.

Three-Way Conversations

In the time I have been in DC, I have realized that the phone can be used for evil or for good.

I call Golden Horizons to speak with Beau, but first I speak with Lysa, Sonya, and even residents Rose and Chet, who seem to be happily dating. This is all good and does my heart wonders to remain in touch. The real disconnect begins once the call is transferred into Beau's office.

"Hello? So glad you called," he says a bit like a real estate agent rather than a boyfriend.

"I'm glad you're glad. How are you doing? I've missed you."

There is silence and some paper shuffling it seems. "Hey, I'm great."

A long pause follows and the sounds of the activities in the hallway seem to fill the receiver in place of sweet words I had hoped for.

"Lots going on there? Your doorless office sure adds some clutter to phone conversations," I say, still hoping we will turn a corner from chitchat to heart-to-heart any moment now.

He laughs strangely. "Actually, can you believe it? I put the door back on. Seems there are some perfectly good reasons to have a door."

"But it was such a nice statement. The staff loved it. Do they understand the change?" I fondly recall the door removal ceremony. It was the start of a new leadership philosophy for Golden Horizons. I am disappointed and Beau knows it.

He decides to answer a former question, a more manageable one. "Just taking care of some last state reports for this month. Oh, and that cruise-themed night of entertainment you suggested was exceptional. We sailed right through it without one complaint."

I appreciate the praise, but this is all so much more formal than I expected for one of our rare conversations. "Wasn't this the time you suggested I call?" His obvious busyness and attention to distractions makes me want to hang up.

"The residents are acting up a bit in your absence. They miss you."

They miss me.

Who took over the heart and soul of my fabulous boyfriend? That's what I would like to know.

"Should I leave?" A woman's voice asks a question within range of Beau's phone.

"Beau?" I ask once again, being more polite than I want to be. "Is this a bad time?"

"No." He says clearly, causing my lungs to take in air again. Until I realize he is talking to the other voice. "Stay. We need to go over these projections."

I'm getting the picture. This wasn't a good time to call. Beau is going right along with his business.

Now he speaks to me. "Can I give you a call this evening? So we can be..."

"Alone?" I say coldly.

"Yes, exactly. I do appreciate your call. Bye, you."

"Bayou? Or Bye, you?" says the woman whose call is so very appreciated.

"Funny girl. Talk to you soon."

Click.

Disconnect.

Familiar Faces

Get out of here! Is that you, Mari?" A loud voice startles me and causes precious ounces of my Americano to spill over the top of my Alexandria Roasters paper cup. I'm still licking my thumb when a woman approaches me and gives me a side hug.

"What?" I look up and into the eyes of my former high school locker partner. "Rachel Reynolds?"

"Yes!"

I stare at her funky, close-cropped haircut, black silk jacket, and ruby camisole and recall her days as a tomboy basketball player. "When did you give up rugby shirts and gray sweatpants?"

"After a year of playing ball for the community college I decided to go to art school. Can you believe I'm a sculptor and a jewelry designer?" She spins as though she is on the runway.

"You always were creative," I say honestly.

"And you were always nice." She resumes walking, so I join her. "I heard you were somewhere crazy like Mexico."

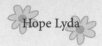

"Tucson." Pause. "Arizona. You weren't too good at geography, as I recall."

"Oh, no. You want to ruin the nice reputation so soon?" She playfully punches my shoulder. "So why are you here?"

"My folks needed an extra set of hands at the center for a while."

"See? Nice. I was just about to pick up some lunch and take it back to my studio at the Torpedo Factory. Want to join me?"

I check my watch, but I'm not wearing one.

"It's almost noon. Or were you trying to fake busyness?"

"I am busy. I'll have you know that today I was going to map out a field trip so I can bring the kids here next weekend and then to Williamsburg the following week. But even a working girl needs lunch."

"We can do one better than lunch. Remember Cheyenne?"

"Porter? Are you two still feuding over what's his name?"

"Vinton."

"Yeah, Derek Vinton." I think of the baby face of the most popular boy in school.

"As in Cheyenne Vinton. She won that dispute." She throws her head back and fake laughs so hard she has to hold onto me for balance.

I feel as though I am sixteen again.

Once she regains her composer, Rachel steps in front of me and walks backward to keep the conversation going. Passersby look at her with fascination and step out of her way, just as she expects. "Cheyenne and I are friends, I'll have you know. She is the only person from high school I stay in touch with, other than Derek, of course."

"How is she?"

"Great. And my point in mentioning her is that she is assistant director of the Williamsburg tourism department. I'll have her meet us at my place, and then we can officially arrange that tour for your kids."

"Hate to remind you, but Williamsburg is not exactly a hop, skip, and a jump away from here."

"She lives here, in town, and today is one of her days off. The woman

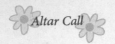

works nearly every Saturday and Sunday for events, so she has the luxury of midweek weekends."

"Lead on, then."

The employee door at the renovated Torpedo Factory is propped open with a brick. We climb two flights of stairs with our bag of Caesar salads and maneuver a catwalk-like corridor until we come upon a bright blue door adorned with a star and Rachel's signature across it. She removes a pink rabbit's foot key chain from her jean pocket and unlocks the door to her small studio.

A jewelry case runs alongside one wall and a worktable matches its length along the opposite wall. A small window up near the ceiling and amber-colored bulbs hanging from black cords provide gentle lighting. My eyes fall upon a necklace pinned to her work platform. Sapphires and topaz stones are placed on strands of silver; it is as intricate as a spider's web. On the opposite wall, above the worktable, are four long shelves with various sized ceramic sculptures and vases. The delicate hand-painted forms are whimsical and dainty.

"I'm impressed." Actually I am shocked at the adult life of my friend who refused to wear nylons and a dress for the ninth grade choir performance. She showed up in slacks, a white blouse, and a tie to protest.

Rachel waves away my admiration. "I can barely afford the rent anymore. I like creating art, but I'm not so good at the selling."

"The Torpedo Factory is a pretty visible place. I'm sure things will happen."

"I can hope."

"Hey, how'd you recognize me so easily? I haven't seen you in years."

She opens her hands in a helpless gesture.

A knock at the door precedes the entrance of Cheyenne Vinton, who looks like a more mature version of her very pretty teen self. Dark ringlets frame her bronze, distinct face and wide grin. "It sure is you, Mari."

"Cheyenne. Good to see you."

"You haven't changed a bit." She eyes me and good-naturedly adds, "I swear that is exactly what I remember you wearing."

"Yep, pretty much," I agree.

As she comes over to hug me, I realize that in addition to similar clothes, I also have many of the same insecurities I had when sixteen. Cheyenne always was too pretty. I look down at my T-shirt, jeans, and Tevas. Angelica, Caitlin, and Sadie would all be appalled by my fashion regression.

My reestablished friends and I spend the next hour plotting my future field trips and randomly bringing up our shared histories. The two seem excited by my return to DC, and in some way, this is the reception I had hoped for at home.

Cheyenne licks salad dressing off her fingers like a trucker might rid his of onion ring grease. I like her more than ever until she brings up the topic I had hoped to avoid.

"So Marcus is in town and Mari is in town. That sounds like some potential drama." Her deep brown eyes expand to take in my reaction of stern disapproval.

"Next subject."

Rachel repositions herself on a work stool so she can lean in for the gossip. "Now we are getting to the story. And you said you were here to help your parents."

Cheyenne smiles. "Exactly what Marcus is doing."

I feel the need to correct her. "He is here finishing his counseling program at Georgetown."

"Ah, yes. But he is living at the Urban Center to help your parents. Which would mean that you two are sharing the same dwelling."

I look at her through a veil of hair recently blown into my face by the over-active air conditioner. "Seems like you know an awful lot about Marcus."

Suddenly her enthusiasm dwindles, as if she has said more than she would like. "I've just seen him around town."

Rachel tosses a plastic fork toward Cheyenne's feet. "And?"

"My husband and I have gone out with him a few times." She pauses and tosses her hair back before adding, "Him and his girlfriend."

"Girlfriend?" Rachel shouts while my stomach does a flip with a half twist.

"Girlfriend?" I say as casually as I can—which means my voice is shaking and a bit shrill. This shouldn't be such a surprise. Why wouldn't Marcus have a girlfriend? He's a fantastic guy who logically would be dating while living here. In truth, I cannot believe some fortunate, undeserving girl has not yet married him.

Cheyenne backpedals a bit. "But I don't think it's serious. She would love it, but he seems to keep a bit of emotional distance. I always figured that distance was approximately the length of you."

"That is crazy. I'm dating a fabulous guy in Tucson—and Marcus and I had a talk last year when I came for Thanksgiving. He knows there is no…"

Rachel wags her finger at me and interrupts. "If you say chemistry, then you will have to take the lie detector test."

"I was going to say chance—no chance of us being an us."

Cheyenne looks at Rachel and Rachel looks at me.

I stand up for my integrity. "That is the truth."

Cheyenne repeats, "Is there a chance?" over and over and over. A Chinese word torture method, apparently.

And after saying "This is so immature" I finally say something I hope my mother never gets word of— "*Maybe.*"

But, I swear, it was only to get her to shut up.

From a Distance

He what! Isn't that out of the blue?" I hold the faded yellow, archaic phone to my ear in case I didn't hear Caitlin right the first time.

"Totally out of the blue. I don't know what got into him. We don't talk for weeks because he is in Mexico, and then we go out to eat a few times, hit a couple of bad movies, and he springs this on me."

Noises from downstairs echo in the receiver. I pull the phone closet door to. When will I adjust to living in a house with more than a dozen other people?

"Start from the beginning."

"How long have you been there?" Caitlin asks.

I squint, trying to recall my arrival date. "I think it has been three weeks. Does that sound right?"

"Yes, right. Well, Jim and I had a great time dancing at your going away party. After that we talked a lot more on the phone, and it seemed we were connecting. Then yesterday morning he calls and asks me to meet him at the park. Well, we've hiked a few times so I show up in my sweats carrying

a backpack. And he is dressed in a *tuxedo* and standing by the fountain with a picnic basket."

"That is so romantic."

"And embarrassing. I think I still had sleep lines on my face and this guy looks like he is ready for the queen's coronation."

"A *little* embarrassing, but you have to admit it was a lovely gesture."

"That is why I didn't run back to the bus stop like I wanted to. I understood he was really putting himself out there, and so I walked over to him."

"And just like that, he asks you to marry him?"

"No. We sit there and eat a meal his mother made for us. Then we talk about life, the weather, those bad movies, dentists, Mexican art, and last but not least, the cost of gourmet cheese."

"Cheese?"

"Apparently he loves cheese."

"Then he asked you?" My mind cannot settle down. I've barely been gone and one of my best friends gets the question of her lifetime.

"Yes. After his comparison of world cheeses he popped the question." She squeals, but I cannot yet figure out if it is delight or delirium.

"And you said?"

Before I can get the answer about her answer, there is knock on the closet door.

"Go away," I say.

Knock, knock.

"Go away. This is important." I reach for the knob and push out to get a glimpse of my annoyer. It is Marcus. "Emergency call here. Go."

Marcus bends over to stare at me. The space between frame and door shows only a sliver of his forehead and nose and lips. "I'm expecting a call," the lips say.

"We have call-waiting. I'll let ya know."

"I'd rather you just get off the phone."

"Too bad." I pull the door toward me again to end the conversation on this side of the phone and return to the other, more pressing side. "What was your answer?"

"Guess."

"I think you are spontaneous enough and optimistic enough to say yes. My guess is yes."

"You've got to be kidding! I've known him for what—less than a year? And two months ago I thought we were through."

"Sadie and Carson knew each other much less than that. And Jim was taking care of his grandmother during the non-breakup," I hear myself listing reasons against her decision; I shut my mouth quickly. "Sorry. Your choice makes total sense."

"I am about to make a huge decision about whether to move to New York. And did I mention that I got approval for the small business loan?"

"That's great!"

"But does that mean I am supposed to stay? What if you face two open doors...how are we supposed to know which is the right direction?"

"I wish I could answer that. Maybe the answer is to just move forward and trust."

"My heart is the New York scenario, yet how can I possibly add Jim into the mix? He's not going to transfer. A yes to him means a no to Isabel and the trendy shop and the separation from my parents and a new attitude about life."

"I hear your pain. But I also know that when you move far away, as I did when I left here for Tucson, you don't really leave your attitude or your family issues behind. Believe me. After a day back here, I felt as though I were twelve again."

"But in New York, I'd have a chance to know who I could be."

"How did he take it? The no."

"Like a gentleman," she says, sighing. "And then he asked me out for next week."

My devil's advocate mode continues. "You want distance from your parents, but do you really want distance from this relationship?"

"I want to be *me* before I am part of a *we*. You know?"

"I do know. In a way, it's like Angelica's decision."

There is silence on the other end. "Oh, great. Now, I'm making choices like Angelica."

"Don't go there, Caitlin. Angelica happened to make a very good decision for her life. And you will too."

"Mari, you are so lucky. You don't worry about the outcome of every decision you make. You left your boyfriend and your job for an undetermined amount of time to help with the kids…"

"I didn't *leave* Beau." What is it with everybody? I take a family medical leave and suddenly I am the girl who left her boyfriend.

Caitlin makes up for the slip. "Of course not. I'll bet you two are stronger than ever."

"We're great," I lie. I'm not yet ready to spoil Caitlin's version of my life.

"Did I make a mistake?" She sounds worried.

"No, we are stronger. Distance makes the heart grow fonder, right?" I sound fake and stupid. I want to turn my words off.

"I meant about Jim."

"He obviously wants to keep dating. Who says you have to end it?"

"Nobody," she yelps into the phone. "I'm confused."

"Pray about it. I'll pray about it too. Oh, hey…there is someone trying to call."

"Maybe it is lover-Beau," she offers, sounding a bit more encouraged.

"Probably," I lie again. "I'll call you later."

I press the receiver down to click over to the other call. For a moment my heart is expecting the static of long distance. Maybe Beau and I were thinking about one another at the exact same moment, and he just had to call me to say he misses me.

"Beau?" I say hopefully and a bit loudly in case the connection is bad again.

"No. This is Lonna." A confused voice responds.

Pause.

"For Marcus," she says, as though I should know.

"Oh, right. One minute." I push open the door and Marcus is seated just inches away from the closet.

"Lonna," I say casually.

He nods and changes places with me.

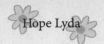

As I limbo under the yellow cord to get out of Marcus' way, I consider Cheyenne's interpretation about Marcus' relationship and wonder if his emotionally distant dating and my geographically distant dating are very far apart on the unhealthy relationship scale.

The Shadow Knows

Mainly, I just need a friendly face in the crowd. Not that my constituents are not friendly, but usually I would have…"

"I am happy to be at this city council debate," I say cheerily so Mom doesn't have to finish her sentence. Dad is her usual friendly face, but he couldn't muster the strength to sit through a two-hour meeting. Marcus said he would do his research from the house instead of going into the library so that I could attend Mom's first public event as a candidate.

"Debate sounds so scary." She looks at me a bit worried.

"I meant discussion. Citywide discussion."

"Thank you." She squeezes my hand and then keeps hold of it as she waves to a focused, well-dressed woman approaching us with fast, efficient steps. "Kayla! Over here."

"She looks like she is about to hurdle us," I say quietly.

Mom drops my hand and gives me a look I know well from my childhood. It means "Stop it immediately or you are going to the car."

As the woman hugs my mom in a professional but sincere way, there is something about her profile that seems familiar. I'm trying to figure it out—one of our volunteers, a community supporter, a former schoolmate?

"Kayla, I'd like you to meet my daughter, Mari. Mari, this is my brilliant campaign assistant, Kayla."

"Pleased to meet you. I'm a big fan of your mother. She'll go far, you know." As the words leave her ruby red lips in a voice that mimics Katherine Hepburn, with a slightly haughty undertone, I know exactly who this is.

During my senior year of high school, my guidance counselor suggested I do an internship to boost my scholarship potential. He arranged for me to job-shadow Kayla, who was a former graduate of my high school, just out of college, a bit wet behind the ears in her city public relations job, and more than a little upset that she had to provide me with a chair in her office and an occasional word of explanation about what she was doing.

"We've met. Remember your city job? Me in the corner…in the chair. Taking notes. Following you."

Mom looks back and forth between me and her friend with confusion.

Kayla ignores my comment and our shared memories altogether. "Nice to *meet* you, Marni. And you, Mrs. Hamilton, you will shine today. Let's meet up next week." She does the European kiss on the cheek departure with my mom and walks right by me on her way to shake hands with the mayor.

"What was that?" Mom asks.

"No kidding. Did this woman enter the witness protection program or something? Or are her days as a mere PR flunky such a blemish on her record?" I laugh a bit at the absurdity of the pretentious woman.

"I meant what was that attitude you gave her? I introduce you to her, and you act strange. No wonder she left in such a hurry."

"Mom, I know her. Don't you remember my internship with the city? And the mean woman who thought her supervisor had planted me as a spy when she got busted for padding her overtime? That was her."

"I remember that situation, but this cannot be the same person. Why would she act as though she doesn't know you?"

"I'm telling you, she's *loco*." I circle my finger around my ear a few times to emphasize just how crazy this one is.

"Kayla Newcomb is a highly regarded professional."

"*Loco,* Mom. Watch out for her."

Mom is getting exasperated with my line of reasoning. She gives me the crazy signal. "I think *you* are losing it. Isn't it about time for you to go and visit your friends? You are cracking under the pressure of all the work we have you doing at the house."

"I leave soon for my second dress fitting."

Mom leans in. "Until then, and even after—no more talk of this. Whoever Kayla is, she is one good campaign consultant and she is doing it for next to nothing because she believes in me."

"I will not say another word about it." *Today.* "Let's review your notes so you are ready for your speech."

This calms my mother down. We focus on the importance of after school activity and nutrition programs, more teaching assistants, and weekend tutoring sessions for homeless children.

But my mind cannot shake the image of Kayla scowling at me from her makeshift desk of file cabinets and Plexiglas in her basement office at city hall.

Flavor of the Month

"Mari, get up. Get up," Daisy squeals. She pulls my hand from my book and tries to drag me from the couch.

"I just got settled, Daisy. I told you I would help you make a house out of the cardboard box this afternoon."

"It's the ice man."

Matty comes up behind Daisy and reaches for her other hand. "She means the ice cream man. Come on, Daisy. Give Mari a break."

I strain my ears and can barely make out an instrumental jingle version of Sly and the Family Stone's "Hot Fun in the Summertime." "Thanks, teammate, but he's playing my song. Let's all go."

Daisy claps her hands and hollers, "Ice cream time!"

Everyone in our house heads outside. Dad even decides to leave his latest crossword puzzle to join us.

As we step into warm sunshine, doors open and close throughout the neighborhood, and a steady stream of children pours from apartment building entries. The song gets louder and the line forming by a fire hydrant gets longer. We step in behind the neighbors from across the street.

"Hi, Mrs. Jamison," I say.

"Well, hello, Mari. I wondered when we were going to see you in the ice cream line. You waited until the last week. Are you being good?" This single mom has a warm laugh and three adorable boys with thick black hair and hazel eyes.

"I haven't been paying attention. I think my dad deliberately sends me on errands during this time of day. He wasn't fast enough today."

"I heard that." Dad steps up next to me in line. He is using a cane and seems much more mobile. "Frank, are you ready to work on the carburetor?"

Dad teaches the eldest boy how to work on cars. It keeps Frank's mind off not having a dad in the picture, and it keeps my dad's mind off his limited abilities right now.

"Yes, sir. I'd like that."

"Don't forget us." Marcus comes rushing across the street with Wallace riding piggy back just as the ice cream man stops at his usual driveway and opens his traveling refrigerator for business.

"Can we take cuts?" Wallace asks.

Dad looks behind us. "If the two people behind us say it is okay."

Marcus and Wallace ask permission and return to our gaggle of family.

Mrs. Jamison looks at us all with a big smile. "This is just like old times. Except Frank was just four then. And you two were teens. Remember how he used to call you something funny…what was it?"

She is pointing to Marcus and me. I try to act like I don't know what she is talking about, but Marcus is eating this up. "Love birdies."

"That's it. Sounds silly now, but you two really were old souls. Kindred spirits, I guess you could say. I look at Frank, who is about to turn eighteen, and I cannot imagine him finding the love of his life this young. He's still my baby."

"Aw, Mom." Frank blushes and turns his attention to the ice cream man. He then realizes that he needs money from his mom so he holds out his hand for the dollar.

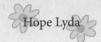

Dad reaches across her shoulder with a twenty-dollar bill. "All my kids get treated today. Including you, Cheryl."

She laughs and graciously accepts the offer. I gladly accept the distraction from the line of conversation.

Marcus handles all the orders and doles out the flavors one at a time. "Carmel nut for you."

"Thank you. Still eating cherry chip, I see."

"Nothing better."

"Except our own creations, of course."

He smiles. "Goes without saying."

We walk in silence for a while enjoying one of the last days of summer. I feel seventeen again—all tied up inside with life's questions and joy. It was the point in my life when I realized I was an individual and could have my own future someday.

"If you had asked me thirteen years ago what I would be doing right now in life, I would have rattled off so many things."

"But not this?" Marcus jokes softly.

I slant my head toward him. "No. Anything but this."

"Have your dreams served you well?"

"They have. I went through a phase when I was dreaming of the wrong things, but I think I have that figured out."

"I did the same. Realistic is better."

I pause in our walk. "Yes, realism inspired by dreams and faith is best."

"Here's to dreams, then." Marcus tips his cone toward mine.

I take a bite off the top of my ice cream swirl and hold it on my tongue as long as I can stand it. Another carryover from seventeen. Marcus does the same.

"You swallowed. I'm the best!" I say after a couple minutes. Though it comes out more like, "Thoo swawod, I'm thu beshed."

"Hey, love birdies, beat you to the house," Frank says from behind us. He and Dad are also heading to the house.

I notice Marcus smile shyly at our nickname. Then bravado takes over. "You're on. I'll beat Frank. Mari, you outrun the old man with the cane!"

We take off for the house. Each of us running in awkward, silly strides. By the time we reach the front step, we are winded, covered in a smattering of ice cream, and laughing.

The taste of pure joy hits me hard. And I am surprised by the sweetness of childhood contentment.

Forty Licks

"Mari, I always drink water with lemon when I have a mailing like this to do," Kayla says in a tone that declares she is much wiser than I will ever be. She places a glass of tap water with a lemon wedge floating on top in front of me.

"I was thinking a cocktail might help more." I smile at her with an open mouth like a ventriloquist dummy might.

"Mari!" Mom slaps the back of my head on her way to her seat at the table, where piles of letters and envelopes and stamps await our folding, stuffing, and licking.

Kayla acts hurt. "I just meant the lemon helps you salivate, which in turn helps you lick all those envelopes and stamps. Once again, I'm terribly sorry that I only had enough self-adhesive envelopes for your mom and me."

I do the smile again and this time add really wide eyes. Now I am a circus sideshow puppet that comes alive at dusk.

Mom throws a pen at me this time. "Mari, I swear, you'd think you were a child."

"Gosh, I remember my childhood. Back in high school. Remember

when I was in high school, Mom? I did homework and special projects and internships. Remember that?"

Kayla ignores me completely. She gives Mom a snuggly-wuggly smile and shakes her head. It is a "those kids and their strange humor" look. Mom laughs but gives me a very stern scowl when Kayla bends over to retrieve more envelopes from a box under the table.

"So, Mari. Your mom tells me that you read to old folks? That is such a servant thing to do."

"Actually, I'm the recreation director for a retirement and assisted living facility. I do lots of things. I teach classes, I schedule special events and activities, I coordinate the volunteers, you know...like interns."

Mom kicks me beneath the table and offers Kayla a snack. It is so obvious where the love is in this room. Far, far from me. Deservedly so. I don't know why I cannot let Kayla alone in her psychotic world of make-believe. Why does it matter if she wants to pretend she does not know me? It occurs to me that maybe I really am that forgettable. I did only job-shadow her for three months. Maybe my personality does not come out until month four.

"These are delicious, Mrs. H." Kayla begins to eat a biscotti without dipping it in coffee first. As I watch bits of shortbread and almond tumble from her lips and onto the letters in front of her, I suddenly have a flashback.

We went on a double-date together.

Kayla was supposed to go out with a senator's supposedly boring son, Rob, and she didn't want to go alone, so she invited me to tag along as the blind date of the boring son's friend, Thane. When I protested that my parents would never let me go, she insisted that I sneak out of the house and pretend I was twenty-one.

Sadly, I did both under her wicked spell. Turns out the only bore that night was her. As she ate like a wild animal with a broken jaw and harassed the waitstaff, the two guys and I watched with horror. Finally we ignored Kayla, who seemed frozen in her inadequacy, and we embarked on interesting conversation about politics and baseball. When nine o'clock rolled around, the nice young men said it was time to get me home before my parents found out. I was not excited that they were on to how young I was, but I

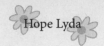

was relieved to get home before curfew and the interrogation that would have ensued had I arrived home after ten.

"Mom, do you know whatever happened to Senator Bob Munroe?" I ask as casually as possible. I watch Kayla's eyes widen.

Gotcha.

Mom presses down on a stamp and thinks for a bit. "I think he and his son are quite successful in business real estate these days. You know, I should invite him to my next event. I always liked him."

"Wow," I emphasize, "he and his son are really successful, huh? That sure is good to hear. Don't you think so, Kayla?"

For a brief moment, there is a look of recognition, of avoidance, and finally of denial on Kayla's face. She shrugs and bites into another dry biscotti.

"Thanks again for the water with lemon idea, Kayla. I feel like I could spit all day."

"Mari!"

A Fitting Response

Passenger Mari Hamilton, please report to the Fly Right gate." The overhead is blaring my name every ten seconds. I try to act as though my fast shuffle down the airport hallways isn't a direct response. It is like casually exiting to turn off your lights when your license plate is announced at a restaurant.

"I'm Mari Hamilton," I say while juggling my laptop and an overnight bag. "You paged me?" I look up into the stern eyes of Clarissa.

"Your friend tried to get past the gate to greet you with a special package. We don't allow that. Tell any friends that if they want to meet you at the airport, they must meet you in the baggage claim or here. Got it?"

Gulp. "Yes, ma'am. Can I see my friend now?"

Clarissa does her extreme pointing. I follow the shell pink, polished nail and see Caitlin looking sheepish next to an airport security guard. It is the guard who last time removed the necklace Beau made for me.

"Maybe you should send a memo to your friends. Surprise gifts at the airport are not such a good idea," says the guard.

"I got that message from Clarissa, but thank you. Can my friend go now?"

He nods and Caitlin hurries toward me.

Clarissa is helping another customer but finds it necessary to add one more round of wisdom to this day's lessons. "Maybe your friend could dress in something recognizable too. She wouldn't be such an obvious one to pull aside. Okay?"

I wave and smile and reassess my friend. I am so accustomed to Caitlin that even after a month's absence her clothing taste did not faze me. But now that I take a second, fresh look, her multi-colored headdress is a bit conspicuous.

"Don't worry. This isn't one of my designs. I borrowed it from a friend. Thought I would show up at the dress fitting with this on to tease Sadie."

"I'm thinking that is a big risk, my friend."

She fingers the tufts of feathers that extend about two feet above her face. "I wouldn't want to upset her. I thought it'd be funny."

Am I really the only one who understands that Sadie is on edge?

When we pull up to the dress shop in my ratty car, we are met by Valerie, who is beaming beneath the awning-covered entrance. Her hair is up in a very formal style, and she wears a floor length, blue satin dress.

"Should we hope that Sadie changed her mind about the striped numbers?" I say before we get out of the car.

"No. I even asked. In a discreet way, I promise." Caitlin nods with grave seriousness. "That's why I thought the headdress might be good comic relief. Angelica told me that even her size four thighs were not meant for this challenge."

"We just have to deal with the dresses. That stays," I give her a Clarissa directive for her comic relief prop.

"I'm glad we returned the dresses for a second fitting," says Caitlin.

"So it wouldn't be in your apartment, sucking you into its mesmerizing vortex of cataclysmic, stripy..."

Caitlin can spot one of my adjective-filled run-on sentences in a few syllables. She holds up a hand to stop me. "I stress ate for a week while making the New York decision. I needed to move the hips back out to the fuchsia stripe."

"I passed the fuchsia stripe months ago. Now, put on your 'I love looking like a Bond girl' face. Our friend awaits."

Sadie is peeking over Valerie's shoulder, excited to see us. She looks beautiful in a white suit and lavender blouse. We cannot disappoint our friend with bad attitudes. And we don't. Not even when two of us put them on backward in confusion. We are perfectly agreeable.

"Where are those little sandwiches?" Angelica looks haggard and is sitting in an unladylike position on the bench. Or off the bench. She is on the floor with her feet propped up on the cushions. She says it is to relieve a backache, but I think she has vertigo from the stripes.

Sadie doesn't seem to mind Angelica's pose. In fact, she seems more chipper than ever. "We should have food now. Has everyone been pinned?"

"Yes, Miss Verity," we say in unison, eager to get to the free food. Well, free to us.

Once Valerie has offered us a splendid assortment of sandwiches and salads, Sadie asks if we can have the parlor area to ourselves. Once alone, we all four sit on the floor and get comfortable. My brief visit with Rachel and Cheyenne in Arlington made me homesick for this circle of friends.

They all want to know about the shelter, the kids, and my dad's health. And all I want to know is how Caitlin is handling her relationship with Jim, postproposal.

"So, Caitlin, any change of mind or heart?" I ask openly.

Caitlin looks down at her sandals. Angelica and Sadie appear puzzled and curious. I realize I am about to blow a secret. "...about how you plan to wear your hair for the wedding?"

Caitlin plays along. "No. I wanted to see what Sadie thought." She gives us all a few hair poses.

Sadie considers the possibilities. "I like the hair up along the sides but long and a little wild down the back. Do you think that matches the feel of the bridesmaid dresses?"

We all hold our breath—just for a moment.

As Angelica opens her mouth to speak, I close my eyes, anticipating the worst comment possible.

"Believe me, 'a little wild' fits the dresses."

Surprisingly, it is the perfect answer.

Filling in the Blanks

"Call me when you want me to pick you up," Caitlin says as I heave myself out of her low car.

"I'm sure Beau can drive me to your place. What time will you be going to bed?"

"Early. I'm wiped out. You know, with the whole proposal thing. By the way, thanks for not bringing it up. I feel funny. Like if I stick with my no answer, I will offend Sadie somehow, and if I say yes, I will let you and Angelica down."

I stand on the curb and lean in through the passenger window. "You worry about disappointing everyone, Caitlin. I'd be so happy for you if this was the right thing. And only you can decide that. You and Jim the Cop."

"I've been envious of Sadie for so long, ever since I've known her but especially since her engagement, and now that it is a possibility for me, I realize that a lot of questions go with that one big answer."

"I hear ya."

"Angelica would totally be against the idea."

"There you go again. And to let you in on a little secret, I predict Angelica

150

is going to come out of her self-appointed isolation. She's a lot more like you and me when it comes to figuring out the love stuff."

"You'd never know it." Caitlin starts her car. "Can you really see me married?"

"I can see you married *and* having your own store. That's what I see."

After I watch Caitlin's car pull out of the parking lot, all my thoughts are of Beau. Happily I feel weak in the knees and my heart is racing. After our not so great record of phone conversations recently, I was afraid I would approach this time with him too cautiously, or worse, with hurt feelings. Instead, I am taking the stairs two at a time to his upstairs condo.

I can hear clapping and what sounds like the laugh track for a 1950s sitcom—rising and falling in an orderly way.

Knock. Knock.

More clapping.

Knock. Knock.

Chuckle. Chuckle.

Finally I hear motion on the other side of the door. Or commotion rather. Something heavy hits the floor, there is another thud, and then a small crash. I stretch my neck to peek in the window just as the door opens. My heart skips a beat when I see Beau standing in the doorway looking bedraggled and slightly disoriented.

"Were you asleep?" I ask instead of hugging him like I want to.

He rubs his eyes. "Come here." He reaches out and pulls me to him. The awkwardness of the phone conversations disappears as soon as I look into his face.

"You are working too hard. It's only eight thirty and you are falling asleep in front of the television," I tease him, but not long ago this was my life every night.

"I just turned the television on to help keep me awake. Guess that wasn't such a good remedy for fatigue." The word fatigue apparently triggers Beau's thoughts of my dad. "How is your father's condition?"

"Better. He's stronger each day and more feisty. I think he is going a

bit stir-crazy, but it is way too early for him to tackle anything close to his past routine at the center. And the kids have been great. It does them good to tend to some of his needs. A few of them are really blossoming under the role of caregiver." I smile, thinking of Jon, Katie, and Alf taking turns blending Dad's vitamin shakes.

"Come sit down. It's so good to see you, Mari."

"It is?" I love it when he says my name.

"I have missed you. And this report is killing me."

"Then we should go out for ice cream or for a walk at the rock gardens. You need a break from all this work."

He scratches his head and then his oxford-covered stomach. "Actually, I was thinking you could help me with some of this."

"Oh, sure," I say not too convincingly.

He reaches for the hook on the wall past me. Holding up his keys, he says, "Tell you what. I will go get some ice cream and toppings and you can sit back, relax, and maybe take a look at that printout there. Something is missing, but I'm too tired to figure it out."

I kiss his cheek and readjust my expectations for a romantic stroll or a nice dinner out. If I had not been gone the past month, I would love the chance to help him with this project. In fact, it is exactly what I was asking for before I left for Washington—involvement, inclusion, connection.

He is out the door and down the steps quicker than I can say "extra caramel sauce." I sit back on the couch and wonder what it would be like to be married and living here with Beau. The furnishings and decor are sparse, and moving boxes remain unopened, even after all these months. Yet Beau is the kind of guy who can make a place feel homey. The couch is cozy with pretty pillows and colorful throws. He has a candle arrangement in the fireplace and up on the mantel. Sure, it is the exact arrangement they have on the cover of Pier 1's sale flyer, but still, for a guy it is a nice touch.

Maybe staying in and working together side by side is just what we need. We only have a few hours, and here we have no distractions from waiters, and we can relax and enjoy the precious time.

Wheel of Fortune's theme song is screaming at me. I turn the sound down,

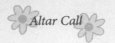

but keep the television on so I can guess the words. Spreadsheets cover Beau's polished pine coffee table. No wonder he has been working so hard; this project seems daunting. Jumping in midway isn't easy, but soon I recognize stats and charts from my work at Golden Horizons. It seems he is showing how facilities with high program involvement have a greater success rate for improving the quality of life for patients who have Alzheimers, dementia, or mobility problems. It is something we all know, but it is not necessarily easy to prove that dollars toward programming are dollars well spent.

I continue examining the reports from various facilities. A standard questionnaire has been completed for each location evaluated and there are additional notes jotted down at the bottom of the sheets. I notice some are in Beau's boyish printing, and some are written in cursive.

Paige.

Just when I had stopped thinking about her, I see her name scrawled at the top of one of the evaluations. Of course it is her handwriting. She is his mentor. I get up and walk across the room to the sole bookshelf and the sole picture of me and Beau. It was taken after the Tucson Trot, a fund-raiser walk last year. I look terrible. I had just found out that Tess, my favorite resident at Golden Horizons, had passed away. The skin around my eyes is sort of puffy and my face is a bit shiny from the heat. But there is a sweetness in our couple stance. I am leaning on him, and he is giving me a tight sideways hug, supporting me in my sadness. His eyes are not staring at the camera as people usually do when they know a photo is being taken—his eyes are fixed on me.

The phone rings right beside me and nearly sends the frame flying from my fingers. Instead, I catch it between my arm and my thigh and save it from brokenness. The phone keeps ringing. Even after many months of dating, I don't feel comfortable answering Beau's phone. Then again, it could be him wanting to know which sprinkles I like best. I smile. No, wait. He would have called me on the cell phone he bought me. I, unlike him, usually have mine turned on.

The last ring is cut off and Beau's voice comes on. "Try, try again. Leave a message at the beep."

"Hey, it's me. I hope you are figuring out what we are missing because I've been working on this since we left the restaurant earlier. Maybe you are taking a much-needed break. Remember, I've got you all weekend, so be ready to work first thing tomorrow. *Ciao.*"

Ciao? Who says *ciao?* And I've been Beau's girlfriend for more than ten months and I still identify myself when I call. Paige works with him for two months and bypasses her name and throws around "Hey" and *"Ciao"* as though she's an overly flirtatious waitress at the corner bistro. My finger hovers over the delete button. But I can't. It would somehow be admitting that I really think I need to worry. And I don't. Beau is not that kind of a guy. He's the kind you take home to meet the parents. He's the kind you marry if you are lucky enough to get asked.

I force myself to return to the couch and focus on the data, not the dame. This seems to work as I am on the edge of figuring something out when Beau comes through the door with three freezer bags full of selections.

"They didn't have your favorite, and I couldn't remember what you like second best, so I bought us a buffet of ice cream. And toppings." He turns to show me yet another bag tucked under his arm.

Now that I see his smile, I think of Paige. I pray he doesn't play the message while I am here. There isn't room for the three of us. "I'm sure I'll like one of those."

"Did you figure out what is missing?" Beau eyes the notepad where I have scrawled out some notes.

"I have ideas. I'm not sure if it is what you two are looking for." I did what I thought I wouldn't do—I indirectly brought her up. But Beau doesn't notice my phrasing. He doesn't know that it takes every ounce of self-control in me to not say the word "Paige" right now, out loud, and to his face.

"That is great. I knew you'd have an eye for this research."

Then why wasn't I asked sooner, know-it-all?

Beau plops down next to me and hands me a large spoon and a carton of peppermint stick ice cream.

He is forgiven.

"You have a cat. Can you fill in the word?"

"Excuse me?"

Beau points to the television and the about-to-be solved puzzle. "The missing word? The guy missed it, but I think the woman knows it. It is 'cat' blank," he says, wiping chocolate sauce off his mouth with the back of his hand.

I look at the board on the screen and shake my head in disbelief. It can't be. But clearly it is. "Ciao," I say.

Beau looks up a bit startled; there is recognition on his face. Then it melts as quickly as the ice cream left on his chin and he looks back at the television. "You're right. Cat *Ciao*. That was incredible. You didn't even hear the clue."

"Oh, it's nothing," I say. "Just playing the game, right?"

Etiquette

"More croissants, Mari?" Lola Swanson, who smells of lilac linen spray, leans over me to secure a pretty pastry with metal tongs.

"Yes, please," I say in a very dainty voice. I am participating in the final presentations of the Elders for Etiquette club hosted by Golden Horizons. I don't remember agreeing to this for one of my rare weekends home, but Lysa assures me I did.

"I always love these." Lysa smacks her lips three times after nibbling a miniscule sandwich.

"You just flunked the manners portion of this session."

"Ya think?"

"I think. Now, Sonya is a shining star. Look at her."

We glance over at our friend, who is sipping from a porcelain cup like a queen.

"If this is an Elders *for* Etiquette event, do you think on the other side of the tracks there is an Elders Against Etiquette activity?" I have not had coffee yet.

"Oh, let's go." Sonya says, laughing.

Lysa turns to me. "Don't your breakfast buds meet at Freddies on Saturday mornings?"

"We met yesterday for the dress fitting instead. But really, the Saturday breakfast ritual was hardly happening—not since DE-day."

"D-day?" She wipes watercress from her chin with the back of her hand.

"Diamond engagement ring day."

"Changes everything. I've seen my sister twice since she got married a year ago. We used to go shopping at the Farmers' Market every Wednesday."

"Now?"

"Not once."

"Are you doing anything with our bossy boss?" Sonya dabs the corner of her mouth with practiced flair.

"We hung out for a while last night." I pout. "His mentor is in town, and they need time to go over his proposals for the program."

"He'll do so well. That is worth a weekend now and then."

I wave my napkin casually. "Oh, yeah. It's worth it. I just wish…"

Lola comes out of the kitchen a bit flushed to apologize for the delayed baked Alaska. We graciously tell her not to worry.

"That it wasn't *your* weekend?" Sonya asks sympathetically.

"That too, but—this is silly—I wish he had a male mentor."

"You are crazy to worry. Beau is the most stable guy I have ever met. And he is absolutely smitten with you," Sonya says, telling me what I already know.

Greta Banfeld prances into the center of the sunroom. She has on ballet slippers and seems to be our unscheduled entertainment. Clearly a ploy to keep our minds off being deserted by dessert.

We cannot take our eyes off of her. She reminds me of a music box ballerina on a spring coil who bends when the lid is closed—her spring might be loose.

"I'm getting dizzy. Make her stop," whimpers Lysa.

I turn to laugh, but I see she is holding her stomach and turning a shade shy of a shamrock.

"Maybe you had better excuse yourself. I'm pretty sure that…"

Lysa bends over and places her startling green face in my lap. She also knocks a dish of tapioca all over me.

"…this is not polite." My impulse is to jump up and run far, far away, but I place one hand on her head to comfort her and with the other try to scoop up the pudding.

A few moments later, without attracting more attention than necessary, I half lift, half drag Lysa to the hallway. In her sick mumblings she mentions a tuna allergy.

"Can I help? Lysa, do you need a ride home?" Sonya joins us in the hallway near the bulletin board decorated like an aquarium.

Lysa looks up at a colorful, paper version of a betta. "Tuna."

"A nursing student should know not to mess with food allergies, especially not at a function," I reprimand my friend just as we turn the corner toward the bathroom.

"I wanted to be supportive," she moans.

I look up in time to see Beau and a stunning woman walking down the hallway.

Beau, looking curiously at the scene and trying to piece together what is going on, asks, "What happened?"

"Lysa's allergic to tuna."

"Tuna," she echoes pathetically. Lysa's mouth is now open as though she has been drugged.

I'm trying to stay focused on Beau because I don't want to look at Paige. I see she is dressed in a polished, tailored suit, and this is not my best moment. I realize this is poor manners. So be it.

"Sonya?" Paige's voice glides over me toward my friend.

"Paige? What are you doing here with…" Sonya pauses.

I know why she stops the conversation. "With Beau" does not sound proper. After all, Paige isn't *with* Beau. This is all my mind focuses on and seems to avoid the question that would be asked if people asked the questions they wanted to instead of politely stepping around issues: "How do Paige and Sonya know each other?"

I don't ask it, and I still don't look up.

"I'm Beau's mentor. Can you believe it? Small world, isn't it? We have lots of work to do this weekend. We are on our way to look at some of Beau's research here at the office. This project is his heart, but I think I can offer some guidance. Together we have a good chance of earning our grant stripes on this, right, Beau?"

"Yes," Beau says, and I can tell by the volume of his voice that he is facing me. "Mari, can I help you and Lysa? She looks awful."

"She's had a bad day. We'll be fine. Excuse us." I am giving him the brush-off. I am also counting the number of times Paige used "we."

"Mari, do you want to use my office? Lysa could lie down on the couch in there." Beau is trying to acknowledge me in this situation, and I don't take it. Yes, I did beg him to introduce me to Paige early on, but this is not the moment.

"We'll just take her home. Paige, good to see you. Maybe we can catch up during one of your visits," says Sonya.

"We will be busy, busy, but perhaps coffee sometime. I'll get your information from Beau."

I am already in the women's restroom splashing cold water on Lysa's face and mine when Sonya finishes saying goodbye to Paige.

"You didn't tell me it was Paige," Sonya says with a bit of shock evident in her voice.

I use the soap from the hand dispenser to wash my face and hands. If the sink was bigger, I'd try to dive in. My erratic motion turns the substance into many suds. I'm wearing a halo of bubbles as I look into the mirror. "I didn't realize the name Paige meant anything. How do you know her?"

"Well, you know that Beau and I knew each other as acquaintances in college. Paige introduced us."

"She thought you two would want to date?" Lysa asks the question because once you almost throw up in public, you do not have to abide by the proper question rule.

"No." Sonya manages a polite laugh. She is yanking paper towels and wiping up the mess I have made. "Goodness, we may need to give you both a shower."

"What aren't you saying, Sonya?" I ask.

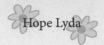

She keeps cleaning and avoids looking at me. "This is a conversation for you and Beau."

"If it is something you would want to know, tell me."

She considers this and nods. "Paige and Beau dated."

"My eye. My eye!" Soap has dripped into my field of vision.

"Flush!" Lysa pushes my head under the sink with the force of full recovery. After a few seconds she pulls me back upright and wipes my face. "Open your eyes, Mari. Try to focus on my fingers. Your eyes will water for a while, but you need to open them."

My instinct overrides my common sense, and my eyes remain tightly shut.

I'm not ready to look.

Amazing Grace

Caitlin lives walking distance from my church, and while I thought I would not be up for it after yesterday's big news flash, I am decidedly very much in the mood to be back in my home church.

I didn't even call Beau because I figured he would be working all morning with Paige. I let myself acknowledge this without going down a path of dark thoughts or jealous rants.

And when I see him entering the church from the other side of the sanctuary, I am only glad, relieved, and happy.

He scans the crowd, notices me, and rushes over. His hand reaches for mine and doesn't let go during the service, which makes taking communion difficult and makes experiencing communion attainable. When he gets the chance, Beau looks at me and mouths he is sorry. Later he nudges me and whispers it in my ear.

A part of me wants to strangle him right here in the pew we have chosen as our favorite spot. I figure that is about 49.9 percent of me. One of my biggest fears in a relationship is to be made the fool of, to be taken advantage of, to not be cared for in some way that is important. Beau's lack of being forthright is shocking. If anyone else was dating a guy who did this, I would be skeptical. I would be a love atheist or at least a romance agnostic. But this is my Beau. The one who treats me well, laughs with me, and cares about the people I care about. The view is much different from here by his side.

Which brings me to the 50.1 percent that wants to readily forgive him. I want to hear his reasons and believe him wholeheartedly. I want to be the giver of grace.

I have not heard his reasons for keeping the truth from me.

I don't have to imagine them because I know them well.

I have not yet told him the whole truth about Marcus. It never occurred to me to reveal that Marcus is not just a good-looking, good-hearted guy who is helping my parents, but someone I had a relationship with. A young, teen relationship, but nevertheless one that affected me and my heart deeply at that time in my life. If Beau visited me at the center, he would see how closely Marcus and I work together. And should he stumble across the detail that we once dated, I would be standing in the same place of guilt by omission.

I am ready to give grace because I know I need to ask for it as well.

On the steps of the church, I confess to Beau that I dated Marcus many years ago. Beau says he felt jealous of Marcus from the beginning, but only because Marcus was close to me, geographically speaking. I laugh and say it was the same threat I perceived about Paige.

We come clean about our past enough to reassure the other that it was our past trials that made us who we are today. There you have it, love professed in clichéd story morals.

Best of all, we both agree it cannot be geographic distance that keeps us together or tears us apart. The faith we have in our future stems from the grace we are giving to one another this weekend. It is a clean slate that we don't disturb with lots of exuberant promises or vows. Doing so would only remind us how fragile this relationship is, and we both want to give it a real chance at survival.

Today, as I hand Clarissa my ticket, there is no extra security check. Beau does not give me more ways to stay in touch with him, and I follow

Clarissa's rules carefully. I think I even see her smile as she recognizes my name and driver's license image which is, sadly, hard to forget.

As I sit on the plane flipping through the airline publication and pretending to read, I figure out that the camera phone, the calling card, and the necklace Beau gave me last month were less about Paige specifically and more about the fear of what distance can do to a relationship—and what the nearness of others can also do to a relationship.

I reach into my bag and pull out the gaudy necklace. The chunky chain and mother of pearl goes around my neck—once again. It is my act of faith.

Stranger and Stranger

Could you get that, Mari?" Mom calls from upstairs. I am cleaning up yet another weekend breakfast mess after losing an arm wrestling wager with Jon. Now all the kids have invited me to an arm wrestling challenge with dreams of being chore free for the rest of their young lives.

I head to the front door and look in the security monitor. Kayla. Then I look down at my messy apron, frayed jeans, and broken flip flops. Oh, great. She will pretend to not know me all over again with this getup.

Kayla enters the door by first poking her head in, as if checking to see if the coast is clear of kids. She seems relieved until she spots me standing by the soda fountain bar holding up a spatula.

"Goodness, Mary. They've put you to work."

I don't correct her. She knows my name—just as I know hers. "That's right, Kale. But you know what hard work volunteering can be, don't you? After all, you've taken on my mom's campaign out of the kindness of your big heart. It's not easy to be so generous."

She fluffs the back of her hair with platinum adorned fingers. "Well, thank you. It is worth every backbreaking minute of it."

"Mom!" I call for backup.

"I'm here, Miss Impatient Pants."

I turn to Mom to thank her for the humiliating nickname, but when I see her beautiful outfit, all I can do is praise her. "Is that what you bought last week? It's wonderful. That jacket is very stylish, and the necklace is fantastic."

"Those were my selections, Marsha," beams Kayla.

I stare at Mom, giving her a "see what she does?" look. But Mom is on an adrenaline high and does not tune into her daughter's hypersensitivity to being called by the wrong name.

Kayla does a quick check of Mom's makeup and outfit and her notes. "Perfect. They will love you at the Friends of the Library function. This group represents people we want to back us all the way."

"To the White House?" I ask mischievously. Mom is running for city council, not a senate seat, for goodness' sake.

I get a kiss from Mom and a sideways glance from Kayla.

"Have a good time on your field trip, Mari," Mom calls back.

I hear Kayla say, "That is so cute, a field trip," as they walk down the front steps.

"Oh!" I yell when they are out of earshot.

"Don't worry, dear. Nobody can replace you."

"I'm not worried about that." At least I wasn't. "I know her and she knows me, but she won't admit it. That is just strange behavior."

"Did you like her back then?"

"Not particularly."

"Maybe she wants to start over. Your mom seems to like what she is doing for the campaign. Think of it differently?"

"Okay. Thanks, Dad. Will you round up the kids for me?"

"Marcus has got that covered. They are all out back doing drills. He wanted to wear them out a bit before driving them in the van."

"I'm taking them. Me. Not Marcus. I planned this field trip to Williamsburg." I start counting off all the things I have done to prepare for this day. "I researched places to go, I arranged stops with the restaurants and retailers, I scheduled the colonial reenactment actors…"

"This is your show. But you know how we were talking about your mom and me being a good team—it is out of necessity. You don't take fourteen kids on a field trip alone. For one thing, it is not even legal according to our center policies, and two, it is much more fun to blame another adult if something goes wrong."

"Good point."

Dad turns as quickly as his body is able these days and snaps his fingers. "Say, didn't you go by the name Chanel last year for a while?"

I huff defensively. "It was for my job at the resort. What's your point?" Though I think I know.

He raises his eyebrows. "That is just strange behavior," he says, mimicking my words.

With a grumble to hide my smile, I gather my stuff together and walk to the back door. Just as I am about to open the screen door, I hear Alf "shush" everybody. Marcus stands up straight and keeps his hands behind his back. The kids do the same.

"What's going on?"

"Nothing, Ms. Hamilton," they say in practiced unison.

I wag my finger at them all. "I will find out one way or another what you are up to. Now get in the van!" I pull a whistle from my pocket and give it three short blasts.

Reenactment

Marcus and I are sharing a picnic blanket at the back of the group. A presentation of life in 1720 Williamsburg is going on, the kids are engrossed, and we both seem distracted by the other's presence. We've barely spoken during my first month, and I miss the fun of constant banter with my old friend. Could it be I hurt him more than I thought last visit?

"You seem…"

"How long…"

We speak at the same time and then are both embarrassed. Our conversations have never been work. Now they are pure labor.

"Go ahead," he says while watching Lou and Daisy pull each other's hair and giggle.

"I was asking how long you and Lonna have been together."

"Oh." He pauses and looks down at his hands as though they have the answer. "We've known each other for about a year. It evolved into dating, I guess." He laughs at himself. "I don't even recall making the decision, you know?"

"Were you dating when I was here last?" I'm ready to call him on this. After all, he indicated he wanted to date me then.

"No." Another pause. "Just after."

Oh. "Is it serious?"

"Can we switch to a new topic? Conversing with you about the whole girlfriend thing is weird, to say the least."

"Sure. What were you going to say?"

He moves his head side to side in an endearing, nonchalant way. "I notice you seem a little different since your trip to Tucson. Did that go okay?"

"It was a bit rushed. When I got back here, I felt the tug of two worlds."

"Makes sense. That is a lot to be dealing with. Things with your job okay?"

I give a "pshaw" wave of my wrist. "Fine. Fine. That won't be a problem. The trip was good. It was just pretty emotional for a long weekend."

"Because?" he eggs me on.

"Talking with you about the whole boyfriend thing is weird, to say the least."

"Fair enough," he says, laughing.

Out of the corner of my eye I catch him looking over at me several times during the performance, but I keep my eyes focused on the kids and the entertainment provided by Cheyenne's connections.

"I guess if you wanted to talk to me, you could. About the guy. As you know, I've moved on. We can have conversations like old friends."

I give him a look.

"What? You don't agree?" he asks innocently.

I release my tight shoulders and flip my hair, which is back in a ponytail, so the effect is minimal. "You are the one who said it would be weird."

"I'll warm up to it. Maybe I will start as the listener. But even if it is too awkward, we can certainly talk about other things like we used to."

"I suppose we could. My parents would love it."

"Yeah. Your dad asked if the cold war had been resolved while he was sick."

"No surprise. They'd love nothing better—"

"Yes?"

"Nothing better than to see us talking and working together. They like peace in their house." I try to cover up my near-mention of Marcus and me in the couple form.

He grins. "What is your impression of how things are going with your dad's recovery?"

I'm thankful for the change of subject. "Well, if Fabio keeps up the good work and Dad keeps up the hard work of taking it easy and eating right, I predict I will be back home in a couple months."

Marcus looks surprised. "You'd really stay that long? I gotta tell you, Mari, I thought your visit would be short and sweet. Nothing against you. I know you'd crawl to the ends of the earth for your folks and the people you care for, but I also know this place—the center—does something to you. It brings up too much stuff from the early years."

He knows me so well. I look over at him for a second. I confess, "It did. Not so much anymore. I worked through a lot of feelings last year. A part of me felt ripped off from all those years sharing Mom and Dad with the others." I pause and then look at him, realizing that he was one of the kids who had me feeling left out with my own parents. "No offense," I add with a bit of guilt.

"None taken. You had to give up a lot as their child. At a time when a kid should get loads of attention in her life, you were part of the crowd. Of course, your folks didn't really view you as just one of the group—but it had to be confusing."

"Thanks." I pluck a clover from the patch of grass just beyond the blanket. "It's all good now, so no worries. I don't resent anyone. Not anymore. Now I can respect how their passion carved out their lives. It is something to model, not fight."

Marcus pops his knuckles one by one, much to my annoyance.

"Could you stop that?"

"It feels good."

"Well, it is incredibly annoying."

He waves all his fingers at me and says, "Not this. I meant us talking. It feels good. Like how we used to act."

On the way home we start a round of I Spy in the van. One benefit of being around a lot of people—they don't usually notice if you decide to step out of the conversation. I am deep in thought about Beau's misstep and about my comfortable afternoon with Marcus. My time with him is completely innocent. I have no reason to suspect or expect any less from Beau and Paige.

Funny how one perspective change can turn a back-of-the-mind dilemma into a solution. I consider how God works with my thoughts and how often he has to untwist them before I see clearly. My dad's suggestion that I think differently about Kayla seems to be ongoing good advice.

I am so buoyed by this simple revelation that I turn my attention back to the game.

"What are we looking for?" I ask Marcus, who is laughing at one of the kids' guesses.

He turns to peer over his shoulder at Camden and nods.

"What are we looking for?" I repeat snapping my fingers to get Marcus' attention back to me and the road ahead.

Camden clears his throat. "I spy something pink."

"Pink?" I scan the neighborhood houses. We are getting close to the center; there are several old cars and bikes, but nothing pink.

"I want a better clue. Pink and what?" I say, turning to face the game leader.

Camden raises his hand. He is armed with a can of Silly String. They all are. "Pink and *you!*" He sounds a warrior cry, and I am covered by strips of sticky, gooey string in a matter of seconds.

We have pulled into the driveway before I can clear off my face enough to glare at Marcus. "You! You are going down!" I start to chase him around the yard and the kids start to chase me.

We all careen around the corner and nearly smack into Dad, who is barbequing on the patio. First Marcus falls, then the kids, and me on top.

Dad barely glances up from tending to his pork ribs and deadpans, "Honey, there is a pink Hostess Snow Ball attacking our children."

The response giggles are so loud that none of us hear the sound of the screen door and the click of a hose nozzle.

Final Words

"Hello." I click on my phone quickly so nobody in the small, used bookstore will judge me.

"Mari, it's me, Bernie."

"Bernie who?" All I can think of is that Bernie sounds like a politician and must be a friend of Mom's.

"Fabio."

I slap my head with my free hand. "Of course. Sorry, Bernie. Do you need me to pick up a higher set of weights for Dad? Or maybe a straightjacket?" I laugh and a woman in my aisle snaps her head at me in obvious disapproval.

"Where are you?"

"Shopping in Georgetown."

"Good. I need you to meet us at Lincoln Memorial right away. Your dad fainted."

"Why would you take him sightseeing?"

"Lincoln Memorial Hospital, Mari, not the tourist attraction. He fainted while working in the yard and hurt his leg."

"And you were there?"

"No. Daisy called me using your dad's cell phone."

"Daisy! She's five."

"Your dad's last words before he fell down were 'Don't tell your mother that I'm out here,'" Fabio says, chuckling, "so she called me. Smart girl."

"So who is with Daisy?"

"Marcus came home to watch the kids. And your mom will be coming from the American Food Shelter board meeting."

"I'm on my way."

As soon as I hang up, the woman next to me opens her mouth to say something. I stop her with a wave of my phone.

"I don't like people talking on their phones in public places, either, but my dad is in the hospital. Step aside."

Her face softens and she pats me on the shoulder as I squeeze by her along the dusty, historical literature shelves.

To avoid thinking about my dad during the drive to the hospital, I worry that my departure line sounded like something from a terrible low-budget action film, and if I got in a fatal car accident, that would forever be my last spoken line.

I start singing "Amazing Grace" aloud—a much better final sound bite.

Bedside Virgil

As soon as I see the white *H* on the blue sign, I am nervous. My hands are clammy. I scan the large foyer without really seeing anyone. Then a kind face steps into my line of vision. I grab the man belonging to the face.

"Excuse me. I need to find my father."

The tall, young man with red cheeks and wispy bangs leans his mop against a door frame and folds his arms across his chest. "Who is your father?"

"Ted Hamilton. He…he…" I start tearing up, yet another telltale sign of my anxiety.

"Oh, I'm sorry. Was he brought in by ambulance?"

"No, a silver Camaro. 1960s refurbished."

The friendly janitor looks at me confused, and then he motions for me to follow him.

"What is your name?"

"Mari Hamilton."

"I'm Virgil." He turns to the woman on the other side of a white counter. "And this is Sandy."

Sandy is a plump brunette. She wears one of those old-fashioned nurse caps. The kind that resembles paper sail boats.

Virgil serves as my liaison to locate my dad and kindly escorts me to the fourth floor. Just as the elevator doors open with a "bing," Dad is being wheeled toward a room, his left leg wrapped in bandages and sticking awkwardly in front of the wheelchair.

"You poor thing!" I rush to his side and begin fussing. I adjust the neckline of his hospital gown and wipe a bit of dirt off his face.

"I'm fine, Mari. It is just a sprain, so I can go home this afternoon. I hope you didn't tell your mother."

My nervousness turns to frustration when I see that he is okay. "You don't think she will notice the splint?"

He pretends to pull his gown hem down over his leg.

"Not funny. And what were you doing working in the yard? Bernie told you to only exercise in the house and when someone is present. Someone other than Daisy." I brush down stray strands of his hair. I find a piece of twig and a leaf.

"Bernie?"

"Fabio."

"Oh, yes." He nods.

"And why were you the only one at home? We have a schedule carefully figured out. There is to be someone with you at all times. What happened?"

As I discipline my father, the nurse and Virgil transfer him to his bed.

"I am a grown man. A babysitting schedule is not necessary."

"Ted!" My mom comes rushing in. She bypasses the fussing and begins the scolding. "What on earth were you doing? Who was supposed to be with you?"

Virgil brings in a couple more chairs for all of us. Mom remains standing, so Virgil sits down next to me and leans forward resting his elbows on his knees as though ready to watch a football game on television.

"It doesn't matter who was supposed to be there. I was supposed to be there, as I was reminding our thirty-year-old daughter. I *am* a grown man. I don't need supervision."

Virgil turns to me. "Thirty, huh? I would have guessed younger."

"Oh, thanks." I think.

Just then the phone by Dad's bedside rings. Mom grabs it. "Marcus! No, just a sprain. I don't know what happened. We had such a good schedule. Who was supposed to be with him?"

Dad reaches for the phone but Mom steps back. I notice her face fall and she closes her eyes. The phone goes to Dad.

"What is it, Mom?" I ask.

She sits on the edge of his bed. "I am the one who was supposed to be there." Her fingers smooth over Dad's knuckles.

I try to defend Mom to herself. "Things have been crazy, and we switched up the schedule last week, so nobody has figured it out."

"I need to quit campaigning. I promised myself and him," she points to Dad, who hangs up the phone, "that I would postpone the city council campaign if it interfered with the family." Mom's shoulders slump.

"City council. In this town that is quite competitive. I'm impressed." Virgil stands up to shake her hand.

"Mari, who is your new friend?"

"This is Virgil. He's a janitor."

"Head janitor," he clarifies, returning to his seat.

"Well, Virgil, I was running for city council. I haven't been elected yet. But another year, perhaps."

I know her. This is her final decision. "Yes, definitely another year." I cheer.

"You are lucky to have such a supportive daughter," Virgil adds.

Dad squeezes Mom's hand and looks over at me and then to Virgil. "You should know that my daughter has a serious boyfriend. Very serious."

"Dad!" I stand up and put my hands on my hips. "Unbelievable. A man offers me help while I am in a state of panic and you assume he is hitting on me. I find that to be extremely offensive, not just to me but to..."

"Virgil?" Dad asks.

"Yes, to Virgil." I turn back to point to my helpful friend—and the chair is empty.

Definitely Fall

The window to my room opens reluctantly. A summer paint job has nearly sealed the cracks, but with persistence I free the window and allow a cool morning breeze into my small space.

I shudder. Not from the temperature but from the realization that fall is here. My life in Tucson seems so distant, even with the trips back and plenty of phone conversations with the girls. While I have told everyone I feel so fortunate to have two homes, a more honest answer would be that I feel I have no home.

The urge to run away is overpowering. Fall does this to me. There is a longing to go away to school or to follow the season through the Eastern states. I will settle for a breakfast at Locals' Landing, the corner café.

Excited, I dress in a pair of jeans, trail shoes, and my first sweater of the season. I keep my hair down and let the slight natural wave from a night's sleep fall where it may. Hoping to sneak out unnoticed, I place most of my weight on the handrail and tread lightly on the stairs. As I set my gaze on the back door, the floorboards announce my arrival and everyone at the breakfast table turns to look at me.

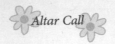

Marcus is, of course, the one to comment. "Mari, you are supposed to sneak out *after* curfew, not at nine in the morning."

"Hey," Dad scolds and flicks a wadded up napkin at him.

"Sorry." Marcus turns and addresses the kids. "Nobody should ever consider sneaking out after curfew because our security system is very sophisticated."

Mom pipes up with, "And because it is unethical—which is the better reason."

I point toward the door, which stands between me and temporary freedom. "I was just heading out for a walk. It's fall."

No more explanation is necessary for my mom. She nods and smiles.

Dad waves and says, "You won't recognize the place. Take the route past the school too. The playground has been renovated; you'll love it." He knows right where I am headed.

Josiah makes a gagging sound. "School. Yuck."

I cannot help but smile at strangers on my way down the street. The mixture of colorful houses, large brick apartment buildings, and small businesses seems a testament to the efforts my parents have made to bring revitalization efforts to this community. There were years when I was not allowed to walk or ride my bike home from school without an adult, though the two-story brick schoolhouse was only a few blocks away.

When I see young professionals sipping coffee at bistro tables outside the café I have to double-check the sign above. Only inside do I see the faces of the old neighborhood seated at regular booths and torn, red vinyl stools at the bar.

Since the place seems busiest outside, I decide to occupy an indoor booth. Most comfortable as an observer, I choose the corner table and sit facing the street. Nobody seems to notice the girl seated alone, not even the waitress. Instead of flagging her down, I reach for a pen from my purse and several napkins from the metal canister on the table.

I get lost in my rambling thoughts as they come from somewhere in my mind and onto the folded sheets that absorb ink quickly and make my letters large and nearly indistinguishable from one another. It won't matter. Some life notes are meant for later reflection, but some, like this morning's, are simply intended to purge the backup files of the subconscious.

"Darlin', you back in town?"

Pulled from my self-absorbed thoughts, I squint up at the waitress. Morning sun is her backlighting, and all I see is an eclipse of bouffant hair.

"Margie...Hemphill. I used to babysit at the home."

The home. It gives me chills and a few flashback emotions, but Margie was a great volunteer. She used to give the younger kids piggyback rides up and down the stairs and let them use the walk-in freezer when we played hide-and-seek. Mom and Dad's liability insurance agent probably made sure she never returned.

"I cannot believe you recognize me. I am back." I intend to add *for a short time,* but my mouth stops moving as my eyes start tracking a girl who just entered the café. She has on a green suede dress with five link belts coiling around her waist. It is a look that could only be rivaled by...

"Caitlin?" It couldn't be.

Marge looks over her shoulder and then back at me with a look of "what'll they think of next." "I will let your friend have a few minutes to look at the menu."

I follow Marge to the front counter and keep my eyes on the girl who is looking through the window at the yuppie crowd. "Caitlin?" I ask the question again, but still in disbelief.

The woman, who is indeed Caitlin, turns around and runs over to hug me. I take her by the hand to my booth and we stare at each other for a few minutes and then she laughs as I speak half-phrases like "What are...When did...Why on...?"

"I'm on my way to New York, and at the airport it occurred to me that I was stopping at Dulles. So I asked the woman at the ticket counter—"

"Clarissa?"

"Yes! And she said she remembered my headdress from that time I picked you up. Isn't that amazing?"

"It was rather unforgettable."

"So when I explained how much I would love to have a full day here to visit you, she changed my departure time from Dulles to JFK so I could have a few hours. Isn't she the sweetest?"

"Let's just say this is a new side of her." I cannot stop smiling. "Caitlin, I really needed to see you."

"I felt it." She places her hand on her heart. "And I really needed to see you. Your dad looks good. He is the one who showed me how to get here."

"He recently had a setback, but he was pushing himself too hard. The doctor says he is doing well in his recovery."

"I'm glad." She beams, and then she adds with a grin, "I had hoped to see someone else while at the house." She raises her brows a couple of times for emphasis.

"You might get that twitch looked at before becoming a New York City girl." I say while folding up my napkin notes and shoving them into my backpack.

"I wanted to see Marcus," she says as if I didn't get it. "Angelica told me that you two were once involved. I never heard of him until this trip of yours. Now, every time we talk on the phone you mention the guy. Don't act coy."

"*Involved with* sounds like a soap opera romance. What we had was a hand-holding, high school dreamworld crush. That is it."

I notice Marge approaching, so we scan the menu and make the fastest and strangest co-order ever. "Waffles," we say in unison.

"We *are* in sync. We never ordered the same breakfast food before." I motion out the window. "You gotta have waffles in the fall."

"Gotta." Caitlin's eyes follow my quick gaze to her left hand. "No. There is not a ring on my finger. You are not very discreet."

"Just checking."

"You are trying to change the subject. But I will let you because we have so little time together."

"Thank you." I bow my head to her in appreciation. "So why do you need to fly to New York again?"

"This trip will be my final. That is, before I make my move. I told Isabel that I could start after Sadie's wedding. I figure this gives me time to—you know, say goodbye to everyone."

"You really are doing this?" I sprinkle salt on my palm and lick it.

Caitlin looks disgusted but continues. "I really am. It's true that I might look back on this decision in three years and regret what I am leaving behind..."

"Namely Jim the Cop?"

"Yes. But training with Isabel is the education I have been wanting. Let's face it, how long have I been researching opening my own store?"

"*We* have been researching it forever."

"Exactly. And all this time I have been avoiding the truth about me—I am not ready to go solo. I don't want that kind of responsibility. But I do feel ready to learn from someone else. I figure last year's fashion show was your way to get back to Golden Horizons, it was Sadie's venue for engagement, and it apparently was my connection to my future as well."

My head leans to the side as I take in my friend's newfound confidence. "This is a great choice, Caitlin. I see that now."

"Sadie thinks I am running away from Jim and a possible commitment."

I wave my hand in the air to brush away opinions of those not present. "Doesn't matter. Look at me. People think I am crazy to leave...to be away from Beau."

Caitlin looks down at the waffles loaded with berries and whipped cream. "Like me. Sorry."

"Don't be. I get it. Maybe I am pushing the boundaries of a relatively vulnerable relationship."

Caitlin stops a forkful of breakfast midway to her mouth, "What do you mean, vulnerable?"

I wave my own opinion away and take a huge bite of fruit.

"What do you mean vulnerable?"

I keep chewing, stalling while I figure out what is going on. "We are fragile right now."

Caitlin looks down at her fork and places it back on her plate. Her face falls into blankness. "I cannot believe anything except that you two will end up together forever."

As much as I don't want to let down my romantic friend, I am desperate to talk about this. "Beau and I had a good conversation during my last visit home—I just sense we could lose each other." I am surprised by the lump in my throat. The doubts I have kept tucked in my mind have escaped their confinement and sound more like fact than theory once out.

"Mari, Beau adores you. He talks about you all the time to anyone who will listen. That night at Golden Horizons he held you so close. Nothing will undermine that."

Caitlin is being Pollyanna for me. And maybe for herself as well. We want to believe that true love conquers all.

"The distance feels overwhelming."

She reaches for my hand. "A few states between you is not enough to come between you." Her forehead wrinkles as she figures out what she just said. When she determines that it was indeed what she meant to convey, she nods emphatically.

I don't have the heart to tell her I was speaking of emotional distance, so I shorten the distance between me and a huge bite of waffles and whipped cream.

Tourist for a Day

Do we have to tell them where we are going?" Caitlin asks as we descend the escalator to the Metro.

"We give the machine our money and then we can go where we want to."

As we make our way to the landing, I skim the sign to determine which side to stand on. "We'll take this to the Metro Station and then switch lines to get to the Mall."

Caitlin scrunches her nose up.

"The area from the Capitol to the Lincoln Memorial is referred to as the Mall."

She is relieved. "I brought a disposable camera so I could get a shot of the White House and the Washington Monument."

"Are you going to be okay in those shoes? It's a lot of walking after we get off the Metro." I stare at Caitlin's plum suede heels.

"These things? Piece of cake. Besides, I paid a small fortune for them from Isabel's collection. Figured I'd show her my great taste. I want to arrive wearing them tonight."

"If you're sure, we'll walk by a few of the museums, and then we have

to see the Lincoln Memorial. There's a hot dog stand nearby. We can grab lunch on the way and have a picnic by one of our forefathers."

"Who are the other three?"

The train arrives with a gust of air. "Three? This is our ride, so get ready to enter when the doors open."

"Lincoln is one. Who are the other three?"

I shake my head in amazement and point to an open orange seat. I have the feeling that seeing the city through Caitlin's eyes and mind will make for a most interesting day, not the kind you read about in travel books.

"I strained my neck looking up at that thing," Caitlin says, pointing to the Washington Monument.

"Do you want to go up? They have elevator rides to the top."

Caitlin gulps and pretends to look at her watch. "Gosh, I would, but I don't want to miss the other sights."

"I hear ya. Let's keep walking, and in just a minute you will see my favorite stretch in all of this area."

We follow a walkway to the crest of the hill and soon we are viewing the reflecting pool that leads dramatically up to the statue of Lincoln, seated and grand. A line of grade school kids marches in front of us. They each hold a sack lunch and the hand of their field trip buddy.

"It's so pretty. I never would have imagined this many trees and green lawns. You were lucky to grow up around here, Mari. It's breathtaking."

"This city is fantastic." I breathe in the air and take in the splendid view. "I've avoided coming down here until today."

She glances over at me, "It's been good for you to be home. I can see it on your face. You seem happier and more together—peaceful, I guess."

"I do?" I hate to tell her how lost I feel.

"Yes, but we need you back in Tucson."

"Tell me everything that is going on. My conversations with Sadie are always rushed; she seems stressed for obvious reasons. And Angelica is getting harder and harder to read. One time she seems more stable, and the next she is sounding overburdened and a bit cuckoo. What's up with that?"

"I'll start with Angelica because I have a bit of gossip."

I rub my hands together in anticipation.

"The three of us got together for breakfast, which was a drag without you, I must say—and Angelica said that she is seriously considering dating again."

"Peyton, I hope."

"She wouldn't say. Sadie asked directly and reminded Angelica that Peyton was invited to the wedding because he and Carson have become friends over the past year. In fact, those two and Beau were meeting for weekly golf games."

"Beau never mentioned that."

"Well, I hope you don't take this wrong or anything, but I guess Beau has been kind of flaky. He cancels a lot and lately hasn't even called. He just doesn't show."

"Beau is super busy these days. That grant project he and—his mentor— are working on is really big for him and for Golden Horizons. He will do so much good for the residents. And there is extra pressure because if he does a good job with this project, he has a chance at getting on with the state board. So the flakiness isn't his nature; it's just that…"

Caitlin holds up her hand. "You are overselling."

I pause for a moment. She is right. "Welcome to the dialogue of justification that frequently runs through my mind."

"Don't worry. Everyone still holds him in high esteem."

"What'd Angelica say about Peyton being invited to the wedding?" I steer us back on track while half of my mind stays stuck on Beau's behavior.

"She actually smiled. That is when we knew we were on to something. But you are totally right; she is a bit unpredictable. However, since she started going to a counselor at her church, she has fewer crazy days."

"Glad to hear it."

The kids start running up the stairs to the Lincoln Memorial and so we do the same. Even the wildest of the field trip clan seem to be calm and reverent in the space surrounding the statue. Silence covers us all, and we just take a few minutes to soak up the grandeur.

"Was he the fifteenth president?"

"Sixteenth. Between James Buchanan and Andrew Johnson."

"So you're the student who actually retained that information."

"No retention. Several of the kids are learning the presidents this year, so I told them that if they learn the list before I do, I will do their chores for a week."

"They must love you."

I look at the kids, who are now quietly reading aloud the inscriptions on the wall of the memorial. One of them reminds me of Wallace, all serious and earnest. "They are growing on me, that's for sure."

After some photo ops, we head to a food shack and load up with hot dogs, chips, sodas, and plenty of mustard packets.

"Does life get any better?" Caitlin bites into her relish-covered dog and closes her eyes in rapture.

"I'm telling you—after walking all morning, this is the most satisfying meal imaginable." I wipe a bit of mustard off my chin and get comfy on the backless cement bench. "Sadie update now."

Caitlin takes a swig of soda. "Yeah, right. Okay, Sadie is gearing up for Harry's visit. They got the whole living situation figured out. Harry will stay with Carson and Harry's mom will stay at Majestic Vista."

"Perfect. She'll feel pampered and not excluded, and Sadie will be a lot more comfortable than she would have been had they all been with Carson."

"No kidding. So that is working out. But Sadie's sister and mom are making her bananas. They are coming in early also. When they heard about the Majestic Vista arrangement Carson had made for Harry's mom, they jumped on that bandwagon."

"They're good people, aren't they?"

"Yes, but they get under her skin. And we all know Sadie's sister is a bit strange."

"We do?"

"Hello? The dresses?"

I throw up my hands and smatter ketchup on my sweater. "How could I forget the dresses?"

"I remember them every day. I seriously have to cover mine up at night

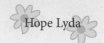

so I can sleep." Caitlin burps and wads up her hot dog wrapper. We both have finished in record time.

"I think we should set her sister up for a psychiatric evaluation."

"My guess—jealousy. She is not married and is a bit older than Sadie."

"Well, at the bachelorette dinner we can keep an eye on her."

Caitlin slaps her forehead. "I knew I forgot to tell you something. That elegant dinner at the *Chateau d'Or* is now a Western-themed outing. Complete with horse rides and chicken potpie."

"Chicken potpie?"

"Or whatever they serve out of chuck wagons."

I shake my head a few times in an attempt to to retrieve logic and sanity once again. "Don't tell me—the sister?"

"Yes. She said that she and the mother never get out to Tucson, and they want a real Southwestern experience."

"I should think Majestic Vista and an order of quesadillas would be sufficient."

"Sadie has the disease to please, as they say."

"Don't we all. What is it about women especially? Guys don't seem to worry about pleasing everyone else all the time. They don't develop ulcers if someone isn't happy with their decisions or actions or how they wore their hair that day. Beau is a perfect example. He is barely available to talk to me and dodges golf games with his new friends, but he probably isn't up all night worrying about letting me—them—down. We take on all that. We practically beg for it."

"Hey, you're preaching to the choir. I grew up trying to please my parents, but by age sixteen I understood it was impossible to do that *and* be myself. Either they were going to know and like the real me, or they would have to settle for a very civil relationship."

"And it is quite polite."

"Positively proper. We never have conversations about dreams or purpose or life's meaning. Nothing that could involve opinion or dissension. I'll bet your mom and dad are very real. I could tell by looking at them."

"They are very authentic people, but I still had to go through the same rebellion."

"How'd you rebel? Did you refuse to do extra credit in one of your classes?"

"Let's walk over by the pool on our way back."

"Good tangent. Spill the goods."

"I broke up with Marcus, for one."

"That was to rebel against your parents? You lose a perfectly good relationship because you happened to be dating someone they liked?"

"It was more complicated than that. They had our whole future figured out. I felt trapped. I wanted to see the world. You have to understand that the Urban Center was not exactly the coolest of addresses to call home. My whole childhood was spent waiting to be old enough to break out on my own and live someplace I chose. But my parents practically had Marcus and me married off and stepping in line behind them. I couldn't see the great part about what they did. I could only see me in ten, twenty, forty years, stuck in the home I grew up in. I thought my only out was to break up with Marcus and start applying to colleges far, far away."

"Mission accomplished. Tucson is pretty dang far away."

"And Tucson has really grown on me." I stop walking and fold my arms across my chest. Suddenly, the air seems chilled. "I'm torn, Caitlin."

"You are considering staying, aren't you?"

"It has crossed my mind. I thought it was just the good feeling of being back around family, but lately I've wondered if my Tucson life was about running away. I adore Golden Horizons and when we are on track, Beau and I are fantastic. I just don't know if it is enough. How messed up am I? I don't know which life I am running away from."

Caitlin hugs me. "Didn't you think things would be easier by the time we hit thirty? Here I am moving clear across the country to finally do what I love. You are torn between two lives. Angelica is still finding out who she is. And Sadie is trying to stand up for herself and create a new life with someone who has been married and who has a child. It's like we are all just beginning to live."

"I like the perspective that we are just beginning to live. It does feel like a birthing experience. Painful and scary."

"And yet hopeful, right?"

As I agree with Caitlin's words, I'm wondering when my crazy friend became so darn sane.

She continues. "I'm excited about my decision. And you will be excited no matter what you end up doing, Mari. How great that you have people who love you and support you in both places. You are blessed."

"I am. Thanks for the perspective."

Caitlin looks around at our surroundings. "Could you get a picture of me by the water? Get the monument in the frame, too."

I reach for her camera and direct her toward the reflecting pool. As I am about to take the shot, Caitlin starts to wave at someone behind me.

"Sir, could you take a picture of me and my friend?"

An elderly gentleman wearing a baseball cap and suspenders over his flannel shirt is most agreeable.

"I'll take my heels off so we are the same height," Caitlin hollers as I hand off the camera to the man. I'm showing him the point-and-shoot method when I notice the accident about to happen. Caitlin has one shoe in her hand and is bending over to unhook the other shoe's strap. I think she will regain her balance until the first shoe is flung into the air. Caitlin would never throw away a perfectly good shoe.

The splash directs the attention of countless tourists and the laughter of several school children. Caitlin flounders about in the murky water until the man, Hank from Wisconsin, and I can fish her out.

"This is suede, dang it. I love this dress." She starts crying from embarrassment and over the loss of a fabulous outfit.

Now this is the Caitlin I know so well.

"Caitlin, you poor thing. Let's get over to those restrooms. Hank, thanks for your help, but we won't need to record this moment."

Hank hands me the camera and reluctantly walks away once I convince him we are going to be fine.

And while Caitlin is distracted by the sound of her green dress sloshing against her thighs, I steal a photo of my mermaid friend.

Rhyme for Reason

You can't say no," Rachel says while chomping gum on the other end of the line.

"It's our poetry pizza night." I step on a chair to sit on the kitchen counter. "And I promised to be here tonight."

"Cheyenne's husband is driving her nuts with his fantasy football picks, and I just decided not to resign my studio lease. I can only imagine the stress you have had lately. We all need it. Besides, we didn't really get to catch up during our last visit."

"Maybe because I was being interrogated?"

"So this is a yes?"

"I guess I could leave after the readings."

"That's the spirit. We'll even come pick you up so you can stay as long as possible at the poetry thing."

Rachel is so transparent. "You mean Cheyenne told you I drive a fifteen-passenger van these days."

"That would be the more important reason," she confesses.

Wallace waits by the front door with his hands behind his back. Every few seconds he stands on tiptoe and peers through one of the narrow windows.

"Do we get it free if it takes more than half an hour?" I holler from the top of the stairs on my way down to the kitchen.

"Naaa. That's the other place with the rubbery pepperoni. Besides that doesn't count when you order eight pizzas."

"I suppose not."

Several of the children are following behind me. Lou is pushing on my lower back to hurry me up so I wedge my heels into the wooden slats to resist.

Daisy presses her tiny self against the stairwell and sneaks past us. "Slowpokes."

"Art is here. He's coming."

"Art?"

Wallace turns around quickly and gives me a disappointed shake of his head. "The pizza guy."

The pressure builds behind me and finally I give way to the herd. They clamor to greet Art, the apparent celebrity du jour in this household.

"What's the rule?" Marcus shouts from the doorway of the walk-in freezer.

A choir of children's voices respond, "Don't buzz-in unless its kin."

"That's right. That is my job. Or Mari's. We will do it."

I look down at him and he looks at me. *He just made us a we.* Poetry night turns my thoughts into rhymes.

"Mari, I will get the door. You get the name jar."

I head for the cupboard above the stove and retrieve a mason jar filled with torn strips of paper representing everyone in the house. Several names are pulled out for each poetry night and those kids have to read. We don't cycle through the stack again until everyone has faced the crowd.

"Josiah, go get Mom and Dad. They are in the flower garden out back. Tara, get the paper plates and towels out of the hall closet. Grant, set up the karaoke microphone." I joyfully give directives like a pro.

The wheels of an organized gathering are set in motion. By the time Mom and Dad enter the room, everyone is seated and ready to pray over the pizza and get the night underway.

After the first round of slices is distributed, Marcus nods to me. I stand with the jar and with an exaggerated move, I crack my knuckles.

"Gross," says Elsa, but the boys giggle.

"Silence!" I shout to reinforce my moment of dictatorship control. I roll up the sleeves of my long-sleeved T-shirt and wiggle my fingers.

"We'll never get to the poetry," mumbles Grant.

"Silence!" Marcus shouts as my dedicated assistant.

More giggles as I reach in slowly and remove three different slips of paper. All eyes are on me as I call out those who will be put on the spot to either read something they have written, make up something in that moment, or read aloud a portion of literature or a poem they have selected. The real cruelty of this night is that, of course, everyone must decide in advance what they will do in case their name, scrawled in my dad's handwriting, is on that piece of college-ruled paper.

"Jon."

"Camden."

"And…" I pause and look at everyone in the eyes. Wallace is a nervous wreck and taps his fingers on his forehead. I look down at the paper and turn toward Marcus. "And…Marrrr."

"Marcus!" shouts Tara.

I snap my fingers in an aw-shucks way. "I wish."

"It's Mari!" cries Wallace. "Praise the Lord! My piece is not perfected."

"Who added my name to the jar, anyway?" I look over at my parents, who are standing at the kitchen counter shrugging.

Marcus raises his hand. "I did, Ms. Hamilton. It is only fair. You did start this tradition."

"Well, your name will be surfacing soon. I guarantee it!" Outwardly, I shake my fist at him, but inside, I feel the warmth of inclusion.

While everyone digs into the pizza, I rush up to my room to search for one of those napkins from the Locals' Landing. I discover the missing one wadded up in my jean's pocket. It will reveal too much of my thought life, but it is all I have.

"Jon. Jon. Jon." The hungry crowd begins their call for the first poet. Jon is typically all bravado, but tonight his long bangs cover a reddened face and a shy stare. Hands in front pockets, Jon looks down at a piece of notepaper on the floor. He has scrawled out a poem in large markers.

"Nobody laugh till I am done. Okay, here goes it." Jon licks his lips nervously and begins in a cracked, puberty-ready voice:

> *There was a time when I was sad.*
> *There was a time when life was bad. I always felt alone.*
> *And when I was the most scared, someone came along who cared...*
> *and that day I found a home.*

We all burst into applause as the young boy brushes back his hair with a shaking hand. His grin is broad and sweet. I watch as Jon accepts a sideways embrace from Marcus, his biggest fan. Their backs are to me and I notice the similarities between these two—broad athletic shoulders, trim torsos, and long, strong legs, dark hair—these two resemble father and son more than mentor and pal.

Camden wastes no time getting up on the short performance platform. He has his eye on the last of the sausage pizza so he reads just a few stanzas of Poe's "The Raven." Of course, he reads enough that the young ones are sure to have nightmares.

Dad stands. "That was a fine reading. and since you are so eager to give us the *Reader's Digest* version, I think we should ask you to present it in full for Halloween."

"What's *Reader's Digest?*" asks Camden innocently.

"Not the point." Dad tosses a wadded up napkin at him and laughs. "You will read us the rest for our harvest party. Mari, you're up."

As I stand, the doorbell rings. Wallace pushes the step stool to the intercom and loudly proclaims that it is poetry night and we are not to be disturbed.

"Sorry," I say. "Cheyenne and Rachel must have come early."

Wallace pushes the buzzer with authority. "No, it's Lonna." And Wallace, who never does anything comical, walks across the room in what must be Lonna's style—hands on hips, swinging strides, and little curtsies.

I stifle a laugh. I can feel my face growing warm. Marcus stands and walks over to the door. He is ready to greet his girlfriend. The girlfriend I have not yet met.

"Mari, hon…your turn." Dad places his hands on my shoulders and directs me toward the stage.

"No. We have a visitor. I will go first next time." I reach for one of the last cartons with pizza remaining and hold it up. "Who wants Canadian bacon and pineapple?"

Marcus is now talking to Lonna, who is standing in the doorway. I cannot see anything except an expensive purse on a slender, tan arm.

"Mari. Mari. Mari!" My dad conducts the yells of the kids as though he is forming a precious symphony. They end with an earsplitting, high-pitched yodel.

I will only receive more and more attention the longer I put this off. I walk to the stage and hear the door shut. My heart is racing, and I pray that Marcus and Lonna have left for the evening. Slowly my feet turn to face me toward the audience and my eyes close briefly. When I open them, all the kids are attentive and Marcus and Lonna are sitting on the soda fountain stools waiting as well. I don't mean to, but I look directly at Lonna. Like a kid told not to stare, it is all I want to do.

I shake my head to return my mental focus to the scrap of napkin in my hand. With what I hope is an undetectable movement, I shift my feet slightly to the left so that my parents are in my line of sight rather than Marcus and Lonna. My voice begins nearly as warbled as Jon's, so I cough and begin again.

> *Along my way, I am finding what I left behind*
> *Through worry and wonder I walk on*
> *Waiting for shadows to leave*
> *Hoping for light to lead.*
> *What used to be comfortable now seems distant.*

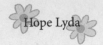

I tethered my dreams to certainties that have defied gravity
and taken flight.
It is cold here in the unknown
But as I look around
I see the freedom of possibility.
Along my way I am finding my future
In the pieces of yesterday.

There is applause and then I see it. I see it before I can read the expressions of appreciation on my parents' faces. My eyes glance over, in the wrong direction…the direction I warned them about, and they see the furrowed line on Lonna's brow. Confusion. Frustration. Anger? She is looking at Marcus and Marcus is looking at me, and he is smiling, but not with the silly grin he gives me when I have made a fool of myself. It is a smile of recognition.

He understands me.

I step off the stage quickly and return to my seat, which is thankfully far from the soda fountain and front door. From here I watch Marcus and Lonna leave. I see his hand on the small of her back and it gets to me.

One of the kids makes a joke about curfew. I don't hear it all, but everyone laughs…so I join in to cover up my nervousness.

Lucky in Love

"Where are we going?" I ask from the backseat of Rachel's VW Beetle—the old kind. I am wedged between piles of heavy boxes. "And what is this junk?"

"Junk? I'll have you know that is future celebrity, rent, gas money. I have to get used to not having much storage space anymore."

"Huh?"

"It's her sculpting clay." Cheyenne turns in the passenger seat to look at me. "We thought we would take you to a place that would feel like home."

"The Southside Youth Shelter?"

"Austin Grill."

"You do know I have been living in Arizona, not Texas?"

"They eat enchiladas in Tucson, don't they?" Cheyenne inquires.

"And the Alexandria location is a great place to take in the view of local men," Rachel offers as a food alternative.

"Um, Cheyenne is married, and I'm spoken for," I say a bit loudly. A night with old girlfriends I was up for—a night on the singles scene I was not.

They look at each other and smile.

"What? What is your little inside joke?" Paranoia is leaking out of my mind.

"You say you are spoken for. We just want to know who is doing the speaking?" Rachel singsongs while trying to parallel park.

"Enchiladas sound good. Inquisitions do not."

Rachel holds up her hands in submission. "Okay. Okay." The car jolts forward and hits a curb. A box of clay lands on my foot and curbs my appetite.

"That large slab of concrete resembles a speed bump, but it's actually a sidewalk," I say angrily while rubbing my ankle.

"Rachel, you were right," says Cheyenne as we step out into the nice evening. "Mari needed the night out even more than we did."

I hobble along the cobbled sidewalk and wait for some sympathy. I know better than to wait for empathy. As we near the Austin Grill sign and hear a band tuning up, Rachel turns on her heel and glares at me.

"This hopalong bit is not going to be too helpful inside those doors."

"But your clay landed on my ankle. It hurts," I whine. "I think it is swelling."

"I'll order extra ice with my margarita, but please act normal."

Cheyenne looks at my ankle to be sure they are harassing me for good reason. It isn't swelling, only red. "You are okay, Mari. Rachel, on the other hand, is a bit sensitive about tonight. She is hoping to run into a particular someone, so she wants to make an impression."

"A *good* one, in case you need clarification." Rachel adds, staring at my rolled up pant leg. "Make yourself presentable. I'll go put our names down for a table."

"Whom are we impressing?" I ask Cheyenne once Rachel is inside.

"Phillip Wallis. He manages Trampled, the band playing tonight. Good guy, but a bit full of himself. He thinks he is single-handedly responsible for the music scene in this area."

"Is Trampled successful?"

"Not yet. But he is putting a lot of energy behind them, so they might do well. He really is a good businessman, but I personally could not handle the..." her voice trails off as we see Rachel approaching.

"No waiting necessary. Phillip says we can share his booth by the band."

She is giddy and her face is flush with excitement. I look to Cheyenne to finish her sentence, but she only shakes her head and acts innocent.

"Great," I say. "Who is Phillip?" I join the innocence.

"Okay, you got me. I had a couple ulterior motives in choosing this particular place for our night out. Phillip and I have group dated a few times, and I'm hoping to go to the next level and get a one-on-one."

"Do you have to try out for him or something?" I am being sarcastic.

Rachel is serious. "Sort of." She touches the tip of her gelled hair. "He could have his pick of women. Tonight could be the big night that he asks me."

Good grief. "You'd think the girl was getting a proposal for marriage, not a pass to a one-on-one date," I whisper to Cheyenne. Rachel has bounded into the club, and we are about to be accosted by the techno sounds of Trampled.

As we step into the bar area, it doesn't take long to notice Rachel. She is doing a little show-off dance near the booth. Clapping her hands above her head, she looks as though she would be put on a solo platform for *Soul Train*. The image of her doing a desperate disco move strikes a familiar cord in me.

Angelica.

I had never made the connection between my high school friend and my college pal. Even in Rachel's jock days, she was a tad boy crazy and more than a little off balance when it came to crushes and infatuations.

It makes me wonder if we have adult versions of most of our childhood friends.

As Rachel does a low shimmy, I see her prey and the object of Cheyenne's near comment, and I have to stifle a yelp. It's not that Phillip isn't attractive, but the guy is wearing more eye liner than Rachel.

"Eek!" I say in Cheyenne's ear.

"Told ya."

"But a good guy, right?"

"Generous. Not sure if I'd be banking my future on him, though."

Rachel points toward us and Phillip waves a very generous wave. As he does, I notice his eighties ponytail.

"Oh, no." I mutter.

Cheyenne turns toward me and acts like she is pointing to a rack for our coats. "We are so lucky we don't have to worry about looking anymore."

Her statement causes me to step back. Something in me wants to rebel against that thought. Just because I'm dating someone doesn't mean it is all settled, wrapped in a taffeta bow.

Is something wrong with me or is there something just plain wrong about the large leaps women make in hopes of connecting the dots from single to married? Am I a bad friend for encouraging Caitlin to go for her dream instead of the dreamboat?

I watch Rachel nervously vie for Phillip's attention as we and several other friends and acquaintances order a round of appetizers, and I realize that I do feel lucky. Not because I think my future is set, but because I get how crazy women are about love.

Scene and Overheard

My head is pounding by the time Trampled is on song three. At least I think it is song three. They seem to run together. A bit like Rachel's rambles about Phillip's "cool and awesome bands." His ponytail bobs with glee with each compliment Rachel gives him. Two other women, Sara and Mia, apparently also trying out for solo dates with Phillip, are ordering more rounds of drinks to stave off the boredom of neglect.

Suddenly realizing that she is here with friends, Rachel stops her explanation of why Phillip's bands rock the world with a start. "Mari, you should be sitting on this side."

Cheyenne, who has been making origami birds with her cocktail napkins looks up from a wing. "Yes. That's right."

"I'm fine here."

"But you can see the band better from here. Come on, they're great." Rachel pats the place next to her and looks pleadingly at Mia so she will swap seats with me. Mia reluctantly gets up and waits for me to do the same.

I cooperate so that Rachel won't break into a list of 101 reasons why Trampled is great. As I stand, I check the clock on the wall above the bar.

Thirty minutes down and probably three more painful hours to go—this *is* exactly like going out with Angelica.

The silver lining of sitting on this side with Phillip and Rachel is that I won't have to look at them. I kick Cheyenne, who is now across from me. She seems in a daze. This was not the vision she had for a girls' night out either.

"Bathroom?" Cheyenne mouths and points upstairs.

"Yes!" I holler. "Powder room break," I say to Rachel, who is now braiding Phillip's ponytail.

Upstairs it is quieter. There are families dining calmly, completely unaware of the dating disasters going on down below. "Now, this is a happy place," I say. "Where's the bathroom?"

"Down the hall, I think. I actually was hoping we could get a table to ourselves."

I sigh with relief. "Hallelujah. My thought exactly."

The hostess is not pleased we have bypassed the seating list, but a couple is about to leave an undesirable table near the wait stand, so she gives in.

We order a new round of food and relax when a pile of chips and salsa rests between us.

"Boy, your husband's fantasy football must be driving you batty if this is a better choice. What were you thinking?" I reprimand.

"I had forgotten Phillip was connected to Trampled and to the Grill."

"I thought it was your ulterior motive."

Cheyenne licks salsa off her fingers and avoids eye contact.

I press her. "Was there another motive?"

My guilty friend nervously turns her earrings in her lobes and mumbles something at an inaudible decibel.

"Repeat that."

She puts her hands in her lap, sits up straight, and looks at me intently. "Lonna. She is a friend of Paisley, Trampled's lead singer. And when Derek and I ran into Marcus a few weeks ago, he mentioned that they would probably come check out the performance later tonight."

"What are you thinking?" I reprimand again. "That makes no sense. I

see the guy every day. I live under the same roof as Marcus. I am seriously dating Beau. Why would you want me to see him here?"

"It was Rachel's idea. She thought that if Marcus saw you out and about…you know, on the scene, he would see you differently."

"Oh, I see. I go out with girlfriends, and Marcus sees me laughing and having a good time, and all of a sudden I am available? Rachel's sense of things is warped. But why would you agree to it? You're married, for Pete's sake. You know what faithfulness is all about."

Cheyenne folds her hands in front of her to beg for forgiveness. "You are totally right. I got caught up in the whole 'wouldn't it be great to see Mari and Marcus together' idea, and I threw my morals out the window."

"Lonna and Marcus left the house well before I did. They must have changed their minds. So you got off easy this time."

"They said they'd be here around nine."

I check my watch. It is five after. I don't want to run into Marcus tonight. Not after the poetry reading. I saw his eyes. I saw her anger. This is not what I want.

"I'm leaving. Hopefully they haven't arrived yet. You, my friend, are getting me out of here."

"But we'll miss yet another dinner order. I'm starving."

"We'll go grab pizza down the block. Let's head downstairs, you in front of me. And while you tell Rachel that we will meet up with her later at her car, I will try to get out the door unnoticed."

She nods but gives me a once-over. Repeating my words back to me, she points a finger at my heart. "You see Marcus every day. You live under the same roof. You are seriously dating another. So why the nerves? Why the action plan to escape?"

"Tonight isn't a good night. I have my reasons."

"All right. I got you into this; I will get you out." Cheyenne starts down the stairs, and as we hit the first landing, we look out over the bar. "Coast seems clear," my lead offers. We jet down the last few stairs, and she takes up her position by Rachel's booth while I hurry out the door and into the starry night.

It is an active Thursday night in Old Town. People are coming and going out of the area shops and restaurants. I miss this kind of urban experience. Tucson is sort of spread out with popular spots miles apart. Most of the DC metro area is overflowing with great places to meet up with friends or to experience the diverse culture. I miss having four different ethnic restaurants on one block.

Through the window I see Cheyenne expressively chatting with Rachel. The light changes so I cross the street toward the pizza place and feel my lungs starting to take in air again. What was I so worried about? I probably imagined Marcus and Lonna's tension back at the house. I was probably projecting my own relationship woes onto them...just the way I did with Sadie and Carson months before.

I guess I am still a long way away from really figuring out the bizarre nature of my own emotional life.

Up ahead I notice one of those dispensers for apartment guides. I veer toward it and assure myself that it is merely healthy curiosity that motivates such research. Leaning against a brick building, I flip pages and immediately begin to covet the offerings. My Tucson apartment is so new, so white, so lackluster, so square. These photos display old rooms with cove ceilings, built-in bookshelves, hardwood floors.

I am lusting after a one-bedroom in the Woodley Park area when I hear a woman's voice just around the corner.

"I don't want to go in there now. Not together. I'll get a ride home with Paisley."

Paisley? My heart skips a beat. Could it be?

Then I clearly hear Marcus' voice respond. "This isn't what I wanted to have happen. I'm so sorry. Let's just go. I really want to hear them." His voice is fragile and he sounds upset.

Lonna, on the other hand, just sounds matter-of-fact. "You wouldn't like their music. You were only coming tonight because I wanted to go and because you are a great guy, Marcus. A rare thing these days, it seems. Please. Let's get together later. I really want a night out with friends."

From the corner of my eye, I see Lonna and then Marcus walk toward the intersection. I hold up the apartment magazine to cover my face and hold my breath. As I hear them part company, I fold down the corner and see Marcus walk on up the street as Lonna crosses toward the Grill.

Cheyenne steps out just as Lonna approaches the door. As they greet each other, I see Cheyenne's eyes wide with worry, scanning the area for either Marcus or me. I don't reveal my position until they finish talking and Lonna is safely inside the restaurant.

"Over here!" I wave the paper.

Cheyenne dodges a red SUV to get to me. "Lonna said that Marcus couldn't make it. You worried for nothing."

"We're still doing pizza," I say adamantly.

"Fine. Fine. Let's go. It's this way." Cheyenne grabs me by the elbow and leads me down the street.

I casually turn to look in the direction Marcus was heading and catch a glimpse of him just as he turns down a side street and out of view.

I want to know what happened to make Lonna go solo tonight. I want to chase after the lonely silhouette of Marcus and be sure he is okay.

Cheyenne says something to me while my mind is racing and my feet stay put.

"What?" I ask, emerging from my fog.

"I said this will be your second round of pizza tonight. Aren't you worried you'll get heartburn?"

"Too late."

In Hiding

Ding. Ding. Ding.

"Mari, you gave him that dang bell, you respond to it," Mom says from behind her sewing machine. She is making costumes for the annual progressive harvest party our sponsoring churches and neighbors throw for the area kids. Piles of orange, black, and green fabric enshroud the small woman with black reading glasses sliding down her thin nose.

I walk over to the intercom rather than head upstairs to the small reading room where Dad has taken up residence. "You'd think the doctors amputated his legs or something," I shout into it.

The crackle of static is followed by Dad's voice. "Ha-ha. Now bring me my green tea, *s'il vous plait.*"

"*Oui, oui. Un moment,*" I respond.

"You see what your pampering has done to him? You were better off when he was pushing his physical limitations. Now the king of the castle is getting a big head."

"I was worried about him."

"You bought him a massage chair and a GameCube. Let's hope your father does not have an addictive personality or this house will be in shambles."

I start the kettle and rummage for tea packets. The knob on a cupboard door falls into my hand. I quickly screw it back into place. "Don't be silly."

"I saw that."

"I can only find orange spice. Think he'll notice?"

"Tell him it's healthier."

The outside intercom buzzes. I look to Mom and she looks at me and nods toward the door.

"I have to do it all, do I?"

"It's Kayla. Just let her in."

"I thought you were done with the campaign."

"We have some campaign contributions to redistribute. Kayla has kindly offered to call the contributors to see if we can turn their donations over to the literacy program."

"And who will you hire to call all of them to be sure she isn't pocketing the money?"

"Mari!"

"Okay, okay." I trod toward the door with heavy feet to be sure my reluctance is known.

Kayla comes in wearing a new tailored suit and has a matching bag tucked beneath her arm. She immediately goes over to Mom and hugs her.

"That's some expensive outfit, Kayla." I wink at Mom and she frowns.

"Why thank you, Marla. You're a dear."

The teakettle whistles and censors my response.

I traipse up the stairs with a teapot, two cups of tea, and some gingersnaps. My plan is to wait out Kayla's visit. So much for an afternoon on the computer downstairs. I had promised Beau that I would write up a few reports on the Golden Horizons recreation program. When I tell most people that I double-majored in anatomy and leisure studies, they get a very wrong impression, but Beau was thrilled to have my educational background put to work for his project.

Their project.

Funny. I hadn't thought of Paige in days. Weeks. Not since my last visit

to Tucson. Their tight working relationship is only annoying when it affects my time with Beau. From a distance, I don't feel a thing.

Dad has the game volume up on high. Old newspaper crossword puzzles are scattered around the room. Plates from the past few weeks are littering the coffee table. I clear a place with my foot for the tea tray.

"Geez, Dad." Mom was right. Dad's addiction could indeed be the downfall of the Urban Center and this family. I must take away the bad and bring in the good.

"I'm almost through level ten," he says with his tongue hanging out of his mouth like a kid concentrating on tying his tennis shoes for the first time.

"Out of how many?" I inquire.

He stops to think and crashes and burns whatever he is maneuvering from afar. "Darn it."

"Oh, I'm so sorry, Dad." I am evil—but I am evil merely to reclaim goodness and productivity in the Hamilton household.

He adjusts his robe. It is a chenille eyesore and seems to be his only uniform lately. His physical health is improving, but I am questioning his mental health.

"This smells different."

"It's a citrus green tea. Extra antioxidants and all that."

He sniffs it. "Ah, yes. Smells wonderful and healing."

"Can we turn that off? The graphics give me brain spasms."

Dad hesitates. Then spying a pen under a newspaper, he scrawls down his score.

"I'm pretty sure it keeps track of your games."

"Fantastic! I don't know why I refused to get one of these before."

"Because you thought the *kids* would avoid homework, housework, and social interaction." I recall his argument and extend it back to him in hope of personal awareness on his part.

He nods thoughtfully and then laughs. "What a tyrant."

So much for insight. "Kayla is downstairs talking with Mom. I think I will just hang out here for a while, if that is okay."

"I'd love nothing better." His mouth uses the appropriate, fatherly phrase, but I see his eyes glance longingly at the GameCube.

"The flower garden is covered with weeds. Who usually takes care of that?" I ask this knowing full well it has been him.

"The great thing about a good garden is that it can live through a rough season and be resplendent the next. I think Fabio brought a friend by to help out with that, anyway. Seems there is a quick replacement on standby for anything I used to think was urgent." I see sadness in his eyes. Or maybe they are just glazed over from his level ten adventure.

"Marcus noticed that the paint on the front steps is chipping. Which I think makes for a great, old look, but I know he was thinking it might be lead based and dangerous for the kids to be around."

"I replaced the lead paint years ago with a very nice, nontoxic basement paint."

"Oh."

We crunch on gingersnaps.

"I guess we'll have to cancel hosting the harvest party this year. There would be all the cooking and the cleaning and the decorating. It is just too much...with the way things are right now."

"I spoke with the pastor at City Christian, and he and his staff are volunteering this year to set up our house. I don't know why I didn't think of asking them in past years. They nearly cheered at the chance to take part." He smiles, and I see his right hand move toward the remote.

I tried all the tactics that would usually send my dad into a frenzy of worry. Not that I want him feeling negligent, but I do want to pull him from the suction known as the funnel of digital fun.

Desperate measures—I need to show him how much we need him back in the routine.

"Dad, you know that in two weeks I will need to be gone a while for the wedding. Maybe we should talk about a plan of action to cover my responsibilities during that time. Marcus moves back to Chicago in December. It is going to be quite an adjustment for all of us."

The glaze goes away and clarity returns to his blue eyes. He looks at me puzzled.

"You knew that Marcus was taking the job in Chicago, right? Remember, we talked about it when…"

"Mari, I am well aware of Marcus' plans. What I am confused about is your reference to *us*."

Now I am puzzled.

Dad places his teacup on the tray. "Mari, you are not really planning to return after the wedding, are you?"

"Well, I hadn't completely thought through it, but it seems for the best. Look, you are still recovering. Marcus will be leaving. The kids have such busy schedules during school. And things at Golden Horizons are going fine without me."

"And your relationship with Beau? Is that going fine without you too?"

I look over at the television screen for a few seconds, hoping it will spur him back to addiction. I blew it. He is fully in the present moment with me.

"Mari?"

I shrug, and my throat feels tight and achy.

"Your mom and I appreciate all that you have done for us. We couldn't have asked for better help or a better daughter, but you have your own life to lead."

I speak strongly to convince Dad of my importance, my necessity here, but my emotions beneath overcome me and my voice is shaky and uncertain. "There is so much to do. Dad, you don't know what it is going to be like without me. What will the kids think? I will just be one more person who comes and goes in their fragile lives. My relationship is just fine. Beau understands how important this is to me. Besides, he has everything under control and I'm not really needed there. At Golden Horizons or in…"

"The relationship?"

"Stop it, Dad. I don't want to talk about this."

"This cannot become a hideaway for you, kiddo."

I wave about the tiny room which has become Dad's cave. "Uh, yeah. Look who's talking."

"This has become a den of self-pity. I'll leave if you do?"

I come up here to convince Dad that he needs to return to his life, and now he is trying to convince me that I need to return to mine.

I'm not ready.

"Show me how to play this thing," I say, full of youthful enthusiasm and manipulation.

If Dad knows what I am up to, he doesn't point it out. He excitedly pulls up the player screen and gives us both cool nicknames.

Girlfriends

I am waiting patiently—okay, impatiently—for Marcus to come out of the phone closet. This seems to be where we see each other most often here in the house. He is busy finishing his school program, and I am playing caretaker to Dad and carpooler to the kids.

"Are you about done?" I've stepped comfortably into the role of being Marcus' sibling.

He kicks the door three times. Our predetermined signal for "almost done."

I tap twice on the door—our predetermined signal for "five-minute warning." And I wait.

He emerges just a couple minutes later with a notebook gripped in his hands, a pen behind his ear, and glasses resting on his nose.

"All yours," he says, bowing in submission.

"Glasses. Nice touch for your academic career."

He touches the bridge of his wire-rimmed choice. "Just for reading. I was talking to one of my study partners."

"Not Law-na?" I am surprised by my sharp tone. I am even more surprised by his response.

"Look…I don't mention Ben. Leave Lonna out of this."

"Beau. Beau. Beau. You know the name. Why are we dancing around each other? Is there something here that we are hiding?" I decide to confront him completely. We stand toe-to-toe, and I am ready for us to battle this out.

"There is no dancing. You are uncomfortable around me because I told you how I felt about you last year. That isn't my issue." Marcus uses a tone that is stern but calm.

He is right. "You are right."

"We had such a good time on the field trip and in recent weeks. Is our pattern going to turn into this—good time, bad time? It's like you feel threatened."

"Threatened?"

"Mari, I don't plan to interfere with your life or with you and Beau. I'm not that kind of guy. You should at least know that about me."

"I do." I pull on my hair as though going nuts. "I'm sorry. I don't know why I'm having these mood and perspective swings."

"Could it be because your life is not your own right now?"

I nod and then add, "But is it ever? I mean, in terms of faith?"

"Milkshakes?" Marcus motions for the stairs in the direction of the kitchen. We used to spend a lot of late nights inventing milkshake flavors and discussing faith.

"Let me make a quick call. I want to hear about Caitlin's New York trip."

"There might not be any ice cream when you get done. I've timed your so-called quick calls."

I think on this for all of three seconds. "I can chat with Caitlin later."

Taking the stairs two steps at a time, we arrive at the walk-in freezer quickly.

"Which three?" I ask Marcus with my hand on the metal door.

"Peppermint, fudge, and orange."

"Name for creation?"

He considers his invention title carefully. "Patty Goes to Florida."

I take it in. "Very interesting name. Not sure if it will make our all-time favorite, though."

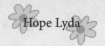

"No. It's hard to beat your Play It Again, Yam concoction."

"That was before we made the rule that we could not add vegetables to the ice cream. But it was a mighty good shake." I hold up two aprons and Marcus chooses the frilliest one.

As I scoop his flavors from the large tubs, he reaches across the counter and grabs sundae glasses from the shelf.

"How is your faith these days?"

My surprise at his question shows.

"I'm not judging you. I was asking. As someone who once was involved in youth group with you, I do care."

"I know you weren't judging me," I say defensively. "My faith is good. I'm trying and kind of struggling to figure out how to really follow God's lead, but isn't everyone?"

"Yep. At least anyone honest."

"The past two years seem to be all about finding that place of contentment and also not settling, you know?"

He looks down at the long spoons in his hands. "I do know. And that is exactly what I have been learning."

"Do you think God triggers certain waves of life lessons?" I wonder out loud.

"In a person's life?"

"More like in a bunch of people's lives. I ask because it seems that my friends and I face some similar decisions and faith struggles at the same time."

"That would make sense. You are all about the same age and you have similar interests and circumstances, right?"

"It goes beyond my friends, though. I run into strangers who are facing the same stuff. I find it interesting."

"I guess I should start paying closer attention."

"What have you been learning about contentment?" I ask while perusing the ice cream options. I point to raspberry sorbet, rootbeer ice cream, and lime sherbet.

He makes a gagging face. "Name for this?"

"Pop-Tart," I say without missing a beat. "Now tell me what you have been learning."

"I..."

The blender masks what he is saying. I try to guess. "You woke up on the lawn?"

"No, genius." His face shows exasperation and a bit of embarrassment. "I said I broke up with Lonna." He pours my disgusting ice cream creation into my glass and avoids eye contact.

"W-Why?" I stutter with shock.

He looks at me. "Don't flatter yourself."

Now I am embarrassed. "I wasn't even thinking that. I'm surprised, that's all. When a guy finishing his PhD degree is seeing someone, I guess you figure he is ready."

"That's a jump in logic."

"No, it isn't. A guy reaches a certain age, and all of a sudden he is ready for forever."

"Isn't that the stereotype given to women?"

"Lots of women do want to get married by a certain age because they want to find love. But most guys don't bother looking for love until they check their own biological clock and decide it's time." I'm starting to wonder what my point really is.

"Is Beau one of these guys in the mode of just wanting to be married, no matter who?"

"Well, I didn't say it means guys throw all discretion to the wind, thank you so much, but..." I pause and slowly nod. "I think Beau is actually a good example, to a certain extent."

"And this works for you?"

"He loves me." My defensive tone returns for an encore.

"Mari, I don't doubt that. However, I find your theory about men quite interesting considering you have how many female friends in serious relationships?" He counts on his fingers over and over, pretending the tally is in the hundreds.

"Two. No, three. Sadie, me, and Caitlin. And we are all in relationships

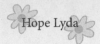

where the guy was ready for a serious relationship before the women were. So there you have it."

"I'm not most guys. It won't be a matter of convenience or age for me when I make that choice. It will be about one thing. No—two things."

I hold up two fingers and await his explanation.

"The woman. And the life lesson we were talking about. I want to really feel that it's God's leading."

"Do you think there is only one person for us?"

"No. I don't mean that. I'm not expecting there to be a huge sign over a woman's head flashing that she is the only one, but I believe God's will is known through the peace we feel in such circumstances."

"I think growth requires discomfort. Not just roses and teddy bears and paths cleared of obstacles."

"The discomfort is followed by the peace. That is my belief. Would you just drink that disgusting-looking liquid?"

"And you didn't have peace about Lonna?"

"No. She's great, but I wasn't in the right frame of mind to start a relationship. She could tell."

"Everyone could apparently. Cheyenne thought you were emotionally distant."

Marcus cocks his head to the side. "Cheyenne? Since when do you ask advice of a former homecoming queen?"

"It's not like I brought up the subject of your dating life. She mentioned seeing you two out together the other night. That's all. I wasn't asking for advice. Don't *you* flatter yourself." Marcus does not respond, but he downs the last of his drink with an exaggerated gulp of satisfaction.

"Do you have peace about Beau?" Marcus asks sincerely.

Instead of answering, I finish what does turn out to be a very disgusting liquid. I don't want to get into an analysis of me and Beau, yet I feel relieved somehow by this conversation. "You know, Marcus, this might be the most helpful girl talk I have had in a long time."

He curtseys in his chiffon apron and says in a high voice, "Give me five, girlfriend."

Champs and Winners

"Nobody use the phone between eleven and twelve today," I command from the stair landing like the captain of an unruly ship crew.

"We heard," says Marcus from the study room. "And for those of us who didn't hear, there is a large sign on the phone closet that is sufficient notification."

"I can't read," states Daisy matter-of-factly.

"Thank you, Daisy," I say, raising my voice, "for pointing out why this announcement is necessary."

"I also am not allowed to use the phone anytime, not just between eleven and twelve," she says innocently.

Marcus starts laughing. "Is the president calling again?"

"I have an important conference call with Golden Horizons. We are planning the end-of-year fund-raiser, and I am in charge of the committee."

"In absentia," adds Marcus and returns to his crossword puzzle.

"Yes. But I *will* be there for the fund-raiser; it is in December—so I will be back by then. I'll be in Arizona, living there—again. In just over a month, I will be in Tucson." I'm saying this aloud to remind Marcus that my gig here is a limited engagement. After my talk with Dad in his GameCube cave, I know it is time for me to begin talking about my return to Tucson. I need to say it so I will believe it myself. But right now I am saying it only to get a response out of Marcus.

The scene where he cries and begs me to stay does not happen. The moment where all the kids understand I am a temporary fixture and fall to their knees pleading with me to stay does not happen, either.

Marcus glances up at me and adjusts his glasses. "And I will be in Chicago."

"Mari, don't worry," Jon says. "We're all leaving for school. That is, if Marcus will get up off his duff and drive us."

Marcus writes in the last few letters of his final crossword solution while the kids gather their lunches, books, and backpacks. In a matter of minutes I stand on the landing in total silence.

"I'm really going back to Tucson," I say to the empty table and dirty cereal bowls. "As much as you want me to stay, I have to get back to my life—after all, it is the life that finally unfolded the way it was supposed to. I love my job. I have a handsome, smart boyfriend. My friends need me. Tucson is my..."

The scene where I declare that Tucson is my home to a room of empty chairs, framed photographs of happy children, and mismatched mittens and shoes does not happen. I settle for singing the Rice Krispies theme song.

By 10:30 my notes are spread out in the phone closet in preparation for the conference call. Beau, Lysa, and a couple resident volunteers—Rose and Chet—make up the fund-raiser committee this year.

I am eager to show everyone that I am still connected to the cause of Golden Horizons' well-being. And despite the air-clearing conversation during my last visit, my phone conversations have been strained and surface level. I want to be a productive part of this committee so that when I do return, Beau knows I am on his team.

By the time the phone rings I have psyched myself up and am incredibly positive about all things Golden Horizons.

"Hello, this is Mari."

"Mari!" a crowd of happy voices fills the room.

I can distinguish everyone's voice but Beau's. Maybe he wants to address me on his own. Personally. Importantly.

Lysa, always practical, starts right in on the business. "The board liked the idea of the holiday craft and food fair. They especially liked that we receive a portion of the booth rental fees and a small percentage of whatever the sellers take in. Good suggestion, Mari."

"Thanks. Do we know if we can have the fairgrounds' pavilion?"

"That is being secured," Rose offers confidently. "Willy Tanner is on the fairgrounds' board, so it is only a matter of some paperwork."

"Willy?"

"He's a deacon at our church, of course," Rose says in tsk-tsk way.

"Oh, right," I say ignorantly and keep waiting for my significant other to address me. When the conversation continues for another fifteen minutes without a peep from Beau, I decide to address him directly. "Beau, is the Golden Horizons' craft committee planning a special exhibit for our fair?"

Silence.

"Beau had a meeting with...his project committee," Lysa offers graciously. "He told us to tell you how pleased he is with all the arrangements we have so far. He thinks it is going to be a real hit, like last year's fashion show. He thought you did such a good job with that he just knows this one will be a smash."

Overselling. My mind repeats Caitlin's accurate charge when I was defending Beau. I'm so pathetic. I have my friends and coworkers caught up in the same hyped up protection of Beau and his precious character. The only problem is, everyone but Beau seems concerned enough about our relationship to say anything in his defense.

Lysa gives it one more try. "The good news is that Beau will be able to reveal his report to us and to the board in advance of the fund-raiser. He'll be able to join the committee for the home stretch on this project by the time you are back."

It feels funny to be informed about Beau's life schedule from a third party.

"Speak of the devil!" Chet shouts, and I sit up straight and hit my head on the angled ceiling.

"Sorry I'm late, Mari. What a group of go-getters we have working on this thing. I appreciate your leadership from afar. So are things in order? Are we going to set records this year?" Beau rattles off words as though he just returned from a team spirit management convention.

I don't want to respond.

Rose, our committee secretary, reads through our meeting agenda and decisions. Beau responds with a lot of "Fantastics." I am searching for an antacid by the time Rose finishes her recap.

We close with a "Go, Go, Golden Horizons" team cheer in which Beau's voice is the loud one and mine is the absent one.

As I am about to hang up, Beau speaks directly into the receiver. "You still there?"

My heart races. I'm sorry I hated how peppy he sounded. I liked it, really. It was supportive and motivating. "Yes, I'm here, Beau. I'm so glad..."

"I want to remind you I will need your final recreational report for my project by next week. I know you're great at deadlines, but we all need reminders."

Like a reminder as to why I was just excited to hear your voice.

"That's all you wanted to say?" My disappointment is expressed openly.

"I'm a nervous Nellie over this project. You have really been my rock through all this, Mari. You are my good luck charm. You're the little angel that sits on my shoulder and guides me. You are my..."

"Don King?" I interrupt, tired of his line.

Beau laughs. I don't.

Not catching the hurt behind my sarcasm, he continues. "Well, you are the brains behind this champ. After all, you were the reason I came to Tucson for this job, and it has turned into the perfect career move. Everything is right on track for me. For you. For us. It's a fantastic time."

Champ? On track? Fantastic?

After we hang up, I walk down the stairs and turn on the French tapes to fill my mind with more words that make no sense.

At one o'clock the phone rings again. I pray as I tromp back upstairs that this call will make the difference. *Let it be Beau apologizing.* I want to hear

the man I fell for last year and not the game show host persona who just participated in the conference call. *Please, God. Make it all right.*

"Hello, this is Mari."

"Mari. It's Kayla. Is your mom there? It's important."

So much for effective impromptu prayers.

"No, she is volunteering in Camden's class today."

"I have fantastic news."

Fantastic. My favorite word of the day. "What is it?" I ask without an ounce of enthusiasm.

"Your mom is the new district city councilman. Woman."

"How is that possible? She pulled out of the race." Wouldn't a campaign manager know this bit of information?

"I know. Isn't that amazing? She so impressed everyone that the majority of voters wrote in her name on the ballot. This has never happened in the history of this district. And it all happened without investing money in the last half of the campaign. Unbelievable."

"What a bargain. But do you think she will do it? When she makes up her mind about something, she usually sticks to it."

"I…I don't know. I just assumed she would be thrilled. Oh, gosh. Do you really think she would decline the position?"

I have deflated Kayla with my downer mood. The woman might have been bizarre a few years ago, but she seems genuinely excited about my mother's success. "She might go for it. After all, Dad seems to be kicking into high-gear recovery, and Mom has seemed sad when there is coverage of the campaign on the news."

"That sounds more hopeful. Mari, do you think she should do this? Or would it create problems for the kids and your family?"

Wow. Kayla not only got my name right, but she has a heart. "I think the family and the kids are ready for this. I know Mom is, if she will just give herself permission to go for her dream."

"When you tell her about the win, please encourage her. And tell her the people have spoken."

"Look, she will be home any minute now. Why don't you come on over?

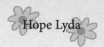

You should be the one who gets to tell her the good news. I'll be here to remind her it is exactly what she wants and needs."

"She is lucky to have you."

"And you," I say, amazing even myself.

Beau Who?

Streamers in autumn colors have been laced under and over the rafters of the main room by the time I have walked the kids home from school. Mom has been manic ever since she got the news of her win. She hesitated for a few minutes, but by the time Kayla, Dad, and I talked up all the good she could do in the position, she gladly accepted her new role.

But now, a week later, we cannot get the woman to slow down. She is making popcorn balls and talking on the speakerphone at the same time.

"Now, Rod, I told you that if I won I would increase the supply of fresh fruits and vegetables to your food bank. But I was just told by a contributing farmer that your guys turned his guys away at the loading door."

"They had boxes and boxes of stuff. We just don't have the refrigeration system for that kind of load. Believe me, we wanted the food."

"Well then, I guess my next call has to be to Phillip Randal, the head of the Star Grocery chain. I'm almost sure he'd love to donate a few industrial refrigerators for a tax write-off."

"He will by the time you get done with him. Thanks, Mrs. Hamilton.

221

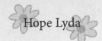

You're already doing more than the last guy," Rod yells, apparently aware that Mom is on a speakerphone.

"That is impressive," I say after she hangs up. "I've always wanted to see a high-powered politician in action."

"You are in the capital Mari."

"Exactly. You are a rarity, and you are just getting started."

"Cynic."

"Optimist," I fire back.

"That was a zinger," Marcus says, walking in through the back door. "Mari's ultimate insult is that someone is an optimist."

"Now look who is cynical."

"I am realistic, not morose or melancholic or morbid or moody or mean-spirited. There is a difference," he offers, full of his wit and alliteration.

"Stop the flattery. You had me at morose."

Mom laughs, and Marcus hands me a box of jugs filled with homemade apple cider. "Make yourself useful, at least."

The front doorbell rings as I am midway through unloading the cider. "Josiah, can you get that?"

"Sure." He waddles over to the door and hikes up his giant stuffed felt pumpkin outfit to use the stepladder. "Who is it? The harvest party doesn't start for an hour."

"Josiah! Be polite, please." Mom ineffectively tries to snap her sticky fingers.

"Please identify yourself, and how can I be of assistance?" Josiah over-corrects.

"It's Beau."

"Beau who?"

There is a thunderous thud, and I look down to see if I dropped a jug of cider out of shock, but it was Marcus dropping a crate of apples.

Mom runs to the sink to rinse her hands. Her eyes are not as wide with surprise as Marcus' and mine. "Let Beau in, Josiah," she says excitedly.

Josiah is amused by the visitor's name. "Knock, knock."

A tired voice responds, "Who's there?"

"Beau."

"Uh, Beau who?"

"No need to cry, I will let you in," he says, chuckling.

There is good-natured laughter on the other end of the intercom, and I find myself smiling broadly and checking my breath discreetly as Mom hurries out the door to meet Beau at the gate.

"You'd think she was the one engaged to him," Marcus says calmly.

"No kidding," I respond, laughing. "Hey, I'm not engaged to him either, by the way."

"Well, like you told me over your Pop-Tart creation, he is a guy with a biological clock ticking away like a time bomb."

"You embellish. Please be nice, Beau."

"Beau who?"

"I meant Marcus. Okay, I'm a little flustered. This is a surprise."

"Run to him, fair maiden."

I toss a hand towel at him and nonchalantly bolt for the open doorway, through which Beau walks looking handsome, tired, and glad to see me.

He meets me the rest of the way and picks me up with a half spin. *This is the guy,* I want to yell. *This is the one who morphed into the salesman of the year just a week ago. He's come back to be mine.*

"Just don't kiss," Josiah says with his hands on his pumpkin non-hips. "That would be gross."

"That would be," says Marcus with perfect comedic timing.

At least he didn't say "It is." That would have started off the night in a very bad direction. The teasing comment alone made Beau straighten up a bit. But then *The Art of War for Dummies* or whatever other management training book he recently read kicks in, and he smiles warmly and approaches Marcus with his hand and a desire for peace extended.

I'm a bit embarrassed at how showy this seems in this setting, but at least he was the bigger man than Marcus, who can only joke when he is nervous.

"Nice to meet you, Beau." Marcus shakes the hand that stretches out from the sleeve of an expensive overcoat. I'm thinking Beau had some kind

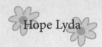

of makeover since we last saw each other. I won't ask him until we are out of earshot of Funny Man.

Mom comes up alongside Beau, who stands a foot taller than her. She resembles an elf as she reaches for his elbow and guides him to the nearest table.

Beau looks around at the decorations. "I'm just in time for the party, eh?"

"Do you want something to drink? Some delicious cider maybe?" I ask sounding a lot like a restaurant hostess or flight attendant.

"Cider sounds most delightful. Thank you, Mari."

Oh, my. Between the two of us, we might never have an authentic exchange.

I look over my shoulder and am comforted to see that Marcus missed the pleasantries. Mom would just view this as two polite people. Marcus would see through it to the awkwardness of the moment…of the relationship.

But Beau is here. That's all that matters. He loves me and understands that our recent conversations have been bad. He gets that we need to talk from the heart. He figured out that a grand romantic gesture was in order. His commitment shines as…

Dang. I'm overselling again.

And overserving—as apple cider pours out onto the counter, I wake up from my thoughts. Dad enters from the back, no doubt alerted to Beau's arrival by Marcus, who seems to have disappeared altogether.

"Beau! Hey, it is so good to meet the special Beau-friend who caught our girl's attention."

"Dad!" I say, embarrassed and very aware of my father's corny nature.

Beau laughs politely and warmly. *He could be a politician.*

Dad moves easily across the hardwood floors without his cane in order to greet Beau with a firm handshake. I've almost lost sight of his progress lately.

"Fabio has been teaching you well, Dad. You are walking like the old days."

Dad looks at Beau and winks. "Don't let her fool you. I'm walking like the young days. Better than new." He does an exaggerated dance move with Mom as his special polka gal. He keeps dancing toward the door while he calls all the kids to help him and Mom deliver pumpkins to the neighbors. One by one little felt pumpkins and cornucopias and candy corns file by us. They are too excited to notice there is a visitor.

When they are out of sight, I lean over and kiss Beau firmly on the lips. He tastes like cinnamon gum.

"Correct me if I am wrong, but isn't Halloween tomorrow night?"

"Harvest night, as we call it around here, is tomorrow indeed. But we always join in a neighborhood-wide progressive party the night before. On Halloween we take our clan and quite a few of the neighbor kids to the zoo early for dinner, and then we stay for the big night."

"The big night?"

"Boo at the Zoo. It's huge around here and sells out in advance. Mom always secures a corporate donor a year ahead of time so we can take as many children as possible."

"I knew I liked your mother," he says, pulling me toward him for another kiss. I check the doorway to be sure it is clear and follow through. "It's perfect, actually. Tonight I'll get to know the clan *and* then tomorrow night, while the kids are at the zoo, you and I can go out for a nice romantic dinner."

I stand up straight. "But that part of the weekend is a big deal, Beau. I must go to Boo at the Zoo." That sounded so much bolder in my head.

"They don't shut it down if you miss one, right? After all, you've been gone quite a few years now," he says, utterly amused by his argument.

Now I am upset. "That is exactly why it is so important to me. I've been looking forward to this as much as they have. Besides, I leave soon for the wedding. I don't want to waste this chance to be with the kids."

Beau looks disappointed and sighs heavily. "I thought you'd be happier to see me. I mean, I cleared my schedule to make this a really special weekend."

I can see he is sincere in his disappointment and part of me feels bad. But there is a voice inside that has been pushed down for a while. Maybe I've

had too much time away to create pretend conversations in my head about this very subject. For whatever reason, I unleash on the poor guy.

"Look, mister. I have been back to Tucson several times for planned trips—planned in advance with a phone call announcing my arrival days ahead so that you could set aside some precious time for us to be together. And yet you were busy each and *every* time. Then you come here, out of the blue, without any warning, and you expect me to drop all my plans. Not even my plans, but the plans others are counting on as well. It's not fair." I catch my foot before it can stomp. I have officially reverted to my childhood behavior.

Beau looks down and then calmly says, "First, I didn't realize you needed a warning before you saw me, and second, I am sorry." He looks up at me. "I am sorry. Come here. I'll just hope that we can steal away for a few minutes together. I have to leave the morning after next, so I got ahead of myself with plans. But those were *my* plans because I didn't communicate with you. Somehow I equated surprise with romance. I'm learning through all this."

The screen door slams as someone exits the back. I don't even care that it was probably Marcus.

I had migrated several steps away during my rant. A bit sheepishly, I walk back over to him and sit down beside him. "I will make time. I'm sorry too. I don't even know exactly where that came from."

"The truth, it seems. I have been neglecting you, Mari. After our conference call last week, I felt like an idiot."

He is saying all the right words.

"Well, and Lysa pointed out that I'm an idiot."

"She did?"

"How bad am I that I didn't even notice how much I was distancing you during all this project research?"

Bad. Very bad.

"None of it matters as much as our relationship, Mari. That's why I'm here. We need to reconnect. I didn't mean to impose or mess up your plans or control your weekend. I just want to be with you, even if it means sharing you with five kids and a zoo full of animals."

Not so bad.

"Actually, it will be more like twenty kids. But I appreciate your sentiment, Beau."

"I love you, Mari."

Not bad at all.

Pass the Sugar

The scent of buttermilk pancakes, bacon omelets, and hash browns draws me out of my deep sleep. My Donald Duck alarm clock indicates that it is earlier than I like to be awake, let alone awake and stuffing my face. But if my scent detector is right, this is all too delicious to miss.

On my way down the hall, I pass Dad's GameCube cave, which magically was converted into a guest room conveniently the day before Beau's arrival. I don't know whether to awaken my sleeping Beau. He was so tired last night—at the fourth house along our harvest party tour, I caught him sleeping against a papier-mâché haystack during Jon's recitation of "The Raven." That was the last house I recall seeing him at all. When I returned from the cycle of a dozen homes, there was a note on the kitchen counter for me that read "Decided to sleep so I can keep up with you and your friends tomorrow. I've missed you. Love, Beau."

I had tucked the note in my jeans pocket. I liked it. Marcus, on the other hand, read it over my shoulder and started fake coughing.

"He has traveled all day. There is nothing wrong with him heading to bed a bit early."

Marcus had shrugged, checked his watch, and said, "A bit early? It would be six o'clock his Tucson time. Or excuse me, *your* Tucson time."

Why do I allow him to humiliate me and Beau? Today, I will be stronger for us. Marcus can just wallow in his aloneness as we revel in our coupleness. I tap on Beau's door and get no response. I peek my head in the room and there is a perfectly made hide-a-bed trimmed with piles of folded clothes—including perfectly folded socks, which I could never be awake enough to comprehend.

And this neat freak loves me? I dare to look down at my ragged sweat bottoms and T-shirt that reads "Win One for the Gipper." I am tempted to retrieve my jeans and a maroon sweater when Beau calls me from downstairs.

"Hey, sleepyhead. Someone would think you were on Tucson time."

Laughter follows.

Did he hear Marcus' snub last night about his early bedtime? My feet tread lightly on the stairs so I can take a look at the scene below before becoming a part of it. Through wooden slats I see Mom flipping pancakes, Marcus pouring juice, and Beau sprinkling grated cheddar cheese on a pan full of hash browns. One big happy family.

I hate entrances like this—everyone has their place and I am on the outside. For years I got up thirty minutes before the first alarm sounded in the youth rooms so I could be downstairs eating breakfast, reading a book, and glancing casually at the rest of the kids as they staggered to the kitchen with heavy eyes.

Great. A neat freak loves a control freak. Can there be a future for us?

"Honey, we got up to make a special breakfast for Beau, and he was already down here working on his laptop. You have an industrious fellow here."

"Why aren't you still sleeping?" I ask Mr. Industry. He and Marcus both have on the frilly aprons. As glad as I am to see them amicably whipping up breakfast, I cannot quite understand what happened between bedtime and morning.

"I crashed last night."

"By the haystack?"

"Just for a few minutes. Then when I woke up, I came back here, worked for a few hours, and then crashed."

"You didn't finish the tour of houses?" Dad asks.

"I thought the party would be at one location, so I could visit for a while and then return to some of the project research." He catches his reference to the project during our weekend together and quickly stirs his potatoes.

"What exactly did you think progressive meant?" I inquire.

He shrugs and stirs. "I dunno. I guess I figured it was some Washington, DC, terminology. You know, politically progressive."

"It's too early for this. Please tell me the coffee is ready."

"Coffee is served." Marcus pours from a freshly brewed pot of Sumatra blend.

We all sit down to enjoy a quiet meal. I wouldn't say this morning feels normal with Marcus, my parents, and my boyfriend all together at one table, but it is comfortable.

"Before the kids storm the kitchen, how about we go for a walk?" I say to Beau.

"Ah, good idea. I ate too much candy last night," Dad says jokingly. "Oh, I'm sorry. You meant Beau. Of course, dear. Go right ahead. Marcus has cleanup duty anyway. And your mother and I have some fun boxes to deliver across town."

"Do you have any area deliveries still? Beau and I could plan out our walk accordingly."

"Splendid," says Dad as he walks over to the clipboard hanging by a nail near the front door. "Thought you would never ask. Here are the last seven deliveries in this neighborhood. They are a bit spread apart, but it's a nice morning. Do you want the Radio Flyer?"

"Yes, please."

Together, Beau and I load the red wagon with decorated grocery sacks containing candy, fruit, grocery certificates, and mittens and scarves for families who are having a rough season.

"These are a fantastic idea," Beau says, beaming.

"Mari thought of this years ago. She is the best surprise gift giver you

will ever meet. Every holiday she invented something just wonderful for the neighbors or the other kids."

"Okay, Mom." I give her a mittened thumbs-up.

"Be sure to have him back for lunch."

"Him? You mean me. Remember me, your daughter? I'm the one who is in charge of lunch today."

"I do remember you and that you are the one in charge of the kids' lunch. That is why your father and I are taking Beau out."

"Fine, I'll have him back by one," I grunt and then push on Beau to get to the door faster. "We must leave now before the morning gets any weirder."

Our first three deliveries are on the same street as the Urban Center. We carefully place the bags just inside the screen doors to protect them from street view and to keep the package a surprise for the family.

"I love this. It is like reverse trick-or-treating. Now this is progressive."

I laugh. It is good to see Beau so joyful, like a kid himself. The sad thing about his job these days is that it removes him from the heart of giving. He manages the care of the residents, but he misses out on a lot of the daily interaction with them. If we make a resident really happy, Beau is analyzing the source of the happiness and turning it into a statistic.

Maybe that is how I was feeling at Golden Horizons and didn't realize it. Being removed from efficiency numbers, state reports, and facility stats has freed me to care in a less mechanical way.

Beau stops abruptly and stands pointing to a sign, "Locals' Landing."

I quit staring at the sidewalk cracks. "Hey, is it okay if I run in and get more coffee? Want one?"

"Yes. Nope. I'll watch the secret packages."

My face warms instantly as I step inside the restaurant. Some of the regulars look as though they haven't moved since my last visit. And Marge's hairdo is just as puffy and fluffy as ever. I'm examining it with fascination when she turns around and catches me.

"This is my extra special Boo-faunt. Look." She leans forward so I can see the plastic spiders and bugs embedded in the layers of voluminous hair.

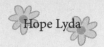

"That is memorable, Marge. Love it. How about a large coffee with cream and sugar to go." I point out the window to emphasize the "to go" part and her eyes follow. They apparently land on Beau.

"Honey, you have enough sugar to go if that fella is waiting for you."

How does one respond to such a comment? I smile and point to the paper cups on the counter, hopefully reminding her of the task at hand.

"He is your fellow, isn't he?"

"Indeed. He's my boyfriend from Tucson."

She finally pours coffee, but her eyes still stray to Beau. "Dear, I figured you only left big ol' cacti back in Tucson." She says this like "Too-Sun." "But if you left *that* back in Tucson, you are plumb crazy."

"Thanks, Marge."

Beau and I make the rest of our deliveries in between lots of conversation and laughter. We forego our mittens and gloves, which are really more for the spirit of the season than necessity, so we can hold hands.

We are a couple.

By the time I turn Beau over to my parents for lunch, I'm seriously wondering if truth has been spoken into my life by a Boo-hive-endowed prophet.

Animal Instinct

Last chance for a bathroom break!" I shout to the excited, motley crew of zoo-bound tricksters. Not one of them steps toward the restroom.

I try again with a more convincing spin. "The line at the zoo could take a while. Please go now if you think you might have to anytime soon."

Marcus pushes me off the platform in the dining area and takes the mic. "This is the last bathroom for the evening that will have guaranteed lighting."

The children immediately stampede to the two bathrooms.

Beau hands me his scarf to wear. "Guess he got you on that one."

"What do you mean?"

"You haven't noticed that you two can be a little competitive?"

I stammer a bit. "Well, well—maybe we both like to do things our own way, but we don't necessarily compete."

Beau nods like a wise professor who decides to let the pupil learn the lesson for herself the hard way.

"Oh, please." I roll my eyes and silently vow to be on my best behavior all night.

"Who's driving?" Dad asks, holding the mini Converse sneaker key chain.

"I am," Marcus chimes from the doorway.

"I…" I won't get sucked into it. I won't. "I think you should drive, Marcus. You are more familiar with the area."

Everyone's shock at my move to acquiesce seems in favor of Beau's theory.

Mom and Dad and the some of the volunteers from our church are corralling twenty children toward the front door. Beau and I reach for another cup of hot chocolate to take with us and follow behind the crowd.

The clipboard is gripped in Marcus' hand, and he is writing down which kids are sitting together. These will become field trip buddies.

When Beau and I are the only ones left in line, I spell out our names and add, "Thanks for driving, Marcus. Beau and I will have more time together that way."

"It is appreciated," Beau adds, wanting to be a part of the fun.

Marcus politely checks our names off his list and blows his whistle ever so directly at my ear. "All aboard. The bus for Boo at the Zoo is now departing."

I am glad when we are finally seated on the bus. Several times during the day Beau had offered to keep an eye on the house for the Halloween evening. Mom wouldn't hear of it. Silly woman, she thought Beau really wanted to go tonight. I could tell he was eager to have some uninterrupted work time. Twice I was this close to rescuing him, giving him the out he wanted—but that felt too much like our pattern in the months leading up to my return to Washington. It is time to see what he is willing to do, wanting to do. After all, he is the one who kept announcing how far he had come and how much he had sacrificed to spend quality time with me. I am merely giving him a chance to fulfill his intention.

Does a normal person evaluate his or her significant other to this extent?

"I'd really like to help pay admission," Beau says, reaching for his wallet when our group reaches the zoo's front gate on Connecticut Avenue.

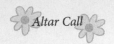
"Oh, no worries. We get the tickets ahead of time," Marcus assures Beau and pats him on the back as a thank-you.

Hadn't I explained to Beau all about our advance tickets?

Each adult is assigned a group of four kids to shepherd through the scary trails and the numerous trick-or-treat stops throughout the park. We agree to meet back at the eating area across from the Giant Panda exhibit in two hours to dine on park food. From there, the little ones will return home with Dad in the van, and the older kids will head back out for more of the exhibits, like the spider show.

Beau and I chaperone a group of four.

Wallace and Josiah are staying pretty close to us while Jon and Camden are eager to strut several paces ahead so as to look independent. A series of high-pitched squeals directs all our feet in the direction of the next exhibit—the gibbons. Ready for their performance, they swing madly along the mesh cage that really is more like a large draping around a natural habitat. There is a wall of the same mesh between a group of white-cheeked gibbons and a couple Siamangs. The two gibbon teams alternately show off either for us or for one another.

A little boy dressed in a ghost outfit turns to a little girl adorned with wings and glitter. "My daddy calls me his monkey. His little monkey. Ooh. Ooh."

I laugh and am about to repeat this to Beau when I see Wallace's face drop. I forget what these kids feel every time another child mentions a mom or dad so casually. This boy's father gives him a nickname, and probably gives him horsey rides and reads the Sunday comics to him. Wallace's father sends him digitally altered photos from prison depicting him playing golf and riding surfboards. I never understood which concept could possibly be more devastating to a young boy—that his father was in a cement room because he sold drugs, or that his father was having a twenty-year vacation away from his son.

"Hey, Tiger, aren't we headed for your habitat next?" I make an obvious attempt with Wallace.

Being the nice kid that he is, he nods politely—a bit like he does when those postcards arrive.

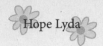

"Allow me," Beau says when we all gather at the snack shack.

"But we have funds for this. Marcus, get the cash Dad gave us," I say, nudging Marcus, who seems to be watching Beau intently.

"I think if Beau wants to be generous, you shouldn't stop him. After all, he didn't get to pay for the advance-purchase tickets, and he really wanted to." Marcus is pushing the issue.

Beau plays his forced hand and opens up his wallet. After twenty minutes all kids have their orders on red trays.

"Who'd have thought the snacks would cost a hundred and fifty dollars?" Beau tries to say lightheartedly, but the number gets lodged in his throat. He takes a sip of a soda that cost as much as a glass of wine to wash it down.

The adults sit together at a picnic bench and let the kids take over several round tables nearby.

"Seeing how serious you two obviously are, I'm surprised we haven't seen you here a lot sooner, Beau," Marcus says earnestly but with an obvious intent.

"How often did you visit her in Tucson?" Beau asks and then seems to figure out this isn't a good comparison to bring up. "Did you and her parents come visit during all her time in the Southwest?" His accent of irritation is revealing.

"I don't go where I'm not invited."

"Mari wanted me here—tell him, Mari."

I hold up cotton candy and wave it between the two primitive males. "Stop whatever this is. Yes, of course I wanted Beau here. Marcus, in a relationship, people don't need an invitation to be with one another."

"Exactly," echoes Beau.

Marcus grunts and nods.

"Let's focus on the kids. Remember the kids?" I appeal to their equally big hearts.

"Sorry," Marcus says, standing up. After taking a couple steps toward the trash bin he suddenly turns on his heel and points to me. "*You* especially don't need to remind *me* about the kids."

Beau starts to stand in my defense, but I won't let him. There is no defense for me. I whisper, "Marcus is right. He has been true to the kids ever since he was one of them. I was the person always looking for the fluorescent exit sign—no matter who I hurt on the way out. I feel much differently now. In fact, since Mom won the election, I've even been thinking…"

Beau interrupts me before I say what I've wanted to tell him all day. In fact, he doesn't even seem to notice I was speaking. "Everyone has a right to live their life, Mari. You act as though you renounced your royal birthright and took up with rebels. Your life has meaning, and if they saw you in action at Golden Horizons, they'd see what light you give others. It breaks my heart that your work isn't valued, respected, or considered a worthwhile investment. Today's standards for success are all skewed." Beau is ranting into the night with a raised corn dog.

I physically turn his face toward mine. "Where is this coming from? My family knows that the work I do is important. Who do you think helped me see that the whole luxury spa idea was crazy for me last year? It wasn't Sadie or Angelica or you, for that matter. As I recall, it was only Caitlin who saw it as a sad move. And…my family."

He looks down while my hand still cups his head. I can tell he has something to say, but he is reluctant.

"What is going on, Beau?" I soften my voice.

"Sonya mentioned the other day that the replacement they hired for you at Majestic Vista did not work out. They're recruiting again. I know Lionel would love to have you back. I saw him at the steak house a few weeks ago, and he could not say enough good things about you."

I sit up and pretend to look around for help or at least an explanation. "Since when am I job hunting?"

Beau reaches for my shoulders and turns me toward him again. His look is so serious, I have to stifle a laugh. "Lionel gets how great you are. I get how great you are. I *don't* see why the spa was a crazy idea. Better pay, good benefits, job security, and a career focused on helping and serving people. You raised the importance of the job because you cared about all of your clients. I told Lionel that he needs your compassion and professional abilities. He agreed."

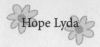

"You talked to Lionel about me?"

"I told you, we bumped into one another, and we have you in common; it was perfectly natural. We even discussed the package he would offer you."

I'm taken aback. "I didn't realize I had left you in charge of my career."

Marcus returns to round up some wrappers and senses the intensity between Beau and me. He makes a quick exit and starts to divide the kids into the group that is staying and the group heading home early.

"I'm looking out for..." Beau seems to be summoning energy to argue a new direction. "Mari, we both know things have been stressful between us. Maybe working together wasn't the best idea. That is my fault. Now I see what you saw last year—how wonderful it can be to work somewhere with perks, with people who can reward your behavior with raises. When was your last raise?"

"Never."

He throws up his hands as if he just won the Tour de France.

"Beau, I don't want to go back to Majestic. I want a job that is meaningful. While I've been here, I sleep like a baby. I wake up excited about how the day might unfold. I feel needed, wanted, and appreciated. And call me stupid, but I think the residents at Golden Horizons appreciate me too. Maybe it is my boss who falls short."

"You know the whole fight or flight theory? When we are faced with conflict, our natural instinct is either to fight off the attacker or run. Well, I believe some people fight for what they want and others run away."

I believe all his project research is going to his head. "And you are telling me this why, exactly? You think one of us is running?"

"*You,* specifically," he says, fully satisfied with how his argument came together in a tidy conclusion.

I find only slight satisfaction in the mustard smeared across his nose.

"This line of reasoning is fascinating!" I say loudly and lower my voice when I notice a few kids looking startled. "I, however, do not need you to get me a new job. I've spent the past several months feeling hungry to do more, to serve more, and to really fulfill my calling. And here you present

the exact opposite. Maybe your heart is changing, Beau. Maybe you should take the job at Majestic."

"I'm trying to lead you to a better choice, but apparently you're too stubborn to see what is best for you and for us as a couple!"

"Lead me? Beau, don't look now, but your God complex is showing."

He stands quickly.

My anger is so palpable that neither of us wants to be near it. I'm too deep in it and too hurt to figure out if I am absolutely batty to be this upset. I point to the short group following Dad up the hill. "You know the van with the little kids who need to go bed early? Well, one of us needs to catch that ride."

I feel dizzy and confused. Beau's power of suggestion is strong. In the face of my attacker, the instinct to run is overwhelming, but my feet won't move, so I sit frozen in the face of grave danger. There is only one thing to do.

"*You,* specifically," I clarify.

Passing Notes

Bleary-eyed and on the verge of tears, I stand in front of Beau's door, poised to knock, but with no idea what I would say to him. I keep walking and push open my bedroom door. What I need now is for sleep to overcome my tortured, waking thoughts. How did today go so terribly wrong?

With head in hands, I sit on the edge of the bed until sleep begins to overcome me. It is then that I notice an envelope with my name in Beau's handwriting on the front.

> *Dear Mari,*
>
> *What happened tonight was so far from what I had come here to do, to say, to experience with you. I wanted this time together to be special. And today was. I was in heaven walking around the neighborhood holding your hand...And then I let go.*
>
> *Please forgive me for all of it. I want to make things right.*
>
> *I realize from this visit that our reconnection will have to happen when you return to Tucson. I look forward to you being close once again.*

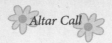

*I changed my ticket to an earlier flight, and your dad is taking
me to the airport at 5:00 AM. I told him I had an emergency at
Golden. Don't see me off. I feel that we need a little space before
we can be together and move on.*

I love you. That is really what I came here to say.

Love,

Beau

*PS. I highly recommend the $7 corn dog and wearing mustard
on your nose while eating it!*

Okay, so the guy writes a good apology. As much as I want to go to him
right now and hash this out, I know it would just make both of us more
tired and edgy. His early departure is the best thing. I sigh with relief that
we have at least had more communication. With my favorite journaling
pen, I add to his note:

Beau,

*Thanks for the apology. I'm sorry too. When I return to Tucson,
it will be better. Please talk to me about how I can be of help.
We keep each other at a distance, and I have missed feeling
close to you.*

The day was perfect. Safe travels, Beau.

Love,

Mari

I slip his note with my addition under his door. I can hear him breathing
softly just a few feet from me.

Back in my chilled room, I stare at the ceiling for hours. As I'm dozing
off, I hear Beau's door open and close and the sound of luggage sliding down
the worn steps. In my half-sleep I follow him down the stairs and tenderly
kiss him goodbye. He gets in the van; he blows me kisses. I wave and have
no recollection of what we were fighting about.

But dreams are funny like that.

Lesson Two

"Good morning, kiddo." Dad tousles my hair at the breakfast table while the kids look on. They smile at one another and some feign disgust at the display of fatherly affection. I know they all crave it, and Dad is the one who provides such kindnesses to them all.

"What's with the scarf?" teases Elsa, who is always impeccably dressed. I touch the cotton-and-wool plaid fabric draped around my neck.

"Isn't it time for school?" Dad looks around the table as though transformed into an ogre. "Nobody had better be late or else..." he lets them imagine the fate of such a sin. His goofy monster voice is enough to rouse them from the table and file in line by the industrial dishwasher. This week my green team has the job of loading it.

Before Matty starts rinsing egg off of plates and wrinkled flakes off of bowls, I step up and offer to do it for him. "I figure I have some chore time to make up after all these years. Best get to school while Dad is still in a good mood." I wink and Matty gladly grabs his lunch and dashes out the door.

"Are you going soft on my kids?" He bellows, looking around to see if any kids remain. Once he knows we are alone he chuckles.

"Don't you think the good cop, bad cop system works? Isn't that the trick you and Mom pulled on us most of the time?"

He grins slyly. "Maybe. But we don't give all our secrets over to anyone, unless they are taking over our spot." He says this last part looking me straight in the eye.

"Dad, I don't even know if I want one kid, let alone fourteen at a time. And this is different for you and Mom. It has been your passion and your vision from the start of your relationship."

"From our first date," he reminisces with a gentle smile.

"See. That is so…" I pause to start up the dishwasher and redirect Dad to the study room to talk. Before I can finish my thought, he has his hand raised and is waving away my thoughts before I express them.

"Silly. Crazy. Naive. But the thing is, we knew that. But we also knew that by doing things the normal way—the supposed right or proper way—didn't bear much fruit. You, me, all of us who are believers have the God-given ability and responsibility to think outside of the box."

Dad rarely gets on his soapbox. I see how this illness has not weakened him but has made him stronger in his convictions.

"It is all three of those things, but what you and Mom have together is rare. Precious and rare. Most couples spend a lifetime trying to figure out what they have in common—or they give up while trying."

"Look at you and Beau. You two share something that is deep and true. You love to serve people in need. It was no different for your mother and me. We've just had more years to polish our act, that's all. It wasn't always easy."

"What if it isn't easy from the start? Is that a bad sign?" I ask, making myself and my concerns an open book.

"I don't believe in signs. I believe in trust and growth and change and inspiration—inspiration is best of all. It changes everything. But you have to allow it. I believe that you will allow divine inspiration to move you forward in life."

"You do?" I say hopefully.

"In my heart of hearts."

I flip our French tape over to lesson two. "Ready, *Papa?*" I say with a terrible French accent.

"*Oui, oui.*" He says, twirling the ends of an imagined moustache.

I press play and go back to my desk. The Frenchwoman's words seem to sink into my brain while I am considering the truths of what Dad has said. I repeat after her as I am supposed to, but I don't know what I am saying. Dad starts laughing.

"What? Did I mess up?"

"Aren't you listening? Some fellow student you turned out to be." He slowly walks over to the cassette player and presses rewind for a split second. "Now pay attention."

The Frenchwoman's voice begins. "*Mon mari est beau. Répétez après moi: Mon mari est beau.*"

Dad orchestrates me from his place at the front of the room. "Come on, repeat after Madame Teacher—*Mon mari est beau.*"

The tape continues. "Congratulations, you have just said 'my husband is handsome.'"

"How about that?" Dad walks over to the chalkboard and writes "Mari and Beau" and draws a heart around the names.

What are the odds of this? I look at the chalk drawing and listen to the Frenchwoman. Our names sound so good spoken in French. I'm just not sure I believe what is in Dad's heart.

So Long, Farewell

We file into the church like the von Trapp family. Child after child walks sideways along the pew to get to the last available spot. The church, a historic building that once was the home of Episcopalians, is now a community congregation—The City Church. It has been my parents' faith home for more than twenty years and the congregants consider them, the center, and the kids an important part of the church's ministry.

Since my temporary return, many of the older members who knew me when I was a teenager have welcomed me back with sweet embraces. When I say I am only here for a while, they shake their heads and say, "We'll see."

I am seated between Marcus and Daisy. Daisy is in thick tights, a knit sweater, and a favorite summer dress she will not relinquish to the season change. Marcus has on a charcoal gray dress shirt and black slacks.

"You clean up nice," I say.

He smiles and does not return the compliment because I am dressed in my usual uniform these days, jeans and a bulky sweater. But today I also have on a cute beret, so I point to this until he tells me it is darling.

When the sermon is about over, the pastor says he has an announcement.

"As some of you know, Marcus will be moving to Chicago next month. Our deep loss is Chicago's blessing. This young man has served this community ever since he was a boy, and now he will do the same for another fortunate community. We want to send him off with resources to help him as he undertakes a noble mission—to establish the Chicago Urban Youth Center."

There is applause and I look at Marcus with surprise. I knew he was returning to his place of birth, but he had never mentioned this vision. I nudge him with my knee and he raises his eyebrows and smiles. He likes that I am surprised.

The pastor continues. "Every week until he leaves, we will take a love offering that will help him purchase supplies for the Youth Center. We are so fortunate to be a part of something so important for Chicago youth. God is good. Let us sing out our gratitude with our closing song."

Everybody stands to sing, and the pastor holds up his hand and leans over the microphone. "I also want to mention that this is the last weekend Mari is here for a while. Agnes Sample has agreed to serve in Mari's place on the fellowship committee, and Harry Zimmer will take Mari's place on the youth board. Of course, nobody is taking her place completely. We hope she will be with us again soon."

People smile and look at me as they break out in song.

"Why don't I know about your plan?" I say out of the side of my mouth.

Marcus pretends he cannot hear me. "Eh?" he says, holding up his Bible to block my face. I bump elbows with him like a sibling to cover up how touched I am that after all these years he is using the Bible I bought him for his high school graduation.

The kids pour out of the church, scratching their itches and shaking out restless legs. They ask Marcus to count up his first offering—a request he adamantly refuses to fulfill.

"Oh, man. We want to know how rich you'll be," Josiah says.

Marcus and I simultaneously recite my father's favorite line to use when we would complain about not having enough clothes, toys, or something we saw in the full-color ad section of the newspaper, "Rich in spirit, poor in wallet."

Several of the older kids groan at the bad line. Marcus and I look at each other and laugh at the familiar response.

Wallace walks between us. "Good thing Mari started the poetry night. You could use a little help with your rhyming, Marcus." He reaches for our hands and we walk, the three of us, with matching strides.

Last Call

"All potential poets who have not yet read will read today. This will be our last poetry pizza night before Mari heads West." Dad uses a megaphone as if he is addressing an unruly crowd, when actually there is calmness among the gatherers.

"Hoorah!" shout the boys.

Mom steps up to the stage and reaches into the jar to remove the last two names. It is no surprise. "Wallace and Marcus."

"Hoorah!"

Wallace holds his stomach and asks to go first. He cannot eat until he is done with the torture of public speaking, he says. Marcus concedes his own desire to get it over with and turns the floor over to Wallace. "This is my poem in honor of our poetry night. For Mari."

I give a little bow, and Wallace stands tall as he reads.

> *Words that share who we are and who we want to be*
> *Are born on the night of poetry.*
> *With pizza for a reward and rhymes to save face*
> *Acceptance as thick as cheese becomes our grace.*

Wallace pauses and grins. We all laugh.

> *And there is something about the sausage, or maybe it's the sauce*
> *that makes us dream in color and forget about our loss.*
> *To this makeshift family, Mari has been a great addition.*
> *To her we owe our thanks for this wonderful tradition.*

A big "hoorah!" and a crowd wave are initiated. I give Wallace a standing ovation and a big hug. None of us notice that Marcus has snuck behind the soda fountain bar until he steps from behind it with a large piece of board covered with a sheet.

"Oooh," I taunt. "The man has props."

He points at me. "You in the back, watch it," he threatens.

"Wallace, you did an outstanding job honoring Mari. I guess we both had a bit of the same idea in mind. I decided to do a poem of images and words combined. So you will all have to gather around this masterpiece to get the message, so to speak. I know Mari hates to have her photo taken, let alone displayed, but I hope she will forgive and grant me artistic license in this instance."

Everyone puts down their pieces of pizza and gathers near Marcus. I stay at the back of the group, unsure of what he is up to.

The sheet is removed and a storyboard of images seems to chronicle my life from toddler days to high school hair mistakes to as recent as the Halloween party. Brief descriptions or one-word snapshots fill in the spaces between photos. Dream. Passion. Service. Kindness. Friendship. Faith. Adventure. Independence. Hope. Purpose. Wonder. One shot is a computer image of a map—of Tucson, to be exact—and the words beneath it read "the Missing Years."

Other words emerge after I have stared at the incredible display for a few minutes. They are written in a lighter shade of marker, but represent the darker or more serious parts of me and my journey. Complicated. Embarrassed. Determined. Stubborn. Willful. Guarded. Uncertain.

Everyone loves it. The kids are laughing at the photo of me with braces. Then they set their sights on that photo of me with the glasses and helmet and bust up all the more. I have to join in. It's either that or hide away embarrassed forever. Mom and Dad express "oohs and ahhs" as they recognize different moments in my life.

"What a great last poem for the season," Dad says, beaming.

Marcus has snuck up next to me. He leans over and whispers, "I'm not in too much trouble, am I?"

I lightly punch his arm. "Not at all. It's awesome. I thought I smelled rubber cement coming from your room."

"Aren't you so funny." Pause. "Are you really leaving?"

"Are you?" I say a bit too quickly, too defensively.

"Yes. But I'm not leaving behind what this is. Look." Marcus hands me a photo of a large old house with chairs on the porch and a tricycle on the lawn. There is a tire swing hanging from a thick rope in the forefront of the shot.

"What's this?"

"The house I'm buying in Chicago."

"It's sad that you have to drive a Big Wheel in order to afford a place to live."

"I put a down payment on this with a grant I got as a result of my thesis. It's the future Chicago Urban Youth Center."

So this is the good a grant can really do.

"I didn't realize you were *starting* the center. I thought you were working with an organization." I stare at the house. The shape of possibility is visible to me. "Have Mom and Dad seen this?"

"I wanted you to be the first. I'd love for you to come and see it."

I look up at him. He is hard to read sometimes, but not this time. I return my gaze to the white house with potential. "When could I? I'm gone for a few weeks for the wedding events, and when I get back, we'll both be loading up to head out again. For good this time." Sadness rushes into my heart. I gulp.

"Chicago does fall somewhere between here and Tucson, you know. Will you come back home for Christmas? Make it a stop sometime after a visit."

"I've missed so much work already. I'm pushing the limits. I'll be here in a few weeks for Thanksgiving, and then I'll be on my way."

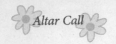

"Why are you even returning after the wedding, Mari?"

I roll my eyes. "You sound like Dad. You always have. It's as if you bypassed being a kid altogether. If you must know, nosey-man, I compromised with Dad. I'll only be returning to enjoy Thanksgiving and to pack up my remains. That way I don't have to mess with lugging all my things back for the wedding trip."

He nods, somewhat amused by my reasoning.

"Okay, that sounds a bit confusing. But you're not always rational, adult, and mature in your decision making. What was Lonna about?"

He shakes his head—he's as disappointed as I am in my response.

I hand him the image of the house. "Forget what I just said. I'm sorry, Marcus. Truthfully, I've loved how stable and strong you've always been. You are exactly what the Chicago Urban Youth Center will need to get off the ground and running."

I've blown the moment, but Marcus is gracious about it.

"Thanks, Mari."

"I love the poem. It really helps me see what goodness I have had in my life. What a gift to have a visual of my journey."

"Your journey?" he says with a smile.

"Who else's?" I ask.

Elsa and Daisy are grabbing Marcus' hands and pulling him to a standing position. "Piggyback rides!" they demand in giggles. They know that soon, these silly afternoons with Marcus will be a thing of the past.

"Guard this," he says, pressing his dream into the undeserving palm of my hand.

"I will."

While the circus surrounds Marcus, I wander up to the board to examine my life in photos a bit more closely. Even those strange years, the ones that seem a bit dark or insecure in my memories, were filled with light and happiness. Why did I forget that so easily, I wonder.

One by one, I trace the photos with my finger. I take time to examine my expressions and recall what I was thinking in each circumstance. When I get to the last image, the one of the recent Halloween party, I look at the

photo of me surrounded by small pumpkins formerly known as kids. My hands are adjusting the stem hat on Daisy's head, but my eyes are looking straight at the camera. I'm happy. Everyone is.

Except for one.

Beau is standing next to me, but he is a world away. He has his cell phone midway to his ear when he must have noticed the photo was being taken. His other hand has come up in a half salute as if to wave away the camera bearer. His eyes first appear to be looking in the direction that mine are, but I realize they are staring off, beyond the room. They are overlooking the moment.

I recall what I was thinking when this shot was taken. *How can I leave this?*

Beneath this photo Marcus has placed the word "Perspective."

The Business of Dating

As the plane circles for a landing at the Tucson airport, I count on my fingers the times Beau and I have spoken on the phone since he left DC that early morning over a week ago.

No fingers needed.

"You seem troubled, dear," the older woman next to me says over the top of her *Glamour* magazine.

I smile and shake my head, hoping to cut off the conversation before it begins. Again. Louise Merrill, a former flight attendant who used to serve this nonstop flight, has been talking nonstop since Chicago. Her incessant chatter, like the voice on museum headphones, has described with great detail the changing scene out the window for a couple hours.

"Boy trouble? I can always tell. My daughter has a terrible case of the boy blues. She's a basket case. One day she calls him constantly, the next day she refuses to talk to him. You know what I told her?"

I wait for her to continue, but she peers at me. Baiting me for an answer.

"What?"

"I told her to break it off with the louse, of course."

I nod gravely, hoping it will end the conversation.

"She said she couldn't because it'd be bad for business."

"Business?"

"She's a matchmaker," Louise says laughing. "I guess it would be like a psychic dying in a plane crash."

"A little."

"Here's her card. By the looks of your book, you could use her services."

About to argue, I glance down at my twisted and mangled copy of *The Five Love Languages*—a gift from my mom—and take the card.

"Is he picking you up?"

My eyes go back to the window and scan the ground below for some landmark I can ask Louise about to sidetrack her from my love life.

She elbows me. "Well?"

"I don't know. It was a while ago that we discussed my flight. And he's really busy. He's managing this important research project..." my voice fades. I'm tired of selling Beau to anyone who will listen.

"When a fella is too busy to pick his girl up at the airport after she has been gone—how long?"

Elbow again.

"About four months. But we just saw each other a week ago. We're good."

"Well, when a fella is too busy to get his girl after four months apart, then there is trouble. Capital T, if you ask me."

I sense what this woman's daughter goes through on a daily basis.

The pilot announces our arrival at the gate. We taxi for a few minutes before the doors to freedom open. I'm quick to gather my bags so I can make it into the terminal before Louise can notice who picks me up. Or doesn't pick me up.

Nervously, I survey the people coming and going near the baggage claim, hoping to catch a glimpse of Beau's shoulders, his dark hair, his timid smile.

But instead I see Angelica standing at the top of the escalators. She is holding up a big piece of poster board and is chatting with a young boy in a three-piece suit. I wave, but she doesn't take her attention from the boy. When she reaches the bottom, the sign is visible. Glittered handprints form a frame around the words: "Welcome Home Mari. Love, the Golden Horizons Gang."

"Angelica, over here!" I finally catch her eye. She rushes over to me. The boy follows her, clearly enamored with Angelica.

"Mari. I wrote down the wrong flight information. We would have missed you completely, but Sadie called to double-check when we are meeting up for breakfast. Thank goodness she had the information in her Palm. Harry and I would have stayed at the mall watching the pet store reptiles."

"Harry!" I say to the nicely dressed young man and give him a quick hug.

He is not shy at all, but rather poised and proper.

"Spitting image of his dad, wouldn't you say?" Angelica gives Harry an incredulous smile.

"Absolutely."

From the corner of my eye, I see Louise in her pale blue track suit shuffling toward me.

"Shall we go? I'm starved."

Before we can get out the revolving door, Louise brushes up next to me and whispers in my ear, "Unless you are dating a midget, hold on to that card, honey."

Break Fast

"Angelica, dear, does Sadie know you have confiscated Harry?"

"Sadie had to go in to work for an early meeting and Carson is out of town for the day. So we are heading to Freddies to meet up with Caitlin and, eventually, Sadie. Besides, Harry and I have been having a very good discussion about love."

I stretch my head out over the front seat. "Do tell. I'm floundering a bit in that area."

Angelica gives me a concerned glance. We haven't talked lately and apparently she doesn't know about Beau's visit. I throw her a "We'll talk later" look.

Harry straightens his tie and begins quietly at first. "It is complicated. That is the best way I can put it."

"Amen!" I cry.

He politely rubs his ear. "Dad loved my mom and they had me. Mom and Dad still love me, but they aren't in love with each other. My mom has Trevor and Dad has Sadie, whom I like very much. And in a way, we all have each other. We just happen to have a bigger circle of love than other families."

"Isn't he smart?" Angelica praises. "I told him about what I have been doing for the past year, and he had great advice. Tell her, Harry."

"Well, Mari, you know Angelica much better than I do. So this is an outsider's humble observation. But I believe Angelica started with a good choice to take love more seriously than she had in the past."

"I agree."

He raises his hand. "But she eventually replaced true love with the fear of love. She's frozen, like a frog in biology class."

"Biology? Aren't you ten?"

His dark eyes peer up at me. "I'm practically at the height of my academic career in prep school."

"Oh, sorry. Angelica, would you agree with this assessment?"

"Completely. I have traded love for fear. I've been stuck. It is all so clear now," she says, half kidding but with an element of serious awareness.

"Harry, how'd you get to be the expert?" I ask our brilliant guest as we enter Freddies.

His small, heart-shaped face turns in my direction. "A girl named Danny."

"A girl named Danny? That sounds like an after-school special."

"Short for Danielle. She's much tougher than most of the girls. Most of the boys, for that matter. I love her."

Caitlin comes running up to me and hugs me tight. Her approach is so quick, I can only get a glimpse of something disturbing on her head. She reintroduces herself to Harry as if he were five rather than a mature ten. I whisper this to her, but Harry hears me.

"I just turned eleven, by the way." He points to Caitlin. "You're the one with the funky clothing store. Very eclectic."

Caitlin raises her thin eyebrows. "Thank you."

"Our old table even!" I say, hugging it tenderly. Was I really thinking I could leave this place that has become my home? This place I love?

"I was here an hour early to secure this table, I'll have you know. I've been drinking coffee since I arrived."

Angelica has scored some laminated menus from the hostess podium. She passes them out with flair.

"Will you take our order too?"

"Anything to have us all here for breakfast one more time." She gives Caitlin a double take and then quickly looks down at the breakfast specials clipped to the inside of the menu.

"Girls! Sorry I'm late." Sadie is barely through the door and wiggling her way out of her coat so she can hug each of us. She plants a big kiss on Harry's cheek. For the first time the little prodigy is unsure what to say.

Our nearly married friend soaks in the presence of her best friends with teary eyes. "You don't know how thankful I am that this is happening right now. I thought I was so together, so organized, and I was so wrong. Right, Harry? I'm a bit of a mess."

"It's a big day you are planning. A little stress is to be expected."

"Listen to the man. I mean…boy! The man-boy. That suit is confusing me," Caitlin says, shaking her head, and I see that the bizarre attachment to her head is actually her hair. It has grown out, and she has formed a strange side ponytail with the several inches of length.

Sadie is the first to crack. Apparently prewedding nerves also becomes a bit of a truth serum. "Caitlin, what is with the hair today?"

Caitlin picks up on the tone of judgment in Sadie's voice and speaks a bit defensively. "Since I decided to grow my hair out, I've awakened to many different kinks and curls and waves. I had forgotten what a pain hair can be. So, I've decided to write a beauty book about how to take the top twenty bed-head problems and turn them into sassy styles. So a person can look in the mirror, decide which bed-head issue they have, and then maximize it while spending less time fussing. Don't you think women will be thrilled to turn flaws into fashion?"

Angelica is tired of this already. "Won't the squirrels be jealous?"

"Squirrels?" Caitlin says, laughing.

I lean over the table. "Our sweet Angelica is implying that your ponytail looks a bit more like the tail of a friendly woodland creature."

"Nuh-uh!" Caitlin is shocked at this comparison.

"Oh, yes," says Angelica, unwavering in her opinion. "When I walked

in and saw your head at our table, I wanted to call pest control and report the restaurant."

"Well, you are in fine form. What happened to your new leaf—flipping it over and being nicer, kinder, gentler?" our little friend retaliates.

"You copped that from a laxative commercial. I'm insulted. But if you must know—I flipped it, I lived it, and now I am getting back to a balanced, midflip existence. Don't tell me you haven't missed me." Angelica's lips form a smile.

"I haven't missed the insults."

"Are you liking Tucson, Harry?" I inquire, reminding everyone that we have a guest today who might not be used to acerbic conversation in the morning.

"Well, I've visited many times before to see Dad."

"Oh, of course. I wasn't thinking."

"But, actually, I'm liking Tucson much more than I did before," he says, grinning and stealing a gander at Angelica, who is fluffing her hair and pursing her glossed lips at a mirror. She is oblivious of her newest fan.

"What?" she asks, putting the compact back into her purse. "You all want me back out there," she circles the air in front of her with a flat hand, "searching for true love. And Harry has convinced me to get unstuck. So if I return to primping before a meal, you all have nothing to say." Her manicured nails form a goose egg zero.

"Harry convinced you, or a certain other attractive gentleman inspired this change of attitude?" Sadie pries.

Angelica wants to dodge the question, but her initial gasp gives her away. "Maybe Peyton's willingness to wait for me has made a good impression. However, I'm still staying away from him until after the wedding. Or at least until the wedding."

Our waitress takes our orders. Angelica has quit eating for three, but Sadie is fervently breaking her rules of math. She has ordered two servings of the chocolate chip pancakes with whipped cream—a concoction that has a scary carb count.

The rest of us smile at one another as Sadie asks for chocolate syrup to be provided on the side.

"I hope Jim is as patient," Caitlin says, sighing.

"By the way, Mari, Beau had planned to surprise you at the airport this morning, but he got held up in a meeting." Angelica tries to explain my boyfriend's behavior.

I pretend to be engrossed in the wedge of lemon in my water glass.

"Something about the upcoming fund-raiser?" she clarifies.

"Yes. It is that time of year again. Can you believe it has almost been a year since your proposal at the fashion show, Sadie?" I try to keep the conversation flowing in the direction opposite of my relationship with Beau. If there was a fund-raiser meeting, I would have known about it. Inside the ache returns. I imagine him sitting at his desk and looking at his pewter clock, knowing I am in the city and yet staying seated. Waiting until he thinks we can see one another. *And why is the time of our reunion for him to determine?* I ask myself, still plunging the lemon into my glass with a red-striped straw. *Why did he get to say we shouldn't communicate until I returned?*

"Mari?"

I am being summoned from the maze of downwardly spiraling thinking. There is physical pain involved in surfacing, even to be with the people who love me most.

"Yes? Sorry. Lost in thought."

"Carson said that Beau surprised you by showing up a week ago in DC." Sadie opens up the vein of my relationship.

"That is so romantic." Caitlin provides her usual assessment of Beau. Even after she and I had that heart-to-heart about my misgivings, she sees what she wants to see. I've probably helped create that denial, me and my sales pitch.

I'd like to order that kind of faith from the menu today. Instead, I settle for the American breakfast—two eggs scrambled with toast and hash browns. The plate is placed in front of me. It is appropriate that I have ordered eggs. Chicken, that is what I am. Too chicken to go to Beau directly. Too chicken

to call him in advance of my arrival. And too chicken to tell my best friends about the ache in my gut.

"Did your family just love him?" Angelica asks a safe question.

"Yes. My mom was smitten right away. And he was quite taken with her recent post on the city council. They are both type A personalities."

"See, you cannot get away from us," Angelica says, laughing. "You are even destined to marry a type A."

The others look at her sternly, as if she has crossed a conversational barrier.

"What?" I ask innocently.

Sadie shakes her head and her newly relaxed waves tumble about her high cheekbones. "Your first day back, and Angelica is teasing you. We should give each other space."

Space? Funny that Sadie is using the same word Beau did in his note.

"Why would I need space?" I ask with a rise in my voice.

"Not just you. Me, Angelica, Caitlin—we all need space for the decisions and transitions we are making."

I'm not buying it.

"What do you know about Beau's visit to Washington? Does everybody in my life know that it was a disaster? That he left without us even talking or saying goodbye in person. Sweet, wonderful, patient Beau couldn't handle the confrontation after an argument that he started. Instead he left so that we could have space. Lots of space. Miles and miles of it. Which shouldn't bug me because that is the way our relationship has been for more than eight months. I have so much space, Sadie, that I'm conferring with NASA about a satellite."

Everyone is sitting with their backs board-straight in their chairs. Even the waitress is standing at attention with the coffeepot.

Sadie breaks the silence. "Mari, we didn't know any of that. In fact, we thought good things were going to happen on that trip. We were all praying that you would have a strong sense of your future relationship with Beau."

"Was this trip announced on the radio, at the Rotary club meeting?

And why that prayer specifically?" *Specifically. That harsh last word I spoke to Beau at the zoo.*

Angelica is about to burst, Caitlin still looks confused, and Sadie is repeatedly pushing her hair behind her ears in a nervous motion. Harry has reverted back to the demeanor of a real child and is licking whipped cream from each of his fingers, completely lost in the world of sugar sprinkles.

"I repeat. What do you all know about Beau's visit to Washington?"

Sadie looks around us covertly. Once she seems convinced nobody is listening to our conversation, she reaches for my hand and holds it tightly. Her gaze is open and fixed on my face. I cannot look away.

"Mari—Beau was there to ask your parents for their permission to marry you."

I try to pull my hand back. But unlike Beau, my friend Sadie won't let go.

Beau Motion

I spend the day doing everything I can to avoid thinking about Beau. Caitlin and I took a load of her stuff to Goodwill, and then we cleared out her spare room for my stay. I met with Yvette and Zane, who are still happily subleasing my apartment and my cat. I brought Elmo back to Caitlin's so I would have his comfort. And I checked on my bank account to verify that I am indeed poorer than poor.

Golden Horizons has kept me on a small retainer for the work I have done from a distance. It has kept the basic must-pay bills, like my cell phone, insurance, and my student loan, from becoming fodder for collectors. I don't mind seeing my low balance because it reminds me how little I need. I've only thought about money a couple of times while in Washington. I've barely needed any spending money because I've been focused on the kids, on chores, and on my parents. It is amazing how frugal a life can be when it is not self-focused.

When I check my watch for the millionth time and see that the workday has ended, my heart plummets. Not one call from Beau. And tomorrow I have to go to the office to meet with the fund-raising committee. How can I face him if he won't face up to our situation?

Caitlin is packing boxes of her fashion creations at the store, so Elmo and I sit on beanbag chairs and continue waiting. We are really good at it. I scratch Elmo's belly for five minute intervals and then sigh heavily for thirty seconds. Elmo then looks up at me curiously and squirms to position another part of his belly for the next round of scratching. Elmo and I have been apart for months, yet we can return to the same level of relationship almost immediately. Okay, two cans of cat food and one catnip toy later—just like old times. I wish human relationships were this easy.

The call I have been waiting for comes at six thirty. My legs are numb from sitting on the beanbag, so I crawl like a soldier in combat over to my purse, in which I left my cell phone so that I would not appear desperate. The phone is just switching to my message when I intercept.

"Hello?"

"Mari? I was just leaving you a message." Beau states what I know and leaves out what I don't know. Like where do we stand? What is he thinking? Is he really sorry?

"Should I listen to it?"

"No, of course not. I'm glad I caught you."

"Me too."

"I'd like to meet at the park."

"Meet?"

"Do you need a ride?"

I would like a ride from my boyfriend. "My car is here at Caitlin's house. I can meet you."

"I'll pick up something for us to eat."

"Great. See you there. Beau…"

"Yeah?"

"I'm glad you called."

"Me too."

I reach the park first. A group of kids are finishing up a soccer game, so I watch both teams shake hands in a gesture of good sportsmanship. They

appear to be grade-schoolers, with nylon shorts dragging near the tops of their striped socks and haircuts that resemble the Beatles—early years.

I stare at the faces and soon see Wallace, Camden, Jon, Elsa, and the others. I've lived in a city completely unaware of the children who reside here. My life has been about work, my friends, and the quest for an identity beyond that of "single." I cannot imagine that I coexisted with all these little people without noticing them.

My phone rings. I anxiously check the car clock before answering. Beau is running late and it bothers me. "Where are you?" I ask as my greeting.

"Where are you, Mari? The talent show starts in ten minutes," Yvette volleys back. "Zane mentioned it today when you were over."

"He did?" My mind recalls a vague reference. "I'm so sorry. Beau is on his way over. I don't know if we can make it. We have a lot to talk about."

"Don't worry. I wanted to catch you if you still wanted to come, but don't feel pressure. Besides, we already have your money for the tickets. That's all that matters," she says, laughing.

Beau's headlights come into view at the south entrance of the parking lot and his car rolls up to the left of mine.

"Thanks for understanding, Yvette. I'll let you know how this goes."

Beau waves the bags of Chinese food happily. It is as if nothing had happened between us.

I roll down my window and he rolls down his passenger window.

"Were you calling the cops? Sorry I was late. They left out the fried rice in the order."

"It was Yvette. I completely forgot about that talent show she is coordinating. It is tonight, and I had bought tickets for us. But that was well before—before recent developments." I string this out slowly hoping he will catch on to our situation.

"Let's go!"

"But the Chinese food will get cold." *And so will our relationship.*

"It's better cold. We need a date night."

"We won't be able to discuss all that space we've had lately."

"I think this is just what we need. We'll have the Chinese tomorrow for lunch."

As we both start up our cars and drive to the auditorium just minutes away, it feels like forever. My heart is racing, but my thoughts are caught in slow-motion mode. "What is he thinking?" I ask aloud. My voice seems low and distorted.

At a stoplight I look over and Beau is parallel to me. He gives me a thumbs-up.

"Who are you?" I mouth.

"I love you too," he mouths back. A crisp Chinese noodle sticks out from the corner of his mouth. I watch it move as he forms words, wide and exaggerated—the noodle teeters on the edge of his lips; it will tumble either onto his tongue or his nice leather upholstery.

I cannot take my eyes off of that noodle, as though its inevitable fall will trigger my very own.

Disappearing Act

The theater is dark.

Beau taps the shoulder of a young woman who is standing at the back handing out programs. He nudges me to retrieve the tickets, which I buried in my purse months ago. I'm still digging when Yvette shows up.

She is surprised to see us, but she takes our presence as a good sign rather than what it really is. "This way," she motions with her arm. I notice she has a velvet *Y* on her suit jacket. It makes me smile.

Beau takes this as a good sign. "See, it's fun already."

Yvette leads us to a boxed-off pair of luxury seats. I'm embarrassed to be in such an obvious part of the theater. Thankfully the fire juggler is having trouble igniting her batons, so we do not interrupt anyone's act—except for Beau's. And only for a moment.

"Isn't this great? This is the kind of stuff we should have been doing all along," he whispers. And when I look into his eyes, they are wide and blank. Maybe he believes we are fine. Maybe we are fine and I have totally distorted the reality.

Was the confrontation in Washington the way I think of it? Wasn't that

moment at the zoo significant enough to shift the foundation of our relationship fathoms below the placid surface of Beau's eyes?

I lean against the soft fabric of the theater seats. In between flashes of fire, the darkness envelopes me and it is comforting. But my heart aches. And I use those moments of darkness to look toward the ceiling. Spotlights and cables are intertwined with the metal pipes and rods that support the curtain. I look past all the innards of the theater and into the darkness beyond. I imagine that is where God is sitting, watching all this take place. *What am I not getting? What is going on with this relationship?* I mentally plea with my Maker.

When the house lights come on to signal the start of intermission, I feel as though I have been napping. Beyond the fire juggler, I did not notice any of the other acts. Beau, on the other hand, is as excited and fidgety as a toddler. I should view this youthful enthusiasm as charming, but all I can think of is…

"Dummy!" He shouts.

"Excuse me?"

"I loved the dummy! That ventriloquist was hilarious, didn't you think?" Beau continues to rate the seven acts I missed. His exuberance is annoying.

"What was your favorite part?"

"Hard to choose," I say unconvincingly.

"'The program shows that there is only one act after this—Lyle the magician."

I grab the yellow sheet of paper and read it with horror. "I don't like magicians, Beau. Can we head out early? Besides, you can catch this guy's act any weekend at Chez DiDi's. I've seen it. Not that great."

His face falls. I'm responsible for ruining this night for him. This stop in his tour of denial is mine to keep in motion. I am the halftime act, and I rise to the occasion. "You are right. We shouldn't leave. It would be an insult to Yvette and to Lyle. Besides, Lyle is getting better." I've nearly convinced myself.

Beau kisses my cheek and goes to get us a box of Girl Scout cookies, the lobby's sole treat offering.

"Samoas!" I shout after him. If I am going to endure Lyle, I want to devour something delicious.

I notice Sadie, Carson, and Harry a couple rows up and to the right. I wave to the small, happy family. The small, happy family waves to me in my boxed set of soft chairs.

I've never felt so alone.

The lights go down while we are still exchanging waves. Crouching, Beau makes his way to the seat beside me. He has a box of Thin Mints and a box of Samoas. I'm feeling less alone.

The emcee, a short, nervous woman with bushy black hair, red glasses, and a tight matronly dress, seems flustered and quite pleased to introduce Lyle. Her eyes follow him as he takes center stage in his tuxedo.

Lyle warms up the crowd with lukewarm humor. I open up my box of Samoas.

He pulls doves out of his sleeves.

I reach for a cookie.

He builds audience anticipation for his finale.

I breathe in the scent of chocolate and coconut.

He wants an audience volunteer and selects Beau, who waved his arm in earnest desire to be on stage.

I eat a cookie.

To an entertained house, Lyle warns me that this could be dangerous. Beau hugs his own body and knocks his knees together like he is scared. Lots of laughter. Lyle says to me specifically that there could be risk. He will attempt the impossible...

Dramatic pause as the audience holds its collective breath.

He will make my boyfriend disappear.

That ol' trick? Beau did that months ago. I eat the entire box of cookies.

Afterlife

Sadie is pacing in front of me in a ponytail. Unless she is going to a gym, this is not a good sign. When Sadie cannot put energy into her presentation of self, something is amiss. And as she turns on her heels and makes a strange "humph, humph," sound, I wish I was amissin' this.

"Use your words, Sadie. Use your words." I pick up my cream soda from its resting place on a glass coaster and settle into Sadie's leather couch. I stop watching her go to and fro so I can sip steadily from my straw. Sadie is my only friend who would even dream of having straws on hand. She also has things like tape, scissors, and a glue gun—items the rest of us take for granted at our parents' house.

"I just wonder what I am getting into."

"You mean because of Harry? He is such a great kid."

Her hands go up in the air like an overzealous cheerleader. "He is a great kid. I agree. But I'm wondering about his dad. About this family."

"I thought we voted your family the scariest between the two."

"Until now. Look at this."

Sadie walks over to her desk and removes a hardcover book from beneath a pile of *Floral Retreats* magazines.

She hands it to me and shields her eyes from whatever evil it possesses. From the colors I guess it is a children's book. "Carson gave this to Harry for his eleventh birthday. Eleventh!"

"I admit this is a little young for the kid, but a lot of guys aren't good at buying age-friendly gifts for children."

"Read it." Sadie cuts off my optimism before it can ruin her perfectly bad mood.

I look down at the title *What Happens When I Die?* I grimace to be on board with Sadie's level of disgust. "This *is* a bit depressing to give a kid, but maybe he wants to teach him about heaven. Maybe this is his father-son faith talk. That is sweet, right?"

"Read on. Flip. Flip."

"I'm flipping." As I flip, I read aloud the reasons for her reaction from the table of contents, "A Living Will Versus a Trust, Your Attorney and You, The Estate Mistake…"

"Stop. You get the idea. Crazy, right?"

"I like the illustrations. This painting of the banker dancing on the desk is lighthearted." I consider modeling the banker move.

For the first time I see the spark of Sadie's personality behind her eyes. "Yes, and the probate officer climbing the gate of the mansion looks a lot like Jim Carey."

"Did you ask why he gave this to his son?"

"Apparently the Curtis family tradition is to mark a young boy's rite of passage by passing along his legal rights."

Then it occurs to me what this really means. "They are *really* loaded. Sadie, you are not just marrying a successful man…he is stinkin' rich. So-so wealthy people would surely wait until a kid was, oh, say thirteen before burying him in living trust brochures disguised as entertaining literature."

"Wealthy is one thing—wealth-obsessed is entirely different. Carson has never acted like this before. I'm wondering if there is a side to him that I have entirely missed."

"He's prepared—like a Boy Scout. Sadie, who is your wedding photographer?"

She is taken aback by this question, and then just plain embarrassed when she tells me. "Kevin Milano. You heard that, did you?"

"I ran into him months ago. He saw us together and he let it slip that Carson had asked him from the very beginning."

"I think it is ridiculous to have Kevin as our wedding photographer. His work is more and more in demand in global fashion circles. A wedding is so beneath him."

"This is my point, Sadie. The Carson Curtis wedding is *not* beneath Kevin. In fact, he is quite pleased to have the gig. So let's not pretend that Carson is just any guy. He is a good person, he is a loving fiancé, and he will be a very kind and honorable husband. He will also be the best provider a girl could ask for."

"Besides God."

I nod. "Good perspective."

"I guess I've tried to keep the wealth far from the limelight. It's awkward for me. My parents worked very hard to provide for me and my sister, and we had difficult times. I don't take wealth lightly. I see it as a huge responsibility; morally, socially, and spiritually. I think my sister and my mom see this union as such a score, as if that had been one of my criteria. So I have refused to acknowledge that area. But the things Carson is doing for this wedding make it impossible. He hired a helicopter to fly his best man in the day of the ceremony because Dave has to work the day before."

"Sadie, just your response about God being your provider shows me that you have nothing to worry about. You will always know where your worth and your love comes from. Do you think we are going to despise you because you have money?" In this moment I understand how my own recent revelation about not needing money has freed me from jealousy.

"My sister does."

That would explain the dresses. Revenge.

"Well, up until a year ago I was jealous of your career and your salary. That is pathetic but true. Since then, I've better understood my place and

my purpose. And Sadie, anyone who makes you feel bad about Carson's success—or your own—has not figured out their place or their purpose. You can extend those people grace, but don't offer apologies for your blessings. The rest of us know what your life is based on, and it isn't this stuff." I wave the book in the air.

Sadie looks relieved and then agitated. "You have to admit that this book is still absurd."

"Carson is going to raise up his son responsibly, and that includes telling Harry everything—from the birds and the bees to the stocks and the CDs."

She laughs. "Aren't you the comedian."

"Want to hire me for the reception? I'm not cheap. Hiring me would tell the world that you are without a doubt one of the richest women in the region."

Sadie grabs the book and whops me on the head with it.

"I'm wanted in global funny circles."

Whop.

Rodeo Rhonda

This is an all-female operation," shouts Rhonda, the leader of our Western adventure. "Anyone who thinks the Southwest or the West was tamed by men will see a new side of history during the next twenty-four hours."

I look at Caitlin and mouth, "Twenty-four hours?"

She motions "oops" with her hands up next to her half braided, half slicked back head of hair.

"We are staying overnight in this place? I only brought this outfit."

Rhonda walks over to me like a drill sergeant honing in on her latest rookie target. "Do you have something to share with the group, Miss…"

"Mari. Mari Hamilton."

"Mari?" She asks as if I might have forgotten my name while under the pressure of silence.

I nod.

"Well, Mari. You just got yourself in charge of bunk duty. You and…"

She points to Sadie's sister, who barks, "Melanie, sir. Ma'am."

"You and Melanie have the pleasure of setting up the cabins for this evening. The sheets and blankets are in the cupboards. The wash basins need

to be filled with water, and the cabin floor needs a good sweeping. And the bunks need dusting."

I look at Sadie, who is buttoning up her cute Western vest and avoiding eye contact.

Angelica steps out of line and approaches Rhonda on tippy-toes. "I don't sleep in bunks. There must be a room with at least a double bed and a private bath. I'll pay." She reaches into her leather purse to produce evidence of the offer's legitimacy.

"You see this?" Rhonda nabs Angelica's bag and holds it up for all of us to see.

We nod earnestly. We see it, we see it.

"You buy expensive leather bags, probably have leather interior in your fancy cars, and yet you have never roped a steer, branded a cow, or rubbed the ears of a calf." She shoves the purse into Angelica's open arms. Angelica promptly hugs and kisses it.

This would be true.

"Is that so bad?" Caitlin asks innocently.

"Darn right it's bad. After today, you'll not only appreciate your whamby-pamby lifestyle, you will have a newfound appreciation for animals who sacrifice everything for your pleasure cruise through life."

"Cruise?" Angelica says deliriously.

Rhonda grabs a feed sack and walks down the line with it. "Cell phones go here. All other so-called valuables will be kept in the main house."

"Is there a safe?" Angelica asks, counting the pieces of jewelry she has in her possession.

"Nobody in the history of the Happy Campers has gotten past Delilah's 12 gauge shotgun."

"Have people tried?" I ask.

"Not people we would honor with a mention."

Angelica holds up her BlackBerry and sadly dangles it toward the mouth of the bag. Rhonda stops her and grabs the device. She flips it over and over in her hand as if examining the value in terms of weight and texture.

"It holds the record of my life, basically. Please be careful."

"Out here, the stars and desert solitude hold their own record of our existence. There is no need for gadgets."

"Why, Rhonda—you are poetic," I say sincerely.

Her gruffness returns and she points a crooked finger toward the long, narrow building a quarter of a mile away. "Head over to the stables and Deputy Delilah will fit you with a horse that suits your personality. If you got one," she says with an evil laugh. I look quickly at her mouth to see if she has all her teeth. Surprisingly so.

Melanie enthusiastically links arms with her mother, and Sadie follows behind them looking exhausted.

I come up beside my friend and adjust my attitude. "I've always wanted to do one of these adventure camps. We are all embarking on life changes, and this will be a great way to mark the wilderness of transition."

"You're being nice. This is a disaster. We could be eating watercress sandwiches or Chef Elliot's penne pasta with cilantro pesto sauce."

"That kind of talk won't help at all. Rhonda is right, in a way. We are pampered ninety-five percent of the time. To experience something else for a day is a gift."

"We can do anything for twenty-four hours. Right?" She brightens.

"That's the spirit. Now, you had best hide your cell phone in a better spot than your vest pocket. Rhonda will see that pronto."

"I have too many last-minute plans before the wedding."

"Totally understandable. But if you get caught, tell Rhonda I tried to convince you to turn it in."

Angelica and Caitlin walk behind us. Their silence is a gesture of goodwill. I can only imagine the thoughts going through Angelica's mind. We all stare into the back of Melanie's head and wonder what is in there, exactly.

Sadie's mother, Francine, is the first to get on a horse. She is nervous and keeps laughing, which in turn agitates her horse, Radar. Apparently all the horses are named after *M*A*S*H* characters. Rhonda's claim to fame is that she was an animal trainer for the popular show set during the Korean war.

Angelica makes yet another comment, another mistake. "Did they even have animals on that show?"

Rhonda glowers, but says nothing. Her next move is to assign to Angelica the horse Klinger, who wears a bonnet and walks as if he wears stilettos.

Our horses do not care that most of us have never ridden before. They know the meandering, short path to the small rodeo corral by heart and hoof. One at a time we are asked to follow Rhonda into the wooden circle, where we wait atop our horses for Delilah to release a calf from the opposite half of the perimeter. One at a time we fall off our horses in an attempt to pin that calf. I suspected our calf was as used to this drill as our horses, so our repeated failed attempts didn't seem to faze him at all. In fact, I think he proudly snorted in our general direction.

I consider myself quite mentally slow as it took until my second visit to the corral to even question this masochistic exercise. Bachelorette parties are supposed to be fun, sassy, and a chance to show off a daring new haircut, pair of shoes, or fashion piece. Caitlin had picked out a top for me to wear for the anticipated occasion—a four tiered, baby blue camisole trimmed with silver metallic sequins. So as I face the nostrils of the calf for the second time, I am thinking about the shimmery fashion statement and also wondering how many reported cases of whiplash show up in the files of the Happy Camper police record.

Rodeo Rhonda keeps shouting "yee-haw" as a source of inspiration. We all want her to be quiet. There is only one moment when her enthusiasm seems to lift our spirits—it is of course, when she announces we have answered the call of the wild and can now return to camp.

As we make our return ride, sore and worn out, Melanie asks if we can sing trail songs. Sadie turns to me and pretends to cry in anguish.

Delilah is, it turns out, quite the ukulele player and is pleased as punch to whip it out and lead us in several rounds of camp songs. The lyrics to somewhat familiar tunes have been slightly altered.

By the time we have finished singing *At Home Without a Range*, my behind is numb. I'm tired of staring at Sadie's back, and I cannot stop thinking about Beau. Lyle hadn't completely finished the trick because Beau was backstage after the show was over. He was jazzed, he said. And when I didn't respond in kind, he defined that term. *Pumped. Excited. Hyped. Wired.*

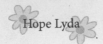

I tried to reroute the walking thesaurus by bringing up past words like space, argument, silence, confusion. But Beau was too jazzed to focus on the past. He practically spit the word "past," as if it were detestable and useless. We left the theater separately with plans to meet up after the bachelorette party.

"I'm so glad we did this. It felt like old times," he had said sincerely.

I smiled because it was all I could muster without tears.

Now on a horse named Hawkeye, the tears start to come. I'm thankful it is dusk.

Rhonda stops her lead creature, Hotlips, and about-faces so that we can see her stern expression. "Francine and Angelica will be our chuck wagon hosts. We know you all are probably pretty tired about now. That calf roping exercise was a bit more difficult than usual. Delilah has never forgotten the actual ropes in our twenty years here. So that was a hoot to watch. You all deserve some fine cuisine. Best in adventure camping."

I find myself salivating at the thought of food. Even settling down for a tin full of chicken potpie would suffice at this point.

"Mari and Melanie, get busy with the bunks. After the meal, y'all will be itching to sleep."

"Please don't use *itching* and *sleep* in the same sentence," Angelica whines.

"Little Miss Fancy Jodhpurs just got herself a stint at KP. Anyone want to help her?"

Sadie raises her hand immediately. "It's the least I can do," she mutters.

Francine and Angelica leave with Delilah to cook up some grub and Melanie and I make our way to the cabin. It isn't difficult; there is a beautiful full moon. The landscape is so surreal in the night light, it has the look of a movie set—a movie about aliens.

Melanie walks at a brisk pace ahead of me. She has the manner of Sadie, and the figure, but not the poise. She clumps along among the sagebrush. We get right to work, each taking a task on the faded list nailed to the wooden door.

"I've enjoyed this," I say to break the silence.

She stops sweeping and looks up through her long, thick hair. "Really?"

"At first, I wasn't too sure. And I didn't know we'd be here overnight. But once we headed out on the horses, I thought it was very exhilarating."

"Me too!" She says happily.

"Sadie has your smile." I offer her the primary status of smile-holder, and she accepts this warmly.

"And our voices sound the same."

I pause and nod slowly. "I do hear the same tone."

She keeps sweeping, and I make up another bunk.

"Mom's kinda worried about the wedding. It's going to be so fancy. That's why she—we, really—wanted to do this kind of party. To feel more…" she stops, seemingly afraid she has divulged too much about her insecurities.

"Comfortable?"

She laughs. "Yes! But the funny thing is, we are hardly outdoors people. I don't know what we were thinking."

"This was good for all of us. It sort of, I don't know—evens the playing field. Just to spend time with Angelica without her dang cell phone was a huge treat."

She smiles again, and I notice that her bottom teeth are crooked. She covers her mouth with a cupped hand and laughs. Then, as fast as the laughter began, she stops cold. "I don't think Sadie sees it as a good experience."

I wave a "get outta here" wave. "This just isn't Sadie's element. Except, did you notice she was writing down the different plants she saw during the road? I think she was inspired by this place."

"Really? I hope so. I'd hate for her to be mad at me. She is so darn perfect, you know?"

"I do know. It is hard to relate to sometimes."

Melanie nods and takes a seat on a lower unmade bunk bed. "It's why I went with those fancy dresses for us. I knew that I couldn't possibly choose something classy like Sadie would. But she asked me to make this one choice for her big day, so I did. Do you like them?"

I fluff a pillow in front of my face to hide my initial expression. "We think they are the most colorful, stylish dresses we've ever seen."

"That's what I thought too! When I touched the silky fabric, all I could think was that Sadie deserves dresses this nice for her wedding. They were really expensive, ya know." Melanie traces a knot in the wood above her.

"Our salesperson in Tucson told us how rare a find they were. You chose something that is one of a kind. Just like Sadie."

Her eyes get misty. "That's right."

From outside we hear Rhonda hollering, "Chow, ladies."

"You heard the woman. It's time for chow."

Melanie reaches for my arm on the way out. "Do you honestly think Sadie will forgive me for today?"

"I'll go one better. I think she will thank you for today."

Melanie sighs with relief, and I send up a prayer. We head to the campfire together, where we are greeted by the aroma of rosemary and basil.

Caitlin is setting a rustic table with colorful Fiestaware and linen napkins. Rhonda helps Francine and Angelica carry platters of roasted chicken, red potatoes, pepper cornbread, and spinach salad. Delilah strums her ukulele as we sit down to a table decorated with votives in crystal holders and small bunches of rosemary and lavender.

"Every time a group of women comes through the Happy Campers experience, we believe it is special. But when one of the women is about to embark on the journey of marriage, we consider it a privilege to join in the celebration. We'll begin our feast with a prayer. Delilah."

Goodness, Rhonda and her sidekick are full of surprises.

Our musician stops playing and stands up. "Let's join hands," she says, clearing her throat. "Dear Creator, we thank you for the opportunity to enjoy the work of your hands today. We join in this time of fellowship with hearts and lives open to the wonders you have in store for each of us. We are grateful for the bounty of your grace. Amen."

"Amen."

We all look around at one another. Sadie is glowing. We all are. Each of us, in this moment, knows full well how lucky we are to be here—together.

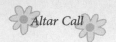

We hold hands for a few seconds longer until Angelica's stomach growls and we all laugh.

The sacredness of the evening, of the day, is not lost in our laughter—it is made even more real. I look around at my friends. Caitlin was so right. We are starting new lives. This day has been in honor of Sadie's beginning, but it is also the end of an era for all of us.

Sadie sips from a goblet filled with sparkling cider and then catches my eye. We are thinking the same thing. She raises her glass. "A toast…to family, friends, and to a perfect day."

"Here, here."

Clink. Clink.

As I raise my glass to meet Melanie's, I wink at her. She winks back and turns to look at Sadie. I was wrong—there is not a bit of jealousy in her gaze. In Melanie's eyes, there is only admiration for her little sister.

That night I don't dream about chasing after Beau, and I don't dream about falling off of horses as Rhonda warns us most guests do. I dream that I am surrounded by a white cloud, and I am happy. I'm running as if my lungs and legs are used to the pace. I don't know what I am running after, but I know it is something important.

All Making Sense

Help, I've fallen and I can't get up," Chet calls to me jokingly as my saddle sore body creeps past him.

"Want to borrow my walker?" Gracie taunts when I walk by her room on the Canyon View wing.

"That's enough out of you two. Chet, I'll tell Wanda you removed numbers from the Bingo game. And Gracie, don't forget I know you rigged your birthday round of pinochle."

Sadly, I don't have blackmail material on all the residents who choose to toss cheap jokes at me during my crawl to Rose's room. Willis decides to race me and nearly wins, except his cane gets caught on the doorjamb. And we had bet Oreos, so I show no mercy.

My knock on Rose's door is unnecessary. She is standing on the other side listening for my arrival. The door swings open, and she gives me the once over before quickly hugging me in a businesslike manner. I reach to give her another warm embrace, which she endures for a few seconds before pulling back to adjust her hair—a self-conscious, unnecessary response because

her hair is perfectly pulled back into a bun with her trademark ornate hair combs creating a jeweled halo.

"Shall we walk to the cafeteria?" I ask, holding my hand out to her.

She waves away the help. "I'd prefer to stay in today. The holiday choir is using the cafeteria for their rehearsals and it is painful."

"Now, Rose."

"I meant excruciating."

"Let's sit at your table then. Do you have the fund-raiser checklist handy?"

"I do. And you will be quite pleased to see that many of the items are crossed off as of yesterday."

"You've all been working so hard. I appreciate that you are taking charge of this. I know my absence has been difficult on the committees around here, but I'll make up for it in the New Year, I promise."

She pulls her head back, her chin toward her throat. It is the look she gives the Scrabble team members when they put down a fake word to gain extra points.

"What?" I ask, awaiting her rebuke in some form. Rose, most of all, will make me pay for my absence in the months to come.

"I suppose it depends on what Paige allows?" Now her eyes examine my face as I give her a look of confusion.

"Paige?" I'm surprised that the residents even know about Paige. Lysa reported to me that she pretty much flits in and out on weekends and has Beau do all the interviews with the residents if they need more data clarification. Lysa sensed Paige preferred the hands-off approach when it came to other humans.

"You don't know what they are up to, do you? Just as I suspected."

"Who, Rose?" I watch her face now, looking for the furrowed brow and the wandering gaze to signal her dementia is taking over.

Her forehead and eyes are perfectly clear as she speaks. "Bonnie and Clyde." Her slender hand reaches up to the intercom, and she presses the button marked "Desk."

Lysa's voice answers. "Ready?"

"Ready," Rose responds.

I ask several logical questions. "Who are Bonnie and Clyde? Do you know what year this is? Who is the president?" to which Rose responds with the extension of her hands to the side, palms down—an umpire calling "Safe!"

Lysa taps on the door within seconds, and then she enters with Sonya on her heels. They tiptoe in as if fulfilling a clandestine operation. Lysa retrieves the manila folder protruding from the neckline of her smock.

"Don't tell me we are changing the color theme of the fund-raiser?" I say with mock horror.

Lysa pretends she will knock me on the head with the folder, but she stops midway and her own look becomes seriously serious. "Mari, we don't have great news."

"The ice sculpture of the manger scene won't fit on the holiday fair stage?"

"You know the project Beau and Paige submitted?"

I didn't know he had finished, but I keep this to myself to protect him and to avoid giving away the fact that Beau has not shared anything real with me in weeks.

She shakes her head apologetically. "I'm sorry, of course you know about the project. Well, I saw a copy of the final report. Beau and Paige had printed it out the night before he left to visit you in Washington. This surprised me because Beau had been asking me to stay late to help anytime he needed to print or merge files or gather data. So I knew he didn't want me to read it."

"And?"

"When he left the next day for the airport, I pulled up the recently printed documents," she confesses, "and I read his report. *Their* report. It has both their names on it."

"Lysa, I knew they were submitting this as a team," I say, pointing to the folder. "Is that what you are worried about?"

"This team report could jeopardize your job," she blurts.

"How could stating the case for effective recreational therapy hurt the person providing that service?" I drum my fingers on the table, passing time until everyone's paranoia comes into check.

Lysa looks forlornly at Sonya, who eyes her back with encouragement. Lysa confronts me. "Their findings, using your data, show that it is more cost-effective to have contracted recreational providers working with several facilities rather than having someone full-time on staff."

"I don't buy it. I make a pittance. Golden Horizons and any other facility with a recreation director still on board gets more than triple their money's worth." My defensiveness takes on a French accent in my head. I poo-poo *l'evidence*.

"Nevertheless, it would cost facilities one-third of your pittance to provide more programming for several units. Or so this says." She points to the incriminating section of the report.

"Mari, what we cannot be sure of is whether Beau would act on these findings. We have to keep in mind that he was creating this report in order to get more grant funding to *help* the programs here. Maybe he is giving the state committee what they want to hear but does not plan to follow through with it at Golden Horizons."

She is reluctant to bad-mouth the best boss we have ever had.

"But…but Beau believes in the work I do. He practically screamed how much he believes in what I do when he visited…" I stop cold and my mouth goes dry.

"What?"

"He stated the case for my value, but then he immediately started talking about Majestic Vista. He told me that you, Sonya, mentioned that the recreation director position was open again."

Sonya adjusts her cross necklace and sits down on Rose's bed. "I never brought it up. I didn't even know it was a possibility. Then, a couple weeks ago I led a stretch class at Majestic, and Lionel mentioned how great it will be to have you back. When I looked surprised, he explained that Beau had told him in confidence that you wanted to return. He asked that I keep this news a secret until you chose to announce it officially."

"And she did," Lysa adds. "But then I showed her the report a few days ago. I didn't trust my interpretation of the situation or of their thesis."

"When I read it, Mari, the possibility that Beau was planning all this without your consent made more sense to me than the idea of you voluntarily leaving," Sonya says passionately, her blond hair falling forward and obscuring her cheek.

My mouth falls open and my mind is closing in on the reality. "During our fight at the zoo, I couldn't understand why he'd think I'd give up Golden Horizons. But he never believed I'd want to—he knew I'd *have* to."

Rose sighs. "Maybe you should have stayed with the *National Geographic* photographer."

"You dated a photographer?" Lysa inquires.

"It's a long story," I answer.

"What are you going to do?" Rose brings us back to the grave matter at hand.

My hands are shaking, but my mind seems quite calm in the midst of the storm. "I'm going to wait for him to do the right thing."

Rehearsal

I need to go over my lines one more time," Caitlin demands, anxious and sweaty.

"Why did you save this for the last minute? I cannot believe you have not told your parents. Do you want to call ahead? Because we could do that and then they could just stand out in the circular drive with the valet guy and you could roll down your window and we could holler something like 'Caitlin's moving to New York and you can't stop her.' Then I'll hit the gas before they can respond."

"Okay. I'm a coward. I could use a little support, you know."

"I'm here, aren't I? We have the wedding rehearsal in an hour, but instead of getting ready or relaxing before the busy night, I'm driving you to your parents' house. Which brings up another question. Why *am* I driving?"

"I got a new old car with the advance from Isabel. A new car would be a dead giveaway."

"That'd be even faster than my idea."

"I'm beginning to think a taxi would have been a good idea." She frowns and juts her lower lip out.

287

"Ah, my point is made. Oh, here we are."

Caitlin looks at me pleadingly before we knock on the door and greet Margaret the maid. "Support."

"I'll say only fabulous things about New York," I vow.

She relaxes slightly, but her jaw is still tense. I'm glad to note that she is wearing her hair in an elegant style, straight with a slight curl at the ends.

Her mother seems to approve as well. "Caitlin, darling. You look beautiful. Hello, Mari. So good of you to join us for dinner."

"Not dinner, Mom. We have to leave for Sadie's rehearsal."

"Yes, of course. We are looking forward to the wedding day after tomorrow. That's strange." She pauses to consider the timeline. "Most weddings are the day following a rehearsal. Is this a new thing?"

I step in to move things along. "Thursday was the only night they could get the church for the rehearsal, and Saturday was the only night they could get the Mesa for their reception. It worked out with everyone in the wedding party to be here the full three days, so tonight it is."

Caitlin's mother nods in full agreement. "The Mesa is worth a little inconvenience. Fabulous chef and the setting is glorious." Her thoughts seem to wander to a previous event and then she resurfaces abruptly. "If you don't have long, what is it you needed that couldn't wait? Your father and I will be at the wedding."

"I know. That's why this couldn't wait."

A flash of worry crosses her mother's face, but it is replaced by the urge to be hospitable. "Girls, come this way. Margaret, could you get these ladies some cookies and sodas with lime?"

We follow Mrs. Ramirez to the living room. Caitlin checks her watch and gives me a hurry-up look, as if I can control *her* mother. I decide to take this as my permission to really step up this conversation.

"Mrs. Ramirez, we are here because Caitlin has big news. It's a bit of a surprise to all of us, but we couldn't be more excited."

Caitlin takes her cue. "A total surprise, but it couldn't be a better move."

"Move?" Mrs. Ramirez raises her eyebrows and touches her fingers to her pearls.

"New York. I got a great job…"

"Career opportunity, really," I interject.

"Yes! And I leave right after Sadie's wedding. Fast, so fast."

From where we sit on the low chaise lounge, we watch Caitlin's mom stand up and begin pacing. Back and forth. Back and forth.

"Mom?" Caitlin says barely audibly.

"You know how we feel about New York, Caitlin."

"Mom, I'll be working with a woman who designs and buys and sells fashions."

"You are moving across the country to go into retail? I'm getting your father."

We are left alone with our nervous energy, a plate of sugar cookies, and two sodas with lime.

"This isn't going well at all."

"Did you expect her to react any other way?"

"No."

"Then it is going as expected. That's a plus." I try out optimism for the sake of my friend's morale. It works momentarily; Caitlin reaches for a sugar cookie and takes a nibble.

Mrs. Ramirez enters the room with her husband. She looks disappointed and he looks weary. "Caitlin," he says, "is this something you have given careful consideration?"

"Ricardo." Mrs. Ramirez expresses her unhappiness with his line of questioning.

"Yes, Dad. I've been researching ideas for months. Ask Mari. She went to the library with me every weekend."

"Mari, what do you think?" Mr. Ramirez says with his arms folded across his chest. A psychological power move, no doubt.

I look at the grandfather clock behind him. We have thirty minutes. I talk fast. "It's solid. Isabel, the woman with the established business, has an excellent reputation in New York. Her roster of vintage fashion clients includes names that we are not even allowed to mention because they are women who had her sign privacy agreements. Politicians, artists, celebrities, and the wealthiest women in the country." I pause to round up more material.

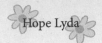

"Look at this great blouse Caitlin chose for me. The girl can do this job." I point to the sheer, flowing layers and the delicate sequins.

This is not received as a selling point. Caitlin's parents politely look away and change the subject.

"Politicians. My, that is exciting," Mrs. Ramirez offers along with the plate of sugar cookies.

"Including a few former first ladies," I say, jumping back on their preferred train of thought.

They nod to one another. Mrs. Ramirez then sits down across from Caitlin, her hand still to her pearls. "Is there health insurance?"

Caitlin nods and smiles nervously.

"And tell her about the classes," I prompt.

"Isabel will pay for me to attend a fashion institute in the city—up to three classes a semester. That way I can learn more about the creative and business side of the industry while putting it into practice each day."

"What is your title?"

"Assistant buyer."

Mrs. Ramirez leans forward and places her hands on her knees while staying seated. "Well, we knew you would leave eventually. It was always in you to spread your wings and fly. This is too fast for me…"

"But…" Caitlin protests.

Her mom holds up her hand to stop her. "However, Caitlin, I can see it is a good way for you to explore what you love. We've always wanted you to commit to something."

"I'm shocked. I've felt…."

I have my arm stretched out on the couch. It is near her hair, so I yank on it.

"Thanks Mom, Dad." Caitlin jumps up to hug them both, and they pat down her sleek hair with tears in their eyes.

This is a Hallmark moment, which needs to be interrupted. Sadie is a taskmaster and we are going to be late.

"Gosh, look at the time. I guess we will see you at the wedding—day

after tomorrow," I say while standing and starting to walk the gauntlet back to the huge front door.

Margaret wraps up a couple cookies for us to take with us for our long ten-minute drive to the church, and we are off.

Caitlin is stunned that there was not a fight for me to break up or a fire to put out. "What just happened?"

"I think that is called support. That thing that just happened…"

"Unbelievable. I've been so worried about this. I've fretted for months. I broke out in hives both the times I rehearsed talking to them. I'm confused."

"Maybe they understand you more than you give them credit for."

"If I had known they'd be so accepting, I would have thrown in the fact that I'm engaged." Caitlin reaches for a cookie in the linen cloth and munches away. I stop the car immediately. The light is still yards away. "What!"

She looks over at me innocently. "I told you that Jim asked me."

"And that you had answered *noooo*."

She slaps her knee and licks her lips. "I am so forgetful lately. I did say no. Then we talked, you and I, and I saw that nobody would judge me if I said yes. So when he said he'd wait for me, I told him I would be engaged to be engaged."

"Like a promise ring?" I say a bit mockingly. Right now I don't have a lot of faith in such romantic notions.

"Without the ring. He wants me to have this opportunity and then we'll see. But we are not breaking up. He's even driving out with me and flying back. Isn't that sweet?"

"What is it about these men willing to wait? It is some sort of phenomena around here. Peyton, Jim…"

"Beau has waited for you."

"Beau has gone on with his life in many ways. You wouldn't believe how much he has left me out of the loop. Do you know that I probably won't have a job after this year, thanks to patient Beau?"

A guy in a sports car zooms past us and honks.

Caitlin puts her cookie down and points to the road. "Keep driving and keep talking."

"Before I left for Washington he was so preoccupied with this big project, and all along I kept thinking it was for a good cause and worth the sacrifice. But Beau is willing to sacrifice a lot more than I am."

"Like what?"

"Like me, apparently."

I reveal the recent fiasco against my better judgment. Speaking it makes it more true. And spreading words that tarnish Beau's reputation feels, at first, like a betrayal. But as the words come out, and I start shaping a perspective of the situation, I feel better.

Caitlin is shocked about Beau's initial report. "He'll fix it. He has to," she says with her hands raised in little fists.

"I cannot pin the guy down for a conversation. My lips are moving, but he isn't hearing me. Meanwhile, he likes the sound of his own voice—he jabbers on and on without mentioning the fight. Or the report, obviously."

"Which means he is sorry."

"I guessed denial."

"The old market is up ahead," Caitlin says full of nostalgia. "Do you know what you need?"

I shake my head in response because I'm finding it harder to force sound from my constricted throat.

"You need a Coke in one of those old-fashioned bottles and some peanuts." Caitlin points insistently at the whitewashed market we are approaching on the right.

"We mustn't be late," I say, sounding like a schoolmarm.

"Yeah. They will probably cancel the entire wedding. Why not look at it as if we are right on time to get that Coke. Is there a better way to mark our last week together?" Caitlin goads, referring to the year after we graduated when a day of job hunting would leave us both tired, depressed, and in need of a drive out of town. We never got further than the Time Stop Market.

I hit the brakes and the reality of this week hits me—it is more than beginnings and endings. Just like that unbearable and exciting year of job hunting, this is a time to harvest memories and sow dreams. Suddenly I have a thirst that can only be quenched by an icy Coke and a hunger that can only be satiated by salty peanuts.

There is comfort in this market with its huge Coke bottle caps on the walls and slatted wood flooring. It smells of popcorn and cigarettes, which happen to be the diet choices of the pointy-chinned woman who runs the register at all hours.

We walk over to the cooler and pass by some men wearing cowboy hats and boots who are tossing cards into a Yuban coffee tin. The youngest of the males, a spry seventy-ish gentleman, stands politely as we make our return trek to the counter with our bottles of cola and bags of peanuts.

Pointy-chin pops the top of our sodas and hands them back to us. The bottle is cool in my palm. I take a large swig as the screen door opens and a couple of college-aged guys enter. The second holds the door for us and we nod without making eye contact.

"Do you do the Macarena?" He says looking at my shirt.

I start laughing and Caitlin nearly loses Coke out her nose. I tell her that she is not to choose a shirt for me ever again.

My friend checks her normal, pink cotton wrap shirt for soda stains as she gets back into the passenger seat of my car. I sense her lightness of mood. Moments before, mine had felt heavy, dark, and determined to remain there. But the burn of the pop in my mouth and the rebelliousness of arriving fashionably late to the rehearsal in my Macarena shirt is inspiring.

"This actually helped," I say to my friend, who is pushing the peanuts into her bottle one by one.

"Told ya," she says, always the optimist. I will miss her.

"Maybe I will confront Beau tonight. Look how smoothly the talk with your parents went. I could be getting all worked up for nothing."

"Beau is charming, generous, and great. And he loves you."

"You see how easy it is to oversell the guy?" We pull into the parking lot just as Beau is heading in to the church. I park the car and watch him. "He is all those wonderful characteristics. Am I crazy to focus on this one minor incident?"

"I don't think being fired by your boyfriend is that minor."

"He hasn't fired me." I roll my eyes.

"He hasn't protected you, either."

This sinks in.

We walk into the old, mission-style church. A violinist is warming up, Sadie and Carson are practicing their big kiss at the altar while the minister discusses the service with the parents. The pianist practices the wedding march. Caitlin grabs my arm and we walk, like a couple, down the aisle.

Everyone notices and starts laughing.

Carson points to us. "Mari should be practicing for the real thing."

Sadie elbows him in the side but keeps her smile intact.

We start to do the Macarena the rest of the way. My shirt shimmies and sparkles. The organist joins in with the song. Sadie and Carson start clapping while Angelica "whoop, whoops" a few times.

I turn to see Beau's expression—he is speaking into his cell phone and covering the other ear with his free hand.

"I can't hear myself talk," Beau barks to a group of surprised friends.

Caitlin looks at me, and Beau looks for the nearest exit.

Up Loading

I always thought you were a minimalist, Caitlin." Angelica grunts as she pushes another vintage suitcase into the back of Caitlin's car. Our goal had been to complete this task by sundown. It is now ten o'clock, and we are all a bit loopy.

"Thank goodness we are wearing sweats. I will just roll into bed when we finally finish," I say.

"Did you forget? You don't have a bed tonight. I took everything that wouldn't fit into my car and donated it to the women's downtown mission. But we have inflatable mattresses, thanks to Sadie." Caitlin goes over to her tall friend and gives her a squeeze. "Sadie, it means so much to me that you are here, the night before your wedding, helping me load my car. What bride would do this?"

"One afraid to let go of her old life," Sadie confesses. "Besides, I get to sleep in tomorrow. My mom and sister are going for pedicures, courtesy of Carson, my angel, and I don't have to be anywhere until noon."

"I miss my What Would Old Mari Do bracelet that Caitlin made me." I lament. "I think I need it."

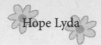

"Did you flush it?" Angelica asks as if this is a normal assumption.

"No, I lost it somewhere. The last I remember seeing it was on my way to Washington that first trip. I wore it with the charm bracelet you all got me." I set down a black hatbox and red lines appear where the ribbon handles had dug into my hand. "What on earth is in this?"

Caitlin glances over at my current burden. "It's my belt buckle collection."

"But of course," Sadie says, laughing.

"Could this really be the last piece of luggage?" Angelica comes out of Caitlin's apartment holding up a white leather makeup case.

"It is, but I need that tomorrow for the wedding."

"Wait? The last piece of luggage? Don't tell me we packed my bag in all this mess!" I say.

"Hey. Important life belongings, please," Caitlin says proudly.

"Is it the one with red ribbon tied to the handle?" Angelica asks, looking back into the empty apartment.

"Yes! Hallelujah. It's still in there?"

She turns back and deadpans, "No. I think I saw you pack it an hour ago. So it should be somewhere in the middle."

"Perfect. There's another hour," I mutter.

"Maybe you subliminally want to go with me," Caitlin says gleefully.

"The word is subconsciously," Sadie corrects gently, and then she claps her hands with a burst of energy. "You all retrieve Mari's suitcase, and I will get the bag of goodies out of my car."

"Goody, we get goodies," Angelica sings.

Suddenly visions of strange, Asian purses dance through my head. I had completely forgotten about our bridesmaid gifts. "Be kind," I whisper to Angelica while Sadie rummages in her trunk several yards away.

"What?"

"When you see the goodies, just remember that our friend has had a lot of stress and that she hasn't made consistent fashion selections during this process."

"Oh, great," Angelica says, crossing her jean-clad legs and sitting down on the median. "I'm not that good at feigning pleasure when I am tired."

I stare at her in unbelief. "I've never seen you feign pleasure."

"Remember that orange angled cowl-neck sweater you got me for my twenty-fourth birthday? That expression I gave you when I held it up to my face? That was feigned pleasure."

"I'll have you know those were incredibly in at the time. And the sales woman said orange would go with your coloring perfectly. It was *the* fall fashion color."

"Well, it was the color of baby food. I don't wear baby food."

Sadie comes over carrying a large shopping bag and a smaller grocery sack.

"First, I have your bridesmaid presents. Mari saw these, but hopefully she didn't give away the secret," Sadie says, grinning, and I cannot help but smile with her and not at her. She is truly happy.

"Bring it on," Angelica says, closing her eyes and opening her palms.

Sadie apparently writes this off as normal Angelica behavior and continues smiling as she reaches into the bag and pulls out the wrapped packages and gently places them one by one into our hands. We reverently peel back the red tissue paper. I move extra slow so that I am not the first one to react.

"I *love* this!" Caitlin screams and hugs Sadie with the force of five little waifs.

Angelica looks to me as if to gain strength and inspiration and then she too goes to hug Sadie. I add, "It is even prettier than I remember," and wrap my arms around my best friends.

We group hug as long as Angelica can handle it, which is all of ten seconds, and then Sadie reaches into her grocery sack. She pulls out a bottle of expensive champagne and four champagne glasses. "This is our last night together as friends who live in the same town."

"And as all single women," I say.

"I'll let the departing dame serve us." Sadie hands the bottle over to Caitlin, who sets her purse down protectively to avoid any spillage.

Pop.

Angelica turns to me and whispers, "She gave us the gifts in the wrong order. The champagne would have helped the whole feigned pleasure thing."

Instead of hitting her in the shoulder as I normally would, I link my arm through hers and hold my friend close. She smiles and lets me.

"To friends," Sadie says holding up her glass.

"To friends," we echo.

The pace of the night has shifted from hurried to serene. I don't want to blink and miss a moment of this. I know that I might never feel the melancholy of blessing and sadness as I do right now, in the middle of a parking lot, standing hip to hip in a circle with the most important women in my life...

...saying goodbye.

Wedding Belles

Is this strange or what?" Caitlin asks, spinning around in her empty living room. My suitcase, Elmo's carrier, and Caitlin's makeup bag line the space that was once occupied by a retro metal diner table.

"Freedom," I say, giving the emptiness a spin.

"What?"

"It feels like freedom to me."

She puts her hands on slender hips and hikes up her polka-dotted silk pajama bottoms. "Could it really be this easy?"

"To move?" I pick up Elmo and smell his fur. He is my living security blanket.

"To change everything. My work, my address, my confidence, my parents, for goodness' sake."

Her optimism is catching. Something fuels the blood in my veins, and I am excited, as if my life is on the cusp of change as well. "Don't forget, we have been praying about your career for over a year. There was a lot of heart labor and sweat equity put into this decision." I resist telling her I have recorded more than a hundred library hours in my day planner.

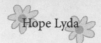

"The prayers I won't forget," she spins twice more. "I hope I have this much faith in my future when I get to New York." Caitlin reaches for the wall to steady herself.

"We need faith in the future God has for us," I say for my benefit more than hers.

"You're right." She sits down where her beanbags used to be. "After all this, I still want to think I'm in control. Now, that is baggage I wouldn't mind leaving behind."

"I do it too. I invest in false securities and then wonder why I am unhappy."

"Like your life makeover last year."

"Exactly. I had reasonable inspiration but not the right motivation. Change can be so therapeutic, but it should move you forward, not just keep you tied to the same old lies."

Caitlin thinks about this for a moment and then falls backward, as if the weight of reflection is too much for her. She stomps her feet and yells. "Sadie is stinkin' getting married today!"

"I hope you aren't planning to provide the toast this evening."

"What time is it?" she asks without changing position.

I spin my Swatch to the top of my wrist. "It is eleven o'clock."

She stomps her feet again. "Sadie is stinkin' getting married in eight hours!"

"Again with the sweet talk."

Caitlin sits upright and stares at me with serious eyes. "My change is easier than your change."

"What do you mean?" I ask, not really wanting to hear her answer.

She looks down at her toes and her ponytail bobs atop her head. She says softly, "I didn't want to think something was wrong—between you and Beau—because it would have meant not believing in the perfect relationship." She stops and looks at the coved ceiling. "Not believing in what I hoped would happen to me."

"I never asked to be the poster girl for the single women in my life. Certainly Sadie has taken care of that."

"But we don't all relate to Sadie. She seems too perfect, whereas you are…"

"This conversation isn't helping my morale, in case that was your objective."

"You are real, Mari. And we were so happy for you and Beau."

"And now that things are not going so well?" I say this with more emotion than I intend.

"We want the best *for* you. And—I hope I'm not overstepping my bounds here—but I don't know that Beau is it. You don't need my two-bits of wisdom, but if you are needing someone in your corner, I'm here for you."

"For another day, anyway."

She gives me a hug

"Look at us—a circus act." Angelica takes in the mirror's reflection of the three of us in our bridesmaid dresses.

"It's not so bad," I say, softening her comments while smoothing out what I think is a wrinkle, but turns out to be a contrasting stripe of gray.

"I'm telling you, we could take this on the road and make good money."

The door to the church's nursery opens up, and Melanie bounds in with her matching disaster. She joins us in our lineup.

I concede. "Okay, now maybe we could travel."

"What are you girls talking about? Isn't this fun? I've always wanted to wear a fancy dress and be the belle of the ball." Melanie curtseys.

I adjust my bangs. "Technically, that would be Sadie's role. Today, anyway."

She laughs and spreads a thin layer of clear gloss on her lips while crouching close to the mirror.

"I like your hairdo, Caitlin," Melanie says enthusiastically.

Caitlin touches the edges of her hair proudly. "It's my bed-head design number twenty-one," she says, smiling shyly. "I woke up with this incredible flip in my normally subtle front curl, so I had to add another hairdo to the list."

Melanie is baffled but still smiles with admiration.

"See?" Caitlin removes the rhinestone clip from atop her head.

"Holy cowlick, bridesmaid!" I say. The others nod, too afraid to name the peaked wall of hair above Caitlin's small head.

Satisfied that her point has been made, Caitlin secures the hair back in place.

"Showtime, ladies." Sadie enters the room, and for the first time we see the bridal beauty in all her splendor.

"Ooh!" We say in unison.

Sadie is breathtaking. Bare shoulders lead to a close-fitting bodice vertically lined with white silk ribbon which flow into a full silk skirt and a long train.

"I wanted the maker of my fabulous veil to do the honors." She holds up the beautiful head piece and layers of tulle to Caitlin. The two of them spend a few private moments in front of the mirror while the rest of us stand in the background pointing out what we like best about Sadie's dress.

A knock on the door alerts us to Kevin Milano's entrance. The groom cannot see Sadie, but the expensive photographer can. He snaps a few candid shots of Sadie and Caitlin and then asks us all to follow him to the church courtyard.

We are all giggling as though this was our first and not our umpteenth round of being a bridesmaid. I become emotional seeing Sadie walk beside the fountain in her dress. Her skin glows, her eyes sparkle, and she looks like the most radiant bride ever. Kevin thinks so too. He is taking countless shots of her as she sits near the water, runs her fingers through the spray, and laughs at our random comments and advice.

"When you walk down the aisle, don't feel obligated to make eye contact with the guests," Angelica says. "It just slows you down, and you always leave out someone important."

"Keep the dangling strands on the right of your head brushed back, or your eyes will be hidden in the photos of you two lighting the unity candle." Caitlin preserves her status as the hair princess.

Sadie starts to look anxious, as if the details are becoming over-whelming.

"When Carson leans in to kiss you, tilt your head up. The last wedding I went to, the bride tilted down and the groom got her nose," Angelica adds.

"Don't tear the tags off of your mattress!" I say with conviction. Everyone turns to look at me and I shrug. I know I have nothing to offer Sadie in this moment except community and comic relief when she needs it.

Aisle Hope

You are in fine form," I say to Angelica, who is tap-dancing in the church foyer while we wait for the processional music to begin.

"Peyton will be here. I'm nervous, okay?" She bites her lip.

"Have you seen him?"

"No." She looks out over the crowd from the safety of a palm plant. "Yes. There he is. He's just sitting down next to Beau. He's standing next to some woman and...I don't believe it." Her face emerges from the plant pale and sweaty.

"What?" I hand her a tissue from a nearby box and motion for her to pat her face. I peer through the palm but can barely make out Peyton's head next to Beau. They are talking and laughing. "He looks good."

"So does the woman next to him." She starts gulping her breaths and bends over slightly to catch more oxygen. "I waited too long. What was I thinking, Mari? Why didn't you and everyone else slap me and ask what the heck I was doing? Why!" Angelica now grabs me by the sleeve.

I try to get a better view, but the woman is wearing a hat. "I don't think she is with him, Angelica. You are overreacting." But just as the assurance

leaves my lips, I see the hat turn, the pretty profile smile at Peyton, and Peyton lean in to nudge the pretty smiling profile.

Caitlin approaches us from the direction of the bathroom. Her hair clip had slipped and the wall of hair had returned. Now she has all of her hair secured in an elegant chignon.

"Can you see Carson?" Caitlin asks, peeking through the crack between the door and the wall.

Angelica does not address the question but continues her panicked ranting, "She grabbed his arm when she turned the corner to sit down. That's an affectionate gesture. I'm an idiot. I'm an idiot."

The music begins and I turn on my wailing friend. "You are not an idiot. You made a healthy choice for yourself instead of doing what everyone else thought was the thing to do. We should all be so smart."

I release my hold on her wrist and realize I am lecturing both of us.

"What?" Caitlin is scanning the room for an obvious disaster and sees nothing.

"Are you ready, girls?" Sadie comes up behind us in the hallway. The addition of beautiful diamond earrings has done the impossible—made her look more breathtaking. She notices my look. "These are the ones from Carson. Aren't they perfect? Isn't this all amazing?"

There is no need to answer her; the evening is undoubtedly perfect. I feel a bit sad for Sadie that we are her opening act down the aisle with Angelica one shallow breath away from a panic attack, but it is time.

Harry and some little girl, who is a distant cousin, start off with the help of the wedding coordinator. She claps her hands lightly to set their pace.

"Caitin, that's your cue." I usher her to stand between the opened sanctuary doors and she has a false start—her Japanese purse tassels get caught on the door handle. I unhook it and push her forward. She regains her balance quickly, but the wedding hostess gives me a dirty look.

Angelica freezes. Her eyes are as big as Ding Dongs, which remind me of my extreme hunger. "I cannot do this," she says with a tremble in her lower lip.

Sadie steps in between us and takes Angelica's hand. "Are you nervous, honey?"

I recognize the voice. It is the one Sadie used with Harry before she figured out he was reading Thoreau and Keats.

"I blew it. Peyton is out there with another woman. She is attractive and confident enough to wear a big hat in public. He deserves someone like that."

Sadie takes the tissue from her hand and uses it to wipe Angelica's nose. "Then let him see what he is missing." Sadie steps back and Melanie rushes up behind her to straighten the train.

I lean in to Angelica's ear as the music begins again for her entrance. "She might have the confidence to wear a big hat, but *you* have the style and panache to wear a psychedelic dress!"

Angelica nods, satisfied with this thought. The wedding hostess positions her toward the altar and gives her elbow a solid tap.

"You see," I say, "sometimes a little force is necessary." I wink. She does not smile but waves like a traffic controller. This is my cue to make up time in the procession by quickly following Melanie. I can hear her giggling nervously behind her bouquet of lilies.

I take my place on the top step and watch as Sadie makes her entrance. Everyone gasps with admiration while the bride elegantly saunters down the aisle on her uncle's arm. I look over at Carson, who is completely enraptured. He wipes his eyes quickly and scratches his cheek to cover his sentimentality.

Our friends are standing as a couple before us, reverently watching the minister and nodding to his words of commitment, covenant, and unconditional love. A soloist rings out a rendition of a song that makes me want to go pick out china patterns. I glance toward Beau, who is checking his BlackBerry, which I didn't even know he owned. But Peyton is looking straight at me. He shrugs toward Beau like "what can you do?" and then he raises his wrist, points just below it, and mouths something at me. I squint to show my confusion. He must think I am giving him a dirty look because he points to his girlfriend with the hat and shakes his head. I squint again—this time intending a dirty look and route my gaze to the nearly weds.

And then I get it.

The purses. Peyton was motioning to remind me about the message in Angelica's purse. I glance at Angelica, but there is no way to communicate with her now.

Sadie and Carson walk toward the unity candle. Like sunflowers trailing the sun, we bridesmaids delicately turn our faces and shift our bodies to follow our radiant friends.

The soloist returns for a song that involves wings and soaring. Whatever it is, I cannot follow because I'm staring at the intricate hem of Sadie's dress. Pearls are sewn into the swirls of silk trim. Sadie told me she envisioned this dress all of her life. I asked when she had this dream of yards of silk. It came to her mind shortly after she dreamed about the man she was to marry. So when she saw the dress in the magazine, and later the man across the room, she just knew.

I look across the room. Beau is keying in a message with his thumbs.

"And do you, Carson, take Sadie to be your lawfully wedded…"

I've never envisioned a dress.

"I do," he says sweetly.

I've never dreamed of a groom.

"And do you, Sadie, take Carson to be your lawfully wedded…"

Will I even know?

"I do," Sadie says with confidence and eloquence.

I'll hope so.

After we had regally made our way back down the aisle I whisper to Angelica, "Open your purse."

She slowly follows my strange instruction and her red eyes brighten and her posture completely changes. Angelica passes the note to me.

On the back of the receipt slip, clever, visionary Peyton had months before written "She's my sister. Now will you go out with me?"

The Elephant in the Room

Could you be any louder?" I ask of Angelica, who is munching on corn chips in my backseat. I have been assigned the role of designated driver from the church over to the Mesa restaurant. Nobody plans to drink, but everyone plans to eat.

A lot.

We have all been dieting for the big day and we are finally free. We are pathetic representations of all that is wrong with fashion magazines, peer pressure, and horizontal stripes.

"I'm calorie deprived. Eating with my mouth open allows me to more fully enjoy the flavors. The oxygen enhances the crunch."

"But if I strangle you, that oxygen effect will lessen," I say, looking at my rearview mirror. Angelica sticks out her tongue and Caitlin claps her hands. They both are seated in the backseat.

"What's with the *Driving Miss Daisy* reenactment?"

"We decided that two women dressed in identical, striped dresses sitting up front is more of a road hazard than two women dressed in identical…"

I hold up my hand. "Got it."

"I'll bet Sadie and Carson will take the long way to the Mesa so they can take in the romantic view of the river. Do you think we will have to wait to eat?"

"I'm pretty sure that is the proper thing to do." Schoolmarm again.

"Is Beau's nose out of joint because we insisted that you drive us?" Angelica asks, licking every grain of salt from her fingers. "He didn't seem very happy tonight. Was something going on with work?"

"For me to know what is going on would require Beau and me to converse. There has been no conversing."

"Trouble in paradise?" My snacking friend doesn't know how right she is. I hear her opening up another bag of food.

"Oh, I love frosted animal crackers," squeals Caitlin.

"If you must know, Beau and I will be facing off tonight."

Caitlin stalls placing a pink elephant in her mouth. "Shouldn't you wait until after all the wedding activities are over? In case..." She bites into the sugar, afraid to go further with her sour thoughts.

"In case things get ugly?" I challenge.

"No. I was going to say in case he wants the chance to fix things."

"Just because I am drowning my single sorrows in food does not mean I am not picking up the left-out-of-the-loop vibe. What are you not mentioning?" asks Angelica.

"I'm tired of talking. I want to celebrate our friend's marriage. I promise to share all the gruesome details after Beau and I talk. But I really want to be in this moment. Everything changes after this weekend."

They nod. We are all silent for the next few minutes as I make the turn down a long, cobbled drive lined with old posts bearing antique lanterns. I had read that they purposely carved lots of slow curves for the driveway so that only the final turn would reveal the beauty of the 1920s mansion to visitors.

The amber hues of sunset showcase the beautiful hacienda that was transformed into a restaurant a few years ago. Sadie had been invited to the opening weekend, but the rest of us have never been here. We have, however, been salivating over the thought of its renowned blend of Spanish and Cuban cuisine for months.

"This is the most romantic place I have ever seen. Even in my dreams." Caitlin unfolds from the car after Angelica.

"Hey, the sky looks like the color of that gaudy birthday sweater you gave me," Angelica offers her lack of romantic notions as she adjusts her slip indiscreetly.

A Cuban Charanga band welcomes us with high energy conga players, inspiring us to dance our way to the entry. Sadie and Carson did not take longer than us but are at the door greeting their guests.

We walk to the punch fountains and fill our colorful flute glasses. I hear Carson greeting Beau. My half turn places me in line with him as he peers over his friend's shoulder at me. He winks.

"There's your guy. Now I will go find mine." Angelica gleams. "That feels good to say. Am I being presumptuous?"

"We'll find out," I offer with a noncommittal wave. I can see on my friend's face that this was not very encouraging. I set aside my own trouble for a moment and look her in the eyes. "You've avoided love long enough. There were times we all wanted to slap you—for many reasons, but mainly to point out that you were risking a really good thing. The guy's wedding date is his sister. Go get him."

She gladly leaves me by the punch and the mini poppy seed cakes with pink champagne icing. I hear Beau laughing and congratulating Sadie. He says "What a beautiful ceremony" as if he had not been emailing during the entire service.

I say a quick prayer that I will not chicken out—I will not let festive music and romantic candlelit tables sway me from pursuing a real conversation with my boyfriend.

A Proposal Accepted

"When two people are in love, they move on from things. They don't keep rehashing them." Beau leans against the porch rail holding a shrimp skewer and pointing a finger at me, the rehasher.

His line sounds like something I told Marcus back in high school, except I was stating the case for friendship. Neither fill-in-the-blank relationship makes the statement entirely true or fair to the person wanting to talk.

"I don't think couples in love dwell on the negative, but they at least have conversations about important matters." I am wringing my hands and wishing I was wearing something more breathable for this uncomfortable moment.

"Exactly," he says.

"So let's have a conversation…" I plead.

"About important matters," he finishes the sentence.

"Yes."

"You mean matters of the heart and forever after?"

I give him a sideways look.

He puts the skewer down and runs his hands through his hair a couple times. Then he scratches his scalp and makes a strange face. I'm thinking of a Jane Goodall special I saw last week on public television when he finally blurts, "I think maybe we should get married."

I step back, my knees unable to remain strong for me. My hands start shaking. There is complete silence around us. Through the arched windows I watch people dancing to the festive music. On the back lawn wedding-goers are laughing and talking boisterously.

But there is no sound beyond blood pulsing in my ears.

When words come to me, I don't recognize my voice as I speak boldly. "You think we should get married? Beau, the fact that the words *think* and *maybe* are a part of the proposal might be a warning sign."

"You're twisting this. Mari, I love you. You love me. We've been dating almost a year. Our lives are going well. I've asked your folks' permission—and *they* were happy. You're back for good. It's the logical next step. It's the right thing to do."

"I'm tired of logic. I rarely let myself feel what it is I need or want in a moment. I don't even know if I have ever truly trusted God's leading in my life because I want reason to rule every move I make."

"Then forget logic. Let's focus on love. We have a heart for each other and others. We could build a very good life together. I'm so envious of Carson and Sadie today." He looks away and shakes his head.

I force myself to step closer to him. "Beau," I say softly, "I'm a little jealous too. I understand the desire to want these good things in our lives—love, connection, and the whole forever-after scenario. But you think doing the right thing is abiding by a specific timeline. I see doing the right thing as doing right by the other person. Do you understand what I'm saying?"

"Do *you* even understand what you are saying?" He bites his upper lip and finally looks at me.

"So there isn't anything going on in our lives that should be brought out and discussed and resolved before you want to march down the aisle and promise for better or for worse?" I force him to talk about the real life we are sharing and not the fantasy.

He hesitates. "There are some things going on. But work is work. And our relationship is not based on sharing the same business address."

"I thought it was based on trust and mutual respect. We were so disconnected when you visited Washington. You were selling me on Majestic while I was sharing how deeply I feel about the work at the Urban Center. I wanted you to see that with open eyes and an open heart during your visit, but you had an agenda."

"Asking your folks for permission to marry you isn't some awful agenda. A lot of single women would be happy if the guy they've been seeing for a year had that agenda. Do you get that?"

"That's not the agenda I'm talking about. Why do you want me to consider Majestic, Beau?"

He motions for a server to come by with a tray of sweet potato cakes. He places half a dozen of them on his plate

"Those are loaded with spices," I warn him.

I watch him eat four of them, one right after the other with a defiant look in his eyes. He starts sweating profusely, and not until two glasses of water later is he able to compose himself. His lips are swollen and his eyes are red.

"If you are so big on trust, why don't you just say what you want to say instead of playing some game with me?" His voice cracks and he coughs.

"You are submitting a report that will eliminate the job I worked so hard to get back last year. You know how much I care about those people."

"We are submitting a report that shows how to provide better care for more units. That is called progress, Mari."

"There's that warm fuzzy word again. Is that how we measure people now, in units?" My mind keeps circling around his use of the word "we," and I feel dizzy.

"I was referring to facilities. Not to people." He enunciates this last statement, as if I am a slow learner.

Apparently I am.

"Exactly. You are focused on facilities and not people. Which is amazing because the people love you, respect you, and trust you. What statistics are in your report to show the increase in function, memory, and happiness

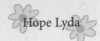

when residents engage in regular exchanges of friendship and care with permanent staff?"

"You can't measure happiness, Mari," he says with the gall to let a laugh slip from his swollen lips.

"Pull the report. You know stats can be used to prove any point, Mr. Businessman. Your grant proposal does not have to turn into a statement about reducing staff, for Pete's sake."

"That isn't fair. We've worked hard on this. And it will bring funding to the state and status to the Golden Horizons' program. I didn't know what Paige and I would find at the end of this report. Not until the research directed us toward this conclusion."

"You must mean *status to you*, because there is no program. There won't be if you don't cancel this report."

Beau arches his back and rolls his neck side to side. He is limbering up for the rest of the conversation. "They accepted the proposal, Mari. They loved it, and they want me to personally oversee the changes for the state." He says it with pride.

My heart breaks.

"When were you going to tell me—the day I got a pink slip?" I ask when I can manage to breathe again. Angelica and Peyton walk by holding hands.

"Mari, I figured it all out."

"Yes, I know. You got me back on at Majestic without telling me."

He shakes his head. "After our blowout in Washington, I saw that I was wrong, totally wrong. I fixed all that."

I stay silent, waiting for the details. *Do the right thing,* I think over and over, hoping Beau gets the message.

He loosens his tie and leans against a column adorned with bougainvillea. I put my hands on the porch railing, but keep my eyes fixed on his face.

"My follow-up report to the state committee includes a stellar recommendation for you to be the contracted director. It's a promotion. You would oversee the programs for several facilities. We'd still be working together,

but it'd be less awkward because you wouldn't have to report directly to me but to…the state supervisor…"

The missing word stands out like a caution light. "The state supervisor?" I ask only because I want him to fill in the blank this time.

Do the right thing.

Do the right thing.

He waves away the response as he gives it. "It'd be a new position also established by the grant. But you would have free reign, other than complying with state laws, of course." He laughs nervously and undoes the top two buttons of his shirt. He is perspiring, and not from spices this time.

He didn't protect me.

"Say something, Mari."

"What should I say? That I'm so happy Paige is going to have a state-level job thanks to your great interpretation of my data, my life's work? You haven't done right by me, Beau. Not for some time."

He opens his mouth but nothing initially comes out. His chance to do the right thing came and went. I feel a bit sad for him. His naive view of this night was that one accepted proposal would lead to another.

As I try to find a different way to explain my feelings, I notice a woman with a blue dress standing behind a potted, flowering cactus. When I step a bit to the left, a manila folder is visible and so is a splash of red hair.

"Is that Paige?" I ask, incredulous.

Beau reluctantly follows the lead of my pointing finger. I can see him gulp like a cartoon character entering a haunted house. A trickle of sweat slides down his face.

"You invited Paige to the wedding reception?"

He turns back to me. "Don't be crazy. She emailed me during the service and said she had the final papers to be signed before she could fax them to the state commissioner. He's waiting on them or I wouldn't have suggested she interrupt the reception. It was an emergency."

"Then go sign off. We don't want the state to fall apart just because we are having a vital conversation about our lives."

He hesitates. Paige peeks around the cactus plant, but when she sees me she recoils back undercover. Beau's mouth moves but nothing comes out.

"Go sign." I say grabbing a chicken kabab from a nearby waiter's tray. My eyes remain fixed on the meat as I nibble.

Beau stays standing. Then his hands go to his pockets and he shifts his weight. "Um, she needs your signature, Mari." He lowers his head.

I make him wait for a response while I eat the chicken.

"The state needs the plan secured on all levels."

Nibble. Nibble.

"I'm not signing. Believe me, you'll be glad I didn't take this job." I lick my fingers aggressively.

"I didn't mean for all of this to happen in one night."

"Beau, it isn't the timing. It's how you handled it and me. There was never a *we* discussion about this job change. You expected me to play along if it served you best."

"I'm sorry I let you down, Mari. But clearly, an apology won't be enough. Our views of this situation are so different. We thought you'd be happy about this."

Now, there's the we. "Who are you talking about? Just to clarify," I inquire.

"The board. Others I've talked to," he says nervously. "Everyone except you, apparently."

"You talked to everyone except the person you supposedly want to share the rest of your life with…" my voice falters. There is a metallic taste in my mouth—the taste I get when I am about to get sick. The small string of lights above the porch twinkles and casts strange shadows on his face. I cannot recognize the shape of his eyes any more than he or I have been able to recognize the shape of our relationship.

"This is beyond awkward. I thought this was going to be an amazingly special night for us—a beginning, not an…" he can't finish the statement.

"Ending," I say quietly, filling in the blank for both of us.

Something Borrowed

Sadie is surrounded by congratulatory people. I rudely step up to the front of the crowd and grab her by the hand. She sees the expression on my face and immediately walks us both over to a secluded corner.

"I'm leaving. Angelica and Caitlin will need rides tonight." The words tumble out.

"Mari, what's wrong."

I want to pretend I'm sick or just overwhelmingly tired, but Sadie looks at me with deep concern. "Beau and I, we're done. Things haven't been good for some time and tonight it was just clear—really clear that we want different things out of this relationship."

She hugs me close, and I can sense my composure is about to crumble. "Tell Caitlin I will..."

"Tell me what?" Caitlin comes up behind me holding an entire tray of hors d' oeuvres. "These shrimp thingies are divine, Sadie. Mari, what is going on?" She hands the platter to Sadie, who obliges.

I am shaking my head side to side nonstop like someone in a padded room. I need to get out of here, and there are so many people and tables and pleasant smiles to walk through in order to reach the door.

"They broke up and Mari needs to leave, so we'll find a ride for you and Angelica."

"Jim would take me home," she says, tearing up, "but I want to go too. Let's get to my place. I need to get rested for tomorrow."

"Tomorrow?" Sadie and I say unison.

"Jim and I decided we were too ambitious. We're leaving first thing in the morning. Come on, Mari. I'll field people for you."

Sadie brushes imaginary lint from my psychedelic dress. "I'm so sorry. Carson and I have been praying for you and Beau. You did what you needed to do." Sadie comforts me with her words. It never occurred to me, in my past naive beliefs, that pain would accompany doing the right thing.

"We'll need these," Caitlin retrieves the tray of appetizers and we head out to the parking lot. Two guests try to reach for a cilantro-lime shrimp and Caitlin slaps their hands. "These went bad. Wait for the next tray, please."

"I want to go home," I say as soon as we step out into the night air.

"You take the tray, I'll drive. We'll be home in no time."

I stop walking, peel off my heels, and leave them behind on the rock lined driveway. "I mean my home. Washington. I want to go tonight."

Caitlin looks worried. "You're already going back later in the week for Thanksgiving and to finish packing, right?" She speaks slowly and with precision.

"I want to go home for good. I ran away from it for almost twelve years. But it is where I need to be right now. That's all I know."

"It's almost ten o'clock—at night. But let's call and get something scheduled for first thing in the morning. I'll take you to the airport myself."

I nod. I'm numb and hungry. I notice my cell phone flashing. I have a missed call from Mom and Dad from a few hours before. They'll see me soon enough, I think. By the time Caitlin pulls up alongside her overstuffed, parked car in the apartment lot, only orange translucent shrimp tails remain on the tray. "I'm a stress eater," I say as my explanation for devouring nearly twenty-five shrimp.

I sit with my head in my hands unable to move. Caitlin gets out of the car and comes over to the passenger side to help me out.

"I feel as though I've been hit by a truck. The love truck. The breakup truck." Rambling is not the only side effect of heartbreak. My tongue is thick

and my scalp tingles. "The bad luck truck—it zoomed over me tonight."

She laughs softly and pulls me to my feet, extending her arm around my waist for support.

"I'm really cold," I eek through chattering teeth.

"You're in mild shock." Caitlin props me up against her car while she rummages through her trunk. She emerges with an oversized cashmere cardigan. "Here."

I crawl up the stairs to her empty apartment. Caitlin quickly gets my air mattress prepped for me while I sit in a corner, wrapped in the dreamy sweater.

"Do you want to change out of your dress?"

"Too tired. Took nylons off in car," I mumble and lie down. Caitlin covers me with a blanket.

"I'll call my parents' travel agent and get you a flight first thing. Should I let anyone else know you're leaving? I could call certain people...someone..."

Even in my frozen mental state, I know what she is getting at. "Just Angelica. I don't think communication with him is a good idea. Not yet."

I drift in and out of consciousness and can hear her making phone calls to various people.

"I love this sweater," I say when she hangs up and turns off the light.

"You should keep it. I'll like knowing you have it with you in Washington," she whispers. I hear the sound of slumber parties from days of old—the zipper of a sleeping bag. "Your flight is at eight. Jim and I will drop you off on our way out of town. Angelica will come and get your car. She said don't be upset if she exchanges it some day for lunch at the Taco Store."

I laugh. Elmo cuddles up next to my face and starts purring.

"The sun will come out tomorrow," Caitlin says.

There is silence until I start laughing, "Um, Annie wants her line back."

A pillow comes sailing toward my head and we both laugh some more.

I'll take the borrowed sentiment—and the sweater. They both bring me surprising comfort as I stare at the ceiling, keeping an ear close to Elmo's rumbling. My eyes are heavy with sleep and the weight of loss.

"Thank you, Caitlin," I say before fading.

"For what?"

"For not asking what I am going to do when I get there."

Fear of Flying Solo

Leaving a relationship, especially one mid-proposal, is a lot like quitting a job with medical and a pension plan. Once you take the plunge, everyone you bump into is lamenting their own leap from security and offering wisdom that is too little too late.

I discover this phenomenon at every stop along the trip.

The ticket counter: "I thought your license photo was bad, but this is worse," Clarissa points to my face. "When the heart breaks, it shows in the lines around the mouth. Don't you lose faith in love, you hear?"

"Too late." I reach across the tall counter and grab my ticket.

The security gate: "If we searched your emotional baggage today, I suspect we'd find disappointment. Am I right?"

"Geez. What is it with you people?" I put my shoes back on and shake my head with indignation.

And now in row 24 of the 747: "You've got the look. She's got the look, doesn't she, Sammi?"

Sammi, who sits on the aisle, leans across her apparent twin and eyes me without discretion. "You are right, Sally. If Sally spots it, you've got it."

320

They both stare at me expectantly, dying for me to ask, to enter into dialogue with them. I refuse to. I don't want to know what Sally sees in me.

I smile and reach for my book, opening it to a random page and begin reading as though I cannot get enough of the words.

They laugh. Sally nudges Sammi. "That's a sure sign." More laughter.

The flight attendant approaches our row with the beverage cart.

"What do you want, love?" Sally asks me.

"Diet Coke."

"We'll take two club sodas with lime and Miss Lonely Hearts will have a diet Coke. She needs something stronger, but she's asking for a diet Coke."

The flight attendant looks at me apologetically and hands me the can and a plastic cup with four ice cubes.

"Must be fresh," Sammi says with an overdrawn frown.

"Your heartbreak is recent, is it?" Sally translates. "He just broke up with you."

"There is nothing as sad as a woman flying solo." Sammi sticks her lower lip out and sucks in her breath as though she might cry.

Before my rational, private self can stop the prideful self, I set the record straight. "I broke it off with him, if you must know."

"Oh, sure you did, hon." Sammi reaches over and pats my arm.

"Really. He proposed and I broke it off."

The twins wink and nod at one another, their matching turquoise elephant earrings swinging in unison. While their clothes would make them ringers for the retiree set, Sammi and Sally don't appear to be more than forty. Neither of them has a wedding ring on.

"If he proposed, where's the ring?" Sally prods, seemingly reading my mind.

I put the book down in my lap and turn my body toward them. "We didn't get that far because I broke it off."

Sammi waves her hand. "That was a big mistake. Believe us." She draws a line in the air between her and Sally. "The benefit of a breakup when you are that far along in a relationship is to have an addition to your jewelry collection. See this?" Sammi unbuttons her royal blue blouse down to her cleavage to show me a diamond pendant necklace. "This was from a broken engagement. I got word he was breaking up with me, so I handed the ring to Sally for safekeeping before our dinner date, and when he ended things before the appetizer came, I told him I had lost the ring that very morning. I swear I did."

"She did. She did." Sally slaps Sammi and they laugh in harmony.

"You'll know better next time." Sally adds her wisdom in place of a rich story about deceiving a former love.

Sammi playfully slaps her sister's hand. "There won't be a next time. She won't make the same mistake twice. Girls these days have learned from our generation—they are getting married, settling down, and having families well before they turn thirty. You have a couple years left, I'll bet, but don't lose too much time crying over the one that got away."

"I am thirty. And it wasn't a mistake. The mistake would have been to go through with something that wasn't right or good for either one of us."

They nod to one another again and turn to me with wide, sorry eyes. "It's fresh. You're still in the denial stage of your grief."

"Beau—flaws and all—is still funny, handsome, sweet, smart, and all those things we think will be a part of our personal version of Mr. Right."

"We hear you."

"And then he wrote some dumb report—using my information, mind you—to change everything. He wanted to make his mark in his professional field, and he sure did. He marked me off the employee roster." I mime the heinous act of crossing my name off a clipboard master list.

"That is awful."

"However," I raise my hand to add drama for my jury of two, "I am guilty of skewing the statistics in favor of what I wanted all these months. I didn't allow myself to see what the data and the results were really pointing out about my boyfriend—or about us as a couple. I was in denial *then,* but not now. "

"Statistics?"

"Figure of speech."

In another ten years, will I be cornering some unsuspecting, younger

woman and telling her about my big mistake at age thirty? Will I twist the situation in my memory so many times that Beau becomes "the one that got away?" instead of a good man—but not the right man—whom I dated during an important year in my life?

From my bag I pull out a box containing a beautiful, gold-edged Bible I bought for Marcus while in Tucson. When I saw that he carried the one I gave him in high school, I knew I would choose a special one to give him for his graduate studies graduation gift. I gently rub the etching of his name on the front cover with my finger and turn to the front page where there is a space for a dedication. I have put this part off, unsure what to write. I am digging for my pen when Sally jerks off her headphones and hits my arm with her elbow.

"We saw this movie last week on our flight to the single twin convention. Sam and I had a double date with this ferociously handsome set from Bosnia."

"I've never heard ferociously used quite that way," I respond.

"They were amazing. And very polite."

"So what happened?" I cannot believe I am encouraging this conversation.

"Religious differences." Sammie winks and points to my Bible.

Sally finishes the bit. "They wouldn't worship us!" Lots of laughter.

"That's a good one. I think I need to use the restroom. Will you excuse me?"

My face is hot and my clothes are sticking to me as I wander up the aisle. If I saw an emergency parachute, I swear I would strap it on and head for the exit.

A flight attendant is walking down the aisle and crooks her finger, motioning for me to approach her. Her name tag reads "Allegra."

"I couldn't help but overhear some of your conversation," she says in a loud whisper.

Great. Here we go again. Another person with advice and warnings about my future as an old maid.

"Are you with those ladies or are you flying alone?"

"I am traveling by myself. And I don't find that sad at all." I puff out my chest and the guy seated next to where we stand in the aisle gives me a curious look.

"I have an extra seat in first class. You are welcome to have it. I thought you might need some…space."

I nod yes emphatically.

From my luxurious, reclining chair in first class it becomes crystal clear to me—a woman flying solo does not need advice, warnings, or fear-inducing stories. Nor does she need guilt. All she really needs is a comfortable chair, a glass of fresh-squeezed orange juice, a couple wafer cookies to melt in her mouth, and some glorious space to recover.

When Everything Fits

Nobody is answering the phone at the center. I check my cash supply and find that I have only enough to get a cab home if the driver gives me a less than typical fare. I go from car to car explaining my situation, and finally a young driver, Edmond, agrees. He says it has been a slow morning, anyway. Why not be charitable?

"I don't know why nobody has answered. It is rare for everyone to be out of the house at one time," I say and go on to explain my living situation.

"You seem very happy to be going home. Have you been traveling for work?" Edmond asks innocently.

"For work and for life. But now I have a better idea as to what I want."

"What is that?" he asks, curious and kind with his questions. "Maybe you have the secret to life?"

"Well, I was just going to say I want what I didn't have in Arizona. But on a deeper level, I want to fulfill my purpose by serving others and..."

"And what, Miss Mari?"

"That's it. Don't we all just want to find our God-given purpose?" I give him the answer appropriate for the length of our relationship—exactly forty minutes. Had we a longer drive, perhaps I would have divulged the rest of my gut response. I want to be with someone who helps me fulfill my purpose. Shouldn't this be an elemental understanding? Why hasn't it been my guideline all along? All the people who love me would say this is an essential part of what I need—Caitlin, Sadie, Angelica, Mom, Dad, Marcus.

Marcus.

I had been hoping he would answer the phone when I called from the airport. He would have interrogated me as to why I returned early, and I would have grumbled about telling him the embarrassing truth about Beau, me, and the relationship that barely ever was. But it was what I was hoping for nonetheless.

It occurs to me as we turn the corner and head for the Urban Center that everyone is at the retreat house in Virginia. Every year my parents are given use of the retreat center either the weekend before or the weekend after Thanksgiving. They use it as a time to set goals with the kids, pray for the year ahead, and focus on the blessings of the past year. They also create a lot of crazy games to help the children bond before they face the holiday, for some their first ever, away from family.

When Edmond pulls up to the house, I hand him all the money I have including my change. He waves and wishes me luck with my purpose. I punch in the security codes and waddle to the front door with Elmo in his carrier in one hand and my roller bag in the other. I enter without having to explain anything to anyone. I realize this is the best way possible for me to return. I will have time to make sense of the past twenty-four hours and put them into perspective before retelling my story.

I tromp up the stairs to my room. I wonder if this will remain my room if I stay. *If I stay? What am I going to do?* Somehow I think there are more answers here than back in Arizona. The pull to return was beyond strong. It was undeniable.

No denial now. I decide this will be my motto for whatever comes next. I write it in bold letters on the dry-erase board next to my desk. Somehow this appeases me. I have no job. No specific plan. Only the urge to return to my childhood home—and I am at peace. I take this as a good sign.

I want to pray. The phone closet used to be my makeshift prayer closet, so I walk down the hall and ease open the door with my toe. I am half-expecting Marcus to be seated on the floor with the phone cradled on his shoulder, begging me for five extra minutes. I smile and kneel.

I figure I need a lot of work. I have had a good life, God. And I appreciate everything you've done and shown me over the past few years. Even recently. Especially recently. But I'm ready for the truth now. No more denying the desires you have placed on my heart to find a way to work with kids like my parents have for nearly forty years. You guide them. And I trust you to guide me to the next step. Let this risk not be about running away, but about coming home to your purpose. Show me the rest of the way. Amen.

I stay seated on the floor. My head rolls back and rests against the cupboard door for several minutes. I could sleep here. My slumber would be deep and peaceful, I know. As messed up as this seems, I'm glad for everything that has happened. It took something as huge as heartbreak to get me back here.

Yet heartbreak doesn't fit the freedom I am feeling. There is the ache of loss. There is the twinge of regret for taking so long to wake up to life. But my heart is more full than broken. I whisper a thank-you prayer and return to get Elmo situated with some food and water. I decide to go round up some garden dirt for his litter box.

It is chilly outside but the sky is blue. A few early evening clouds are rolling in. I like the mysterious point of the day when dusk is about to descend upon the landscape. I pause to look up at the last leaves of the season.

"Mari?"

I look to see Fabio coming toward me. His reaches out his gloved hand to help me up.

"What are you doing here?" I ask.

"I just talked to your dad a bit ago and he asked me to tidy up the yard while they are gone. He also likes the idea of someone checking on the house. Funny, he didn't mention you'd be here."

"Nobody knows. It's a surprise." I take a shortcut through my story.

"Well, the kids will be thrilled. Daisy has not stopped talking about you.

In fact, they all have a Mari story close in mind." He chuckles and grabs his rake.

I gather my dirt in a cardboard box that once held cans of green beans.

"I'll be upstairs if you need anything, Fab…Fabulous Bernie."

He laughs and keeps raking.

When I get to my room, I cannot find Elmo. I search beneath the bed and under my desk before I hear his small cry from above. He's perched on the top shelf of my built-in shelves. My gentle coaxing is useless; he backs up further under the covering of the alcove.

"Be a man," I mumble. "Oh, I guess you are." I am talking to myself—Elmo has clearly stopped listening. Even a cat avoids my sarcasm.

I drag my chair over to the cupboard and climb up to be face-to-face with my poor traveling companion. He doesn't know this will be his home for a while.

"Elmo, kitty, kitty. Come on, sweetie." I reach for him, but he proceeds to jump onto my shoulder and to the floor. The force of his leap causes me lose my balance. I reach for the top shelf to regain my footing but grab a large white box instead of the wood. My tumble backward is cushioned by the bed.

"Bad kitty!" I reprimand, but Elmo is settling onto a pile of blankets, turning round and round to search for the ideal position. A crease of cardboard is wedged into my lower back, so I follow Elmo's lead and roll over to secure a more comfy position.

The box is flattened and the white contents spill out. Beneath the lid I discover a card and a dress. My hands go straight to the neckline of the dress. I hold it up and can barely believe my eyes. It is not just a dress—it is a wedding dress. And it is not just a wedding dress—it is *the* wedding dress featured in the fashion show I sponsored last year. I cannot believe my eyes.

Without a second thought, I strip down and pull the dress over my head. I am thankful for the recent prewedding diet. It glides over my body with only a mere tug or two. I didn't let myself try it on last year—last year when I was securely dating Beau and hopeful about my future. Yet now, in

the chaos of drastic change and uncertainty, I readily slip into a dress that seems to represent so much faith in things yet to come.

I pull my hair up and let it fall back to my shoulders. I do it again. I kiss the air.

There is a knock on the door and a gruff "Hello?"

My heart stops but my dress keeps swishing back and forth. "Yes?"

"It's Bernie. Marcus had something in my car for you. I have it here."

I open the door to Bernie holding up the large poster board poem. "Oh, yes. Thank you."

"Wow! That is some fantastic dress. I got to say, Mari, we are all pretty excited about your wedding."

"My wedding?" I ask this as though it is an absurd assumption for a man facing a girl in a bridal gown to make.

"Your folks announced that Beau was asking you to marry him while you were in Tucson. Everyone was excited for you. Well, mostly," he adds pointing to the poster board.

I take it from him and slip it against the wall. "And why did Marcus give you this?"

"For safekeeping, I reckon. He didn't want the kids to add black moustaches or anything like that."

We both laugh. The craziness of my getup is getting to me. "Well, my coach changes back into a pumpkin soon. I had better change back into sweats."

It takes him a second and then he howls with laughter. Bernie is down the steps and heading back out the door when I realize I did not clarify that I am not getting married.

I shut the door and allow myself another few hair and smile poses in front of the mirror. There is something to this princess for a day thing. I'd never been the girl who married off her Barbies or practiced walking down the aisle with girlfriends—well, until Caitlin and I did at the rehearsal. But standing here in this remarkable dress, I feel more emotion than I did when standing beside Sadie as she spoke her vows. I understand, maybe for the first time, how beautiful it would be to walk in such a dress toward the man who loves me completely, unconditionally.

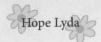

I sit on the bed. In the mirror image of this somewhat pathetic scene I notice the card to my right. Or left. I reach for it, assuming it is a receipt. At least I will find out who bought it. My mother's handwriting is on the front. I tear it open and a piece of folded stationery and something colorful falls out.

> *Mari,*
>
> *We couldn't be happier for you! Beau is such a lovely man. Marcus saw this dress on your fashion show website last year and told us about it. We knew when we saw it that you were destined to wear it—so we purchased it. We had no idea it would be a part of your life so soon. We are thankful you are with us this Thanksgiving. It will be our chance to say goodbye properly and to celebrate the upcoming event—our little girl's wedding!*
>
> Love, Mom and Dad

The postscript is in Dad's handwriting:

> *PS. We found this and decided it must stand for What Will be Our Mari's Dress. We've always known that when you made this choice, it would be forever. You can trust the heart God gives you, Mari.*

I quickly put on my WWOMD bracelet and smooth the skirt of the dress with my hands several times. My nose and eyes sting and my throat aches. I had told everyone I didn't want it, that it didn't matter to me. And I never let myself inquire who purchased it so I could secretly imagine that it was mine.

But they all think I said yes to Beau. What a disappointment it will be.

I walk over to the poster board and pick it up. There is an index card paperclipped to the top.

The thing is Mari, the poem is my journey too. Love, Marcus

He is right.

Most of the photographs include Marcus. There he is handing me my

birthday package, tying my roller skates while I stick my tongue out at the camera, raking leaves while I jump on the pile. There is a recently added black arrow drawn at the bottom of the poster. I flip to the back as it indicates, and there in the center of the board are two photos that cause my heart to flutter.

Marcus taped a picture of the house he bought with his grant money—the site of the soon-to-be Chicago Urban Youth Center. He wrote the word *Future* in blue marker. Below this image is a shot of Marcus and me sitting on a park bench. Jon is standing by Marcus, tugging on his sleeve, and Elsa is leaning against me. It was during our field trip to Williamsburg. Marcus is looking at me and smiling. I am laughing with my head tilted toward Marcus. Beneath this is the word friend.

Friend.

I stare at the word and the image. Then I focus on the one who was always there to make me happy, to work by my side, to serve the same beliefs and purpose that I did. This is what I will write in his Bible. I retrieve it from my bag and start my inscription—*You have been by my side for so many important moments. May this encourage you along the rest of your journey.*

I am about to write "your friend, Mari," but my hand stops moving across the page.

The word "friend" looked strange earlier, and now it sounds funny in my mind. It doesn't fit what I feel inside.

You can trust the heart God gives you, Mari.

What Is Normal, Anyway?

Can it really be this easy?" Caitlin's words come back to me. Can all the pieces suddenly fall into place? Are we given moments of clarity and understanding after years of denial?

These are my thoughts as I rush down the stairs and out the front door. Bernie is raking the leaves beneath a maple tree, wearing headphones and nodding to the beat.

I stand before him in the dress and my tennis shoes, looking what I imagine to be a bit maniacal. Bernie slips his headphones off. "You are a bit overdressed for yard work."

"When Dad called, did he say what time they would return?"

"They are at the retreat until tomorrow afternoon," he says, rubbing his chin.

I look around at my vehicle choices. The 15-passenger van is parked at the curb. I could change clothes, pack a bag, and get to Virginia in no time. I'll tell them all I'm not getting married and then I'll ask Marcus if we can talk. Really talk. About matters of the heart and forever after.

"But your dad didn't call. I was there, just this afternoon."

"Why?"

"To pick up Marcus."

I glance around like a frantic bird. "So what'd you do with him?"

"He decided to go to Chicago early. I hope you won't take this wrong—but I think after your folks announced your engagement, he seemed eager to get moving."

"He's gone? Gone without saying goodbye?"

"I think that was the idea."

I step backward and my foot hits a divot in the ground. I nearly fall into a pile of leaves.

"I don't usually have this effect on women," he chuckles. As Bernie puts out a hand to steady me, he holds me for a few seconds and looks into my eyes. "When I dropped Marcus off at the train, he looked downright sad. He almost got rid of the poster with the photos, but I convinced him you'd want it."

I'm nodding. *Yes, I do.*

"After all, the guy put a lot of work into it. Just because you are getting married, it doesn't mean…"

I do.

Slowly I return to the present moment and interrupt Bernie midsentence. "Train?"

"Yeah. I just dropped him off at Union Station."

"I'm not getting married, Bernie. We broke up!" I shout loudly, raising my hands and the Bible I am still clutching in the air.

"I think there is someone who would love to hear that." Bernie pushes a space between his work gloves and his sweatshirt sleeve. "Train doesn't leave for another thirty minutes," he says this with a crooked smile. "If you left now…"

I glance at the dress, as does he. There is no time to worry about looking like an idiot if I want to catch Marcus. I run into the house to grab my purse and the van keys.

"Miss! You cannot go past this point without a ticket." A male security guard stops me before I head to the tunnel for the train to Chicago. He and his female partner seem glad to have an obvious person to pull from the crowd and question.

"I'll buy a ticket. I have my purse. How much? I need to get down there." I am flustered and barely able to get my wallet open. The emptiness of it is a fast reminder that I gave Edmond every last bit of money I had.

The heat of tears makes its way to the corner of my eyes. "I'm not a crazy person. I'm normal. Or pretty normal. I need to get to the tunnel or I'll be too late and..."

"Are you part of that Vera Wang photo shoot?" The female security guard asks a bit dubiously.

"Yes!" I point to her with a shaking finger. "And I'm late. And nothing against Vera, but for such a petite woman she is really tough. She might hurt me. I'll definitely lose my job. Please." I curtsey and beg. It seems the thing to do.

The man pulls at his ear lobe and looks me over. He shakes his head. "When did the grunge look hit the bridal scene? What's with the tennis shoes?"

"It is for next year's fall lineup," I say while scanning the crowd on the other side of the gate.

The female winks at me and pushes a button to let me through the ticket-operated door. "Men don't understand fashion, honey. Better go before Vera slaps you around."

"Thank you." I go through the turnstile but my dress gets caught on the metal arms. A couple rough-looking boys in black leather gently wiggle the mechanical pieces until I am freed. "Thanks, guys!" I wave at them backward and keep running.

The crowd parts as they let the crazy woman in a wedding dress make her way through the station and toward the train about to depart.

"Marcus! Marcus!" I'm hollering like a lunatic and cannot believe my fabulous luck in not getting arrested yet.

I see the photographers and the actual Vera Wang models. They all wave to me and watch me pass by. One photographer starts taking pictures, and